Owen Marshall is considered New Zealand's finest contemporary writer of short fiction. He is also a novelist, editor and poet. His previous novel, *A Many Coated Man,* was a finalist in the 1995 Montana Book Awards and *Harlequin Rex* won the Montana New Zealand Book Awards Deutz Medal for Fiction 2000. He has won numerous other awards and fellowships, including the ONZM for services to literature in the Queen's New Year Honours 2000. He lives in Timaru, working as a full-time writer.

To Iam,

With best wishes in your art and writing, and with shared memories of the 2005 Methven Summer School.

Owen Marshall

OWEN MARSHALL
Harlequin Rex

𝑉
VINTAGE

The author gratefully acknowledges the award of the Katherine Mansfield Memorial Fellowship in 1996, during which time this novel was begun.

A VINTAGE BOOK
published by
Random House New Zealand
18 Poland Road, Glenfield, Auckland, New Zealand

First published 1999
Reprinted 2000 (twice)

© 1999 Owen Marshall

The moral rights of the author have been asserted

ISBN 1 86941 395 4

Printed in Malaysia

HARLEQUIN

Harlequin seems to have originated in a mythical figure known in Old French as Herlequin, or Hellequin. Herlequin is identified with the earlier King Herla (in Old English Herla cyning), a legendary person associated with the chief Anglo-Saxon god Woden.

In medieval folklore Harlequin was a devil celebrated as a leader of the Harlequini familia, also known as the Wild Hunt and Furious Horde, a frightening flight of witches, demons and the souls of the prematurely dead. This group would ride through the air and the streets at night, while inhabitants barricaded their doors. Harlequin is Herne the Hunter, whom Shakespeare talks of haunting Windsor Forest in *The Merry Wives of Windsor*.

By the mid 16th century Harlequin had lost his demonic nature and become one of the principal stock characters of the Italian Commedia Dell'arte. A cunning, covetous, amorous and comic servant — a Zanni. The character underwent further change and eventually entered British pantomime as a mischievous fellow supposed to be invisible to all eyes but those of his faithful Columbine.

Harlequin in drama was originally dressed in a peasant's shirt and long trousers, both covered with coloured patches. His costume gradually became tight-fitting and decorated with triangles and diamond shapes. He was often masked and carried a batté, or slapstick.

REX

Rex means King, but the word is also used in the expression to play rex, which means to play pranks.

In memory of my mother, Jane Ella Jones (née Marshall), who died before my clear recollections begin.

ONE

From each place known well we take something when we go, and we leave something too. Both acquisition and sacrifice are utterly beyond our control.

The bus came over a small rise fringed with red hot poker plants, and there was Havelock, the dipping main street, little changed at first glance from the place David had often visited as a boy. As well as those recollections, he couldn't deflect the odd association that always arose: Havelock Dark pipe tobacco, which his grandfather had smoked in a silver-collared Peterson, deeply curved. Towards the end of his grandfather's working life, the pipe had been an excuse for a breather, so that old George could straighten his back in the yards, or the shearing shed, or turn off the tractor and allow the sound beats to fade like wings into the distance.

Havelock — with its one short stretch of clumsy, honest buildings, the steep, bush-clad hill behind it tipping towards the much longer stretch of the mudflats at the head of Mahau Sound. The police station, the post office, the town hall, were bravely painted. The hall had four thin pillars at its entrance as a pioneer nod to the classical culture of social superiors.

As the bus slowed further, he noticed the little town had put on a pretence of finery to attract the tourists. A gem-cutter's, an antique shop, a fishing and marine travel centre, the Pelorus Jack Café, the backpackers' hostel. A large wooden building had its frontage covered with a mural of what looked like a tuatara, and the length of a tin fence provided undulation for a dolphin and the words, 'Sea Kayaking', as if the speed at which most people passed through the place meant that only the largest scale and simplest advertising message would register.

But he left the bus, the only passenger not going on to Nelson, bought a Coke at the Four Square, sat on the worn steps of the wooden Methodist church, which had been deserted by the living, and become a place to celebrate the dead — a museum with photographs of whiskers and waist-coats, and the hulking tools of the logging days. And as he sat there quietly, the original Havelock, the real substance of the place, peaceful among the haunches of the hills, was clear again. The old-fashioned boats and derelict cars in people's sections, the weatherboard sheds askew with age, lawns, vegetable gardens, an armchair in a porch — all within a hand's reach of the road. And the camellia bushes which, in their season, spread red and pink flowers upon the foot-path of the main street.

He bought egg and chive sandwiches, walked down the short slope of a side street to the sea and turned away from the camping ground and new, rather incongruous marina, towards the working part of the shoreline. Small builders, one-man businesses, fishing boats propped by timber on dry land so that their deep hulls were revealed, a rusting pontoon, a loosely tethered barge that brought sheep in from the island farms, and yards close to the sea for those sheep, which added their warm, dungy smell to the air. The tide was going out, yet most of the mudflats were still covered, and the sea had corralled in the corner between shore and breakwater a jostle of driftwood, plastic bottles, nylon twine, cellophane bags, broken angles of blue and white polystyrene, beer cans, a light bulb, sodden stalks of rushes and grass, and the body of a small, short-haired dog with its swollen stomach tight as a drum. And further out on the shallowly covered mudflat were cast whole trees with black shags on the bleached branches. Along the shoreline away from the town were rushes; grey and russet streaked, and also in stiff, slightly raised patches on the mud.

David ate his sandwiches by the side of a boat-building firm, Nottage & Son, whose business premises were the size of a double garage. The double wooden doors were open, and showed a clinker-built dinghy, bottom up on hurdles. Nobody was working there; nobody came. He sat in the sun with his back supported by the warm outside timbers of the shed, and wondered how the Harlequin epidemic and the Slaven Centre related to what was around him: how the local people took to something which, as far as they were concerned, may as well have come from another planet.

The road to Mahakipawa was a diagonal cut on the hill further down the sound. A rural delivery went through each day, he'd been told; from Havelock past the scattered houses in the small bays and on to Picton.

Everything to do with people was at the low altitude: the unbuttoned straggle of buildings, the few roads, the launches and yachts, some of the small ones lopsided on the mud, three young people after flounders in the channels, a farmhouse or two in the middle distance on the flat at the head of the sound. The bare, flashing arm of water was very blue. On both sides the hills rose in ridges and gullies and flanks of rough grass, pigfern, broom and gorse. There was bush on the high slopes behind the town. The skylines were unfettered strokes where hills met the sky.

David threw the crusts to the gulls, and walked back up the short road to the township. He had the feeling that always came to him in such quiet, settled places. A feeling that time itself was eddying there, and more, that some immense, quiet suction was at work, so that things might well drift from the surface of the landscape, from the warm roads, from the mudflats, the clustered, quiet town, from the lazy paddocks, into the endless, pale sky.

The wooden post office had a low door and facings freshly painted in green and red. David thought maybe he could catch the rural delivery man there. 'Give him a ring yourself, to be on the safe side,' the post office woman said, 'but he gets away from here about one thirty most times. Use our phone behind the counter.' The woman had tracksuit pants with two yellow stripes down the outside of the legs, and a white T-shirt proclaiming MAINLAND KIWI. She had a bright pink scar, or birthmark, at the corner of one eye, as if she had shed a single scalding tear. 'Come far?' she said to show good intent, rather than curiosity.

'Through from Blenheim today, but I've been further south.'

'Bryce doesn't mind taking someone over usually, if he's got room. There's a bus comes through from the Picton side later today, but you've missed the only one this way.'

David told her that he was heading for the Slaven Centre. 'Yeah,' she said. 'He calls in there all right. It's getting to be a big place. Look,' she said, when he explained he had work there, 'why don't I ring him for you? I'm Bev. With you working over there, I'll get used to your name in no time. I do all the sorting for the centre's mail right here. I know all the staff names, though never met most of them. You're not a doctor, though?'

'No.'

'You just sit down in the sun by the door, and I'll ring Bryce for you.'

He did just that; sat by the door, hardly noticed the odd car passing, looked instead to the hills beyond the sound and the place, Havelock, which he'd visited with his father years before. 'It's all jacked up,' said Bev cheerfully. 'No sweat.' His father had crushed a little finger in the mechanised wool press shortly before one of their fishing trips, and David remembered the tight bandage, white at first, but becoming grubby over the three days spent mainly in the boat.

Bryce drove a blue Toyota ute, and had pale, worn trousers pouched at the knees, and slender arms that were almost hairless. David helped him put the larger packages in the back, then waited in the cab while Bryce checked over final things with Bev. It was obvious that for her the rural delivery departure was a high point in a less than hectic day. A swelling MAINLAND was half in the doorway of David's side of the Toyota, as she saw them off. 'Oh yeah,' she said, 'it'll be a really beaut day on the track. Just watch out for any visitors coming back from the centre. Some of those city people, Jesus, they've no idea of driving a secondary road.'

'Some of them should be patients there,' said Bryce drily.

'Don't get me started on that place.' She was going to, though, the MAINLAND KIWI expanded as she took breath for it, but then she remembered David, and that he was off there to work, so she let out her breath harmlessly, waved her hand before her face and theirs to indicate the myriad accounts she could give of the Slaven Centre. Her farewell to David, a stranger of no consequence to her, was as full and genuine as that for Bryce, whom she saw most days of her life. It was the helpful, outgoing nature that he remembered; the striped pants, the careless hair, the track of a scalding tear, seemed incidental enough.

'Good on you,' said Bryce. He smiled as he drove along the short, flat road at the head of the sound before the Mahakipawa Hill. The mud left gleaming by the receding tide had slight green and purple visceral tints like fresh goose shit, and the few buildings of Havelock settled down, dwindling, in the sun. 'Yeah, good on you,' said Bryce again, though David had said nothing. The view of Bryce's smile was a side view; the teeth so heavily filled that the enamel showed a shadow from within.

'She seems a good sort.'

'Old Bev? You betcha,' said Bryce. 'She used to be a real one for the leg-over, but three kids podded in six years simmered her down a bit. She's all right. A trooper, is Bev.'

The ute growled during the pull up the Mahakipawa hill. Gorse, broom, bracken and taller pittosporum. There was flax close to the shore; some pongas and native trees in damper gullies. Whole slopes were in a flowering of gorse and broom, but no New Zealander confuses the two: the bumble bee yellow of the gorse and the butterfly yellow of broom.

Bryce had the easy manner of someone in familiar country. 'This your first time out to the Slaven Centre?'

'Yes.'

'Some family in there?'

'No,' David said. 'No, I'm not visiting anyone. I hope there's a job waiting for me. Nurse aiding, supervision, therapy — stuff like that.'

'Good one. I hear they pay not too badly. Most qualified people aren't too keen, because they're not sure about — you know.' Bryce was going to say about it being dicey because no one knew for sure how the thing spread, but he sidestepped that. 'The isolation's a bit of a bummer I'd say.'

'Sure, for city guys maybe,' said David. 'I suppose the centre is left pretty much alone? Doesn't have a lot of contacts outside?'

'Pretty much. Well, there's people come to visit patients, of course, but they're usually in and out, or if they need to stay a while then the centre has motel-style blocks of its own.'

The road wound up the hill. Poor country most of it: the cuttings exposed the soft, flaky rock and yellow soils. Bryce stopped at occasional farm gates to do his thing — letters, deliveries, a new tyre at E.P. Rossiter's. One or two of the gate boxes were as big as dog kennels.

'Most of them are harmless, I suppose,' David said.

'Harmless?'

'The patients.'

'Never given us much problem that I know of. They do things to each other, I hear, and half a dozen have drowned themselves for a fact. There seems to be something about the water when they're desperate, the poor buggers. But you'll get to know all about that.'

The sea to the left glittered enticingly in the unobstructed sun.

'So the cops aren't there much?'

'Nah. There's no need for any of that.' Bryce crossed the median line and pulled up on the wrong side of the road, but next to the wooden box with just 'Meek' on it. There was a little rise and then a dip in the road ahead of them as they sat there. David tensed for the few seconds that it would have taken a vehicle to rise from the hollow, sweep over the crest and hit the ute head on. Yet he knew that Bryce must have been watching the road carefully long before they stopped, and didn't give him the satisfaction of a query, or complaint.

Soon after, they came down from the hill and on to a small valley flat with a stream to the sea. Just a few willows and a fresh breeze. The little, open valley rose into the hills, partly cleared slopes with some green, irregular pasture, then gorse and broom, then the native bush holding out on the tops. A raw road led up to the Slaven Centre, boldly new and incongruous on the hillside.

Bryce nodded towards the buildings. 'That's her,' he said. 'Stuck there like bulls' bollocks.'

At the turn-off, a timber slab mounted on two stone cairns bore the name of the centre carved deeply and painted white. SLAVEN CENTRE — nothing about Harlequin, nothing about the threat from Africa and the lure of the sea.

Bryce turned in and rattled up the unsealed drive to make his deliveries. 'I come back past usually about three thirty.' He burrowed in the ledge beneath the dash when the van was stopped and David had paid his five dollars, then wrote something on the back of a courier ticket. 'My cellphone number,' he said. 'When you want to get away for a day or so, give me a call and I'll be able to tell you how I'm going for time.'

'Okay. You want a hand in with things?'

'Nah. You get yourself sorted. I hope things work hunky-dory for you here.' He was gone, with a plastic bag of letters and a string bag of bigger stuff.

David took his pack and put it on the grass by the car park. He looked over the tilt of the land to the sound, and across that to the steep country on the other side. He had a strong inclination to put the pack on and walk away into the landscape, but he'd tried that option several times before and it had never worked out.

The Slaven Centre had been built hurriedly and with economies of scale. There were bright, prefabricated panels, covered walkways, aluminium and glass annexes like greenhouses, a car park bulldozed into the pale clay of the hillside. Most of the buildings were close to the ground, yet lacking integration: a bright scatter in the natural colours of the hillside. They reminded David of school buildings, a fresh, brazen campus rather than a hospital. Maybe that was the impression intended: something to distract the mind from the real function of the centre, which was to treat a sickness not much older than the buildings themselves.

He wasn't in a mood for pity, however, not for anybody else, no matter what their misfortune, and not for himself because he knew that the course which had brought him to Mahakipawa was the quite consistent consequence of his own mistakes.

TWO

The dormitory buildings had the Maori names of birds, but the largest, multi-storey block was indicated by a sign that read, RECEPTION AND MAIN TREATMENT SUITES, so David set off in that direction, followed for a time by the unabashed gaze of a large man with his fair hair in a pony-tail, who sat with his face shaded by a newspaper on the verandah of the nearest block. TAKAHE in blue letters was painted on its northern end.

A new chum again, that's what he bloody was. Just like arriving at boarding school and feeling that resistant, psychological membrane which separates you from people and things that already have a working relationship. In death, even, you'd be a new chum, he supposed: somewhat on the outer in heaven, or hell, until you learnt the ropes. In both there'd be some perks, some prime possies, some in-house tricks, which were gained only through seniority and obsequious usefulness to those in authority.

Reception had an airy, Mediterranean décor — tiles, bricks, roughcast and concrete simulating tiles and bricks, and all in biscuit, yellow and ochre. 'Your name again?' the receptionist asked. She knew nothing about David; his arrival was a mystery to her. She retreated into the back office to confer and seek advice. Her back to him, she spread her hands on her colleague's desk and leant there. There was a good deal of flesh at the top of her shoulders and her action bunched it there, above her blouse, so that it formed a pale swell of lard below the back of her head. She placed the letter from Dr Mousier at a distance, as though it were some insolence imposed on her. In a few weeks they might come to know each other, like each other, sleep in each other's arms perhaps, or hold a persistent grudge instead, but at that time he intruded, and was naturally resented, even though her job was reception, even though she had been to the in-service training days on customer contact, first-up impressions, body language, empathy simulation. Well, at least those training days were outside the madhouse, she had told Louise.

'Dr Mousier will be out shortly,' she said. 'Have a seat anyway.'

'If he's going to be out, then is there much point in my waiting?'

She didn't smile, made no response; ambiguous semantics held no frisson for her — David took a seat anyway.

Dr Alst Mousier was conspicuously home-grown, despite his name, which was the corrupted legacy from a Swiss cartographer who came to New Zealand in the 1870s to escape an unhappy marriage.

'You know old Stenness then?' said contemporary Alst. He led David back into his office, holding the application and reference in his hand. 'You've done some general rehab work? It's not so much counselling, or recreational therapy, that's the thing here — more a sort of benign supervision. You know anything about Harlequin? The Slaven Centre is all about that, you realise?'

'Only what I've read,' David said. 'Some new degenerative disease, right?'

'Basically it's a neurological thing, though eventually there are a whole raft of physical manifestations. Not psychiatric in the normal sense, but more akin to Tourettism. You know that?' He saw from David's expression that he didn't.

Mousier had a reduced face, in which his soft, dark, lemur-like eyes caught any light. Yet there was nothing passive, or furtive, in his personality. He was, and frequently asserted himself to be, a man of no bullshit. The thin paws of his hands rustled among the papers of his desk, and the hair was luxuriant upon his knuckles, as if eyebrows had been transplanted there by rubbing. 'We're not into bullshit here, David. You understand? We don't quite know what we're dealing with and so we need to work as a team, admit how much we have to learn.'

'But it's not catching, is it?' asked David. He remembered what his friend Chris had said not long before in Wellington. 'I mean people can work safely with this Harlequin thing?'

'As far as we know there's no direct contact transmission. No indication so far that it spreads within a family, for example. It's one of the aspects we're working on. Who knows, maybe it's one of these predisposed hereditary things. Maybe there's some environmental trigger — some food additive, some pollutant, some stress level exceeded. Our lifestyle is changing so fast that we're creating bow ripple diseases.'

'No nurses or anything looking after these people have caught it, though?'

'Not in greater numbers than sections of the community quite removed from them, but then Harlequin is so recent that any data and any deductions from it are provisional. We don't see dangers there, but can't give guarantees. That's the truth of it.'

David thought of the priests who set up the leper colonies, and finally brought the disease on themselves, but then wasn't there more threat for him outside the Slaven Centre than within? He said nothing of that to Mousier.

'Why don't we give it a go?' said Mousier. 'We need

someone right now with a modicum of experience.' He put his sprouting knuckles to his face, drew down his cheeks so that his great, soft eyes were about to spill. His office was all the modern age, all the business of human focus, all compact technology, winking lights and screens, but beyond the window behind him the hill ridges were still in an abandon of weeds, pigfern and gorse. The Slaven Centre was a sudden dome of uneasy civilisation in the old land. 'A trial period say, of one month, and then if either you, or we, aren't happy, it's bye-bye time. Fair enough?'

'Fair enough,' David said.

'Come into the main office and we'll do the official paper-trail thing,' said Mousier. 'You'll find yourself in Takahe block with Raf, who's a mad hatter much loved by the guests. That's the prevalent euphemism here — guests.' His lemur eyes were sad and lustrous, as if a poet were imprisoned within the administrator.

After the documentation, during most of which the receptionist kept her considerable back to them, Dr Mousier walked with David up to Takahe block, passing Hoiho and Weka. The flower beds, like the buildings, were new, and not even the shrubs above head height. A sensible allowance had been made for growth, but in the meantime the small, yellow conifers, birches and azaleas seemed each in quarantine. The lawns were landscaped and well kept, but here and there, darker than the introduced grass, were tiny sprigs of gorse: the primitive landscape not yet completely repressed. 'We have a simple orientation programme for new staff,' said Mousier. 'Just a couple of sessions in which we help you to see how the place ticks, and there are regulatory guidelines. But, if you've got common sense, you'll learn best by doing the job.'

They were nearing Takahe, and being observed by the same big man who had watched David go down. Raf Hewson, so Mousier explained. Raf sat on a yellow, blow-up seat. Its back was against the wall and the dark valves stuck out from it like cows' tits. Raf wore just togs and sunglasses; when he sat up as the doctor and David neared the steps, they saw on the inflated rest the deeper yellows from the sweat of his back. Only in his size was there any intimidation, for he took off his dark glasses and the newspaper as shelter when Dr Mousier introduced him, and met David's eyes amicably. The soft, fair hair was drawn back to the pony-tail, and his considerable stomach was brown in the sun. 'Welcome to the Bluebird of Paradise Motels,' he said.

'You'll get used to his bullshit,' said Mousier, 'and he does a fair job.'

'You're a hard man, doctor. I hope never to fall into your clutches as a practitioner.'

Mousier just flapped a hand at him, wished David good luck, reminded him of the orientation and began walking back to his office.

David sat on the verandah edge and felt the heat from the wood on his thighs. There were few signs of patients, little noise from any; just a group at a distance putting up a volleyball net by the car park, and one quickfire laugh from inside the block. 'Most of ours have gone down for a swim with Titi,' said Raf. 'We haven't got a pool at the centre yet. The place seems pretty quiet, doesn't it?'

'Seems okay.'

'I wish I could see it all as you do just at this moment,' said Raf, 'as I did when I came eleven months ago. A new place has that clean, special impression on you, don't you think, and then after a while it becomes coded with your experience.'

'Maybe you wise up,' David said.

'You do that, all right. See that fire-escape on the main block? That's a case in point. Reg McConachy did a bungy jump from there after a concert by a visiting jazz trio, but he didn't have a rubber band, did he? For me now, Reg always lies there.'

David could see only the zig-zagging iron steps on the end of the high building and the white concrete beneath in the hot sun. 'It's pretty weird here, then?'

'Well, it's just that no one knows quite what we're dealing with,' said Raf mildly. 'Two years ago there weren't any residential centres for Harlequin in the country: now there's several, though this is still the biggest. Even the doctors are working day by day. Round here precedent isn't much of a guide. We pretty much make things up as we go along.' Raf's back had made a sweat suction with the inflatable seat, and when he leant forward they parted with a squeal. 'Jesus, I'm frying here,' he said. 'And anyway, you'll want to put your stuff away and that. This's as good a time as any, while most of our mob's in the sea.'

They walked down the corridor of Takahe. Forty-five people to each block, Raf said. Most of the rooms were singles, with five doubles for people unable to make any contribution to their hospitalisation costs. No locks were allowed. Tolly Mathews was doing yoga in his room, rather than swimming in the sound. There was an edge of freneticism to his actions which didn't match well with yoga, but which David was to come to see as typical of someone on the cusp of a Harlequin episode.

'You okay, Tolly?' asked Raf.

'I'm going down to Treatment again soon to get stuff.'

When David was introduced, Tolly took his hand with sudden fervour, touched all the nails fleetingly and released it as urgently. A sudden grin split his face, yet his eyes flickered past David. As Raf led David further down the corridor to their own rooms at the far end, the sounds of Tolly's yoga were anything but calming.

'In time almost anything can become routine,' said Raf. His hair hung fair and limp from his pony-tail, but pulled tight from his face, and he gave the half-glance, half-smile, that David was to know so well.

Raf's room looked over the approach and the sea; David's,

on the other side of the corridor, had a view of the steep slope beyond the centre, and he had to bend to bring any sky into view above the bushed ridges. It had the bland practicality of an institutional room: not even lived in long enough to gather much hybrid character from people who had come and gone. A cabinet bed with drawers beneath it, a recessed ceiling light, a table desk at the window, a built-in wardrobe with a sunken lock like a cat's arse. Three cream walls and one mint green. A laminated Toss Woollaston print. How many such rooms do you have to live in, David wondered, before you die, and enter another such, except perhaps the print is one by archangel Raphael — or Lucifer.

'When you've put your stuff away,' said Raf, 'come back into the lounge room. I'll shout you a beer — probably the only one you'll get out of me — and run over a few things before the others get back from their swim.'

David found just one thing in the room that hinted at an occupant: a small, maroon handled screwdriver on the ledge above the window. British Made, it said, 5000 V, it said. The metal shaft was almost black with the slowest of rusts. That one tangible thing passed between the last occupant and David.

'What happened to the last guy?' he asked Raf, who had been along to see Tolly Mathews, and was buttoning a striped collarless shirt before he sat down in the Takahe lounge by the bench, Zip and fridge. All the chairs had the same fabric covering, in the same two shades of speckled green and speckled yellow.

'Prue? How'd you hear about him?'

'I didn't.'

'Prue didn't last long. He started up his own church here, his own faith rather, and it caused friction between those he converted and the rest. There was actually a scrap one night between the two groups and Prue got his marching orders. He's taken his missionary zeal to Patagonia, or somewhere. He was a pretty fair volleyball player, that's the worst of it. How are you at volleyball?'

David told him that it wasn't his thing particularly, but Raf gave him a beer nevertheless, and they sat just far enough back from the lounge window to avoid the full glare of the sun, while Raf talked about the job.

And as he talked, David saw people straggling up the unsealed road, peeling off from the Titi group to head for their own block. They carried towels and their hair was mussed and only half dry. He continued to hear Raf's voice, helpful yet characteristically flippant. David would hold those people in his mind's eye as they straggled back from the shoreline. Later each face, each posture, would be quite familiar to him, although then they appeared as strangers. Howard Peat in front, of course, not wanting any of his fellows in his field of vision; that way it was easier to deny where he was and why. Then Abbey and Jane, self-conscious of their appearance, but full of trivial talk that might give their outing some guise of careless recreation. Jason Brown and Sarah Keppler, who so often consoled each other with their bodies, and thought it a secret safe between them. Others also, in twos and threes, and all with the fear, the anger, the loneliness and despair, carefully buttoned away. Harlequin, Harlequin, come out to play.

'Here they come,' said Raf, breaking off from a summary of routines. 'They don't know what's wrong with them, and nor do we. Today it's them; tomorrow it may well be us. For what it's worth, I find it best to keep my sympathy until it's asked for, which isn't often.'

How do you account for the role you find imposed on you in life, places you inhabit without design, people who surround you, obligations that come uninvited? So bright the sun as David watched the people of Takahe come home. Harlequin, Harlequin, out to play.

A great staircase leading from the hall, a landing at its turn with a green and red poppy plant window, and the stairs then again angling up, up. He would sit and rock on the landing when he should have been in his bed, and listen to the voices below. The landing was a halfway house, a fringe zone, a no man's land, a pushmi-pullyu, between the up and down. The lights reached just that far from below and the dark encroached that far from above. He would rock, and hold the smooth, wooden leg of the stair rail until it was egg warm beneath his arm. If he held on and leant far back with tipping head, he could see the oval landing window, which was almost black unless there was a moon behind it, and in its darkness was the glimmer of the poppy caught in the faintest hall light, as a goldfish gleams with indistinct allure in a brown lily pond.

The life downstairs was trivial and transient, no doubt: neighbours in for birthday drinks, an election night get-together, former friends passing through the district once again, his mother's committee to make submissions on the beautification of reserves. Nothing of significance; nothing of remembrance beyond the time of it, unless recalled hazily from a diary entry, or more emphatically because linked with incident — Tommy Concoran's heart attack, lightning striking the woolshed, Dot Maddox seeing the risen and glowing Christ walking down Hotten's Spur.

But for David then, the voices, scents, opening and closing of doors, the spilling of warm light along the hall, all had the enchantment of adult life of the night. And uniqueness a part of it, because not set among street lights, flashing signs, comings and goings, any companionship of buildings. Their house, surely, was the one bulwark against the night in all the world. If he stood and stretched to peer through the clear glass lozenges at the base of the landing window, what he saw, indistinct and restive, were the macrocarpa at the tractor sheds, the hill behind flayed with sheep tracks if the moon shone, the gully flowing darkness where the creek bore water for the day.

And from his bed he could hear the sound foam away

from the great ships that tossed among the pines, and spray on wet nights was slung like gravel against the windows of his room. Quiet nights, too, with the furtive rattle of a dog's chain, the punctured cough of a ewe, the stark benediction of the morepork who sees all there is to see without need of sun, or moon.

In the yard was the dog tucker ewe hung high in a tree by the kennels to beat the flies, and with a split sack to cover it. His father would unhook the rope and run it down the pulley, and swing the carcase on to the broad stump that served as butcher's block. The heavy cleaver was never lifted high, but bit through the ribs as if they were kindling, and his father would throw a part shoulder, or leg, to each dog without moving from the block, and each dog took it according to character — with a snarl and twist to subdue it, with a fawning uncertainty, with a quick snap and retreat into the kennel. Usually his father tossed the meat with an odd, backward flip of his hand, as a card sharp deals in a routine display of skill.

And when his father had gone on to the next chore, David might watch the dogs eat, the tucker in the sack sway high again, the white leghorns and the sparrows pick the meat and fat from the cuts in the stump. In time it was his own turn; with the same cleaver grown less mystical and the stump so much reduced, and the dog tucker in an old freezer under the tractor shed overhang, instead of strung and idling in the aromatic macrocarpa branches.

At nine he was old enough to make mash for the chooks each morning before his own breakfast, while his father milked the cow, taking down to the fowl house one bucket half full of warm water and another of kitchen scraps, and mixing in the mash meal with an old butter pat. There were wooden troughs in the runs, and in the winter the mash steamed as he ladled it in, and the frozen chicken droppings glittered like agates in the first of the sun. When he dished out the mash, he always left the run gates open, because there were some leghorns that roosted in the sheds and trees of the yard, and they would come stupidly running, late for their share, beaks agape.

Nothing of this is ever lost, Alst Mousier and Schweitzer would say, though it may be inaccessible. The white leghorns run stupidly and incessantly, the dog tucker carcase sways on high, the glass poppy gleams in the faintest of light. Forever.

THREE

Pedder Culhane was the director of the Slaven Centre at Mahakipawa — the Great White Father of the place. Everyone said how lucky they were to have him. He'd been born in Bulls and gone on to a world reputation in some of those fearsome shape-shifters coming out of Africa: Lassa fever, Ebola, HIV. He could have stayed in any of the world's research institutions, but he came back to Mahakipawa to do what he could against Harlequin. Schweitzer, people called him at the centre, and only partly tongue in cheek. There was pride and gratitude that someone of such ability, and with such career options, chose to be heading up things at the Slaven Centre. He had graced the cover of *Time* magazine without becoming convinced of his own divinity. He had a wife and three daughters in Wellington, and every second weekend flew out from Nelson to visit them. All other days but those, he was on call around the clock.

David saw him first on the orientation day for new staff. Three male and four female nurses, Polly Merhtens and David who were block aides, a visiting radiologist from Adelaide and a pudding-faced payroll guy from central admin. They were such a small group, that after Alst Mousier had taken them for a tour of the facilities, and after the nurses and radiologist had displayed a deal of medical knowledge while Polly, David and Pudding Face added little, they were all able to fit into Mousier's office, which was roomier than most because he was chief administrator. It was hot, and Mousier altered the slat blinds to keep out the glare of the sun.

Mousier's secretary brought in glasses of dilute and artificial orange drink, and Schweitzer carried one too when he came. He had a candy-striped straw in his, though, and he sat on the end of the desk with easy informality, and his cheeks sucked in as he drank. Then he said, 'You won't have been in any place like this before, and neither have those of us you're joining. We're not sure at all what we've got by the tail here, but it's sure as hell some sort of tiger.'

He sat amid the trays and papers on the desk, while lifeguards pursued bikini babes as screen savers on Mousier's computer. He wore very light, blue fabric shoes and no socks. On his left ankle a vein curved over his Achilles tendon. He had a tight, nimble body and a heavy shaving shadow on his cheeks and neck. Sustenance for the follicles there was perhaps drawn by gravity, for by contrast the hair on his head had retreated to accentuate the brow.

'The aetiology of this one is so lacking as to be both ludicrous and scary,' Schweitzer said. 'The pathology of it, on the other hand, is all around us, and dauntingly complex. The treatment we're making up as we go along.' He paused, and seemed to concentrate on an even swing of his blue shoes. 'But that's enough reassurance for you on arrival at Mahakipawa,' he said. Had there been more of them for induction they would no doubt have laughed, but as it was, intimate within Mousier's office, they smiled and leant back in their vinyl chairs.

He had presence, did Schweitzer. You didn't listen to him long before admitting the intelligence, the concern, the quiet confidence, and only that degree of unconscious arrogance which arose naturally from a long time living with the deference of those around him. Schweitzer himself had coined the name Harlequin, which was increasingly used for the illness, because he thought primal brain regression inaccurate and unhelpful. 'After all, primal brain dominance, if you must. The regression is from powers more recently acquired. Over hundreds of thousands of years higher brain functions evolved which imposed control over more rudimentary responses, and what we seem to have in Harlequin is the failure of these later functions for some reason, and so the archaic response of primal brain, the thalamus, hypothalamus, limbic system, are set free again. Our original soul: call it what you will.'

'And it's an odd brute,' said Alst Mousier from behind them. 'Evolution can never go back to the drawing board. It's had to build on what's there.'

The sun glowed at the chinks of the blinds, Schweitzer went on to explain how the Slaven Centre worked; and all the time the primal brain, old Harlequin, was biding its time in them, and rampant within the patients they were there to help. The only difference was that, with the guests, he was already able to slip his collar and come out dancing. It never paid to bait the monkey man.

How had they all come to be there: the nurses, Polly, the Aussie radiologist, the pudding pay man? And which of David's many poor decisions had brought him to Mahakipawa when all his ambitions had been different?

'I hope that your choice will prove a happy one for us and you,' said Schweitzer before he left. David noticed that he had wound the candy-striped straw around his left index finger as he'd been speaking, and that there was a slight sheen of sweat on his frontal baldness.

The farm was named Beth Car by David's great-grandfather, who had come out from Wales. It was near the head of the valley, and Coal-pit Road went only a few kilometres more past their gate, and finished in a trivial reserve where there was a picnic area among the broom and lupins, a shallow swimming hole under heavy willows, a concrete fireplace smudged black, and beer cans in the lank grass within throwing distance. The place altered little, and was too far from town to be under any pressure of use. Occasionally the Palliser kids, or the Mercers, would pedal up in the shimmer of a summer afternoon; sometimes in the evening a local guy would take a girl there, the family Commodore, or Falcon, throbbing through the dusk.

The creek ran through Beth Car, and the farm sloped up to the west, steeper and drier, although still with limestone beneath it which sweetened the soil, so that grass came away quickly with the rain. The house David's great-grandfather built was tucked behind the macrocarpas, close to the business of the farm — the yards, the old concrete dip, the shearing and equipment sheds. The new house, built over forty years ago, was higher up, to claim a view and get above the shit, shingle and shout of the working area. It had a feature stone chimney that was visible both inside and out, and feature greywacke boulders covered most of the house end that could be seen from the road.

For years the lower house was used by married couples. David had recollections of them coming and going. The Lawsons and Hayters stayed the longest, and were the only ones David remembered well. The Lawsons had a daughter he had his eye on, but, before David was old enough to make anything of it, Gavin Lawson went into a mussel farm partnership.

John Hayter bred border collies, and took over his wife's washing machine for weeks on end to make home brew. She had a thing with Stella Jones who taught at the Waipounae primary school, and it was the talk of the district until the three went their various ways. Hayter went to Ashburton and set up a business making mud and cement bricks, but the booze got him, which was always the likely outcome.

After the Hayters there wasn't another married couple. Times were tighter. David was old enough to do more at weekends and holidays, and his father would also get casual labour in. His mother didn't like the idea of renting the old house to people they had no connection with, so it was just shut up for a few years, and then downgraded by random convenience to a storage place. Eventually it was gutted, and used for hay and super. On winter feed-out days, David would haul bales from a window through which he once saw Wendy Lawson inspecting her new breasts.

He'd been out with the .22 after possums, which swarmed in the walnut trees in season, and he walked back past the yards with the dark, shifting macrocarpas behind him, and the air gathering the weight of night. There, clear as you like, was Wendy Lawson having a look at herself in her mirror. She held her arms at different angles; she leant and turned. It was as if she were trying on a garment and liked the fit of it. So did David. Tits of a thirteen-year-old, but shapely, high, the nipples more pronounced than he expected.

The next morning he caught her up as they walked down to meet the school bus, and looked her over carefully while talking all the while of Podge Nicholson being strapped for insolence. There was hardly any sign that she had good tits at all. It struck him that those girls who had a show in a dress, must have a real pair on them when stripped. At school he told his friends of his hypothesis, but they were more interested in their own stories of the female form observed.

The old house was made of timber pit-sawn on the property, and it gave way only grudgingly to the cold rot of neglect that came as the trees enclosed it. The laundry and dairy had been lean-tos, and the lavatory, originally a long drop, was a short walk from the back door and shielded by a trellis of roses. The last time David had looked at the old house, a red hand-separator had been rusting on the dunny seat, and moss bulging on the crumbling concrete of the path. The trellis had suffered a soft collapse, but there were small rose flowers, fresh and white in the shade.

He was forced to sell all of Beth Car, which three generations had built up for him, and had nothing to show for it but echoes, fugitive scents, the flicker of things seen there — the Lawson girl before the mirror, hills white with frost as the sun rose, pencil tallies on the wall of the shearing shed, a hand-separator on the dunny seat of the old house, the poppy window at the bend of the stairs in the more recent home, his mother in the garden, his father on the hill.

All of these memories should have been enriching but, instead, each was stained with guilt.

FOUR

'I'm taking my lot for a dip,' Raf said. David told him that they were his lot just as much. 'Ah, but I'm the senior aide, though,' Raf said. 'It's like that strict army hierarchy: even if you're gazetted only minutes before someone else, you take absolute precedence in field command. In your case you're well behind. Fucking useless, in fact. I should by rights be taking half your pay.' Raf scrutinised his port bottle while he talked, as if reading his lines from the label. 'Bloody stuff's made in the North Island,' he said despondently.

'They can't all go,' David told him. 'Abbey, for example. Abbey's been peculiar all morning. She's going to blow.'

'Let her blow. If it happens, then the mudflats are ideal. All give, yet complete retention. She'll be better there than down at Treatment.'

Raf began going through the block urging people to go down for a swim. Some rooms were empty, but most of Takahe had walked back after lunch for want of any more pressing destination. Ham it had been: a great mass of green salad it had been, slick with a clear dressing, as if dipped in sweat.

Many of the guests had been significantly decisive in the

lives they had before Harlequin, but their confidence was knocked, and most had become resigned to suggestion. Only trivial or peevish expressions of self-determination were shown — like not waiting in the car park for all to assemble as Raf wanted, but straggling down the long drive to the sea. In time over twenty were on the move in the hot, still afternoon.

David noticed how clearly their order of march reflected their state of health for the day. Gaynor Runcinski, Eddie Simm, Howard Peat, Big Pulii and Sara Keppler were in the front, and interacting as a group. They could quite well have been a seminar syndicate on super nova, or a progressive dinner party between courses. At the back, however, and falling further behind, were the odd-gaited and self-absorbed like Abbey, Wilfe Orme and Jason Brown. Like mob stragglers with foot-rot, they wavered and wandered on the gravel drive, kept generally in the direction of the shore only by Raf's insistence. Jason was smacking his bare arms and assuring himself, and others within earshot, that the cork in his arse would prevent him from bleeding to death.

'God won't be mocked,' Dilys Williams was saying peevishly. 'Why won't people take any notice of the things going on in this place? Surely in a hospital there should be godliness and better meals.'

Across the public road, down a runnel of a track through the matted grass and stiff, yellow-brown rushes to the shore. Short rushes, thick as an upturned scrubbing brush, and holding aloft small pieces of driftwood and other flotsam as a sign of some stormy high tide. The mud was there all right, a dark kidney lying heavily inert, but there were also tide channels across it where the currents swept away the mud, and the bed gleamed with runs of compact pale sand, blue-grey stones, shell pieces, dark shards of wood heavy as the stones. The whole mudflat was pocked with crab burrows and, as the first of the group came down, the crabs stopped fossicking and fighting, and scurried home. One receding flicker of movement across all the wet slick, and then nothing for a time. The sea way out was very blue: like a child's ocean beneath the sun, but flexing and with fleeting pinpoints flashing white, violet, gold, because of the breeze blowing up the sound.

The track ended by the largest of the channels, which had become a swimming point for the centre. It must have been a good possie long before that, too, a place from which the deeper water could be reached, for there were three dark piles left as the remains of a jetty, no higher than a man, and these filed out from the shore like people also — thin and dark, with nothing to say of their former usefulness.

'I'm getting in before the droolers arrive and start pissing in the water,' said Howard. Like most of the others he wore his togs beneath his shorts, and in seconds he had stripped, clamped his towel on the peak of the first pile and begun wading into the channel. 'Corker,' he said in his old-fashioned way. He turned back to see Gaynor fumbling with her dress. 'I'm going a fair way out,' he said testily, as if there'd been some move, or murmur, to restrain him. His white legs seemed even thinner beneath the water, and were refracted away in apparent deformity. 'No one's to touch my towel, remember.' He remained facing the sea as he called.

'Yes, my liege,' said Gaynor.

'Silly old prick,' said Sara.

'I'm leaving my sneakers on this time.' Undressing so informally made Gaynor rather prim. 'Remember Sonya McDonald slashing her toe on something in here.'

'Fair enough,' David said.

Gaynor waded softly into the clear channel, the water at first just lapping her ankles. As she went deeper and further she lifted her arms up, and the water rose around the blue and white checks of her costume. The laces of her sneakers writhed, and the soles sent up puffs of mud and sand. The wind moved on the broad surface of the sound far beyond Howard. More people gathered at the shore, not quite as eager as Howard and Gaynor to get in. 'Look at the tits on her,' said Dermot Sweeney with institutional frankness. Gaynor blushed, lowering her arms and folding them across her chest as the water reached there to make her shiver.

She was a textile artist of renown in her field: she had taught at the Palmerston North Polytechnic, and been awarded a travel grant to Tuttle, North Dakota, to study indigenous weaving. Her large piece, 'Maui Fishing', hung in the National Gallery. Nothing of that gave her credence as she waded in the mudflats. She was just a guest — an overweight woman not good enough to make the Takahe volleyball team, and diagnosed only eight weeks before as suffering from Harlequin's. All was different now. All bets were off.

'Oh, it's very bracing,' she cried. She didn't turn round. The tears ran over the curve of her cheeks. Is that how dying is: joining with strangers in a place that means nothing to you? All bound on the wheel, but trying to avert your eyes from the agony of others. As her sneakers trod the channel bed, she must have been aware of the kidney mud stretching fatly beside her, the crab holes gaping like anuses to the splendour of the sun. 'So refreshing, but there is that glare on the water,' Gaynor said, and was immediately aghast at her own empty civility.

Gaynor was known to hold her breath in the latrine until her head went dizzy, but she swam well and swallowed in a sea that was shat in by a thousand creatures for a thousand years — sperm whales, conger eels, fur seals, penguins, purple-topped men-o'-war, Taiwanese fishermen and birds migrating to the other side of the world.

Behind Gaynor, others were stepping into the sea, making their own comments, and behind them more of the group again, arriving and beginning awkwardly to take off their clothes. Abbey had brought no togs, and was to swim in T-shirt and white knickers. She was too confused to feel demeaned.

'Now this is the life,' said Raf firmly. 'Everything you'd get at Club Med at a fraction of the price, and you provide your own cabaret.'

There was a deal of wading to be done before the sea was deep enough to swim in. Some of the group were only paddlers and potterers anyway: working shells from the bottom with their feet, bending to inspect the reduced creatures which, on close view, could be seen to populate the apparently barren mud. Small crabs were the most numerous — green-backed and with flashes of yellow beneath their pinchers. They held a transfixed posture of minor threat, or vanished at a snap; seemingly no movement in between.

Raf stood yawning amid the rushes. His mouth stretched immensely, his eyes were forced to close, he gave the high-pitched sound that accompanies a full yawn. A sound that no doubt had preceded speech and now, millions of years later, was inexplicable. His hair, drawn back to the ponytail, was damp at his temples with sweat. 'Jesus George,' he said. 'It's an odd way to make a living, isn't it? Leading a bunch of Harlequins to water. It's just as well we've no way of knowing our future, otherwise we'd never be happy. I thought I'd be rich in the city by now, and here I am as a minder, watching these good people by the sea, maybe killing myself in the process.'

'There's worse things to be doing,' David said.

'You reckon.'

'Well, almost everybody here is worse off than us, after all. It's all relative, isn't it? In the country of the blind, the one-eyed man is king.'

'Ahh–h–h–h–uh.' Raf yawned to the sky and rubbed his eyes. He then made a seat of driftwood so that he could sit down in the rushes without getting his bum damp. David knew that Raf came down in the evenings when off duty, and swam far into the sound, his long, maidenly hair flowing out behind him.

The tide began to turn. Small surges were at first

contained within the channels, and then fanned out over the mudflats. Black swan were at a distance, and a single blue heron. A few pied oystercatchers and mallard ducks followed the tide in, fossicking for advantage along the water line. The guests began coming in also: well, at least those who had made any appreciable move away from the piles. The first in to swim were also the last out — Howard and Gaynor. Howard had an intrepid air about him, but no one praised him for being so heroic, so far out. Gaynor had mastered her self-pity in the privacy of the deeper water, and was cheerful and considerate once more. She put a dry towel around Abbey's shoulders and began walking with her, after the others, towards the road to the centre. 'There's a broadcast of the Ivashkin recital tonight,' Gaynor told her friend. 'Rossini's "Une Larme" and something by Astor Piazzola.' The surface of the sound glittered between the hills, except where ruffled and dulled by a passing wind. A stock truck rumbled by to Havelock.

David had accepted the responsibility of being tail-end Charlie, and did a quick check of the shore by the channel and weathered piles. The grass and rushes trampled somewhat, the gathered driftwood people had been sitting on, just one floppy, green hat, which he thought was Jason's, and he put it on before leaving the mud crabs to salute the tide.

'I reckon we're heading for a drought,' Wilfe was telling Eddie Simm as they crossed the road. Anything was welcome which took attention from their affliction.

FIVE

'Dragnet, Dragnet,' shouted Raf as he opened David's door and leant in: one hand anchored on the doorframe, the other on the knob and spilling him forward, although his feet remained in the corridor. Such was the length of his arms and the extent of his large body, that his head reached far into the room and was outlined against the corridor light. The crop of his pony-tail frayed into the glow behind him; his large nose was a restless shadow on his hung face.

'Jason's running berko on the hill,' he said. A tone almost all urgent and genuine concern, but with some joy of the spectacle. 'He's lost it altogether, the poor bastard. He's blown. I've buzzed the main block. He's got some stuff from somewhere, and he's setting fire to the goddamn hill.'

It was one of those moments when you're unsure if you're emerging from sleep to reality, or moving from the world to nightmare. It wasn't the first time such bewilderment had gripped David in that place. Nowhere, surely, had a more indistinct boundary between real and unreal. 'Jesus,' David said weakly from the bed, and then, trying for a stronger voice to match resolution to the event, 'Right, Jesus, I'm with you.'

'Come on, come on,' called Raf. His voice was flung away,

as in one movement he swayed from the room and made off down the corridor. 'Get something on your bloody feet, though.'

In the time it took David to reach the verandah, Raf had a torch, was over the fence that kept stock from the centre's grounds and was a bounding shadow on the slope of the hill. Further up flared patches of gorse and bracken fired by Jason. The night enhanced the flames so that they were blood red and glittering, but the smoke was denied its true colour, and rolled away black as liquorice except immediately above the flames.

David could hear the duty team coming up from the main block and, wanting to be on the hill before them, he slipped through the fence and headed up towards the fires, using his own issue torch to find the best way.

There was nothing fugitive, or furtive, about Jason. As David passed some of the earlier fire patches, already dying down, he could hear him shouting exultantly ahead. Raf had taken the can of petrol from him by the time David arrived, and sat on it, trying to catch his breath, his pale pyjamas almost luminous in the night. 'Look at him,' he puffed. 'He's well away. Happy as a bloody sandboy.'

Jason Brown stood agog before his last fire, his high laugh of release matching the jumpy energy of the flames which caught gorse barbs, or fern whorls, in a sudden grip and gave them brief, incandescent beauty. Jason wore a long, blue coat, unbuttoned, and his head rocked in excitement, his voice raced at the eternal fascination of fire: the threat and wilful power, the heat, the primitive wonder of it. Jason was unable to keep still. His mind and body were in spasm. His hands and feet and eyes had the sudden movements of the fox and ferret; his voice had release and abandon. 'Look at the bright cunt,' he shouted. He was dancing, as if in imitation of the flames. 'Woosh, you beauty, away you go. Burn it all up, you fucker.'

'He could have started on the buildings,' said Raf. 'Now,

without the petrol, he can't do much harm. We'll let him bounce around until he wears off some energy, and then take him down for the shots.'

'Let it all burn to buggery.' Jason waved on the flames fiercely. He wanted the whole world consumed.

'What's the cocky going to feel about all this then?' asked David.

'I imagine he keeps well away,' said Raf. 'Do you know who's coming up?'

David hadn't been able to see any faces behind him, but thought he'd heard Dr Sheridan's voice, and sure enough he came puffing behind Colin Squires, who was one of the duty nurses.

'Everything's jake,' said Raf, as Colin continued over to Jason, and Tony Sheridan made a special effort up the hill over the last few metres. 'He can't do anything without the petrol.'

'I swear he picks the bloody nights I'm on,' said Colin. 'Who knows what mad thing he'll get up to if we don't get him down for treatment.'

'Just leave him,' David said. 'Probably the excitement of the fires was all he needed. I'll help Raf bring him down.'

Colin pulled Jason's long coat closed, and buttoned it for warmth as the last clump of fired gorse died down. He did it with no more sense of human contact than if Jason had been a scarecrow, and received as little reaction. 'Yeah, I think I'd better go back down. There's bound to be some other cracker about to blow. Okay, doc?'

'Sure,' said Tony Sheridan. He was still bent forward, hands on his knees, his face disappearing as the flames contracted to embers. 'I'll be down myself soon with Jason. I just need a breather here for a bit.'

They heard Colin going back, the light of his torch winking down the slope towards the steady, broad glow of the centre buildings. And when the fires were no longer a dominant glare, the natural variations of the night could be realised again. A certain sheen to the dark sky, stars even, the absorbent black of the bush on the high slopes, a scaly glimmer from the distant movement of the sea. Raf and David moved over to Jason, and stood with him for warmth by the last fire. The smoke in their faces was powerfully aromatic, and David could feel the faintest touches of ash on his cheeks when Jason flipped branches with his feet. The last sparks flitted up and were gone. Jason still twitched and talked, his hands roved to make compulsive touches, but as the fire dwindled so did his euphoria. The red of the flames, the black winging of the smoke, were almost lost to him, and the accustomed profile of the hill crest against the sky came up quietly again. Fire wasn't freedom for him after all, just an expression of some tyranny within. Atavistic responses are the heart of Harlequin.

'Burn, you fucker,' he said bitterly.

David and Tony Sheridan walked with Jason down to the centre. Raf followed behind, with the sound of the petrol sloshing in the can to locate him. David had nothing on over his pyjamas, and felt cold when the excitement was over. His concern for Jason was partly overtaken by a wish that he'd thought to pull a jersey on before following Raf up the hill. He used the torch to keep to the clearer ground, but his light trousers were filthy with ash stripes and the dew from grasses and fern.

'I'm okay, okay,' said Jason. 'It wasn't a reversion.'

'It's the third time within a fortnight. Must be at least,' said Sheridan. There was a morepork crying through the darkness from the shore. There was a small wind which rustled and fingered on the hill. There were embers which glowed briefly at its touch.

'Jesus, I suppose I'm for it then.' Jason said it with both fear and defiance, as a soldier might who can't turn back. His head went up, and he gave an odd turkey cock cry which drifted on the dark slope. He walked in a way that made the long coat swirl about his legs.

'You'll be all right,' David lied.

'Once you have some stuff, you'll be fine,' lied Raf from behind them. 'A time will come when you'll look back on all of this, and have a laugh. All of us will. Won't he, doc?'

Tony Sheridan was busy climbing through the wires of the fence, and on to the lawn of the centre. He didn't say anything, but the morepork floated a reply out of the darkness that was both sea and land. 'I wouldn't mind so much,' said Jason, 'but there's this girl in Napier.' None of them asked about the girl in Napier, or Sara Keppler closer to hand. They had enough with Jason right there at the centre; seeing anything of the life that he had come from could only make it more difficult. It was better, as a form of protection, to keep him in focus as a patient. Was there a point at which you drew a line and allowed no emotional concern, not even curiosity, to go past it?

They took Jason back to Takahe, but only so that he could collect overnight things for the treatment room in the main block. Most of the others were awake, and had been watching from the verandah. Sara couldn't bear to approach. She wept for him and for her loss of the sweet consolation that is a lover's body, but some of the others saw him off, magnifying, or diminishing, the significance of it, depending on their way. 'Rely only on your own resources, Jason,' said Howard Peat dogmatically. 'The fight is with yourself.'

'God won't be mocked, you know.' The voice came from Dilys Williams's window. She must have been standing there with her light out.

'You'll be all right, Jasie. Hang in there,' called Abbey as Jason walked down from Takahe with Sheridan. 'See you, Jasie.'

'See you, Abbey,' mimicked Jason. The voice exactly hers, and exactly Harlequin's — not mockery from Jason. The coat swished around him, its blueness coming and going as he walked through the pools of light cast from the buildings.

'He won't be back,' Raf said softly. 'No chance.' Blue

faded to black; black was refurbished to blue. Jason's head rose and fell because of the unnatural energy of his walk, whereas Tony Sheridan's gait maintained him at an even height. David realised that Jason was building to blow again. His hands were raised as he talked urgently to the doctor, almost as if he were conducting an orchestra out of sight of the rest of them. Swish blue; swish black. See you, Jasie. The morepork was quiet by the sea. Swish blue, swish black. The guests began to withdraw to their own rooms. Sara had already gone in and closed her door.

'Go back to bed,' Raf said to David. 'I'll hang on a while till everything's settled.'

No one wanted to talk about what had happened, for they knew exactly what had taken place. It was old Harlequin, wasn't it, coming out to play.

Chris came to Collegiate at the start of the fifth-form year, when his parents shifted to a diplomatic posting in Berlin. The same dorm, the same form, as David, and so an opportunity for friendship. Not immediately, however; Chris was too much a showman to encourage early confidences. It was his way of settling in: attack as the best defence until he was accepted in the place. He was shrewd for his age. Within a fortnight he had to face up to a fight with the malicious Coddy Joux, and knew that to appeal openly to the masters was as bad as chickening out. So he appeared eager for a meet behind the library after prep, but set up such a din, swearing and shouting as they fought, that the hostel staff got wind of it before Coddy could do more harm to him than a torn ear.

Chris was accomplished at art, at fives, at loyalty and at getting girls. He was hopeless at maths, science, honesty and keeping to any rules. His mother was part Chinese and passed on just enough to give him a smooth complexion and very dark, straight hair. When he was in the seventh form, an ex-Rangi Ruru girl in her first varsity year, and not half bad, asked him to partner her to an orientation dance. She lived near the school and had picked Chris out. It was almost as if girls liked the smell of him. David and the others had to work harder to be noticed, but they came to accept his appeal as just one of those things — like being born with odd-coloured eyes, or having the knack of holding your breath under water longer than anyone else.

Several times Chris went home with David to Beth Car, where he charmed David's mother, amused his father with general irreverence, and failed only with the dogs, which must have been averse to the pheromones that worked so well on women. Neither Chris nor David talked about school realistically to those outside it. The hostel was a separate life, a foreign land, and they kept it that way, tacitly acknowledging that special values and rules applied there.

When you are young, friends are often made instinctively, without any assessment, any calculation of their intrinsic value as people, or the outcome of commitment. Only years later did David realise that Chris was amoral, and later still that perhaps that had been part of the attraction all along. Chris was a jesting plunderer of other people's lives.

By the sixth form they were so close that Chris hatched a scheme for both of them to score well in Sharkey's history exam. Every system has a weak point, Chris said, that's the thing to bear in mind. The staff were very aware of the need for security before and during the exams, but he sussed out an opportunity to cheat afterwards. Sharkey was their house master as well as their history teacher, and they knew his procedure well. Each question was answered on a fresh sheet, so that Sharkey could bundle them together and mark question by question, rather than script by script. And Sharkey never started marking until the weekend. On the night after the exam, Chris and David rewrote the three weakest of their answers from their class notes and took them to the flat the following afternoon while Sharkey was coaching junior rugby. Chris was a favourite with Sharkey's wife, of course: she could barely keep herself from patting his gleaming black hair. Had she watched his dorm imitations of Sharkey giving her one, she might have felt differently. While Chris entertained her with school gossip that Sharkey never thought to pass on, David went into the study and readily found the question bundles on the desk.

Chris was complaining about exam stress when David came guiltily back. 'If only you could sit down after the exam and have another shot without the nerves.' His smile was ingenuous.

'I bet you'll do all right,' said Sharkey's wife. Looks must be commensurate with ability after all.

'Actually,' said Chris, 'I've a good feeling about the history, but then we're lucky with the teacher there, aren't we, David?'

'I don't butter up that easy,' said Sharkey's wife, but of course she did. She buttered up until she gleamed with it, and Chris could have trussed her legs for roasting.

David got top marks for history that year, and the next year too, without any cheating, and at the university he was an A or B plus student in it, even though before Chris's plan he couldn't seem to get the hang of the subject. He thought it strange, because dishonesty was supposed to turn out badly, yet that one instance of cheating seemed to benefit him year after year.

SIX

Tolly Mathews was having a good patch. He brought a bottle of vintage port, and Raf, along to David's room. Tolly was a designer and manufacturer of bathroom fittings. His business employed seventy-four people, and had plants in Auckland, Palmerston North and Christchurch. Mathews shower boxes with their non-drip doors were used all over the country, and exported to Australia. 'Let's sit down for a bit and enjoy ourselves,' he said.

'I'm on duty,' said Raf.

'So they know where to find you then, don't they? It's exceedingly conscientious of you not to leave the block. You'll probably get a bloody medal.' Tolly still had all the money he'd ever need, but he'd agreed with his family that he wasn't running the business any more. There'd been the evening when he drove a forklift through the window of a rival's showroom, and an indecent assault upon a lingerie mannequin. 'Anyway,' he said, 'most of the others are watching that quiz thing on television. Abbey reckons it has a calming effect. So many nutters on the outside perhaps, that it takes the spotlight from our own behaviour.'

David admired Tolly. Even though he was secondary stage

Harlequin, and privately horrified by it, most of the time he kept an interest in other people and happenings. He had an expensive telescope set up at the window in his room, and was teaching himself astronomy. Sometimes he focused on Amelia Struthers getting undressed in Weka, but that didn't detract from his serious study of the heavens. His enthusiasm was persuasive, and he'd given talks to societies in Nelson and Blenheim, as well as his fellow guests. Amelia had twin dimples low on her back, where the curve of her buttocks began, and the light of her room would cast them into oscillating saucers of shadow.

That night, though, Tolly was more interested in drinking vintage port and enjoying a time free of symptoms. He fronted to the cool air from David's window, and inhaled the complex smell of the mudflats. He held his port glass at head height. 'This in defiance of the shape shifter,' he said. 'We're not dead yet.'

'Really top wine could prove to be the cure,' David told him. 'The boffins are finding more and more benefits in it.'

'English squires thrived on a bottle a day,' added Raf. 'Mind you, the rest of the population probably starved to death.'

Tolly had an alert, boyish face, with only a hooked nose to spoil it. All his front teeth were immaculately capped. As well as design and business flair, he loved music and had a talent for squash, and that, unlike the other things, had been accentuated by Harlequin, as physical abilities so often were. 'I've never played better than when in the grip of it,' he said. 'All sorts of athleticism becomes possible, or you think that it is. If Harlequin ever really takes off—'

'What would you call it now?' said Raf.

'Full scale, though, then I reckon it would revolutionise professional sport. It might kill you, but Jesus, how much better than any performance-enhancing drugs. Harlequins will out-jump, out-run, out-wrestle and out-lift all the rest.

You see it here with volleyball sometimes, don't you, just before someone blows?'

Tolly poured more port for each of them, and the taste of it was oddly mixed with the aromas drifting on the air from the sea. Tolly could afford the best of port, and it was darker even, more aromatic even, than the night. Raf's flagon variety didn't deserve the name. Was there any hierarchy among the three of them? Tolly was officially an inmate, and Raf and David his keepers. Tolly was rich, and Raf and David were not. Drinking and talking there, they were equal in the simple enjoyment of the night, and the shared ignorance concerning the illness moving all around them.

'With the telescope,' said Tolly, 'I've become aware of a scale of things that bears no relation to how we live here. Yet, after spending hours looking at solar systems beyond our own, I feel a micro-organism's need to piss, or eat rissoles with onion.'

'Or switch to a view of Amelia Struthers,' David added.

'That most of all,' said Tolly, 'though I bet it's likely to provoke old Harlequin.'

'Then we're all sufferers from the same disease, if the odd hard-on is a symptom,' said Raf.

The small, impersonal room was briefly made a close sanctuary by friendship and tacit acknowledgement of a quiet moment, before time surged on. Life no doubt whirled as ever further out on the circle, but the thin walls, the lines of attention to each other, allowed them to forget it for a moment. A sheet of hardboard can sometimes separate agony from ecstasy. Tolly's stars lay in the velvet of the sky, and myriad crabs gave their pincered salute from the mudflats.

'What's the news on Jason?' said Tolly after a time. His voice was diffident, almost casual. David had earlier that day asked Dr Roimata Wallace the same question. On the way out, he'd been told, and knew that Jason wouldn't be walking when he went.

'Not so hot,' said David.

'Meltdown,' said Raf.

Tolly allowed a brief pause for respect, then turned the subject to fishing, so that they could stay cheerful. Fishing from the shore was useless apart from flounder, but Tolly's money gave him options. He'd bought a large dinghy and kept it tethered in the mudflat rushes of the tide line. He found out the best fishing spot, which was about a third of the way across the sound, and on the slope of one of the deeper channels that brought a flow of nutrients. He anchored a craypot marker there. It was faded to a blush pink, and bobbed persistently in promise of sport beneath.

David spent whole mornings, afternoons, evenings, in the dinghy, sometimes with Tolly, or another guest, mostly alone, rarely with Raf because of duty rosters. Fishing provided an accepted withdrawal from the world. The dinghy would snout on its anchor rope into the breeze, or the tide, the chop slap against the dinghy's clinker sides, the shallow bilge water slop under the duck boards, the hand lines veer off sharply underwater, refracted, until lost in the intensifying green depths.

Blue cod were the most common catch, sometimes tarakihi, occasionally the slim menace of a barracouta, even a starfish, or conger eel, if the bait had been long on the bottom. For David, none of them was more than a gratuitous justification for being isolated there in the long arm of the sea. From the dinghy, the Slaven Centre became only a small part of things again, though he could recognise Takahe, the walkways, the treatment block, the tractor mower revolving like a blowfly on a polished table, even Bryce's blue ute going up with the deliveries. David thought some emanation from the centre should be visible: transpirations of bewilderment and defiance, fear and desperation, comfort and selflessness, stoicism and compassion — all rising up over the buildings. But there was nothing of that: no distortion of the mundane buildings unless just a shimmer from rising heat waves.

Perhaps a faint diesel plume from the high, stainless steel boiler house chimney.

As David talked with Tolly and Raf, enjoyed a rich man's port, he knew that the faded float was out there on the dark water, holding against the fluid, tidal bulge towards the bone-dry moon.

SEVEN

Agony and beauty co-existed at the Slaven Centre: David suspected at times they coalesced, though he shied away from any serious consideration of that. Often when he sat at a lounge window while on night duty, or when sleep wasn't easy, the sound was a pale trough between the hills rising from it, and the moving air bore scents of the salt, purpled mud, the bracken under dew, and the shellfish in all the small bays. The morepork was insistent, yet invisible. The stoat and weasel made no noise, but they struck as happily.

It was a morepork-cum-stoat-cum-weasel night when Lucy Mortimer came to the centre. Big Pulii suffered several sudden attacks that left him almost dazzlingly euphoric, and after David and Raf had strapped him to the power trundler and delivered him to the main block for treatment, they came back just in time to see Jane Milton begin to die. She had wedged herself between her chest of drawers and the wall. Her fingers were already fully curled, which was a gloomy sign, and she had kicked in some of the hardboard so that the timber framing showed beneath. Abbey was sitting beside her, stroking her hair. With Tolly's help, Raf and David got her face up on her bed. She was seriously regressed.

'She was grooming most of the afternoon,' said Tolly, 'and while you two were away with Pulii, she blew. Everything except walking on the ceiling.'

'Did you do anything about it?' asked David.

'Sure, sure, I fucking cured her, didn't I. What do you think? Abbey stayed in here while I rang the main block and told them what was going on.' Jane drew her knees up suddenly and shivered. The tissue white skin of her ankles was marked with little sunbursts and twists of red and purple from her veins. Two nights before, David had been interested in her description of ballooning in south Italy: ugly Brindisi at a distance and the green olive groves, the white charcoal field kilns, slipping past beneath. Harlequin reduced her to grimacing at the light fitting, snoring for air, checking the parts of her body with fluttering hands.

'Well, you did what you could,' said Raf.

Jane began to baboon, turning her head and drawing back her lips to show the dog teeth. She stopped breathing for longer and longer periods, even though Raf gave her shots. No sign of the higher responses: all well gone, and even the involuntary functions were failing.

'Jesus,' said Tolly.

'Remember you're not here,' said Raf. The protocols were insistent that fellow guests were not to be part of such observation.

'I never thought she'd go downhill anything like as fast,' said David.

All so animalistic at the end, which made it easier for them — well, easier for Raf, David, Abbey and Tolly; something of a performance, though, for poor Jane.

Afterwards, restful on the power trundler, Jane looked her old self again — the self of humour and acceptance. The pale face, glimpsed in the security lights as the trundler took them past the buildings, was civilised, apart from the wild hair across her forehead. Briefly, while still soft in the first of death, she was allowed her natural configuration. Tolly and Abbey were left behind. Officially they had no part at all in any of it once they'd rung the main block. Raf and David would have to write out their reports, and the duty doctor would have a good deal to do before Jane's body went to the morgue annex — the locker room as it was called. Abbey went quietly around the Takahe rooms to tell her fellows what most already knew.

Nearly two hours later Raf and David stood in the dark on the lawn outside the block, and looked down to the glimmer of light on the surface of the sound. When Tolly joined them quietly, they understood his need of companionship. Two of their people seized by massive Harlequin episodes in one night — Jane fatally, perhaps Big Pulii as well.

'Christ, eh, I wonder if we do any good at all,' said Raf.

'What about me?' said Tolly. 'How do you think I feel? I'm the bloody patient here. I'm the one that's got the frigging disease. You can walk away from it.' He gave a stifled laugh as a release, which started the other two off.

'Jesus, what a night,' said David. 'I can't take much more of this.'

'Another few days and we'll probably have everyone in remission again,' said Raf.

'Ah, Indian summers for us all.' Tolly's laugh was barely audible a second time.

A land breeze through the sweet darkness from Havelock was cooling the greasy sweat on David's face and neck. Labour in death's service is arduous. Car lights were coming far away, winking, disappearing, flashing, vanishing again along the winding road which was itself invisible. Lucy Mortimer was on her way to the Slaven Centre.

'Give us a joint,' said Raf, and David went to his room and came back with the flat Abdullah tin, an old friend, in the palm of his hand. Thank God for Chris's Picton contact who made a regular drop. Raf's lighter guttered briefly.

'Maybe this is the stuff that's doing it,' said Tolly with

no hint of alarm. He brought his hand to his face. Even unlit, the shit had a comforting smell.

'No,' said Raf. 'They've been through all that.'

The car turned up the drive to the centre, close enough for the two headlights to become distinct. 'Maybe it's the hearse for Jane,' said Raf. 'You know the pressure on bed space here.'

Flippancy, like shit, might help them through the night. All three moved towards the car park quite unashamedly: decorum had little place in the centre on such a night. They were curious, sought distraction from Jane's death and Big Pulii's ordeal, were more desperate than they knew, so they wandered over the new lawns in which the small sprigs of indomitable gorse still came up. The lights became a dazzle, and the tyres scrabbled on the final, loosely gravelled corner.

'Maybe it's a rush delivery of a cure found in a secret government laboratory, and we'll all end up laughing at the end.' Tolly had a strong drag, cupped his hand about the joint protectively.

After the station-wagon stopped, there was a small shock of silence and, when the lights were cut, the trio were blind for a moment before their eyes adjusted to the dim cast of the security light on the barge-board of Takahe. The smell and taste, indistinguishable, were of the fine clay dust drifting in behind the vehicle. David always found the taste half comforting, half disturbingly evocative. Country roads, take me home where I belong. Much of his life was printed in the senses.

There were two people. A tall woman, and a small man who opened the back on a great number of cases. 'Look,' Lucy said to the little guy, 'this must be the bearer party.' A full, even careless voice. Only when they both laughed did David realise how Raf, Tolly and he must have seemed, standing rather vacantly in the poorly lit car park of Harlequin's domain, itself sent to Coventry in an expanse of rough farmland and bush and sea. Tolly wore lime green shortie pyjamas and a grubby headband which he said absorbed perspiration while he slept. Raf had on grey sweatpants, and a borrowed T-shirt cutting into his great arms and chest. His hair was free of its pony-tail for night, and flowed biblically over his shoulders. David wore a blue singlet, and faded yellow shorts with a perished elastic waistband, so that he had to keep hitching them as he walked.

Nothing could change their appearance, but Raf cranked his vowels up for the introductions as he became aware of Lucy's poise. Tolly stepped back a little, accepting for the moment, and before strangers, his official subservience as a guest.

'Lucy Mortimer,' said Lucy Mortimer, 'and this is my agent Laurie Connor, who's delivering me to this place, but then gets to escape.'

'Hi,' said Laurie. He continued to pile cases by the side of the station-wagon.

'I know you,' said Tolly to Lucy. 'You're on television and radio. Christ, I never thought that this thing would get someone who was on television.'

'You and me both,' said Lucy.

'Maybe you're just using a cover to do a programme on the place,' said David. His mind worked that way, and he also felt the need to make some feeble resistance to Lucy's smooth hair and assurance. He was aware of what easy suckers they were, and how clearly it showed.

'That's not a bad idea, is it, Laurie? Remind me of that when I'm cured, or get bored waiting.'

They did become the bearer party of course, a second time that night, and only just sufficient for all the stuff she had. Lucy had a way with her that made almost everyone a willing accomplice and assistant in her life. Clutching cases, the five straggled through the night towards reception, moving out cautiously from the security of each block's lighting into the gloom, and then more confidently into the glow of the next. Laurie griped a bit. 'Jesus, Luce, what've you got in here?' and 'How far is this bloody safari?' He was a small man, not young, and maybe familiarity made him rather less susceptible to the honour Lucy was doing them all. David's only worry was that his shorts would fall down as he walked, and he held one of Lucy's cases hard to his groin as a precaution.

Tony Sheridan was the duty doctor, and, having settled Big Pulii for the night and completed an examination and report on poor Jane Milton, he was kipping in the duty room. He had enormous feet which, Raf told all the women at the centre, were of course indicative of an equally prodigious cock. Tony was wearing suede shoes, two-tone mustard and purple, and they rose up at the end of the squab like figure targets on a shooting range. Raf prodded the soles of the doctor's suedes with a rolled-up vacation magazine from the rack. 'Sorry, Tony. There's a special admission.'

Lucy stayed in the doorway, aware of the courtesy that prevents you from looking down on the vulnerable, sleeping face of a stranger. David got his first look at her in good light. She wasn't beautiful, her face was too broad for that, but she was tall, and supple with youth and physical health, her dark hair glinting, the sharp whites of her eyes catching attention.

'It's Lucy Mortimer from television,' said Tolly.

'I don't suppose the poor beggar ever has time to watch any,' said Raf. The brighter, inside lights showed the habitual creases on Tony Sheridan's grey slacks, and the stubble of his chin and neck. Observing the slovenliness as if through Lucy's eyes, David wished that Sheridan's perception, kindness, the compassion, were more apparent than those physical features which meant so much less.

Sheridan had a large, whitebread face, and a bald top with soft, grey hair like thistledown on the three sides apart from his brow, yet he was less than fifty years old. The thistledown undulated as he jerked upright. He drew his fingers down his face to arouse himself and, until he spoke, his bottom lip remained oddly exposed, the pink moistness showing the blood absent from his pale face.

'She's come all the way tonight,' said David. 'All the way from — wherever she's come from.' He was establishing himself as moron, he thought.

'All the way from Nelson. We flew down from Auckland this afternoon, but there was some muck-up with the times, and then Laurie and I had one or two friends to see. Anyway, I'm to be a personal patient with Mr Culhane. He knows all about it.' Lucy took this inclusion in the conversation as sufficient introduction. She joined the others standing by the couch, and watched as Tony Sheridan sat, then stood up, working a little to assert his position after being found at a disadvantage. His shirt had red and white stripes; furrowed a little at the buttons with the strain. He had an inoffensive smell of deodorant, the institution's lasagna, the mild perspiration of sleep.

'Quite,' he said. 'Let me welcome you to the centre. Just a brief formality of admittance, and then we'll find a room for you. A meal if you haven't eaten. I'm sure that Mr Culhane will want to meet you in the morning, and I see you've already met our Takahe staff.' His gaze hardened when it reached Tolly, who knew that he shouldn't have come on through into the doctors' duty room, knew that he must draw back from the beguiling proximity of Lucy Mortimer. Lucy spotted his withdrawal, though, and thanked him for bringing her large, green case down.

'Couldn't have done without you,' said Laurie, who was still sitting on it, getting his breath.

Later, Lucy told David that she'd been fascinated by the size of Tony Sheridan's mustard and purples. And appalled by the doltish inconsequence of the behaviour she saw around her.

She knew nothing of Big Pulii and Jane. Later again, of course, she became one of them, and found that doltishness was a commonplace means of getting by.

All the advice had been to have at least the first year in a hostel: that in itself was good enough reason for David not to follow it. And after five years of boarding school he had experienced enough bonding to be cynical of the team ethic, and be attracted to a more individual and selfish life. So flatting then, with Louise and Kevin, whom he'd not known before, in Christchurch, in Avonside, in the back rooms of a jerry partitioned wooden mansion whose decline was obscured from the road by great elms. The tree roots humped up even the brick and concrete wall, so that cobwebbed cracks were there, and the wall had an acquired sinuosity in old age. The branches rubbed on the frayed guttering, and kept out the sun, so that in winter the weatherboards of the south side had a constant green mould; a verdigris that spread even to the windows.

Lamar Haven was the name of the house, proclaimed on an Ozymandias bronze plaque on the main gate, which was pushed back permanently in to the hedge. The branches grew through the bars of the gate, and the twitch covered its raised footing, matted like a Clydesdale hoof. 'Llama Heaven', they rechristened the house, for students can rarely leave a word alone. Poverty has no power when you are young. They rejoiced in the almost derelict squalor of the place, for they foresaw great futures for themselves. Even as they lived there, they consciously stored experience so that they could retell it to great effect — when they had surpassed it, of course.

The world of tacky, ill-partitioned flats, tall weatherboard boarding houses festooned with rusted fire ladders, working class homes that took in lodgers, pawnbrokers, second-hand furniture, fish and chip shops, bright, defiant op-shop clothing, bedroom televisions and computers, corner dairies and draught beer pubs, welfare grants and student loans, and garage sales. That world shook together alcoholic solo mums, emphysemic retired wharfies, ageing whores, perpetual victims, hard men grown old, ranting prophets of a new order, the marginally and criminally retarded, failed poets and illegal Island immigrants, the shickered and the shattered, bankrupt pyramid sellers and old women with visions of the crucifixion — and the students, just passing through. Young intellectuals experience poverty and the failure of others, as a bridal party passes through the graves of the churchyard.

Dan Posswillow was challenged to provide a meal on a moneyless Sunday, and he went out as a baron into his fiefdom. He stole onions and carrots from a market garden in Heathcote, potatoes from a pensioner's allotment by the Shirley golfcourse, a pineapple from a still life in the foyer of the McDougall Gallery, and under a small bridge in Hagley Park he caught two mallard drakes with a whitebait net. He should have been dared, like Maui, to pull down the sun.

Motorbikes were stabled on the verandahs of Llama Heaven, where once Canterbury tea parties had been held. Weeds covered the gracious curve of the drive. Where roofing tiles had failed, they'd been replaced by sheets of second-hand corrugated iron. The leadlight windows on either side of the main door retained a few wonderful pieces of blue and gold; the gaps were covered with plywood and carton flaps, past which pollen, scraps of blossom and the winged insect husks eddied into the hall. Some vanished tenant of better days had hung three wire plant baskets on the west verandah, and they had filled up with cans, fried chicken boxes, collapsed candles and unmatched sneakers stiff and dark with sweat and toe jam.

Llama Heaven, with some engineering students from the Coast in the front flat, a Baha'i couple in the side one, a retired jockey in the single room behind the garage. Llama Heaven, where David and Kevin played poker when they should have been working, partied when they should have been working, read Roth and Updike when they should have been working, lay on their beds and agonised over their lack of academic progress — when they should have been working. Louise, on the other hand, was diligent and organised, evenly friendly, and fitting in more sex than either of them — writhing and calling to her maker with a married solicitor who came through her window late at night to lay down the law.

Come to Llama Heaven on a summer afternoon. The overgrown drive mottled with shadow and gold from the trees and the sun. David and Kevin join with all the engineers, but one, to throw screwdrivers at a centrefold target on the trunk of the cherry tree. They leap, shout, push each other, and shake the branches like a band of chimpanzees. Nick, the last engineer, lies on a stretch of verandah boards that has direct sun: all his underclothes make a modest collection, drying on twine slung above him, and he has a dishcloth to keep his cock from sunburn. The Baha'i woman has her foot on her window sill to cut her toenails, and her hair is free about her face. The retired jockey is obscurely within his lean-to as usual: just his sharp coughing to represent him, over and over, as if he tries to kick-start his life. All the youthfulness, promise and summer joy is a bitter surfeit for him perhaps.

Come to Llama Heaven when a winter smog caps the city; when the elms sweat coldly and the mould glistens, but not quite able to match the iridescence that the drizzle unfolds from the oil where the motorbikes have stood. In a shallow puddle before the front steps the worms have come to die, pale and swollen, and dark leaves are star tramped on the hall floor. Each downpipe has a slightly different tune, and the colour supplements of junk mail plastered on the pavement by the gate catch the soft, winter light in a transient gleam. The swollen cupboard doors refuse to close, the one bar heater fizzes by David's desk as he reads his mother's letter from Beth Car, the engineers bicker in front of a video of violent heroism, Louise completes another A+ academic assignment, quite at ease because she is the lawyer's brief for the coming night. The Baha'i couple make familiar love beneath a patchwork quilt, and the jockey, his professional recollections roused by that sound of energetic riding, coughs the more urgently.

Louise achieved a doctorate and became something between a linguist and an anthropologist. She elaborated the history of people through their languages, and died suddenly in Andalusia of food poisoning. Kevin finally managed a BA in education, and became a futures broker in Melbourne. David met him afterwards only once, in an Irish pub in Sydney. They laughed each other silly over their reminiscences of Llama Heaven, and then had absolutely nothing else to talk about.

'It's all relative, though, isn't it?' Kevin would say in each discussion, or argument. His hair was straight, stiff, and like a sparrow's wing jutting above his face. He would fluff it, bent over his desk, and then collect the dandruff into a small heap with his finger. He won brief fame when he pulled a schoolgirl out of the creek when she rode off the path while cutting through the campus. A thin, flat-chested girl, who wasn't able to reward him immediately in any substantial way, he said.

In the second year David was at Llama Heaven, the Baha'i woman had a need for him early in her pregnancy. 'It's not that I don't love my husband just the same,' she said. 'It's the energy I need.' She never took him into their bedroom but, when her husband was at work, David would go to their small laundry and there she'd kneel and take him in her mouth. He never forgot the white parting in the centre of her long, free hair, and the flash of her eyes as she would look up at him to share his pleasure. A stage in her pregnancy, just two months or so, and then she dismissed him, and they were mere acquaintances again.

Llama Heaven became in retrospect almost the whole of his higher education. Of the books, lecture rooms, plump, bearded academics, the assignments, the wider student population, numbing examinations, virtually nothing remained. All spun out of his recollection by the powerful centrifuge of Llama Heaven. He had the feeling that it was all still there, like a bright carousel, and that if he stepped aboard, all would start up again, just as before. Those who have no good times for regret, have regret indeed.

EIGHT

Lucy Mortimer went into Kotuku block, with Colin Squires and Polly Merhtens as the aides, and Roimata Wallace as physician nominally in charge of her treatment. Most patients had to park their reputations, and enter as uncomplaining equals until they proved themselves to be intrinsically more, or less, than others, but Lucy's moderate media fame remained with her; set her just a touch apart. Not so much by admiration, certainly not envy, rather a sense that they knew her, when it was only recognition. And they saw in her the unexpressed, sad proof that no one was beyond the reach of Harlequin.

Schweitzer himself had diagnosed her, after being contacted by someone high up in the TV business, and he took a part in her treatment with Roimata Wallace and Tony Sheridan. Lucy was resting privately because of overwork and stress, it had been announced. Schweitzer told all staff not to draw attention to the more high-profile guests. There were some far more newsworthy than Lucy — like Celia R who was the daughter of the deputy prime minister, like the Olympic triple gold medallist who had cut his way into the tiger enclosure at the Auckland Zoo, like Chandiwala and

Bazarov, drawn from so far apart to Mahakipawa by Schweitzer's reputation. The deaths that occurred at the centre shouldn't be discussed either. People outside weren't in a position to understand, Schweitzer said.

David made no initial effort to approach Lucy. Guilt conditioned him to keep his distance. His self-esteem had taken a beating over the previous two years. Lucy, though, had smoked pot moderately for years, and made it her business to find out that David was one of the few guys who could supply the stuff. After three weeks she came over in an evening that had a sweet, fine rain drifting in from the sea. David was in the lounge room with others, sitting with Abbey and old Mrs McIlwraith as he helped the latter to glue a break in her reading glasses.

Lucy wore a navy blue jersey, and the tiny droplets were caught on the fabric, and on her dark hair. She had a bruise beneath her left eye, from a fall in the night she said, but her tone didn't invite commiseration. 'I don't want to be a pain, particularly if you're not on duty.'

'Can't hear a word,' said Mrs McIlwraith.

'She's not talking to us,' said Abbey.

'Eh? What's that?' Mrs McIlwraith had a hearing aid, but made no adjustment. She didn't appreciate the progress on her repairs being threatened.

'Just a minute or two if you've time,' said Lucy. 'I'm told you might be able to help. No hurry, though.'

The low clouds were grey, the sound was grey, the drifting rain was silver grey, the bush high on the hills behind the centre was massed green-grey. It was still warm at eight o'clock as Lucy and David stood on the verandah of Takahe for privacy.

'David, you've still got my superb glue,' shrilled the old lady.

'She means super glue,' David told Lucy. Why should he feel a need to explain?

'Take no notice of her,' called Abbey.

'Look, I'm in no rush.'

'It's fine,' said David.

'The thing is,' said Lucy, 'I need a few joints. Something to while away a wet evening in this paradise of yours.'

'Schweitzer's against it. You know that. It's banned within the centre. Some people say it even sets Harlequin off.'

'This is to jack up the price, is it? All the difficulties you face, the risks. I gather there's others you're happy enough to help.' It was disconcerting the way that she kept direct eye contact: not aggressively, not at all flirtatiously, but to get the two of them talking on the same level if she could; make some connection she was able to assess.

'I'm not a supplier here or anything,' he said. 'I give some of my own stuff to a few friends, that's all.'

'I didn't mean it about jacking the prices up. Sorry, that's shitty. I've been an occasional user for several years now. I could get Laurie to send it in somehow, but that takes time. At the moment I'm a bit down to it in this place. I haven't got the knack of living here yet, you see.'

'It's not so bad.'

'Compared to what!' Lucy seemed to think she'd made a joke, and laughed at it herself. 'For you it's a job, isn't it? Well, I had a life and job out there, and now it seems likely enough that I'm in this place for keeps. What's a little happy baccy if it'll schmooze the days.'

David couldn't come up with any reply that wasn't fatuous, so he just smiled, lifted his hand as a sign that she should wait and went to his room for his stash. He had some in his pocket as he came back through the lounge room, but no one was paying any attention. Abbey had joined several others who were watching TV: lives almost as far removed from everyday existence as their own. Mrs McIlwraith was left upright in her chair, grasping the armrests like Abraham Lincoln. He could have injected himself with heroin before her face and she be none the wiser. Her eyesight was okay, but there was nothing in her past that gave awareness about such things. Indoor plants were what she knew, brass and copper antiques, and dinner parties in Merivale for six, or eight at a pinch. The Slaven Centre, and the episodes Harlequin imposed on her, were incomprehensible and therefore best ignored when possible.

Lucy was well back on the verandah to avoid the drift of rain, and she took the four tinnies David offered and closed her hand softly over them.

'These might do something for you,' he said. 'Some good head shit, and not just cabbage.' She asked the price. 'A little gift,' he said, and she thanked him, but showed no inclination to stay and talk. 'I'll come over some time and see how you're holding up.'

'Okay, yes, but not for a few days,' Lucy said. 'I'm no company at present, and getting a fair belt with initial treatment.'

She stepped into the greyness of the drizzle, and her dark jersey and hair bobbed through it towards her own block. What a thing it was, that she should get so far in her life and then be dragged down through no fault of her own. You can't know how you're going to act if such a thing happens. David wasn't a great one for television, but she used to front a show about the lives of single people, he remembered. A documentary-style programme full of assured, artistic or professional people of a sort he rarely came across in his own life. And Lucy, with so much going for her, had stood out among them.

He didn't think that he'd go and see her, despite the sharp black and white of her looks, and her approach for shit. Who wanted to be a witness when Harlequin put her through the hoops? Who wanted to give up the personal secrets that a sincere friendship demands?

His father had just cut a lettuce, and the milk of its blood marbled his hand. He stood upright, then swayed back that little further to ease the spine after stooping. The lawn, the vegetables, the trees and pasture beyond were part of Beth Car. 'Someday,' he said, 'you'll have to take care of all of this. You know that.' His father enjoyed the exploitation of the cliché and David's smile in response. His father had been to a wedding: his suit trousers were tucked into his dark socks, and he wore unlaced, old shoes from the porch. And he'd removed the red and black tie from the collar of his best, white shirt. A cool, scoffing day, and the breeze brought the smell of the rain that was falling in the hills at the head of their valley. With his free hand, his father drew the collar ends closer across the base of his throat, and tugged at the grey hair tufted there. 'Your mother's already begun to worry whether there'll be enough graduation tickets. She wants a mass of clan witnesses again.'

'You know how boring it is. The stage so bloody far away, and it seems like thousands going up to get their degree. It pays to be well up the alphabet: the clapping gradually gets less and less.'

'In my day there was just one ceremony for everybody.'

With a twist, David's father took the rank outside leaves from the lettuce and spun them towards the compost heap. Greenfinches and sparrows darted over the garden. A couple of the dogs rattled the pipe and netting gate, wanting attention.

'Congratulations, anyway,' he said. 'A good degree. No one can take that away from you. People think it's all brainpower, don't they, but there's no end of bright students who can't hack it for one reason, or another. No discipline, or something going wrong in their life — just loneliness even. Cheever said that loneliness is a kind of madness.'

Had he been more than a passing fancy of pregnancy for the Baha'i woman of Llama Heaven, maybe David would himself have remained a perpetual, contented student. Sex can be a kind of madness too.

'Gordon Aimes complained to me that his daughter never used her degree,' continued his father. 'As if it were a power *saw, as if you can go through those years and then live without any influence of them. Right?' His father extended a cool hand to shake, slightly wet with the dew from the heart of the lettuce and its white blood. 'Anyway, go in and see your mother,' he said. 'She's been so looking forward to you coming.'*

'Come in with me,' David said.

'I'll be in shortly.'

As long as he could remember that had been their way: neither of his parents comfortable in the presence of the other when they wished to express their feelings. It was a courtesy perhaps that they had developed in order to live together. How much of marriage which is called natural, is only customary.

As David walked from his father in the garden, his mother appeared from the sunporch, came impetuously on to the steps. How he loved her. Yet, as always in that home, he felt passed from one affection to another, rather than included in their united love. 'Oh, wonderful to see you,' she called, and they went in together. Looking smart as ever, his mother. Appearance was for her a competition, like all else in life: against one's earlier self, against every other woman in the world, though the intensity of the struggle rarely showed. She had a brief, fierce pressure when they hugged, and again David was her special boy, her vicarious opportunity. 'Good for you. Good for you,' she said. 'I'm so proud.'

'It's all the help I had from you and Dad.' Forgotten, then, all her actively expressed reservations about Llama Heaven, and the population he lived with there. Forgotten, her anger at the drunk driving charge, her exasperation with his failure to write, her objection to his obscenity and idleness. Remembered truly the love and letters, the financial help, the absolute knowledge of being in her thoughts every day of her life.

His mother's mid-brown hair still had a sheen, when that of most middle-aged women had become drab. The cream linen was crisp to his hand as they hugged, and she wore a perfume bought on her last trip to Sydney. How well David knew his mother's pride, from long experience as its main object and the main source of betrayal. As he'd grown up he had felt a sense of helplessness before such love, sensing that there was no way he could stop his achievement, or failure, from being felt in her heart. Through the dimpled glass door behind her, he could see the misshapen image of his father coming to the house.

'Anyway,' he said, 'I'm now qualified, but unemployed. I know more about glacial geomorphology than anyone would ever wish to hear, and already I'm starting to forget it.' Sometimes he still woke from anxiety dreams in which he was fooling around at Llama Heaven, quite unprepared for exams.

'Just think of all the opportunities to build a professional career,' his mother said. The prospect made her face young, gave vibrancy to her tone. 'I've told your father that we'll celebrate, of course.'

The shape of him became somewhat clearer behind the dimpled glass as he sloughed off his shoes. Was it David's imagination that she seemed to hurry the things she went on to share with him, before his father joined them? His parents had a civilised marriage, which somehow ached with lost possibility.

The Christchurch restaurants were stuffed with graduation groups on the night. Some wore gowns and hoods with self-conscious relief that, for the night at least, they weren't failures. David and his parents had eaten a meal as expensive as most, drunk South African bubbly, leaned together for the freelance photographer who worked the room on an evening so ripe for business that his cajolery was quite untested. The photo is still in his mother's album: he is between his parents, of course, and still clear behind David is a thin woman at another table, caught just for a moment and eternity in the lives of unknown people. The tendons of her long wrist show as she pauses with a forkful of cannelloni to shout joyously above the noise of the crowded room. She is old, defiant, risible, wears a short-sleeved green dress, and inhabits the family album with as much substance as any other figure there.

David Stallman MA. Even Llama Heaven couldn't last for ever.

NINE

One of their great failures was Alice Bee, who garrotted a male visitor departing from Hoiho. The caretaker's Samoyed found the body beneath the ornamental flaxes far back from the car park. The guy was still in his tie and sports coat: well over six foot and heavy with it, Tony Sheridan said. It was assumed he had walked that far, lain down with little Alice Bee expecting favours, and got more head than he bargained for.

Such a thing is so bizarre that, for a while, the sadness and horror of it can be avoided, but Alice must have remembered it from time to time. She went into the secure unit in the main block, where she made a beautiful wall hanging of angora wool for the reception foyer, before electrocuting herself with wire in the dayroom plug closest to the nurses' station. Gaynor Runcinski, who knew all about textiles, considered it a thing of genius. Alice had written a card for her wall hanging which read 'Fibre landscape: Mahakipawa 3'. There was no evidence that Mahakipawas 1 and 2 ever existed outside her mind.

David was remembering that as he and Tolly went down to Sheridan's office for Tolly's session. There was a cold, steady wind up the sound, and barges of dull cloud were towed overhead. Only slightly lower were skuas, skidding by with fixed wings. The wind set up a resonance, part sound, part vibration, which made it unpleasant to be outside. 'An ideal day,' said Tolly, 'to talk about illness. Don't you think?'

There was one other thing about Alice's notoriety which came to David as they walked: an idle connection really, but that's the way the brain works. The visitor garrotted by Alice had been visiting Lorna Ibbotson, whose brother years before won the Canterbury Closed Tennis Championship. David had been a spectator. He had sat there marvelling at Ibbotson's touch with the drop volley, and none in that small audience could know that Harlequin and Alice Bee were waiting to make such indirect connection in the future.

As an extension of whanau support, all guests at the centre were invited to take a companion to their regular reviews. David noticed that many of the sessions were descriptive and diagnostic, rather than providing alleviation. Maybe there was something therapeutic in just the opportunity to talk: to spill out the fear and fascination that patients felt for Harlequin. For each of them the illness was uniquely personal, no matter how often they saw the same symptoms in their fellows.

'How do you find the Hazlitt spinner?' asked Sheridan, when the three of them were comfortable. Yellow and green dwarf conifers outside his window heeled in the wind, and the caretaker's Samoyed loped past to find its master, or a garrottee.

'It quietens you, doesn't it?' said Tolly. 'Takes you out of the world for a while, but I'd say there's no permanent gain against the demons. No healing in it, seems to me. Healing seems to be the thing that no one much talks about, and yet it's the word most of us are after — that, and a cure.'

'The worst thing would be to build up a lot of false hopes,' said Sheridan. He wore a sports coat with large, blue checks and there was a fair stretch of pale shirt the coat couldn't cover. 'As far as we can tell, Harlequin's a whole new thing and, until we know the enemy better, the outcomes are unpredictable.'

'It's not as if nobody recovers,' David said. He felt that he was there partly to be encouraging.

'That's right,' said Sheridan. 'Ones from your own block, like Edward Simm, who's home and seems not too bad.'

Tolly smiled at the positiveness of it all.

They knew others too, didn't they, like Jason, and Big Pulii, and Jane Milton; like Alice Bee, who had woven 'Mahakipawa 3', which hung in reception only two corners away from Tony Sheridan's office. As they all knew, what they were trying to do at the centre was delay the progression of the disease until an effective treatment could be found.

'Tolly,' said Sheridan, 'you're in the best place in the world to have Harlequin, small consolation though that might seem. Schweitzer's a near genius, and when this thing's beaten, this is where it'll happen.'

'Maybe,' said Tolly. 'I don't want to seem ungrateful, but when you're sick yourself, the big picture is nothing to you, nothing at all. I had an aunt who used to piss me off with that trite saying that your health is all you've got. It's still trite, of course, but now for me it's true as well. Yet from sheer habit I find myself still worrying about my investments, whether my new shower mixers are taking on, and if abstinence will make me impotent.'

'You've been feeling okay?' asked Sheridan.

'Up and down,' said Tolly. 'You know, my sense of smell becomes better than a ferret's at times, just as Abbey said it would. Then I can tell anyone's last meal from a single fart, and I know when the red clover's out in the road paddock over the hill. Cows smell different to steers — did you know that? The blankets on the drying line almost smother me with fragrances, and when I bring my hands to my face I know all the day's activities.'

It was old primal brain again, wasn't it; wonderfully

unfettered power of the senses, which sophistication had overlain. David had caught many glimpses of Harlequin from such descriptions, and the behaviour of patients when they blew.

'This acuteness of smell isn't progressive, though, is it?' Sheridan drew the case sheets to him. 'I mean, it's not heightened every time you have an episode?'

'It's probably growing. It comes on with the demons, of course, but it's certainly lingering on much longer after I come right in other ways.'

No good sign. Tolly must have known that as well, but none of them chose to say it. Atavism was the great symptom of the new plague. What threatened them most at the start of the twenty-first century wasn't aliens, wasn't genetic or technical advance, but something looming up from way, way back. Maybe in the end the conclusive and final predator was their former selves.

'The feeling is at once release, and lack of control.' Tolly was detailing the way his bouts began. 'Everything is self and gratification of self. Everything is now, and it presses out both the past and future. Colour, sound, taste and threat whirl around you. Response is everything.'

David and the doctor knew that Tolly was well in the vortex, but to express it served no purpose. Tolly and Sheridan began to go over the diary that every patient agreed to keep: an attempt to find any triggers, predisposing factors, dietary connections, whatever. The futility of it lay shallowly behind their faces, and David felt it as well. His throat stiffened with the effort to prevent a yawn. His friend Tolly was dying, perhaps, but the horror couldn't be taken head on, and David's attention was displaced to the cool, Mahakipawa day, with the wind coming up the sound, the half-grown gardens of the Slaven Centre tossing, a mixed fruit yogurt six-pack in a supermarket bag by Sheridan's desk, the papers heaped in the desk files, the baleful tweed expanse of the doctor's jacket.

'It must be just a matter of time,' David said. 'Until the causes of it, and a cure, are found, I mean. All these things are cracked in the end.'

'How much time though, eh?' said Tolly, and his face twitched somewhat. Maybe he was able to smell hypocrisy, too.

TEN

In closed institutions, priorities and prejudices evolve quickly, become quite distinct from what's accepted in the general community. Local personalities and issues reform attitudes; things inconsequential everywhere else, are of great significance. A tribal life develops which is both nourishing and cruel.

What was there to mock in the energy, and love, and desperation they sublimated in volleyball? Roimata Wallace had begun it by bringing back the first equipment from Nelson as recreational therapy, and Raf determined its rivalry by organising the team competition among the blocks and staff grouped by occupation. Staff and patients had parity within the confines of the game, and both saw a value in that. Schweitzer himself might be competing with a scrubcutter, a tax collector, a prosthesis technician, a sharebroker grown cynical within his career, a bathroom millionaire, or the most recent laundry employee. And, because of the nature of Harlequin, there were sometimes, in volleyball at least, advantages when the affliction began to stir. There was an ongoing controversy concerning the eligibility of patients to play when they had symptoms, for mild episodes of

Harlequin sometimes gave them spectacular physical virtuosity and intensity. The doctors were still unsure if such activity was beneficial.

Raf was a champion himself: not especially quick, but tactically cunning, physically imposing, and with a spike feared in the business. Only Big Pulii before his death, and Bunt Lorrigan from Titi, could do it better. Others were more unlikely competitors, yet proved themselves adept. Elspeth Jones of Kotuku was thin and pale, but had a superlative skimming serve. Tony Sheridan was an accomplished retriever in back court: the precise hands of a physician, great feet like platters steady on the ground, great cock at the sagging crotch of his playing shorts, which were grey with faded green piping.

Players practised for hours on end, rejoiced or were cast down by selections, argued about the team tactics. A hundred or more people might turn out to watch a routine game between blocks. Rules were parochial; each team had to have two women. New patients and new staff were assessed by guests as much for volleyball potential as any other contribution. Their block allocation was a source of rancorous dispute, with corruption often claimed, and often evident.

Takahe was a good team but, no matter what David and Raf did, they could never inspire a win over Hoiho. The winner's pennant was made of Susan Wedderburn's lilac silk knickers, with TOP DOG embroidered on them in red thread by Sister Galleter. When Hoiho got stroppy they would parade the pennant around the grounds, or fly it from their TV aerial under guard.

The number one court was on the level lawn by the main block. The grass had been established there the longest, and the buildings were a protection from the wind. Evan Beal was the gardener, and knew that strip of grass was more important than any of the flower beds, even those around the director's house. Evan marked the court with weedkiller, and was abused for any miscalculation, until the fresh growth enabled him to redeem himself. He complained of the fetish sport, his real grievance being that he was too old to make one of the competition teams. When games were on, he was usually loitering around behind a wheelbarrow with a transistor hung from the handle.

Volleyball was the present thing that they could fix on, separate from pasts which had cast them out, and from a future too threatening for many of them to consider. Volleyball was both defiance of where they found themselves, and submission to a new order. Within the realm of the centre it seemed no more ridiculous as a preoccupation than religion, or superannuation investment, did elsewhere. We are more easily ruled by custom than by logic, after all.

David and Raf went down with the Takahe team to the number one court to play Kotuku. The team had supporters too, who walked down with them carrying plastic bags, or anoraks, to sit on in case the moisture came up through the grass. Not Howard Peat, whose pride prevented any display of community, not Mrs McIlwraith, who thought civilisation restricted to the indoors — I will not abide a man with hair sprouting from his ears, she said to Tolly Mathews — but Wilfe Orme, Sara Keppler, Jock McPhie. Gaynor Runcinski went from loyalty and an expectation of some tapestry of life about the court, and Abbey, whose talents were also cultural, joined her in the support of friends.

'Easy beats, you Takahe ones,' crowed old Sidey. 'We're going to kick your arse.' Sidey, living evidence that there is no just God. Almost forgotten thalidomide had given him hands without arms and half a leg, then Harlequin joined the queue. Was it any wonder that he had survived by becoming combative? He was avoided when possible, unloved, accorded grudging admiration for persevering with the lost cause of himself till the last. 'We'll piss all over you lot,' he said. He alone broke the rules by having a white, issue bed pillow to sit on when he scrambled from his chair, and he alone would be unchallenged on it. His laughter was as loud as anyone's, his eye as bright. Sidey wasn't welcome, not because of his aggression, but because he made others wonder if their own troubles were unjustifiable self-pity.

'Takahe will blitz you,' said Tolly.

'Blow it out your one-eyed arse,' shouted Sidey, and it was a small victory for him to see Abbey flinch and Gaynor flush.

Raf stood with David, adjusting a blue elastic band on his pony-tail before the game began. 'They don't even want him down below,' he said quietly. 'Old Nick's told the Reaper to leave him up here as a bloody nuisance, rather than have him challenging the establishment among the embers.'

Sidey settled what was left of himself on his white pillow, and began abusing anyone who could be offended, even before the game started. Evan Beal's wheelbarrow was by the azaleas and his transistor provided wistful, on the road again country and western riffs as the Slaven Centre teams played volleyball at Mahakipawa. David didn't want to think about the incongruities that pressed in if he attempted any scrutiny of his life, and was Harlequin's domain any more a puzzle than Paparua prison, a house in Dog Gully Road, or a granny flat in Kaikoura?

'Ahhh, you fucking moron,' said Sidey, delighted at yet one more exhibition of human incompetence.

Lucy played for Kotuku. She had a rangy athleticism without much competitive drive. Her edge had been expressed in her career, and she wasn't going to bruise herself for a ball game. Yet a sweat was becoming on her, fixing the stray tendrils from her pony-tail to her neck and forehead, making darker back patches on her T-shirt. Her thigh muscles blocked when she landed from a leap, and the palm side of her wrists became red and swollen from striking the ball.

'Jesus,' she said, 'I've had enough. I've been putting on weight like a bull calf since I came here.' She gave up her place happily and sat with Gaynor and Abbey, whom she knew had good sense and a range of conversation. From a place on national television, she had declined to volleyball at Mahakipawa, but had the sense to make no comparisons. David found himself looking at her rather than the game. The long, smooth scope of her leg, the small moles like Afghan freckles on her neck and arms, the bright contrast of the irises with the whites of her eyes. He wasn't quite close enough to hear what she spoke about with Gaynor and Abbey, and felt an odd pang of exclusion. The conversation of women always seemed to have greater warmth and intensity than that of his own sex. He accepted that women were the superior nation in all communication.

More than her looks, David was impressed by Lucy's determination not to go down easily. Maybe the hooch was helping her, and he should show more willingness to supply it. What warmth and animation she had, how Abbey and Gaynor responded to it with their own generosity and intelligence.

Volleyball, then, for the flock of Harlequin and the keepers. The ball soared against the sky, and old Sidey's sarcastic cries joined the adulation and the laughter, the country music from the gardener's wheelbarrow, the private conversations quite unconnected with the setting.

The farm was part of the skin of the world: always responsive to the elements that played over it, blossoming frosts, the fierce or pale-yoked sun, distinct, quartered winds, rain of imperious impact, or tremulous accumulation. And beneath the skin the close-packed flesh clays, the limestone bones, the secret flows of arterial water that would tug the willow wand of the diviner down.

He had lived that land, hadn't he? He had circled on the tractor, while the paddock undulated as a mirage beyond the hot engine. He'd stood in leggings and parka with his back to the southerly buster, and pulled lambs from their Romney wombs. He'd stooped on the shearing board so that sweat dripped from his nose on to the dark wood, where oil and blood and sweat and shit had been worked by shuffling sack slippers to give a burnish that hostesses would covet for their furniture. He'd had smoko sitting on bales of first-cut lucerne hay, and eased the skin back on palm blisters, while honkers went high overhead towards the lakes. He'd fed out the same hay, dropping the sections between the wheel marks in the snow, and looping the bright bale twine around his neck with numb fingers. He'd sat quietly on a diesel drum in the dusty yard and noted where the hens came cackling from, and gone and found the egg caches. He'd spent nights in the back of the truck with a mounted spotlight, shooting rabbits that were eating out the downs. He'd had a dog make a fool of him, and experienced times when he was accorded tacit respect. He'd switched off the Case combine and walked away with his face a mask of dirt, and heard gradually the cicadas come back in chorus, the sheep cough discreetly like curates and the magpies sweep passionately from the pines towards the river.

On the day that David made up his mind to go overseas, his father was fencing along one of the ridges of the hill block. Successive makeshift repairs over the years were no longer enough, and he was putting in a new strainer post at the gateway. He was silhouetted on the ridge line as David climbed up to him. The wind grew stronger, flinging away words and, after one attempt at talking over distance, during which his father just shrugged and smiled, David kept climbing and his father continued to work.

Even though the older man was using the big, iron-tipped rammer around the post, and the muscles of his shoulders shook with the impact, David couldn't hear the thuds. His father wore a green army singlet, shorts and steel-capped boots. And oddly studious glasses that mitigated all other appearances. The sweat in his hair made it more noticeable that it was thinning on top. Even in that strong, cooling wind, he took off his glasses and wiped sweat from beneath his eyes. 'Ah,' he said, 'I'll be glad to get this big bugger in.'

'Give us a go.'

'Good on you.' His father sat down thankfully in the grass, and blew his cheeks out in the wind. His boots were downhill, and he rested his forearms on his knees, so that the hands hung from the wrists. His fingers remained partly set in the grip for the rammer. 'This fencing lark's not much by yourself.' He must have cut himself with wire earlier in the day, for there was blood dried black on the back of his left hand, and a red, moist centre.

David wondered what his father thought about during all those working days and years on his own. Classical Greece, he supposed, and Rome, as well as the stuff of farming. That was his father's degree, and when he'd done his thesis on Sulla, that old Felix, and spent the five university years that had been agreed on by his own family, then he'd come back to the farm, as if it had been the most natural progression in the world. Maybe it was, and maybe that combination of historical detachment by training and affinity for place by birth, was the reason that, whatever failings he showed, malice was never one of them.

'I reckon I'm going to go overseas for a while. It seems a good time to have a look around before settling in here to help you.' David hunkered down close beside his father, so that they could talk despite the wind. He held the handle of the rammer loosely, conscious of its surface, smooth from years of use. 'Will you be okay to do without me for a while? A year maybe. No longer.'

'Go for it,' said his father. 'I can get by fine. I just won't put much crop in, because that's the heavy work.'

The two of them sat close in the short grass by the new strainer post, and the wind raced up and down the slope, plucking at the words passing between them about places overseas not to be missed, about the isolation of their own country, about opportunity and the old world. David's father talked of his visits to the village of Spaniakos in Crete, and the family who at great risk had hidden his own father from the Germans in the war. He urged David to go there and meet them again.

Such symmetries are attractive, but actuality takes no account of them. David never reached Crete. There came instead an evening in Gattinara, northern Italy, when David had a phone call from his mother asking him to come back. His father had suffered three strokes within a day. It was afternoon in New Zealand, his mother said, and David could see in his mind's eye the view from the phone table by the large window — her summer garden immediately, and then the family land of Beth Car sloping to the hills. Almost he could catch the fragrance of white roses his mother would have in the heavy blue vase, yet his actual view was the pale, damaged ceramic tiles patched with snow and the cobbled streets of the old quarter beyond the hotel, the chunky girl, dark and sleek as a dormouse, who watched as he spoke to his mother, the smell of shoes, trivial histories and wine in the old hotel. The loose floor tiles clinked like silver beneath his feet, and the light fitting had a wizened fabric shade like an apricot corset.

'You know what he's like,' his mother said. 'He won't ask outright, for anything, but he wants to see you.'

'Guai, allora? Sei nei guai?' the girl was saying.

David was home in three days. He was amazed how quickly his father had lost his tan: maybe it was that the blood had gone from his face. He sat rather awkwardly on a wooden garden seat facing up the slope of the farm, just as David had imagined it in Gattinara. A drought summer, as most of them were, and the dry grass was worn back from the ridges. Only the lucerne paddocks, the thistles and the windbreaks were green, and the willows and occasional poplars that followed the course of the creek. His father was quiet but calm: dispassionate concerning the cycle of growth and decay so apparent to him both in classical history and the seasons of his farm. He talked of the arrangements he had made for his wife and David, then he talked as calmly of what he wanted for himself. And he rested a hand on David's arm in a way quite natural and habitual, despite the self-sufficiency of his nature.

All done without the presence of his wife, of course.

He talked slowly and with little inflection, but it was clear enough. 'The thing is, I don't want to linger on — no good to anyone, least of all myself. And you get to that time when you're too sick to be at home, and so you have to pay the bloody earth to stay in some institution. A thousand dollars a week maybe, so that money that should be for your mother is gobbled up and for no reason. The professions close in when a family's at its most vulnerable, and rip out what they can. You understand what I mean? You saw where your grandmother was — one of many in chairs lining the wall of the Eventide Home's sunroom, their mouths open, but speechless, queuing even for death.'

'What does the money matter if it gets you the very best of care?' said David. How could it be that the farm was exactly the same, no matter what was said: that the drought persisted both dispassionate and remorseless, until the pine cones broke in submission and shed dry seeds with only one wing.

'But the very best of care isn't what I want,' his father said. 'I don't want to be on my back for months, staring at the ceiling, clicking my tongue, having my bum wiped for me. I don't want to be dismissively tended by nurses whose mothers would have blushed to meet my eye. It seems to me that you put up the best fight you can, but when the writing's on the wall you pack up and go. That's the best care — best for all.'

And he never spoke of it again. Just the once, as if he wanted the record to be straight. When things got bad soon after, David feared sometimes that his father was going to ask him to take some action, or that he would choose the old Roman way in the large warm bath: all his blood easily tempted out. Sulla had died badly at the end. His father never contemplated any such drama: he had, on diagnosis, found a way to get the pills he required and, having persuaded his wife to go and play golf one cool, autumn Thursday, he took the lot. A stockman knows when a cull is needed.

His body was surprisingly pale and unthreatening, and with signs of wear. David noticed his father's hands had enlarged through years of farm work, that the sun had scarred his face, that his lips were pursed in a prissy way they had never been in life. Just a husk it was, with no power to move him. The man's calm, quizzical yet loving presence was elsewhere.

'He'd have to be by himself to die, wouldn't he,' said David's mother. 'I wondered what was up, when he was so keen I go to golf. How he hated any fuss at all.'

ELEVEN

Lucy's single room in Kotuku looked across the gardens to the treatment suites, and to Schweitzer's house further up the slope. Like David, she had no view of the sea at all.

David didn't need to go there to give her shit. She wasn't heavily into it, and it was just as easy to give her some stuff in a paper bag on the way back from meals, or leave it in an envelope at her mail drop. But after talking to her briefly at the volleyball, and watching her there with Abbey and Gaynor, he was curious about her. What sort of life could she make of it at Mahakipawa? Did she have someone in her bed perhaps? What did she dream of once her ambitions were lost: did Harlequin release a new woman maybe?

Lucy was writing an email letter on her laptop computer. She would send it to her acquaintances, she said, with just a few changes each time to personalise it. David watched her scroll it. In her letter the centre became quite a different place, a subterfuge to keep from all but her family and closest friends the truth that she and old Harlequin were drawing nearer. It gave David confidence to think that both he and Lucy were in hiding in a sense.

'You brought some stuff over?' Lucy asked.

'No. Just thought that I'd come over for a chat.'

'You're all dressed up.' Lucy's half-smile showed she knew it was for her, and she made that direct eye contact as ever. David had put on his new denim shirt, and aftershave. Of course he thought her attractive, but her easy reading of his visit exasperated him. 'It's all right,' she said, 'I'm flattered. I only said it because I'm grotty myself.'

She wasn't at her best. She had on a loose halter top which had slipped to show her bra straps: trivial, yet a thing that always put him off. There were bands of sunburn on her chest and upper arms. Her heavy hair was held back with a practical elastic band.

'It's just that I've an hour or so before I take over from Raf, and I thought I'd look in. That's all. See how things are going.'

'I had a full session with Schweitzer yesterday,' she said.

'How come you're so privileged then?'

'Charm,' she said.

'Right.'

'Anyway, it was the works. The thing that pissed me off most was that I've gained almost a kilo.' Lucy smiled again, but kept watching him. 'That's the way we are, maybe. You have Harlequin threatening to tear your mind apart, but what you can relate to is the fear of getting fat. Eh?'

'Well, it's a coping mechanism, isn't it?' He held back just a little from responding to her easy way. 'You know the bullshit the psychologists give you.'

Lucy pulled out of Windows and switched off, even though David said he could come back another time. She shifted some of her clothes from the one chair, and he sat there looking out through the window, and across the newly cut lawns to the treatment block. 'How about I give you some of your own stuff?' Lucy said. She closed the door, then took a brass trinket box from her wardrobe and came back to the bed. 'A magic carpet for the evening,' she said.

'I'm on duty soon.'

'And the more suitably prepared you'll be for it.' Lucy sat on her bed, curling her legs beneath her.

Both of them concentrated on enjoying the joints, for that way they were less self-conscious with each other. They sat in the evening privacy of Lucy's room and smoked some fair shit. But it took a while, because Lucy was down to it after her session. David drew in and held on a long time. Ah, Jesus, that friendly weed, and the very best shit, from the Coast. One thing he knew about was cannabis. An expertise that he'd suffered for, but he never considered giving up the stuff. A lot of his life was in the kick and smell of it, so that people and places, and even states of mind, rose up as he smoked, and were there just behind the superficial tableau of Lucy's room in its stroke of present time.

Who would wish to be restricted to that? All the life and success that Lucy had known, the affirmation by others who wished they could achieve as much, and then reduced to one bed, one chair, one room, and a joint with a minder, and no future that she could bear to think about. There was the single advantage as far as David was concerned — Harlequin had laid Lucy low enough to be with him, and even though she was sunburnt and sad and uneasy, almost a kilo up, even though her hair was greasy, he knew that he wanted the opportunity to be with her. He wanted to slip his hand along the inside of her thigh, but he wanted also to hear her talk, to make something of her life. It was a long time since talking had been any sort of priority in his relationships with women.

'People get better, you know,' he told her. 'Even the doctors know bugger all about Harlequin, and some people beat it and walk away. Why shouldn't you?' David tried to remember the last guest who had done that — walked away from the centre with a clean sheet, rather than wrapped in one. Even Eddie Simm was about to come back, he'd heard.

'What is the bloody cause? If they could find that for a

start.' Lucy stretched her legs out, and put a pillow between her back and the headboard.

'Out of Africa. I reckon that's what Schweitzer thinks.'

'Out of Africa! I love it.'

'You know. The monkey stuff mutation, or the mahogany rats. Ebola and all that.'

'Jesus. And this one's come all the way to us,' said Lucy slowly. 'Why some African rat or chimp disease over here, for God's sake?'

'Some carrier, I suppose. Who knows. Tony Sheridan says that there's strong overseas opinion that it's a result of cumulative pollution, but I don't think Schweitzer goes for that.' David wasn't supposed to be talking so frankly to Lucy. At orientation he'd been told that only medically qualified staff should answer questions about Harlequin, but rules were never that important to him. That's why he'd ended up at Mahakipawa, instead of still farming at Beth Car.

'Is it pollution?'

'I'm only an aide, but it seems strange, doesn't it, that incidence rates here are just about the highest in the world, when we've been the clean, green people. It's Africa, I reckon, or maybe some evolutionary crack-up. Tony says that's something else that Schweitzer and Alst Mousier are on to. That our brains have reached evolutionary self-destruct, become too sensitive and complex to cope any more.'

'It's all beyond me,' said Lucy. 'Sometimes you're surprised by your own reaction, aren't you? I thought that I could put up a hell of a fight against something like this, because I have so much that's worth fighting for, but a lot of the time I'm ready to give up. I'm just about resigned to anything in store for me.'

'The first impact, I suppose. It must be numbing, but you'll bounce back.'

'No. I don't think I'm going to feel any different about it. Helplessness is what you mainly feel.'

'Maybe this shit we're on isn't helping?' He watched as, for an answer, she drew deeply and smiled at him. From another room was the persistent sound of weeping; from the Kotuku lounge at a greater distance a fierce burst of combined laughter. 'Maybe it's just this bloody place,' and he smiled in return. 'How can any of us take our lives here seriously? A sort of purgatory maybe.'

'I find it more like a jester's hell,' said Lucy, 'yet I've got this preoccupation with food. All sorts of stuff I've had smuggled in, and I dream of going to a half decent restaurant.'

'I'll work on it.'

'I didn't say to share with anyone.'

Maybe Harlequin really was the end, the final catastrophe, but how was it possible to conceive of that? All you could do was go on from one day to another, one personal experience to the next, and leave the grand outcome to the forces powerful enough to shape it.

'Can you get stronger stuff?' asked Lucy.

'This is the best there is. All head from the Coast.'

'No, I mean other stuff altogether. Heroin, say — ecstasy. Can you find that shit if need be?'

'I don't play around with any of that stuff.'

'Not even if someone was going right under to Harlequin?' An option was what Lucy was after: a recourse if she was going down and couldn't pull out. David couldn't blame her for wanting that, but neither could he buy in.

'Jesus, Lucy,' he said, 'have you any idea what the doctors have got in this place? They've got legit drugs that could whack a blue whale. Don't you worry about that.'

'You don't mind me asking?'

The sobbing and laughing from other rooms in the block had stopped. It was the still, low ebb of the day, before guests and staff began their night routines. The joints made David and Lucy less aware of each other, and so oddly more comfortable together. That's what shit did — it insulated you from life. Nothing was going on, and they smoked, and talked only idly of the centre and the people there, as if it were a summer camp. David couldn't see the sound, and he wondered if Tolly might be out there in the dinghy, at the pink float, with two hand lines angling down into deepening colour.

'So how did you end up here?' said Lucy.

'I needed a job.'

'What did you do before?'

'Farming.'

'You don't look to me like any sort of farmer.'

'What do I look like?'

'A travelling salesman,' said Lucy. 'Put you in a bloody suit and you could be a salesman, except you don't talk as much, do you.' In a way she was right. David had been a salesman of sorts in a popular line of merchandise, still had a minor interest in it, and he used to talk a good deal more readily as well. No bloody suit, though. Not everything can be told simply, and he didn't want to get into the story of how a salesman of sorts might end up at Mahakipawa.

TWELVE

They met again when Lucy came to Takahe to talk with Abbey, and the three of them sat on the verandah of the block with Evan Beal's wheelbarrow transistor somewhere out of sight, but bringing Europe's culture to Mahakipawa, much to Abbey's pleasure. A Bartok Rumanian Dance helped to take attention from the argument between Mrs McIlwraith and Jock McPhie in the lounge. Jock was not about to apologise for spitting phlegm into the sink: he justified himself on the grounds that it constituted a natural function, and seemed sure that he had a good point in common law. Mrs McIlwraith was affronted at even having to interact with Jock. She considered him one of those people of such insignificance that they lack the intelligence to recognise it.

Abbey's hair was light brown and stood up even in the still air, as if there were a mild current of electricity coursing through her. And there was the charge of her talent and good will. She hadn't been a presenter on national television as had Lucy, but she'd played with the National Symphony Orchestra, she'd made a tour of Australia and the Philippines, and another to South Africa. She, too, had dreams dispelled by Harlequin. Those things weren't talked about, though, were they.

'It's a natural function, for Christ's sake, isn't it?' protested Jock. 'This is what's happening today: women are denying a man's natural functions, and no one will stand up to them. Women are trying to make men like themselves. Is it any wonder that the whole bloody world's becoming sick?'

'Bartok was one of those precocious musicians pushed on by parents,' said Abbey. 'He gave a public concert when he was ten.'

'I was a great hunter of frogs when I was ten,' said David.

'I could do the splits,' said Lucy.

'Who'd have thought that we'd end up here together? Things go along nicely, don't they, then they change utterly against you to prove that you were never in control at all.'

David had never heard Abbey speak so directly before. He realised that she would talk to Lucy in a way she never would when alone with him, and the reason wasn't that he was staff and she a guest, or that he was a man, but rather that he didn't have the warmth and concern which invited confidence. He had a natural inclination to selfishness and reserve, which experience had strengthened. Guilt is a quiet strangler of feelings that incline towards sympathy and rapport. He listened to Abbey talking of a Basuto man who could whistle through a bullet hole in his face, and who came to her in Port Elizabeth wanting to become a professional performer. For Abbey it wasn't a tourist anecdote, but proof of resilience of spirit. Maybe, although her face was unmarked, she had begun to do her own whistling in the dark to keep her spirits up.

'The man's an animal,' said Mrs McIlwraith. She was out of sight, but still aware of them as an audience. 'I've seen him at the mirror squeezing fat from the pores of his nose.'

David walked part way to Kotuku with Lucy. 'You holding up okay?' he said with some diffidence. What right did he have to ask something so important?

'Did it rain last night?'

'No.' The days had been blue and bright, the nights quickly cooling as the heat radiated towards the clear stars.

'Then I'm heading for an episode. I'm sure I was awake for two long periods in the night, and it was raining both times from the south-west. I got up, even, and watched. The walkway was slick and wet beneath the security lights, and there was that rush of fragrance that you get after rain when it's been dry for a long time.' The grounds were proof that no rain had fallen, but David thought of Lucy standing at her window in the night, and the heavy rain being swirled in by the sou'-wester as it was sometimes. The smell, too, with its sharp flavours of nuts and insects, cats' piss, and swelling, refreshed earth.

'Did you go over to Treatment?' he asked.

'No. Everything's been okay so far today.'

He felt the stirring of that urge to touch her. Partly the touch would have been sympathy and reassurance, but partly also the desire to feel the warmth, the slight roughness of her skin: the brush of her dark hair on his hand, perhaps. But he didn't reach out at all. He continued to talk a while before leaving her outside the entrance to Kotuku, and going on to the main block to visit Howard in the treatment rooms. What would she be like to make love to: tall, slightly gangly Lucy, with good tits and a good brain, with small, dark moles on her strong neck and a wry perceptiveness? What way would she like it? How urgent would she be in the clasp of a man to whom she was attracted?

THIRTEEN

The Slaven Centre was often visited by people of influence — political as well as medical, international as well as home-grown. It was because of Schweitzer's reputation and the need for reassurance that all possible steps were being taken. In any direction at all.

A group was to come from the parliamentary select committee set up in response to public alarm about Harlequin. Alst Mousier would normally have organised a visit of such importance, but he was in Australia to give a keynote address on institutional administration, and Tony Sheridan drew the short straw. He had a morning meeting with ancillary and block staff to go over things. Mist drifted on the upper slopes of the hills and rolling drizzle greyed the windows of the conference room like a vast exhalation.

'Thank God they're not coming today,' said Sheridan. 'Can you imagine it all? Umbrellas, the smell of wet socks and macaroni cheese, the blocks closed up like stables.' He had his hands clasped over the front of the small lectern, and he leant back to bare his teeth to the ceiling.

'It's probably like that in the Beehive all the time,' said Raf from the front row.

'And the same treatment available,' said Polly Merhtens, 'except that they never realise they're undergoing it.'

'All the same, they may come up with more funds,' said Colin Squires.

'You're right.' Sheridan swayed forward and rested his head on the lectern. His vast shoes were like pancakes on the floor. 'I'm a doctor. I just want to be a doctor, not an administrator, or a tour director.' He was on a small podium, low and wooden, with mushroom carpet on its top and small castors obscured beneath. It gave him full view of the bland, new room even when seated, without undue emphasis of hierarchy.

In twos and threes the staff continued to amble in, and to sit as far back as they could. 'Ah, Jesus, come on, guys. You think I'm going to shout back there.' The mist and rain glossed the bush despite the absence of sun, and droplets clung to the windows, were augmented and then ran on the glass.

Cleghorn from Titi had his pyjamas on under his anorak to remind the establishment that it was officially his day off. Had Mousier, or Schweitzer himself, called the meeting it would have been a different story. Evie Masters from registration was finishing her toast and honey. She had won the novice award at the Gore Country and Western Music Festival two years before, and believed in looking after her throat. Sometimes, after her period, she would have an impromptu concert in the dining hall and sing 'Stand By Your Man' and 'Panhandle Blues' with a Southland burr. Surely she had the makings of a star, people said.

'As you may know,' said Tony Sheridan, 'we're having a visit on Tuesday week from members of the Select Committee on Public Health.'

'Bummer,' said Cleghorn.

'All of us are going to be involved in one way or another.'

'Double bummer,' said Cleghorn. After the blue of his pyjama legs there were his thin hairy ankles and heavy sneakers with the laces loose.

'All of us,' said Sheridan firmly.

And sure enough they were, even if only to guarantee that the less amenable and attractive charges were kept away from the official route, and that Cleghorn was glorified parking attendant. Mousier had made only a few changes to Tony Sheridan's arrangements, such as including a more soporific wine at the parliamentarians' luncheon, and increasing the number of women to be in the patient group to talk with the visitors at three o'clock.

On arrival, of course, the select committee members were first to have an hour's briefing by Schweitzer. David and Raf watched them being escorted by Tony Sheridan and Alst Mousier from the car park and towards the offices. Seven of them. Raf could put names to some, but David recognised only Janis Bloomfield, the Minister of Health, because of her height and the bobbed, grey hair seized on in caricature. It was a fine, still day, and the gardens and grounds reflected the extra care received in preparation for the visit. Sheridan's plan B for wet weather, which was substantial perhaps because of the drizzle on the day of his briefing, was untested. Even as a professed non-administrator, he'd rather fancied his plan B.

'So when is it that they reach us again?' David this way emphasised Raf's responsibility for Takahe.

'Ten thirty,' said Raf. 'Just before they have a cuppa. The thought of it should keep them moving. I've got Abbey primed up to talk about recreational and therapeutic programmes if they ask.' Abbey was a sort of trustee of the centre, relied upon, and even put upon to some extent, by fellows and staff. Her capability and good will were taken advantage of over and over again.

How tall Janis Bloomfield was as she passed not far from them, Mousier by her side. Her head and shoulders swayed in a manner intrinsic to her walk, as the head and neck of a giraffe sway to keep a constant point of balance in its progress. 'Oh, there's a climate of opinion without doubt,' she was saying in her stride. 'Without a shadow of doubt.'

The parliamentarians were accustomed to being well received, secure in their right to make cursory intrusions into other people's lives, but even they were conscious of venture at the Slaven Centre. They maintained a compact group, they traced lapels, or pocket flaps, with their fingers, their voices were slightly raised in assurance, yet furtive glances were given to the buildings, as if the visitors feared that a true scrutiny might show the victims of the new plague gathered and lolling at the windows. David watched the party move past the beds of roses and pansies and on to the covered walkway to the main block. For a moment he saw it all as they saw it — from the outside — in the way that it had been for him when he arrived months ago with Bryce the mailman: unencumbered with knowledge, or experience, a matter of physical presence and unequivocal presentation. The modern blocks, the colours, the landscaping, an openness of clear instruction in the signs, the guests secure in their reluctant occupation.

As Raf had predicted on David's arrival, familiarity created successive overlays, until the place took on a depth of ambiguous reality distinct from the blueprints of initial regard. It filled up with associations, the presence of a whole population, incidents and tableaux both randomly futile and vitally consequential to his life. The rough slope rising behind the centre had the shouts and fires of poor Jason; the covered path was the Bridge of Sighs for Big Pulii; in Jane Milton's room he knew exactly the repaired lining. The verandah on which he stood was Raf's court, the chapel for Abbey's diffident, mild confessions, an arena for the antics of Harlequin's children. The car park, steady in the sunlight, required just a switch of thought to put on a cloak of darkness for the arrival of Lucy Mortimer and all her cases.

Where the path ended at the foyer to the admin block, Dr Sheridan stood back to let the visitors go ahead of him, and he saw Raf and David watching from Takahe far away, for he raised a hand. In his brown corduroy jacket he looked like a bear waving a paw. It was a gesture part recognition, part wry dismissal of the role they watched him play. 'Poor old Tony,' said Raf.

'Maybe he can ditch them in Schweitzer's office?'

'No, he'll be stuck with them, you'll see. He'll have to traipse round all day to make up the appropriate number of professional staff for the occasion.'

'What time again?' asked David.

'Ten thirty,' said Raf. 'Could you just check that Estelle and Wilfe have their doors closed before we come past, and that Abbey and Tolly are all set?' Abbey and Tolly Mathews were to be the star turn, caught in apparent spontaneity on piano and violin.

Ten forty-three wasn't bad. A degree of chronological drag is normal in official itineraries. It meant a more compressed visit to Takahe before morning tea. The delay did, however, extend the rather awkward priming of Abbey and Tolly in the lounge room, and Wilfe opened his door against instruction, complaining that he wanted to join in, despite being medicated for a recent episode. Also David and Raf had asked that no one use the toilets in case the parliamentarians wandered in there, and were met by a stench, or poor Montgomery washing his bum at the sluice basin.

David did a last quick check of the block, and came out in time to be introduced with Raf. No handshakes, no break in the procession, just Tony Sheridan's words and the nod of the minister from her height, and then they were all in the corridor. Open doors like a passing carriage, closed ones unquestioned. Piano and violin eased their passage, and Schweitzer, Mousier, Janis Bloomfield, others behind, all came into the lounge to find the musicians, and an artful disarray of their peers listening. Everyone was familiar with the pretence of happy coincidence: for the minister it had become the customary way of life.

Tolly had been bribed by promise of a tinnie, and played

with skill and good will. Separated by his illness from an empire of bathroom fittings, fishing, astronomy and music had become his trades. Abbey did her bit as ever, always the citizen and a supporter of whatever community she found herself in. Surely she was dying, but something must fill up the time that remained. What could she owe the parliamentarians, the Slaven Centre, or even the world any more? But she played that cheap piano with utmost care, and the facility of a genuine talent. Perhaps it was for herself that she played, or for those loving, academic parents who held her hand in childhood's photographs. 'Look, Abbey, how the rainbow forms behind the rain.'

For most of us, pretence is so accustomed that it comes to be accepted as the true feeling, and we're uneasy if it's threatened. Bodger smiled and nodded to the music as if gulping pills had never been on his mind; Mrs McIlwraith wore her patterned silk scarf and emeralds in honour of the deputation; Dilys Williams sat prim with envy that she had no larger part than member of the audience; Howard Peat looked away from the performance and sneered at the gardens.

'It's good, isn't it? They both seem to have a bit of a knack for it, don't you think? And it encourages socialisation.' The lowered voice was from one of the minister's team, leaning towards David. Ah, Abbey, it had come to that: real talent reduced to a knack, by the voice of ignorance and power. Almost as if she desired to be part of the whispering, Janis Bloomfield swayed her badger-grey head down on David's other side. 'And how are these people *in themselves*, do you think?' she asked him. Ah, Abbey, despite the high hopes, the symphony orchestra and the full concerts abroad — it had come to that.

And so Mousier, lustrous lemur eyes and no-nonsense voice, reminded them of the timetable, and Schweitzer, what presence, what acute affability, led the select committee members away. They straggled like grazing animals across the grounds from Takahe towards the hidden rendezvous for morning tea, and although the bald facts of the visit, the historical validation in memo and report, would be kept somewhere no doubt, the actuality of the experience was already wavering, detail leaching away. The minor stumble that the minister made on the paving, so that for an instant her wild oscillation threatened those about her, the fierce blue of the sea as backdrop, the plaintive wheeze of the hydraulic doors to the loos as curfew ended, the sound of violin and piano fading over the centre grounds and the slopes of broom and gorse.

Tony Sheridan told David later that, at the medical staff debriefing the day after the visit, Schweitzer passed on Janis Bloomfield's relief that there seemed no signs of panic, or despair, and that the patients were positive about the centre. Good material to use against those MPs who wanted treatment centres shifted offshore to places like D'Urville Island. Sheridan said that the Slaven Centre could still manage an impressive shop window, but David wondered how people were *in themselves.*

'What really worries everyone,' said Sheridan, 'are the latest incidence figures: up seventeen per cent and with New Zealand and Italy among the highest outside Africa. The minister told Schweitzer in confidence that it was possible that some overseas countries would soon impose special restrictions of entry. It's rich, that, isn't it?' said Sheridan. 'Because for years we've been keeping foreigners out, now we might find ourselves quarantined.'

'Do we really have such a high rate of Harlequin?'

'Well, outside Africa, of course.'

'New Zealand, for God's sake,' said David. 'I just don't get it.'

Somewhere, though, you see, there had to be a connection.

The country team had to have a new coach when Bunny Lyte finally gave it away, and David was disappointed with the new guy from the very first team talk. Remember, Jenner said, that the victor is always the team with the greatest determination to win. It was one of those facile, commentator's views that David knew from experience wasn't true. He'd been in teams that were comparatively gutless, yet walked over others that fizzed with the desire to win. Talent, size, tactics, local knowledge, luck, even, could equally well be a decider. 'If you want it hard enough,' said Jenner, pressing his new, crap artist face towards them and making a fist of his right hand, 'then you'll be a winner.' The assumption that followed was that if you lost, then you hadn't given everything. David knew that wasn't necessarily true either.

Jenner's dictum was attractive in its simplicity, though, particularly for a coach who wasn't sharp enough to spot, or correct, any other weakness, and it conveniently shifted responsibility for failure. David could see that some of the squad bought it easily enough. Brett Anderson was a believer: his freckled face attentive, and his head almost worn smooth of pale hair from scrummaging. Absolutely fearless he was, almost stupidly so, and he trained like a demon, but would never make a first division team because his genes denied him the size.

'That's the thing,' said Jenner. 'Guts is the thing, by Jesus.' There had been All Blacks, hadn't there, with less than Brett's determination, but gifted in ways he was denied. David didn't point that out to the new coach, though: such observations weren't welcome. Subversive, weren't they — divisive and shit-stirring, as Jenner said, showing that you didn't put the team first.

They trained on a winter field that was pock-marked with sprig-holes in the dark, soft soil and flattened grass. A thin mist might trail through the branches of the birches on the west side of the ground, and Jenner's shouts echo into the stubby height of the old wooden stand. The first few times down on the ball, David felt the damp chill of the mud on crotch and belly; at the scrum the steam eddied away from the close bodies as it does from working horses. As he packed down he caught the cooked lobster smell of close bums. The knee cartilage that he told himself had come right tweaked painfully as he was hit from the side in a tackle. 'Back up the bloody ball carrier. Bloody back up the bloody ball carrier,' Jenner would shout emphatically, as if he had that instant created the idea.

'All good players are workaholics,' he would say. 'Absobloody-lutely,' and after the drills he outlined a fitness regime for them all, because distances meant they could practise together only once a week.

A few more sessions with the crap artist, and David decided that he'd had enough of Jenner: enough of the game even. He was driving up the valley in the dark after practice, the headlights sweeping over pasture, or paddocks of winter feed, at the sharp turns in the gravel road. He decided that the only kicks he got out of it any more were the ones he could do without. With his father dead, so many of the accustomed things lost their point; became small shams of an unexamined lifestyle. He imagined that there must be more important ways of living which had essential connections one with another — and with himself.

Growing shit was one of them perhaps. He'd used it on and off since his days at Collegiate, but had no thoughts of getting into the business until Chris came back from overseas. They met again at a wedding in Christchurch; the reception held in a yacht club's rooms in Sumner, so that the guests walked in and out among trailer sailers, and cockle-shell Sunbursts for school kids, and the Best Man's Adam's apple bobbed against the trophy pennants on the hardboard walls.

They talked of Coddy Joux the bully, who had become the boss of a national park, and Sharkey, who they'd cheated over his exams. Chris said that the happy couple would enjoy their honeymoon, since the bride was eager for it, pleasantly tight, and vocal when on her back.

Chris came out to the farm several times after that, twice with a leather-skirted woman for the weekend. She was a telephone pollster from the city, with a quick voice and a manner anticipating hurt. She was dark and slim, with the slightly used, Bohemian look that Chris said turned him on. If the two men left the house and walked out into the farm, she would remain in the lounge looking out apprehensively as they diminished, as if she were inside a space capsule, and the men advancing across an alien world.

All the characteristics that David recalled in the Chris of schooldays were still identifiable, but tainted with disillusion. His charm had run out on the wider world, and not all his adversaries there could be cheated as easily as Sharkey. Even his attractiveness to women had been found fallible in the very cases where power, or advancement, might have been gained. He was that sort of genre Casanova who looks out at you from behind the sliding doors of concrete-block motels; who has a dark onyx ring set in nine-carat gold, who buys with confidence in the cut-price lingerie shop.

He came alone when he had a business proposition. A humid, still day of low cloud, and David had been tailing a mob towards the back of the farm, and was coming back with tractor and trailer to the sheds. His work jersey was stiff with dried blood, the netting rolls jolted on the trailer, the two dogs trotted with their tongues askew.

Chris's Falcon was in the drive, and the man himself leaning on the tubular gate that marked the division between the working area and the grounds of the house. In just the few months since David's mother had shifted to Auckland, the lawns and garden had lost the clear lines and managed display which had been her mark. Not neglect, just that difference between the enthusiast's care and more perfunctory maintenance. Chris waited as David nosed the tractor into the shed, humped gear from the trailer, then fed the dogs. 'Quite the man on the land,' he said, as David finally came up the track towards the house. 'Master of all you survey.'

'The bank runs us all on this country,' David said.

'There may be an answer to that too.'

David had a shower when they went inside, and Chris got a meal under way without any prompting — cold mutton and pickle, cheese and tomatoes. Afterwards they sat looking out on to the garden and drank beer. 'I can't get used to your mum and dad not being here,' said Chris. 'If I look into the paddocks he still seems to be there, and if I look out at the garden, your mum, too, she's there.' David had no comment to make on such a truism.

And they smoked some good stuff that Chris had sent down from Takaka. 'It's what I'm mainly into now,' he said casually. 'It's a living without too much effort. I never was much on the nine to five, you know.' He drew in, long and slow, and went slightly cross-eyed with the satisfaction of the joint. 'The thing is there's some very ropey people in the business, and I'd rather deal with friends for supply.'

That's how it began. A few rows of premium stock planted between the old orchard and the hay barn, and then strips within the shelter belts and along the back gullies. David was a willing enough partner. Cannabis was the best cash crop of all, and he thought that within three or four years the stuff would be legalised anyway. It was bound to come, Chris assured him. Even many of the Health Department boffins were saying that it was less damaging than alcohol, or tobacco.

They'd just be jumping the gun a little, that's all, and when decriminalisation came, they'd be there to exploit the opportunities — just like the first people into angora goats, ostriches, olives or truffles.

At first it was a sideline that David enjoyed as much because it brought Chris's company, as for the profit, but increasingly it became the easy way to do things at Beth

Car. He and Chris would sit on the warm side of the shearing shed putting the seeds into wet cotton wool to germinate, or settling seedlings into trays where they would be left to grow to about milk-bottle height. David had a CD player above the portholes and, when they had talked all they wished, they listened to tracks of trad jazz, or blues. Even better was working in the plots, transplanting, pulling up the useless male plants, or harvesting. Growing cannabis well had all the satisfactions of farming other crops, and a better return. Where could be the harm in such a healthy association with the land? They concentrated on the heads and resin, hardly bothering to try to move cabbage, and they had a good deal of success with skunkweed, which had more grunt than the old stuff. In time they moved into hydroponics as well, which allowed additives, but David never had the same interest in the indoor process and largely left it to Chris.

It was Chris who usually took the stuff away to their dealers, and no gang members, baseball bats or beatings marred the calm of Beth Car. The Romney ewes dropped no more deformed lambs than usual, the nor'-wester was no worse, roses still bloomed in his mother's garden, the creek still ran clear through the watercress and wild mint. What damage to the world was a little more good quality shit? What better economic theory than supply and demand?

FOURTEEN

From the verandah of Takahe, David could see down the slope to the shore of mudflats and rushes, with Tolly's white and blue dinghy bottom up. He was making a pretence of listening to Dilys Williams while waiting for Chris's Picton contact to make a drop for him. 'That woman who's Minister of Health, that Janis Bloomfield, she's made no reply at all to my letters about the goings on here. And the amount of taxpayers' money that she gets too.'

'I suppose she's flooded with requests,' said David.

'I hardly got a word in when she came here. Write to me about it, she said, and I did, and now there's nothing at all. But God won't be mocked, you know.'

'You're right.' David saw a yellow car park by the shore, and a person get out and wander down to sit on Tolly's upturned dinghy.

'You reap what you sow,' said Dilys. There were some patches on her face as red as winter crab apples, and her hands shook with a vehemence out of all proportion to what she could express. Maybe her discovery of ubiquitous sin was the sublimation of her Harlequin fears, and who could blame her for that. David listened to her complaints with more sympathy for a time. 'Is there anything I can do to help?' he asked, but her face remained a vivid and preoccupied mask. Sin was everywhere.

'What could you possibly do?' she snapped. 'If people won't listen to me and the director. If the minister won't act. I know for a fact that personal laundry is being stolen and sold second-hand in Nelson, and there's a bald man in the kitchens who spits into the soup.'

'Right,' said David. He saw the yellow car carry on towards Havelock, and knew that his delivery had been made.

'No one takes things seriously enough here. There's just soothing talk and open slather for any behaviour at all. People have their hands all over other people. Remorse is unknown. No standards, no self-discipline, no rigour. Has indulgence ever solved or cured anything, answer me that? You can't, can you?'

After a time with Dilys the need for relief was considerable and David imagined a full draw on some good shit. Who did he think he was to be offering any help anyway. Wasn't he one of the mockers on whom Dilys wanted to bring down the wrath of lightning? 'Well,' he said, 'if you'll excuse me, I think I'll have a stroll, but I wouldn't give up on a reply from the minister. You never know.' Dilys said nothing, offered no release from the conversation, or thanks. She stared angrily away as he left.

David went down the long drive of the centre until he reached the road. He crossed that, and went to the dinghy in the rushes with the anchor stuck in the ground, even though the boat was above high tide. He sat there for a while with his face tilted to the sun. After all, Dilys Williams might be watching, or someone with Tolly's telescope. Mocking God was one thing; mocking the system was another. After a session with Dilys he fancied some time with a very different woman as an antidote. Lucy Mortimer might be in the mood for one of their talks, and she appreciated a few joints.

He moved the diftwood log by the anchor, and felt in the stones beneath it for the plastic bag left for him. A good, solid package that promised release in its fashion from his past and future, and from the part played by Harlequin in the present. The more he came to know Abbey and Tolly Mathews, Gaynor and Howard Peat, the people in whose service he had agreed to be, the more their suffering oppressed him, despite his being so much more fortunate than them.

He rang Lucy from Takahe when he returned. He heard the guest who had answered his call, shouting her name down the corridor as if she was just anyone at all. 'Hello?' Her voice at the phone. 'Hello?' How he wished he could have said, You're cured, and both of them start on some new life.

'The candy man's been.'

'Well bring some over then, for God's sake,' she said. 'What do you want, a medal?'

'You okay?'

'Peachy,' she said.

'You're sure?'

'Come on over,' she said.

He put on aftershave and a fresh shirt. He left two tinnies under Tolly's pillow where he knew he'd look. He gave his most genteel greeting to Mrs McIlwraith, who had her pearls on for mid-afternoon bridge at the rec rooms. 'God won't be mocked,' he heard from the verandah, and chose another way to leave.

All the original residential blocks were built to the same plan, and whenever David went into one not his own, he had an odd feeling that was a paradox of familiarity and alienation. Lucy's Kotuku could be walked through in his sleep, and yet where was the Presley transfer on poor Jason's door, and who was the stranger comfortable in Abbey's room? Why were the drapes floral rather than plain in the otherwise precisely duplicated lounge, and if he went to room fourteen would the hardboard show the repairs necessary after Jane Milton's head butting with the devil?

Lucy had pillows along the wall side of her bed, so that it resembled a divan, and when she'd jammed a stopper under her door for privacy — no locks allowed — she and David sat there in bars of bright yellow sunlight from the slatted window. Her skirt, too, was yellow, and he noticed that not so much because of the colour, but because she was usually in jeans.

She was happy because she felt well. She was happy because she'd talked with Schweitzer about the possibility of doing a programme on Harlequin that focused on interviews with staff and patients at the centre. Schweitzer was usually opposed to media coverage, but Lucy had emphasised that she had a foot in both camps, that she knew the world of Big Eye television and now that of the new disease. The director had said he was willing to consider a more detailed submission, though he warned that the politicians were apprehensive of anything which would increase public awareness of Harlequin.

'Will you be running auditions?' David asked.

'Only for stars,' she said.

'Will I get a big chance?' She couldn't know how little he wanted to feature in any filming at Mahakipawa: that if it wasn't for the pleasure the idea gave her, he would wish it never happened.

'Maybe you'd have a small walk-on part.'

'Not a lie-down role maybe?' David said.

Jesus, he hadn't seen Lucy so happy for a long time. It was the way she had been before she got sick, surely, and the jolt of that was painful even as he put his arm around her. They lay together with their legs in the sun; their voices became softer, as less and less was said and more and more intended. They began that journey of languorous, almost helpless anticipation, which comes before a first, fierce lovemaking. Have we ever needed an Einstein to tell us that time is relative? Extreme joy or horror can rein in even the Pegasus of time. Lucy's yellow dress was a response to the warm day, perhaps, or a less deliberate one to the possibilities of David's visit. The dress was linen, with an open weave. How coarse the fabric was on the back of his hand, when her thigh was silk to the palm.

'Open your shirt,' Lucy said.

It was unethical, of course: forbidden explicitly in the contract he had signed, even though he was too humble an employee to be professionally related to any treatment. But then what treatment was there at the centre except care, and what more caring restoration than he performed.

'Easy, oh easy,' she said.

It was unethical, of course, but what were such observances within a death camp, where defiant love might be one way of fighting back. Lucy knelt on her bed and above her glossy hair was the slatted view of the gorse and broom flourishing in rough pasture on the hillside. All of it pulsated with the coursing of his blood. Wasn't all of life in the moment? No past, no future, just the plummet of a present that had as much completeness as he'd ever know. His hands were brown and spread against Lucy's back.

'Not so loud, or half the bloody hospital will hear,' she said.

'Was I saying something?' A language, surely, which transcended any script, or grammar, and came quite naturally to all throughout the world who were suffering such joy. Maybe, even, it was the speech of the good twin of Harlequin.

Lucy smiled, lay on her side, and pulled the discarded linen dress across her hip. No other woman he had seen naked was as provocative, even though fucking had flushed her up, so that her neck and collar bones were mottled, and her hair was still ruffled from the bed.

'Well, are you satisfied now it's happened?' she said.

'Blown away,' he said.

'I hope so. I was really in the mood.'

'So was I. Jesus.'

'But men always are, aren't they?'

'Pretty much, I suppose,' he said, and Lucy smiled at the honesty.

It was unethical, of course, but what possible connection did prudent principles have to your real life.

Lucy reached out and, with the tips of her fingers, brushed the hair back from his forehead: that reassuring contact that a woman makes with a man after the passion of lovemaking, and which affirms the satisfaction of it, but affirms also other reasons for closeness. 'You're sweating,' she said.

'From the best work in the world,' David said. Didn't every man go on with the hope of such times.

'Guys always think that at first,' she told him. There was a slight shaving shadow in her armpit, and an indistinct vee of browner skin above her breasts. Fine hairs parenthesised the upper corners of her mouth. She lay comfortably in his gaze once she had the dress over her bush. Her breasts pooled with their own weight as she lay on her back; the nipples shone with his spit. For an instant he remembered the married woman he'd slept with for several nights in Hobart. She had recently given birth to a son, and each time he left her bed to return quietly to his own, he had her milk on his chest.

David experienced protectiveness, admiration, once that fierce consummation had subsided. Lucy's face wasn't beautiful in any fine-boned, profile emphatic way. Rather it was girlishly wide, broad-browed, smooth, the eyes so far apart that she couldn't possibly enter the criminal fraternity. She had Hollywood teeth, though, and when David told her so, she said that all her front teeth had been capped because of her work on television. 'It's my fetish,' she told him. 'Always what I notice first, and television is cruel on teeth.' She never ate anything during a working day, unless she had a toothbrush handy, she said. In a day of appearances she might go ten hours without eating, rather than risk food between her teeth. And no red wine because it stained the natural teeth.

'Keep talking,' said David.

'You're not even listening.'

'No, but keep talking.'

As all on the hillside lost colour, but remained distinct because of texture and plane, Lucy and David lay on the narrow institutional bed. They heard the Kotuku people go down to the dining hall and then come back. He couldn't believe that there'd ever been a better fuck in the Slaven Centre than that. 'Tell me what it's like to be so good-looking,' he said. 'No false modesty now, no bullshit. What's it like?'

'Do you think I am?'

'Answer the question.'

'Success always made me feel attractive,' she said. 'Success not just with men, but in my life. I felt good when I did my job well, and ugly when I got sick.'

As David massaged her shoulder, the curve of her breast trembled in a perfection of arc and subtle movement. Never forget this, he told himself. Never forget this. Some time when he was waiting for death, he would restore the moment as a triumphant solace. Old age becomes the voyeur of its own past. Half alongside, half over her, graceful only because his body followed the line of hers, the whisper of his palm on her shoulder, the tremor of her unconfined tits, a laugh drifting from the lounge, their own candid talk, the faintly salty smell of her hair, shadows, her face with a smile which had complacency, and irony as well because she understood the transience of such idolatry.

'Now that we've done it, you can tell me something personal about you and women,' she said.

'It took me ages to get past the assumption that good-looking women were more interested in sex. Somehow I took it for granted that anyone who stirred up so much desire must be looking for it.'

'It sounds like your excuse for striking out.'

'Maybe that too. Maybe I just grew up a bit,' he said.

'I never made love until I was twenty-two, although I had boyfriends from the time I was in the fourth form. The intensity of men's interest put me off, even though I enjoyed the flattery. I could get them off quite happily with my hand. Many didn't even need that encouragement. I had a good deal of wet trouser material up against me.'

'And then?'

'What?' said Lucy. She turned to look at him directly, the shadow in the darkening, small room moving on her face, her hair falling in a cusp from her cheek.

'The first time. When you were twenty-two.'

'Oh, no. You won't get me started on the jag of talking about other guys that way, and I don't fancy hearing about your adventures in the sack. I was joking before. I'm not into it.'

'What about right now?'

'You know what I mean,' she said.

No other woman is like you, he thought.

How many times would they do this good thing together?

It was unethical, of course, as so much of what is important in our lives is.

Dog Gully Road was in the hills behind Nelson, and it was no-exit, narrow and gravelled, winding up to a fair-sized pine plantation, planted years before when prices were looking good. In the summer the dust from the road was a talc over the nearby pigfern and blackberry; in winter the gravel sank into the slick, yellow clay and the potholes held a rich slurry. The fenceposts tottered alongside, grey with age, scabbed with lichen, sometimes borne down by old man's beard, or gorse. Narrow stock tracks fanned out from the gateways, and eased up the hillsides to the patches of rough pasture among the scrub. The flash magpie ruled by day, and at night the possums hunkered in the branches and the morepork cried to reinforce the silence.

Towards the top of the gully was the wooden farmhouse Sneaky Pete rented, the land around it long sold for forestry. One of the verandah poles had rotted through, and the bowed iron of the roof was lower there. The giant macrocarpa hedge on the south and west sides had been felled to let in some light, and so attract a tenant. Most of the hedge had been scavenged for firewood by successive occupants, but the great stumps still held on, with the scars of the chainsaw on their surfaces. One of the most even was used as a chopping block. Its ringed surface had additional axe and knife marks, stains and libations; there was a scurf of fine chips, fur, feathers and bone at its base. The waxy head of a white leghorn lay close to David's boot as he stood smoking, the comb granulated and the beak ajar.

'I could take half as much again,' said Sneaky, as he splintered the rib cage of an appropriated hogget for his evening chops. 'But I'd want a sharper fucking price, of course. I'm making you guys rich. That skunkweed resin, though, I must say is top shit.' Sneaky was very tall, thin, bald and revealed by his voice as Australian. At rest he tended to hold his skinny arms across his stomach, as if something had caved in there and was causing discomfort, yet all his actions and opinions were resolute, showing that he was in good form.

Sneaky always complained that the price was too high, but he knew that he was onto a good thing. The quality was consistent and so was the supply. Sneaky collected and distributed for more than a hundred and fifty kilometres around, and although the rented place in Dog Gully Road aroused no envious comment, when Sneaky flew to Wellington as Mr Ferris, bank managers came from behind their desks in welcome.

After they had helped Sneaky put the stuff into the bunker beneath the shed, David and Chris went into the old farmhouse and drank Napoleon brandy and coffee. Sneaky was generous with that, but he made no offer of accommodation and David didn't expect one. It didn't pay to become too personal in their business. So they left quietly in the small hours, when the country was beginning to creak with the hardening of the frost, and Dog Gully Road was just the beginning of a long drive.

The pines were very dark and the sides of the small valley kept out the moonlight. The new Holden's headlights swept over the tottering fence posts and the gleam of ice on the mud of the potholes. Briefly, before the demister took effect, the windscreen grew delicate hachures of frost like the blades of a Spanish fan.

'Sneaky must be raking it in, I reckon,' said Chris.

'He has to take more risk though, doesn't he — dealing with a lot more people to distribute it, and some of them very odd bastards with no loyalty, or talking too much at the pub. We can just come up here once in a while and dump a fair load, yet no one knows us except Sneaky.'

'And you don't think that if Sneaky takes a fall we go down as well?' Chris said. 'Come on.'

'I'm just saying that we're doing very nicely and that Sneaky's business, good or bad, is up to him.'

It was odd, wasn't it, that you could be a criminal, and yet, having made that one move from orthodox practice, you continued to expect many of the principles which applied in the legitimate world to hold good. How else could you operate? How was it possible to escape a middle class upbringing even if you stepped outside the law?

On the drive back, Chris told David that coming through Nelson reminded him of a job he did there with two mates before he went overseas. A shipment of spirits and top wines which they knew was stored in a warehouse in Neath Street. There hadn't been a snatch of booze for ages and the place had got slack. They used two stolen trucks and got away with a hundred and seventy cartons as easy as pie, but one broke down in the Rai Valley and they had to ditch it, and then the other one conked before Blenheim. 'Jesus, can you believe that, though? Weeks of planning and we ended up hitching into Blenheim. On the bones of our arse again, and all we took was one bottle each to carry.' Chris had a good laugh at his misfortune from the vantage of better days. 'One bottle of top whisky,' he said. 'That's what I got out of that lot.'

Growing and selling shit was a much better business, wasn't it? Sneaky Pete was doing just fine, and so were they. Meeting the market, you might say.

FIFTEEN

Claire Townes was one of those who slid into a trough and stayed there: one of Harlequin's muted and uncharacteristic ways to go. So predictable were her last weeks, and free of threat, that she was left in Takahe where she wanted to be. Except when sleeping or sedated, and increasingly the two were combined, she called for her daughter, Sandra, who had become an archaeologist and found work in Yucatan. Before her death, Claire wanted above all to farewell her daughter. It couldn't happen, because Sandra had gone ahead, killed in a helicopter accident on the plateau seven months before. No matter how many times Claire was told the news, she blotted it out as more than she could bear. Her conscious hours were dominated by the failure of her daughter to visit her at the centre. Sometimes she blamed Sandra, sometimes she blamed the staff; she even claimed that it was a conspiracy by her ex-husband, as a punishment for not investing in his olive-growing venture just outside Thames.

Claire's night and day cry, 'Where's Sandra?', became integrated into the acoustic life of the centre, eventually losing any intrinsic and personal significance, becoming as generic as the cry of the skuas over the mudflats, or the bellowing steers on the hillside. Sometimes in the darkness and their agony, other guests too, cried 'Where's Sandra?', not for cruelty's sake, but just to share the solace of the familiar.

'Couldn't we arrange for Sandra to come, for Christ's sake?' asked Lucy, in David's small room. She had heard Claire's piercing cry as Raf and Abbey wheeled her to the sluice bay. David was quiet to listen to the calls as they diminished down the corridor. They had become so customary over weeks, that he had to make an effort to register them as having a specific origin.

'What — a seance?' He wondered whether Claire or Sandra would have the most difficulty in crossing over.

'Just an ordinary visit,' said Lucy. She was leaning on the window sill so that the hills above the centre were visible to her. 'Have Sandra come to visit after all.'

'I don't get it.'

'She's going quite fast now. The doctors told you, didn't they? All she wants is that one last thing. Soon she'll be taken down to Treatment to stay, where people won't know her the same.'

'The daughter's dead, though. Tony Sheridan said she was killed in a plane crash in Mexico or somewhere, but Claire won't take it in.'

'All Claire cares about is getting an okay from her daughter to go. A sort of release. At this stage I reckon it could be done by proxy: there's so much need. I mentioned it to Schweitzer, but he said it was dubious in terms of ethical practice.'

It surprised David that Lucy was on such terms with the director, that during her sessions with him she would discuss Claire Townes in such a way. And David shared Schweitzer's unease with the proposal. The deceit of taking advantage of Claire's illness, even if it was for her own good. The assumption of power and decision over what was left of her life. 'Oh, come on. No more than a prognosis held back, or a drug-induced calm,' said Lucy. 'No more than anything else which is the means to the end of dying more easily. We should just do it, and it'll all happen and be over before anybody really knows about it.'

So Lucy began her successful persuasion.

'Where's Sandra?' called Claire on the wet evening they had chosen to grant her an answer. The rain came in on the wind: cats' claws on the windows. There was a downpipe on the outside wall close to Claire's head, and it gave a vigorous orchestration for the performance inside. 'Where's Sandra?' Few people would be moving from block to block on such a night to provide any interruption. The pigfern on the hill slope had a subdued gleam in the twilight. 'Where's Sandra?'

'She's on her way, isn't she,' answered David.

'On her way?' Claire had almost renewed her habitual cry when she realised what he'd said. 'You mean she's coming?'

'All the way from Yucatan,' said Abbey. 'You remember, we've been telling you for days. She's arriving any minute.'

'All that way just to be with you,' said Raf.

The three of them kept on for some time about the visit, the history of preparation and acknowledgement, until the idea was taken up as valid by Claire herself: until she complained that she had grown sick of waiting for what she had long been promised. Yet David didn't see how it could work, and was embarrassed by their well-intended conspiracy against the sick woman.

Lucy walked across to Takahe, and came with a transparent, plastic hood which she almost shook from her head. 'That rain,' she said. 'It's driving in with the wind.'

'Here she is,' said Abbey in a voice of conviction. Unlike David, she entered into the spirit of the performance utterly. As a patient herself, although not in Claire's condition, she more easily acknowledged the supremacy of need.

'Here's Sandra to see you, Claire,' said Raf. He had no

sense of shame whatever, or rather, perhaps, he was willing to be actively ridiculous if it would help Claire. He delighted in the challenge to shallow reality. Well, isn't life after all a theatre of the absurd, in which bit players are forced to take larger parts because a God is lacking.

Lucy went to the bed and seized Claire with a hug. Not a wary embrace for the sick, but emphatic, outgoing, expressive. Claire was startled rather than welcoming. Her face appeared for the others at Lucy's shoulder: the many lines at the mouth emphasising it as orifice, the slight rash around her nostrils, the eyebrows rubbed almost bare.

'I love you so much, Mum,' said Lucy. 'I've come all this way to make sure you know that.'

Claire allowed herself to be held, but looked at Abbey for affirmation. 'You never used to hug me,' said Claire, when her head and shoulders were back on the double pillow. 'You liked your father so much better because he spoilt you rotten. Do you ever see him?'

'I haven't time for any of that,' said Lucy. 'I've only a moment and all I want to say is thank you, and that I love you.'

There was brief eagerness and intensity then in Claire's face which transfigured it, and for the first time David saw something of the personality that had been Claire Townes; recognised a full individual beneath the spoil of the illness. 'Sandra, Sandra,' she said, yet her eyes went up and she tilted her head back towards the gurgling downpipe. She had a full handhold on Lucy's arm, but perhaps she knew better than to regard her gift horse in the face. Lucy had made no effort to resemble the daughter in the bedside photo. 'I've kept all your letters,' said Claire. 'I just wish you could work indoors more in that place. Everything's so dirty in archaeology, isn't it? All that grubbing after what's better buried. And what must the smells be like.'

David found it so difficult to play a part. The whole thing teetered between the grotesque and the sublime: at once a profound reality and a mockery of itself. Perhaps, too, he was reminded of another old woman, and a granny flat in Kaikoura by the sea. He went out of Claire's room and stood in the corridor by one of the windows, which showed the rain and wind moving like shoals in the liquid evening. Raf followed him, and stood and stretched his face oddly as a commentary on what they'd seen, and as relaxation after a long duty. 'She's bought it, hasn't she?' he said. 'She thinks her Sandra has really come to say goodbye, I reckon.'

'She's taking what she needs most, just as Lucy said she would. Heart's ease, no matter what the source.'

'Weird really,' said Raf.

'She's dying.'

'And going very differently than most of the others, isn't she? I guess you have to take any short cuts there are. Self-deception may be even more necessary at death than in your life.'

Lucy was at the door. 'I've got to go now, Mum,' they heard her say, and Claire calling her back for one last thing. And Abbey was talking too: the three of them in conference. Then Lucy was back again with tears on her cheeks and a catch to her voice. 'She needed so much to say things to her daughter.'

'What did she call you back for?' asked Raf.

'She said the doctors kept telling her that Sandra was dead, but she knew it wasn't true because she could see letters from me on their desks. But they never passed them on.'

'Come and have a drink in my room,' said David. He put his hand on her shoulder. 'Let's have a joint, eh?' She was trembling slightly.

'No, honestly I'm fine, but it's got to me more than I expected. I'll come over tomorrow and have a talk then. You can tell me how she's taken it.' Her voice was firmer with each word. She put on the plastic hood again and started down the corridor. 'See you, Raf,' she called.

'See you, Lucy.'

'Is this some strange place, or what?' said David.

'On the edge, mate, on the edge,' said Raf. He pulled one of his half-grotesque, half-mocking faces. He spread out his large arms and balanced up the corridor towards his room, one foot perilously after the other on some invisible tightrope.

Claire and Abbey had bundles of Sandra's letters out on the bed, but they were talking of the doctors, and which of them could be trusted. Animation made Claire look especially ravaged, her face like some glaring, piecemeal, papier-mâché head. She looked up as David re-entered, but her quick smile was for herself only. 'And I'm not going to tell anything to you men either,' she said. 'Maybe you think it's funny, do you?'

'Why should I think your daughter's visit funny?' said David.

'Men still think women are a joke,' said Claire fiercely.

'Yes, go away now and leave us in peace,' said Abbey. And he did; taking orders meekly from those in his charge, because the whole evening had become topsy-turvy anyway, and Abbey was twice the comforter he'd ever be.

In the three further days that she lived, Claire didn't call for Sandra any more. Maybe she was convinced; maybe she knew that the trick wouldn't work a second time. Others continued the cry 'Where's Sandra?' for a time, but eventually, with the source gone, even those mimics of good intention realised that the power of the incantation was lost forever.

SIXTEEN

David did his final late check before midnight. Nothing at Takahe was untoward, provided you accepted that all was untoward. Happiness could not be made mandatory at the centre, but decorum and routine were laid down. David had his long, aluminium-bodied issue torch, which swung like a baton, but, like the beat cop, he knew his round so well that all he required was the spill from the security lights. He paused at one of the lounge windows to look out and across the sound. The sea had shrunk in the great ditch, become almost as still and dark as the hills that contained it. One large moth, like a piece of chalk, was pit-pitting on the glass by his head although there was no light to draw it in. Had he been sixteen again, it would have been a night for possum shooting, with the torch held along the barrel of the .22. Their eyes shone red hot in the beam just before they died.

There was something adhesive beneath the sole of his left shoe which caused a slight noise on the corridor vinyl with each second step, as if the moth was pit-pitting close behind him. Maybe his charges were asleep behind each unlocked door; maybe they had escaped into the lupins and the gorse, and lay with the tears running down the back of their throats. As long as all was quiet, no disturbance, that's the thing. Mrs McIlwraith was snoring, but in a genteel, upper register, and Tolly turned on his bed, because his stiff back didn't allow him to rest long in one position. Nothing to worry about.

David went through the main door and stood on the outside step. Evan Beal had used the roller on the lawn, and forgotten to come back for it. David moved out and found it as a rest for his dak tin while he lit up. After the flare of the match all was black for a moment, until his night vision recovered. Shit burns differently from tobacco, and those familiar with it know also that the smoke acts in its unique manner: heavier and with a more florid scroll in the still air.

Ah, the first breaths of it, and the deep punch of it in the lungs. It reached far back in his life and on the continuity of it were strung so many associations. The first furtive joints with Chris in the old band room late at night, seated on cushions of sheet music and looking through the gaunt lattice of clustered music stands at the moon. How innocuous was that early weed compared with the stuff he later grew and sold. His room at Llama Heaven fugged up with the smoke of it and the fumes of extravagant talk. The glaring heat, litter and traffic noise at the bridge over the narrow-cut Corinth canal, where he waited for five hours for a scheduled bus that never arrived. The warm boards in the open door of the shearing shed at Beth Car, with his own land covering most of the world he could see. Lying with Jocelyn Parks in the spare room of her house, their free arms held up, the fingers twined, talking with the absolute candour of intimate strangers. The tinnies taped behind the light fitting of his cell at Paparua. The water-marked ceiling of the fibrolite bach at Gore Bay, which Samuels Bros. Transport allowed him to use. He would lie there smoking himself silly until the world went away. The smell of it — that old cats' piss, ammonia flavour — was as familiar to him as the smell of his own sweat.

Takahe was as settled for the night as it would become, and David, walking back to his room, found Raf still awake. 'If you've finished being the Wee Bloody Willie Winkie, then come and have a drink,' said Raf. He filled most of the available space in his room, but David found a perch on the bed end. Raf drank cheap port which he bought by the flagon in Havelock. He was in a mellow mood that inclined him to confidences: how he'd flunked out of med school, and then a BSc course, not through laziness, but an obsession with iron man triathlon eventing. A sports career for three successful years but, just when he was starting to make money out of it, he tore the ligaments of his right foot on Mount Kosciusko in New South Wales, and it never came completely right. 'That's what it is with professional sport,' he said. 'A lottery as far as fitness goes, and a quick end to dreams.'

'You could've gone back to varsity.'

'Couldn't face it. It reminded me too much of the time I'd lost, and decisions that didn't pan out.'

'Doesn't this remind you even more?' said David. He watched Raf cradling the port flagon on his lap. 'You could have been one of the doctors here, maybe, and now you're a supervisory aide. Doesn't that stick in your throat a bit? Better to be something completely away from medicine and hospitals?'

'Normally you'd be right.' Raf swirled the ruby port in the unbreakable glass mug from the kitchenette. 'But here I feel so lucky in comparison with those who have to come. It's an insulation, isn't it, and if you don't have old Harlequin for a dancing partner, then any other misfortune seems pretty trivial.'

True enough, but human nature isn't that logical, at least not all the time. There were occasions when David felt down, and the best times were attributable to Lucy Mortimer, not the intellectual appreciation of his good fortune to be free of Harlequin. The past was a very uneasy place to visit, and he normally went there only when pitchforked by sudden, compulsive association — or overcome by dreams which visited without invitation. Lucy was in his present life, and all the apparitions from earlier times, the ongoing sorrows at Mahakipawa, couldn't completely subdue the wonder of that.

'Do you want to make a night of it?' asked Raf.

'Why not. It all seems pretty quiet.'

'I'll supply the port if you chip in with some shit?'

'Only if you agree to get off your backside and help if something comes up later. Okay for you, but I'm on duty.'

'Knock it off, for Christ's sake,' said Raf.

In some ways it was Llama Heaven all over again: just talking and kicking back, leaving all the rest of the world behind the closed door. Raf had it tougher than David as a kid. He grew up in Invercargill and had worked part or full time since he was thirteen, first to have some spending money, and then saving to get himself to university. His parents had only seasonal jobs. He enjoyed telling David about the supermarket work he did in the sixth and seventh forms. On weekday evenings he'd been a trolley and fruit and vege boy. Customers left the trolleys all over the car park and throughout the mall, and Raf collected them in a growing concertina and shunted them back to the supermarket entrance. When he'd rounded up all the trolleys, he then had to bring in the crates of fruit and vegetables which the delivery guys unloaded in the service alley for the next day. In the summer all that was done in daylight, but in winter the car park and alley were getting dark by the time he started, and he and Philip Hika would fool around charging trolleys at each other, and playing soccer with early drumhead cabbage. On cold or drizzling nights the regular staff hardly ever bothered to come out and round them up.

Raf was starting to talk about the owner of the mall when Wilfe Orme came to the door and asked if he or David knew the word for a fossilised turd.

'I can't remember,' said Raf.

'I can't remember, but I think it starts with C,' said David.

'I need it for Scrabble,' said Wilfe. He sniffed the fumes wistfully, and his eyes lingered on the flagon of port.

'Try to get some sleep, eh Wilfe,' said David, but lifted his mug from which Wilfe took a good swig. 'You'll have some of the others wandering about.'

'Close the door when you go out,' said Raf.

Raf said that Mr Ovenden owned that whole mall in Invercargill, though he ran only the supermarket, and leased out the other retail spaces. He had a red Jaguar, and his office was on the floor above the supermarket. It had a window overlooking the car park and often Raf saw him working there in the evenings.

Sometimes he ran Serena Astle home. She would go out and wait by the Jaguar, and later Mr Ovenden would walk through the aisles and the staff would be deferential. They would say goodnight, Mr Ovenden, goodnight, goodnight Mr Ovenden, goodnight, and then they'd watch from the windows as he let Serena into the Jaguar, and the guys would snigger and the women would look superior. Serena was a provincial netball rep and had an arse like a film star, Raf said, and he was in love with her for those two years.

One night when Raf was due to leave, and the sleet was driving in from the south, Mr Ovenden came out to his Jaguar and called out to Raf, told him to put his bike in the boot and that he'd run him home. It wasn't a Serena night: perhaps the windows misted up too much with Serena on such evenings, and made driving dangerous afterwards, Raf speculated. Mr Ovenden knew his name, Raf said, even though he owned the whole mall and had dozens of supermarket employees, and Raf was only the part-time kid. On the way home Ovenden encouraged Raf to go on to university, and said that all his life he'd wanted to be a veterinarian and he knew it wasn't going to happen. Years later Raf heard that Mr Ovenden started up a racing stables with his supermarket money, and when the horses lost all his money, he fled to Indonesia. Even with a mall and a Jaguar you can't escape regrets, Raf said.

David told his story of being accosted by two North Africans beneath a Marseilles overbridge, and escaping by throwing his francs in the air and jumping onto the scooter platform at the back of a passing mobile home. It stopped just past the bridge, and the driver came around shouting in English, and threatened him with a bulky Lonely Planet guide.

Raf's port was cheap enough, but the shit was quality, the company good, the time a pleasant relaxation. As they talked, David had the feeling that Raf's experiences were his as well, just as authentic and detailed in his own recollection as the driver's shirt loose from his trousers, the pale parting in the Baha'i woman's hair in her Llama Heaven laundry, or the thistledown streaming above the summer yards at Beth Car. He saw the chrome of the trolleys glint in the dim car park, he hurled a Giant Rocca onion grenade above the rusted skips of the service alley to the hoots of Philip Hika. He knew the tight furrows on the skirt over Serena's film star arse: he looked into the grey eyes of fifty-three-year-old Mr Ovenden and saw the man's realisation that he was trapped by comestibles.

Suck enough good shit in, and all of experience is as readily available, isn't it? The selfish and self-contained boundaries give way to universal cognisance. Your own life is reduced in proportion, and even Harlequin becomes less than the sum of everything.

The steers bellowed on the unseen slopes, the sound lay invisible beyond the dark window. Raf interrupted himself with a sudden query. 'What the hell *is* the name for a fossilised shit?' he said.

SEVENTEEN

Howard Peat was getting restless, fidgety again, tapping his fingers on the surface of objects as he passed, stepping with a slight exaggeration as if he syncopated with a Walkman, funnelling out his lips, rubbing his face as Harlequin began to itch.

'Yes sir, here we go,' he said. 'Bugger me, the old roller-coaster is pulling right alongside.' The prissy language of the everyday Howard was in retreat; his back almost allowed itself a slouch.

'I'll sign you out a couple of these tabs, and ring to tell them that we're on our way to Treatment.' David had become accustomed to sizing up his charges; to making an educated guess as to how long they had before an episode was fully on. With Howard he thought they had maybe twenty minutes. He watched him standing in the doorway, breathing heavily through his mouth as if he were going to seize the sides, like Samson, and bring the place down.

'Bugger me, yes. I don't know what I'm doing in this place. Buggered if I do. You know, there's a lot of very plain people in this hole. I mean seriously plain — plain ugly. You know that?' Howard followed David down to the dispensary, which was little more than a locked cupboard by Raf's room. He watched while David signed out Schweitzer's magic balls and, without a quibble, walked back to the lounge and took them with a tumbler of water. 'I mean, you're no oil painting yourself, but you're male, so that doesn't bother me. Some of the women, though, some of the women here could holiday in a men's prison and still not get laid.'

David's experience was otherwise: there were guys inside who would mount a broomstick given the chance, but he knew Howard wasn't interested in debate.

'Jesus,' Howard said, 'I don't know what I'm doing here.'

'Let's get your bag of things in case they want you to stay down in Treatment a while. Anyway, maybe when you're better you can shoot through.'

'Better than what? Who knows if this thing isn't as natural as any other way of feeling, eh? You thought of that?'

'Don't start on me with any philosophy,' said David. 'Today I can hardly think of a reason for breathing myself.'

But the unregenerate Howard was barely listening. His eyes flickered to David and away again, as if he were following the flight of a bird trapped in the room. 'Sometimes you get a feeling when it's coming on,' he said hastily. 'Like that flux that hits you in the stomach just before the trots begin, except that it's also in your head. Something dark comes looming up from the depths, and the surface starts to wash away from it.'

'I'll come down with you to Treatment and we'll see who's on duty,' said David, but Howard had tired of him, moving quickly to those urgent imperatives which had been unshackled. He hissed his impatience, and began quickly walking through the block, pausing just long enough at the doorway of any occupied cubicle to toss in an insult, or a quip, to entertain.

'By Jesus, your breath stinks, Bernie, my man. Have I ever told you that? What garbage have you been putting inside yourself. Cheer up, Wilfe, when it's your turn you may make the volleyball team at last. It's a fucking wanker's game, although the way I am now I could see that ball like a fucking pumpkin, that's for sure, and bounce up so high you'd see the treads on my sneakers. Abbey, you intellectual bitch, I bet you'll be a goner before the end of the week even with your music, and I won't be far behind. The bite's fairly on, isn't it? Maybe when you've croaked, we might be able to get someone in your place with decent tits, for the intellect will have its day, but the cock will have its night. I reckon that the supervisors at Kotuku have nobbled the doctors, so that women with a decent pair like Lucy Mortimer and Sally Clark always end up there.'

Abbey knew that it was Harlequin talking rather than the formal, fastidious Howard she knew, but she blushed even so. Wasn't old Harlequin spokesman for the real man after all perhaps?

'Ah, McIlwraith, you stuck-up old cow. You've voted National all your life because you were born to it, and always used a bloody cup and saucer for your tea. You told me off for sitting in the lounge in socks, yet after your fancy cheeses your own hands smell as if you've been fingering the crotch of a corpse.'

'God won't be mocked,' called Dilys Williams.

'Oh, bite your arse.'

But Howard had no objection when David walked down towards the main block with him. 'I reckon I should make a break for it,' he said. 'No reason to hang around here and hope for any miracles. Who knows anything about fixing this Harlequin's anyway, that's what you ask yourself. They're all fishing in the dark, that's what, even the great Schweitzer. No fucker knows. Clear out, make a break for it, that's the thing to do. During the Black Death, you know, the clever ones walled themselves up so that they couldn't be contaminated.'

Howard had taken his coat with him into the grounds despite the sun, as a sign that he was prepared for departure from the centre. He stood on the concrete walkway looking alertly about him — the gardens, the car park, the separate blocks at a distance and the main buildings, the rough hillside behind, the sound blue and expansive at high tide. David wondered how many opportunities for escape, or salvation, Howard saw; what message his mind chose to read in it all. 'Come on down to Treatment,' said David. 'One or two of the nurses there are very easy on the eye. You might strike it lucky.'

'You're right.' Howard knew very well what awaited him: medication to shut him down, so that Harlequin would have hardly any stage on which to strut for a day or two. The receding personality was still just strong enough to contain the other psyche that was bursting out.

David and Howard went down together. David talked of the shooting star the night before, and the busloads of new guests arriving at Mahakipawa. That's how the insurmountable is dealt with, isn't it? Both of them going down to the Treatment block, past the lavender and hebe plots, the small birches, talking of shooting stars, and all the time knowing that the odds were that Howard was for it.

David wasn't threatened in the same way as Howard Peat, but more and more he was aware of the whisper of time passing, the mundane intersections of experience which would never happen in quite that way again. Abbey, say, with her hand on the jetty pile at the swimming hole and glancing self-deprecatingly back; his father, say, looking out under the shade of his palm to watch stock on the next slope; early spring, say, surprised by a brisk southerly so that a snowfall of white plum blossom blows over the yard and the kennels; Lucy Mortimer, say, sliding the sleeves of her dark jersey up her arms as she talks, until the wool is taut around her flesh; Howard, say, walking past the lavender on his way down to Treatment, with tears in his eyes as he talks, and two denim shirts with a single dark sock between them, strung on an illegal line behind him.

Here and gone, so absolute a presence for the moment, a sum of the immediate world, and then so utterly put behind. 'I don't feel too bad,' said Howard vehemently. His eyes jittered. 'I reckon it's not too bad an attack.'

'Sure.'

They went on down. Roimata Wallace was on duty. 'Don't you worry,' she said. What she meant, and what Howard clearly took from it, is that the worst would happen if they worried or not. Look away, is what she told them. Look for some jig of distraction from the known direction of their lives.

'Don't you worry, Howard,' David said as well. 'Raf or I will come down later to see how things are. Okay?'

He watched him walk away with Roimata Wallace. Howard turned at the stairs and gave one ringing Indian whoop: he was jiving up again. David had no great affinity with Howard, yet respected his independence and demand for dignity. He didn't wish him dead; he didn't wish anyone dead. Even in prison he'd not wished anyone dead: well, maybe Grocott. But there were people you couldn't mourn when they did go: people who meant nothing to you, though you made no confession of that, even to yourself.

Wilkin was one of those, and David was unfortunate enough to be accosted by him in the Takahe lounge after returning from Howard and Roimata Wallace at Treatment. Wilkin, too, was getting worse, but he was avoided not because he was dying, but because he was boring. Wilkin had a regular visitation; a giant Irish elk which prophesied for him as its monstrous antlers moved against the sky. The elk had told him who would win the volleyball final between Hoiho and Weka, although that required little enough prescience, also that Wilkin himself would recover and have a second term as president of the National Archery Federation. David and Raf, however, the elk had it in for. They were marked for sticky ends, so Wilkin let slip to Tolly.

It was surprising that more patients didn't see visions, as

the mind's way to seek release from an unbearable reality. Perhaps Wilkin's Irish elk kept all else at bay. The poet Cummings said that the fear of madness is a sign of unjustifiable self-importance.

'Elk' Wilkin was a primary headmaster from the Manawatu, but his life interest was archery. He made that choice to give himself the maximum chance for advancement. He was no marksman, but a tireless administrator at all levels, and finally he received a QSM. He must have outlasted everyone else at the committee table, but it was at the cost of any warmth or spontaneity. From Wilkin's account, even the giant elk oracle spoke within rules of procedure.

'So how is poor Howard?' Wilkin asked, and he stepped just that much further into David's personal space than was comfortable. 'I've tried often to get alongside him, but he's not an easy man to help is he? Not approachable, I'd say.'

Wilkin had a washed-out elegance — ivory wrists and eyes of faded blue china — but his talk transfixed people with a threat beyond even boredom. God knows what he had done to generations of children. Behind Wilkin's words were the sighing of some universal futility and the rustle of chrysalid husks, the drift of wet Sunday afternoons, the gagging stench of railway station urinals, the barking of dog biscuit commercials in an empty room, winter afternoons with the light squeezed out of them before workers could get home to eat.

Death, though, with sleeping tablets: that's what Wilkin had tried. It must have been a day when even the flat tines prophecy of the giant elk was not enough, but a few days later there he was in the Takahe lounge telling David of Howard's unapproachability. Whether in heaven or hell, Wilkin would end up chairing the dress code committee. 'How serious is it with Howard this time, do you think?' he asked David. His QSM was kept in its presentation box on the table in his room. What did it say of David's life that he must make reply to a man who communicated with an oracular Irish elk, while Abbey went uncomforted, and Tolly fished alone on the green sound.

While Lucy Mortimer, who was always in his thoughts, had her special session with Schweitzer.

They got into it in quite a big way in the end, so that he found himself almost wealthy, able to put some aside, which turned out to be a wise precaution. Sneaky Pete had Sydney contacts, and David and Chris took a few days there combining work and recreation. King's Cross was a disappointment to them, in appearance as much as anything else. David had imagined lurid skyscrapers, flashing lights, animated if superficial glamour, the scent of recklessness in the air. Instead, arriving with Chris on a mid-week afternoon, he found a suburban shopping centre with more pushchairs than tarts in the doorways. Only the disposable syringes lying in the alleys and at the backs of buildings hinted at the vivid desperation of the nights. The cafés by the small, ornamental park were half full of package tourists who would be able to say they'd been there, but most wouldn't come back after dark.

Just two or three teasers were out, as proof of trade. The best was at the entrance to the station. She was tall and had red velvet hotpants, a cigarette in the very centre of her lips and nipples outlined beneath the white stretch fabric of her top. She spoilt it by standing with one knee bent like an idle horse. Her face was implacable rather than impassive, deflecting the male glances with studied ease.

'You need to get the weight off your feet,' suggested Chris.

'Got an idea about that then?' she said. The cigarette twitched as she talked; her eyes continued to appraise the people going in and out to the subway.

'Who's got all the good weed around here?' asked David.

'Stumps me,' she said.

'You know where Piney Realty is then?'

'Are you after it or not?'

'*Lawrence Meelan, Piney Realty.*'

'*Fuck off and leave me alone,*' *she said. Her voice was the real thing: like a crack of a whip. A voice that anticipated the appearance she'd have in fifteen or twenty years.*

They found the Piney office by the supermarket, and Lawrence Meelan walked with them to an Irish pub, where they talked about the sort of costings that would make it worthwhile to bring shit in from Christchurch. Once Meelan realised that they didn't have a good source of hard stuff, only New Zealand resin, he lost a lot of interest. He must have misunderstood from Sneaky, he said. Maybe they'd like to pick up a reverse trade in ecstasy?

That was the end of the business side of the trip. Chris spent the next four days with a separated woman he'd met at the Irish pub when David was talking to Kevin, whom he hadn't seen since their time together at Llama Heaven. A good-looking woman, but with such a throaty voice that at first Chris had his doubts. It required a brief carnal interrogation then and there, before she was invited back to the hotel and onto the payroll. David left them to it, and flew to Auckland, spent a few days with his mother, who had a cross-lease town house of concrete block in Herne Bay. It wasn't that he disliked Australia; he liked it a good deal, and had travelled there several times. But it wasn't home. He liked the openness and humour of Aussies, the touch of flamboyance that came perhaps from the old outback characters as well as the middle European migrants. He liked their cities, and the vast heartlands without cities. He liked the gum trees fraying at their trunks, and deep, soft rivers. He liked the vineyards in wide valleys, and the old, façade pubs in the small towns. Beaches that met the horizon he liked, and the flocks of galahs at the artesian pumps. But it wasn't home.

Auckland wasn't really home either. Why had his mother shifted so far away from Canterbury and Beth Car? So far from him? 'You've got to keep challenging yourself as you get older,' she said. 'New places for new starts, otherwise the old population holds you back.'

He had been able to give her an increasing payout from Beth Car, and she enjoyed spending it. How she loved to buy a new blouse, or jacket, with a good label. She dressed herself well on the proceeds of cannabis without realising it. The three days there were some of the best they ever had together, for as well as love for him, and that was never completely lost, she had then respect and pride. What David remembered most of the Herne Bay visit wasn't the new clothes his mother displayed after her shopping trips, or the talks they had on the sundeck, but the memories that she evoked without the subject of them coming up in conversation at all.

Her flat was a model of order and cleanliness, as if in perpetual readiness for land agents and their clients. The reasonable detritus of everyday living was never apparent in his mother's house — no lightly balled long hair under the dresser from her brush, no crumpled tissues, no dockets tonguing from ornaments, no mummified scraps at the back of her refrigerator shelves, no sweat stains as rosettes beneath the sleeves of her clothes. Was it significant, perhaps, that for David her smell was always a perfume, while his father's strong, clean smell of flesh was utterly distinct and individual.

When he was seventeen, David and his mother had spent four days staying with the Corringers in Kohimarama. She instructed him in the etiquette of host and hosted. What should they do? she asked him. A gift, David suggested: flowers and chocolate. He thought it a good answer. He'd seen his mother give and receive as much. Did he think they'd been in a hotel? They were leaving after four days in the Corringers' guest suite, and he wouldn't clean from top to bottom? She gave him a lesson in cleaning the lavatory — the Harpic and brush, the Dettol cloth, the blue liquid squirted under the rim and left for fifteen minutes. Did he think lavatories cleaned themselves? Even in his exasperation, David admired the self-respect that lay behind such demon concern for appearances. On judgement day she would look every past host in the eye with equanimity. David had the uneasy recollection of the under-seventeen rugby tournament in Wellington, and the post-party vomit that he'd wrapped in a duvet and hidden in his host's wardrobe. Always imagine your travel arrangements falling through, and having to come back to your hosts, his mother told him. There were a good many later year hosts to whom David fervently wished never to return.

EIGHTEEN

There was a pub at the top end of Havelock called by locals The Squat, although its official name made spurious claims to dignity. David went there sometimes when he was off duty, taking Raf's little Mazda and driving over the Mahakipawa Hill with its slopes of pigfern and scrub. Very seldom were they able to go together, because of the rosters, and they agreed that was an added advantage on occasion. Friendship is always strengthened by the opportunity for privacy.

David went on the Thursday afternoon after Howard Peat died. It was a relief at such times to be among a population who had a normal life expectancy, and whom he owed nothing. The Squat had an old-fashioned narrow bar, with a snooker table in the end away from the windows and the road. The nip bottles made a fretwork above the stools of the front bar; there was a child's wood-framed blackboard listing the meals in white and yellow chalk. Harlequin was just a hill and a world away. Like Shane in the cowboy book, David sat where he could see the door.

Bev from the post office, her tear scar ever fresh, was having a brandy and Coke with Michael, her neighbour. David had talked with him once before, about night flounder fishing. Just a hill and a world away, but then it takes only a plywood wall in a block of flats to separate hell from heaven. Who was looking after the post office letters, David wondered.

The barman was tall and courteous, his arms so muscular that it seemed an effort of his will was necessary to ensure the glasses weren't crushed as he carried them. He put the drinks before them with a smile, and just a quick, inoffensive glance down Bev's blouse as she scratched her ankle.

'How are things at the centre?' he said. Just a hill and a world away.

'No riots as yet,' said David.

'All that new building though, eh,' and the barman withdrew with a smile to show that he didn't expect a reply. His powerful arms hung empty, at a loss, by his side.

'Michael goes there a bit,' said Bev.

'Nothing to do with the new buildings,' said Michael the flounder man. 'That's all Nelson contractors, but I do a bit of plumbing and electrical stuff when your own people there are pushed.' Michael may once have been bigger, but his body had settled back into a comfortable size. His head sank comfortably into his shoulders and the sleeves of his green work jersey were given an extra roll at the wrists. The back of his neck had a greying, untrimmed fuzz like that on a dog's leg, the sign of a man with no caring wife, or mistress, and who is spinning money out from one haircut to the next. 'In the times I've been there, I've never seen a really crook one. You hear the stories of what they get up to, right off their chump, but I've never seen any poor bastard go off the deep end,' said Michael.

'People are usually put in treatment as soon as there are signs of an episode. Most of the time there's no problem.' Well, not for those on the outside, David thought. 'Some come right and are discharged, go home for good perhaps,' he said. It was better that he didn't tell the stories of Jane, Howard, Jason, or Alice Bee.

'Every now and again I see one or two over here for the day,' said Bev. 'I've had them in the post office, and they often go to see the little church museum. Nothing's ever stolen as far as I know. Mostly they fossick around the shore.'

Schweitzer's policy was that patients could go into Picton, or Havelock, if accompanied by a staff member — one on one, and therefore inconspicuous. The ruling arose not through fear of an episode during a visit, but as sensitivity to the centre's effect on the settlements on either side. They were too small and self-contained to cope with mass therapy visits. Also there was political pressure to draw as little attention as possible to Harlequin's growth.

'You came last with the millionaire — a chap with a Rolex, but no airs and graces at all.' David had introduced Tolly Mathews to Bev. She had seen him with Lucy several times too, but tactfully said nothing of that.

'A millionaire, eh,' said Michael. 'Is that right? You wouldn't think a millionaire would get sick in the head, would you?' Floundering was a good little earner on the side, but Michael had never known big money.

'Well, I don't know about millionaire.' Some mild disclaimer was necessary. Before you knew it the locals would have the impression that the patients were all loaded. But he did know, and what he knew was that in terms of assets Tolly was a multi-millionaire, and that wasn't uncommon any more. There were plenty of houses in Auckland and Wellington worth more than a couple of million. David thought it might be a good thing to get Tolly and Michael together. Tolly could supply the drinks and the news of the world; Michael could share his local knowledge of time and tide: the soft, slanting submarine places where flounder bulged their eye from artful camouflage and suckled in the sand. They'd get on fine.

But rather than thinking of the future, or even the present with Michael and Bev in The Squat, it was his last visit with Lucy that David inhabited. He'd been compelled to go through the formality of asking Tony Sheridan for permission. There had been a moment when they both knew that Tony was about to ask him if anything was going on, but the doctor couldn't quite get it out.

David and Lucy had gone to the museum, as no doubt Bev observed from her window. It was a narrow, wooden church with solid plank chocks under the steps. The pews were gone, replaced by butter churns, pit-saws, dray wheels, sad photos of bullock drivers, bushmen and women with unwashed hair. There were glassed cases of fob watches on chains, sovereign purses, buttoned shoes, trade certificates, and the medals of Corporal Charles W. Riley, who died of disease on the Somme. Right at the front, under sufferance, the church was allowed some history of its own: a simple lectern pulpit made from the timbers of the *Criccieth* wrecked in 1887, and a dry, cracked board with the names of every minister, until all the congregation had been quite preached away.

Lucy and he had gone down to the water too: down the same road he'd taken with his sandwiches when he came to Havelock to take his job at the centre, by Nottage & Son boat-builders again, though the clinker-built dinghy was gone, released onto the sea. They sat by the enclosing breakwater and watched the flotsam moving at the angle between the wall and the shore, like spittle at the corner of an incessant talker's mouth. Lucy broke off pieces of a dock plant and flicked them into the incoming tide which was stirring up a fine sludge that moved over the mudflats as a faint skirt in front of the clean water behind.

She wasn't glamorous that day. Sitting pulled the cuffs of her jeans higher on her shins, showing the stubble there, and her hair was pulled back simply from her face, emphasising her high, round forehead. She had a slight rash behind her left ear, which she stroked with two fingers. He'd never loved her more, and ached to save her. 'I bet you'd never heard of Havelock, had you?' he said. 'Certainly not Mahakipawa.'

'No. Havelock North I know, though.' Her slim fingers continued to snap and shred the dock plants, or trace the inching skin by her ear.

'There's a South Island Palmerston too, but of course it's been forgotten for Palmerston North. You never know where your life's going to, do you? Like a Havelock boy ending up getting shot on some Boer War donga, like an Auckland girl marrying a Yank soldier and then off to Minnesota to live, like a guy in Bulls owning the same dairy for sixty years and being buried beside his parents who had it before him.'

'Like fronting on national television and then getting Harlequin and ending up here, right?' she said.

'Yes, that's it. Can you hack it?'

They could hear small children from the school playground not far away: the delighted shrieks of self-induced terror, the chanting and taunting, the hubbub of energy released. Perhaps what he was trying to say to Lucy was that all the moods and possibilities were there together in an instant, but experienced separately, as white light contains all the colours of the rainbow. Heaven and hell only a breath and a chance apart. The kids climbed the jungle gym, while over the Mahakipawa Hill new buildings went up to Harlequin. The wizened deerstalker, once mighty, choked to death on a cherry stone in the Picton Rest Home, while Abbey at the centre was acclaimed in concert for the playing of Liszt. The police continued to investigate a murder of passion in Kaikoura, while the history of the Te Tarehi Dairy Co-operative was launched with five cardboard casks of indeterminate white wine and seven kilograms of mild cheese.

'I guess it was a pretty exciting life in television,' said David.

'In a way, but you're so busy that the enjoyment of it tends to get squeezed out. There were plenty of parties, but I felt rather hunted all through it by the need to be prepared, to do a good job. People around are surprisingly supportive, but the system itself's bloody unrelenting.'

'So many people keen to get a look in, I suppose.'

'Nothing's settled,' she said. 'Change is always on the way. Restructuring is how the management make a living, and it seems to me that the youth culture drives TV now.'

'You'll go back to it the better for a break,' he said, and quickly wished he hadn't.

'Oh, sure,' she said, 'I'm relying on it.' Heaven and hell just a breath away.

They walked as far as it was possible along the breakwater, and looked back at the small town at the foot of the hill, saw the arm of the sound running up the valley that the road followed to Nelson. Beds of reeds, brush stiff at a distance, lined the shore. They relaxed in the sun, watched the tide coming, said little and didn't kiss, but loosely held each other's fingers. The perfumed wind came up the sound and cooled them. A sheep truck was busy on the Mahakipawa Hill.

'You never say much about your life,' Lucy said.

'A farm, an arts degree, the big OE, a farm, a failure.'

'And family?'

'Just Mum and Dad. Both dead now.' Just a breath away. Just a breath away.

'Raf reckons maybe something went really bad for you,' said Lucy. 'That it's knocked your confidence pretty much.'

'Everyone's a psychologist, don't you think? I'm no more mysterious than anybody else.' It was odd though to be reminded that other people spoke about you in your absence: that they had opinions about your life and behaviour which they'd never think to say to your face. 'Maybe I just didn't find something to hook into like other people,' he said. 'Some were into pop music, or travel, or career success. Sport was big for some, or getting pissed every weekend. I've just never found one thing to concentrate on.' Except the shit, of course, but he didn't like to see his entire life as revolving around that.

'You liked farming, though?' said Lucy.

'Yeah, I did. Well, maybe I liked living on a farm rather than keeping up with all the stuff to be done there. I got lazy, I suppose.'

'And it was round here?'

'No, North Canterbury.'

'I always think of farms being such boring places. The same things done over and over again, and so many animals to be killed. People working all by themselves, whistling and spitting rather than having a conversation.'

'Some things are best done over and over again,' David said. Flippant innuendo was the easy out. What was the value in any defence of the land when Lucy had so little experience of it: when she could sit surrounded by hills and water and read no signs in them at all. David loved her no less for that. Guilt, too, prevented him from being advocate, for he had lost Beth Car, broken the continuity of his family there, and ended up packed in with people at the Slaven Centre, Mahakipawa, even though the quiet country was all around.

No one had seemed disconcerted by their presence in Havelock that day, but when they came out of the pub after a late lunch, there was a carton flap held to the windscreen by the wipers, and on it — 'Fuck Off Crazies'. 'Maybe it's not paradise after all,' Lucy said. It was a careful sign, and placed almost solicitously so as not to damage Raf's car. There were no observers that either of them could see. Lucy took the sign into the car with her, and wedged it between the dash and the glass, so that it faced other people, not themselves. She enjoyed the reaction of the few oncoming motorists as they went back to the centre, and when they reached the car park she took the cardboard with her to amuse her friends in Kotuku.

David paused to admire a splendidly kept silver Audi in the end park, where there was less danger of a door being opened on its paintwork. David recognised it. It had protective clear covers over the front lights and high-performance tyres. The owner was a plain clothes cop who was liaison between the centre and the Nelson police. Such information soon got around. David had seen the detective once as he walked past Takahe to the main block. A tall man with a plain, blue blazer and blue tie, but with the incongruity of white and red trainers instead of formal shoes. No doubt he sought the pleasure of using his own car on business, and thought it worth the cost.

Your own motives and experiences are always in a different category from those of other people, aren't they? What you do yourself is always subject to special pleading. David realised that when he had his first full session with the lawyer who was to represent him. A man of cautious arrogance: physically clumsy, but well dressed and highly recommended. David told him almost the whole truth, and as he did so could see on the lawyer's face precisely how the situation appeared to people on the outside. David as a man greedy, unprincipled and careless, who had assumed that there was some reason why he wouldn't be caught. Someone with a whole heap of natural advantages, and he'd blown them. A private school boy who thought he could sneer at the ordinary world.

David wanted to explain that it was something else, that he and Chris had fashioned a life based on more than money and indifference to the fate of others. He wanted the lawyer to experience the evenings of discussion beneath the country stars, to appreciate the reputation they established for full weight and full value in their dealings, to understand the satisfaction of the work and planning needed for their crop. In the first interview he tried to open all that up, but saw almost immediately how incidental it was to his lawyer, or anybody else: how expressly common rather than unique his crime was, how self-serving and selective his account, how obviously a camouflage for the easy out.

And sitting with the lawyer, whose hands bumbled on

the desk, David understood something of the indignant anger of many accused, at having their complex and subtle experience tossed into a job lot marked fraud, or rape, or theft as a servant, or treason against one's country.

'Maybe in three or four years,' said his lawyer at that first full discussion, 'all this will be perfectly legal and invoke no penalty at all. There's been strong lobbying for years now.'

David had relied on the strength of it, and been made all the more the fool. In the end, although neither David nor the lawyer realised it at that meeting, it was to cost him the farm. Chris made no effort to evade his share of the blame, but it wasn't his property. In reduced form their friendship survived even the loss of Beth Car, but it would never be the same again.

David was grateful that his father wasn't alive to see him take the fall.

The lawyer's firm had just that day moved into new offices of marble veneer and stained wood above a Thai restaurant, and looking out over Cranmer Square. He told David that he was only the second client he'd seen in the premises, and apologised for his files, which were in cartons on the floor until the polyurethane dried in the storage alcove. How narrow was the point of contact between their lives. The lawyer that night talked to his wife of the new offices, the polyurethane, the disagreement with the senior partner on vertical slat blinds, and said nothing at all of David — an overeducated farmer, who had become a grower and supplier of cannabis, and would be sent to prison for it.

'The positive angle,' the lawyer said, clumsily adjusting the computer screen on his desk, 'is that there are no elements of intimidation or violence whatsoever. I shall indeed bring that out strongly, quite strongly.'

Their lives met just briefly on the ricochet, but David's case may still be on disk, and also, as a precaution perhaps, in a manila folder tied with a pale pink ribbon, and scented still faintly with polyurethane.

NINETEEN

The cardboard with its abuse of crazies was still there in Lucy's room when David next went across. It was pinned to the back of the door, directly in David's line of sight as he listened to Lucy talk about herself in a way quite uncharacteristic.

'Maybe it's not all bad. Maybe there's some opportunity in it to understand more about yourself: things that are never able to be acknowledged when you're healthy. Among all the dangers there's the exhilaration, too, of freedom, of letting the old nature dance free of the leash at last.' Lucy was talking quietly, as much to challenge herself as for communication. 'Everyone who has it, talks of that release, as well as the fear that comes with loss of control. The last couple of episodes I've felt something of it for the first time.'

Of course the guests talked among themselves, but David was surprised by the realisation that Lucy sought such comfort, and then surprised by his own selfishness in assuming that, as a lover, he supplied all she needed. 'I'm buggered if I see any opportunity in this thing,' he said.

'There are people who think Harlequin is the beginning of some fundamental psychic change for both individual and community. Did you know that? A leap into the future.'

'Jesus,' David said. 'A leap back, you mean. That's what the clinical record shows. It's old brain emergence, you know that. It can kill you, and you talk about opportunities.'

'Yes, the past too,' she said, ignoring death for the time. 'Sometimes I'm in several places at once — an overlay of experiences. Maybe I'm standing watching the volleyball, and hear a squeaking that I recognise as my sister's trike, smell the faint Rive Gauche of Mum's wardrobe, see the water pellets on the polished bonnet of Dad's Camry, or the faces of a studio audience across the court. They don't move their heads although the ball goes back and forth. In the dining room I put battered fish into my mouth, but taste the metal of the braces I wore when I was ten. I can sit waiting for my treatment appointment, and feel Ron Sanders's hand edging down to my breasts after the leavers' dance.'

'Like this?' said David.

'Better.' Her hand stilled his. 'Something said ages ago comes back again not as recollection, but as an interruption when I'm in the middle of another conversation.'

'Who knows what Harlequin does inside the brain.' Almost he wished that he was a patient too, that there was some way that he could share the thing that was the difference between them far greater than gender, background, or belief. How honest should he be?

Usually they kept Harlequin out of their talk, their love: he had domain enough in other aspects of their lives, but Lucy was for once getting it all out, and she sat up as if the posture helped her to order her ideas. The softest of rain fell on the lawns and gardens of the Slaven Centre, and brought out blackbirds hopeful that the worms would rise. The birds on the ground cocked their heads in alert silence, but those on the gutterings cried 'Ruby, ruby'. Lucy looked out intently as if close observation helped her to focus her thoughts about Harlequin. 'Structures break down, you see. Things don't keep their place, but whirl around. The whole box of tricks starts to shake loose, and finally there'll be no divisions at all. Once your brain starts that — the deceit, I mean — then you're gone. No firm ground any more, even within yourself. Everything you hear is both achingly sublime and ultimately incomprehensible, like hearing your name called longingly in a crowd, but when you turn no one welcomes you.'

'The medics go on about the heightening effects.' David tried to keep talking as if Harlequin was at a distance; as if Lucy wasn't a host; as if his throat wasn't tight with the effort to talk normally. With his tongue he could feel where the utterly smooth skin of her shoulder blade changed to the slightly rougher texture that was more often exposed to the wind and the sun.

'Oh, yeah, Harlequin can take you for a real ride: better than the happy baccy you bring me, better than a good cab sav, better than — go on, ask me?'

'Better than sex?' He tightened his arm around her to comfort them both.

'Well, lover boy, let's make conjunctions, not comparisons. Sex and Harlequin, now there's some hell of a buzz: whirling up from the fire and not knowing when you'll ever fall again.' She knew what he was thinking. 'Of course with you it's like that even without Harlequin.'

'Don't joke about it,' he said. The university guy, Tilling, who had the next room to Lucy, walked away across the lawn and left footprints where he trod the fine droplets down.

'Often I'm so scared I can't sleep.'

'But don't joke about it.' He didn't turn round. He made no further movement of physical condolence — to do so would have brought him to tears.

'You get punished for fucking in so many ways,' Lucy said. 'Maybe Harlequin's in there too. Maybe when you're giving me one, I'm giving it to you.'

'No, that's one of the first means of transmission they checked, with Aids and so on.'

'Schweitzer said an interesting thing.' Lucy had these

titbits from her sessions with the director, but David was thinking about the Black Death: how people thought that it came from the air. A vapour, like gassing in the First World War, because no one knew it was fleas on rats moving from the East. It would be like that with Harlequin. The textbooks would record that people blamed sex, stress, evolutionary degeneration, or pesticides, while all the time it was something right under their noses. '—yet no one at the conference had come across a case of a patient with a properly diagnosed psychiatric illness catching Harlequin. Now that *is* odd,' said Lucy.

'It's like Jenner using cowpox to inoculate against smallpox. You protect yourself from going mad in the new way, by going mad in the old way. Some of the staff here must be trying it, don't you reckon?' He was able to turn to her as they laughed, joking as he'd told her not to, and they stretched out again on the narrow, firm bed. Everywhere their bodies touched was pleasure. Combing his fingers through hers, he noticed how gracile were hers in contrast; how free of the hair and roughness of his own. 'Jesus, though,' he said, 'no known cause, no established mode of transmission, no effective treatment and contradictory statements of essential symptoms. We're doing so marvellously bloody well. If it wasn't for thousands of people dying, we wouldn't recognise it at all.'

'They'll crack it in the end, of course,' said Lucy softly, 'as they cracked the others that people despaired about. People will learn to live with it as they have with cancer and Ebola. But for me it'll be too late. I won't learn to live with it, or die with it either and, because I won't come through it, I don't give a fuck for all those saved later. Is that awful?'

'It's natural, and anyway not everybody's dying. There are some natural remissions, you know that.'

'Eff all. You want me to put balloons up for that?'

'Why shouldn't you come out of this?' he said doggedly. 'You love me and you help me and you'll suffer with me, but you're still glad that it's me and not you.' She said it without urgency or anger, as if she knew the feeling herself, and she traced the lines at the corners of his mouth as if she spoke of love.

'Not as glad as I used to be.' David was galled with guilts and failures, though free of Harlequin as yet, but he didn't want to get into all that.

They lay down face to face, with just a sheet drawn partly up. On her side that way, her breasts lay together in slight shadow, their beauty a reminder that Harlequin left any distortion of the body until close to an end, and then, mostly by chance, did harm.

No physical appetite can be assuaged by recollection, yet the mind retains semblances of joy. Moments, glimpses, a spontaneous sequence, the sharpest focus of experience, ineffable repleteness, become a store of the marvellously erotic on which the spirit draws. They kissed. They pressed closer in the early afternoon: the drift of voices came from the corridors, laughter from those guests before the television in the lounge. Sex gave a brief dispensation from any threat, every weakness: from past and future even.

'Feeling alive now?' Lucy said.

'Blow my brains out,' said David huskily, and Lucy laughed and widened her eyes. Her breasts trembled as they rode together. 'Look at me,' he demanded. 'Look at me.' It was a good time to be struck down, but they weren't that blessed.

And no Nan nodding in the outer room, no whaleboats putting out from Kaikoura, no guilt even, for a few moments. A kiss, with their throats still throbbing, then they lay, cast up, on the institutional sheet. The brief, blithe spirit of abandonment was over, but their warm fingers touched with complete affection. So it must have been all over the world for the fortunate, as women kissed women, men caressed men, men and women kindly opposed their differences, all holding each other with such a passionate intimacy that no distinction was possible between giving and taking.

'I wish the door locked,' Lucy said. Both modesty and caution were too late anyway. David could feel the sweat cooling on parts of him not pressed against her. From the car park the sound of Bryce's ute, from the lawns came the soft scents of grass and flower beds in the drizzle, from the sky a paua glow of the sun hidden by the flimsy cloud.

Yet the unpleasant truth was that Harlequin had brought them together. Perhaps David took advantage of the situation, to be of service, to lie with her on fewer occasions than he wished in the narrow bed of his room, or hers. He felt no guilt at all in regard to ethics, but a sense of the sad yet fortuitous way in which their lives had been drawn together. Everything for Lucy, her life most of all, was put at risk, and yet Harlequin also created his opportunity to love her.

Lucy was never willing to discuss her illness with such candour again. She endeavoured to ensure David never saw her during an episode. She made him promise never to come to her room without warning; never to visit the treatment suites if she was there. Yet he did see her when old Harlequin was in attendance. On a warm, aromatic evening when the several hundred of them had eaten lasagne, so it must have been a Thursday. Pasta was the designated menu on Thursdays: cannelloni, spaghetti alla carbonara. Great trays of pasta, with the Parmesan cheese sprinkled late perhaps, and its odour of succulent decay mingling with that of the mudflats below, and the stainless steel servery turned to ivory by a trick of the light.

A Thursday then, with just that combination, and all of them at the centre, coming, or going, or seated at the laminated tables to feed an inner man — one of the cruel jokes they shared there. Lucy Mortimer then, fighting like a fourth former with a Maori woman from Hoiho, and getting the worst of it: fists dog-paddling, language shrill and unbridled. Had it been anyone else, David would have been one of those who separated the pair, apologised to the Maori woman and soothed the other participant before taking her to the treatment suites. As it was, he kept his distance lest Lucy see him, remained seated before the pasta, watched Polly Merhtens and Philip Tyler smooth Lucy's clothes as they stood close and persuaded her to go down with them to Treatment. 'I won't be shoved about like a bloody five-year-old,' said Lucy. It was a voice he hardly recognised. A voice utterly self-centred, and stripped of all the subtlety that comes from personal and social awareness.

He turned away from Lucy then, not in disgust or dismissal, but in helplessness and loving knowledge that it was too cruel to be a witness. She might catch sight of him. He grimaced over the dining table, and popped his knuckles. The Slaven Centre at such times was just another prison: and Harlequin wasn't big on parole.

TWENTY

David told himself that death wasn't restricted to any institution: that a natural conclusion to life should be accepted with healthy philosophic resignation. Some die because of growths within them, and some because no growth occurs. Some go spectacularly in the jaws of a shark, or a greater white crevasse. Some become small and flat in their beds, with no more movement, or relevance, than the green flecked wallpaper which they plumb-bobbed twenty-five years before. Some with eagerness await the dark angel; others are driven to a fine old Celtic rant before they leave the stage. Death is generous in the variety allowed its players.

Death, that great egalitarian: that customary and modest victor.

Lucy was unwell for some time after fighting in the dining room, and David observed her wish by not visiting. He was left subject to all his old guilt. And the most powerful new one, which was his inability to help her. He had a feeling that the air was congealing, and that after the final agony of suffocation, they would each be set there in time's amber: all movement and resolution abandoned, despite the sea wind, in one last glaze of futile boredom.

Churchill called depression his black dog, and it followed him faithfully enough, drawing closer to his heels with old age. There were traces of white paint where David's nails grew from the skin, yet he had no recollection that would serve as an explanation. Someone's sneakers lay on their side with long laces limp on the verandah, and the stained ivory soles worn through to blue on the pressure points. Faintly yellowed sweat stains showed on Raf's shirt as he leant back with his hands clasped behind his head. It was a poor creation after all: the uncouth gorse on the slopes, the sheen of the mudflats, the blatancy of the far hills' appeal. No wonder that disease came easily. Raf and David talked without much interest in the topic, or each other's company. They were considering an outing for their Takahe charges.

Despair is the sense of loathing we have for the world. David had access to alcohol as well as cannabis. A combined dose when he longed to escape the glint of Wilfe Orme's discoloured teeth, the sound of the inane games show through the thin wall, the crass sweetness of Jungle Glade toilet freshener, the reptilian touch of the communal plastic chairs, the cattle splattering shit on the gorse slope, the partly repressed memories of his more significant failures.

David left Raf's room, rang Tony Sheridan and asked if he could go down and talk with him: it was time perhaps to hand in notice and leave the Plague House before coming down with Harlequin himself. It was a temptation of fate after all, wasn't it? No one could guarantee a lack of contagion. Maybe it would be like those nineteenth-century leper colonies, with the priests at last recognising on their own bodies the lesions that they had been ministering to on others. David certainly lacked sufficient sense of faith and calling to accept that with resignation. The Slaven Centre was a bolt hole as far as he was concerned, not a place of service. He thought about it as he went down to Sheridan's office, but no matter how many considerations drew the scales down on the side of leaving, the single presence of Lucy was more than enough to outweigh them.

'It's natural to have downers here,' said Sheridan. 'All of us in the medical services are acting contrary to our natural instinct to avoid debility, sickness and disease and, though we repress it, that instinct will have its release in some way or another.' He was in something of a philosophical mood, because he had no more treatment sessions for the day. His legs were crossed at the ankles, and his huge shoes were like leather petals from a common centre. 'I'm collating my research on the proclivity of Harlequin patients to experience episodes at much the same time, in the same way that communities of young women tend to a common pattern of menstruation.'

'Or maybe it's the food,' David said unkindly. Silverside every Monday, pastas on Thursdays, Sunday simple salads that could clear out the digestive system of a Clydesdale. The whiff of mayonnaise and hard-boiled eggs lingered through the buildings as a transpiration of religion.

And Lucy was sick again.

David realised he should be interested enough to draw Tony Sheridan out concerning his research, but his own boredom and discontent were more important than the conventions of friendship — or the possible salvation of the world. More than anything else he needed some change of scene, some distraction from the modern blocks of the centre on the hillside and the peep show that was Harlequin.

And Lucy was sick again and there was nothing he could do for her.

'Raf and I thought we might take some of our group on an outing,' he told the doctor. 'The ones stable at the moment. It must be good therapy.'

'Where to, though? Picton and Havelock are out for groups — you know that.'

'Oh, we'd be well hidden from everything but the sun and the sea and the sky. There won't be any witnesses at

Pan Bay. We could all writhe on the ground, and froth from various orifices without inconvenience, or alarm, to the locals.'

Sheridan just wagged the leather petals of his feet, and stirred the baby-soft fluff at the sides of his balding head. 'Go ahead,' he said. 'Sound off. I get paid to listen to everybody work off a shitty mood, but it'll have to be done correctly all the same. You know, the form with the people who want to go for me to check through, the right ratio of staff, an itinerary — the full Scout manual stuff, otherwise it's no go.'

All the needs of bureaucracy were dutifully attended to that week, and on the day they were provided with packed lunches: those with mustard in the sandwiches marked with a green felt pen. Sara Keppler had been declared unfit to go, and she wept, sulked, then disappeared just before the mini-vans left. How she missed her old fire-bug, Jason, who had been friend and lover. Tony Sheridan assured Raf and David that he would find her, that they should go on and not give Sara the satisfaction of spoiling the picnic. 'She hardly knows what she's doing at the moment,' he said. 'Once you're away she'll forget all about it and be right as rain.'

He stood at the car park with the Solomon twins from Titi, who happened to be passing, and the three of them farewelled the Takahe party down the shingle drive. Although only there by chance, the twins remained after the doctor turned away, and waved until the vans were out of sight.

Dilys Williams was in the front seat of the van David drove. She adjusted the seatbelt so that her breasts wouldn't be crushed if they had an accident. 'Those Solomon twins,' she told him as an equal. 'They steal stuff from the laundry room. And when they had a search at Titi, there were dozens of knickers and vests and stuff in their room. Even though some of it was named, they never so much as made an apology. Can you believe that? All this stuff in their room and they were as brazen as you like.'

'Is that so? Jesus.' But what interested David more than the alleged kleptomania of the twins was that they should end up at the centre, both with Harlequin. He wondered what Schweitzer made of that.

Pan Bay was one of the small inlets in the sound, with a creek flowing in a culvert under the road, and a shore of finer shingle — almost sand — because of some protection from the swell. The stiff rushes immediately behind the beach held up scurf from the last storm, and the wind was just enough to ruffle the shallow water of high tide. In all that they could see, there were signs of only one home: the red tin roof of a farmhouse above hedges, a pipe and netting gate at the road, a hand-written sign rigged up in a trailer at that gate which offered unshelled walnuts, and self-pick mushrooms at $15 a bucket, even though not one pale dome was in sight.

The mini-vans were parked to provide shade, and those who wanted to read, or sit and talk, spread their rugs there. Wilfe Orme had a tubular, folding seat that was the object of much undisclosed envy: Gaynor Runcinski and recidivist Eddie Simm set one of the chilly bins between them to act as a chess table. 'A little cell of fucking intellectuals,' said Jock McPhie to the wind, as he went off with his thread line to fish.

Fourteen was the limit that Raf and David were allowed to take away. David wondered how such a regulation ratio was arrived at — one to seven — and what was expected of the one if the seven ran amok. Aides were assumed to be like the little tailor perhaps: seven at one blow. 'Remember,' Raf told them, 'no one beyond the sound of the car horns at any time.' And how would they ever know until the horns were sounded? Mrs McIlwraith spent some minutes gaining a consensus as to which van would be the changing place for women and which for men. Raf said that he'd been on this course where they stressed the significance of delegating non-essential decisions to patients as a way of preventing dependency and a sense of powerlessness. 'All crap,' he said, as he watched Mrs McIlwraith stirring up resentment among her fellows. 'And who would seek an excuse to catch a glimpse of her scraggy bum in any case?'

David, Tolly and a few others went for a swim, but even though the sun was bright and the water warm enough, it wasn't a great success, because you had to wade out and out before the water deepened much at all and, despite the stones of the small beach, they could find only mud as a footing further out. Even though they had light sneakers on to protect their feet from broken shells, the mud clung unpleasantly to their legs, and swirled up into the shallow water when they tried to swim. So they went back and lay with their heads in the shade of a van, bodies in the sun.

Tolly thought that maybe at low tide he would find a channel exposed and be able to walk out to clear, deep water. He was struck by the oddity of fate that had brought him to the place and the predicament. 'Just a few months ago I'd never heard of Mahakipawa, or Harlequin's disease, had no idea that God had a brother called Schweitzer. I had a five-bedroom three-bathroom architecturally designed house and was running three factories. I had women trying to catch my eye at conferences. The bank manager picked me up for golf. Now here I am with you guys: grass stalks up my bum, mud up to my crotch.' He was right. Only the most trivial and the most fundamental concerns seemed to be left, nothing in between, and so the distinction blurred. Extinction, and the failure to win a volleyball game, were equals at Mahakipawa.

'Don't get on to all that today,' David said. 'Jesus, let's just relax here and leave all that behind.'

'I'll tell you what, Tolly,' said Raf. 'I've got two cans of Speights for each of us. Strictly verboten as you know, but David and I have put our distinguished careers on the line for you all. So stop feeling sorry for yourself, and put them in a sack in the sea so they'll be cool at lunch. And because you're such a big businessman, it's your shout all round. Right?'

'Speights,' grumbled Tolly, but he went willingly to get the cans from Raf's van. 'What is it with you people down here and Speights?'

Abbey had replaced Gaynor as Eddie's chess opponent, and they had the doors open in the other van so that music from the radio drifted out to them as they played. The aching falsetto of early Orbison seemed completely at home in a land and seascape that he would never know. Jock was smaller than a thumb, knee deep and casting at a distance; Gaynor, Wilfe and a couple of others were closer, idly looking for shells worth keeping; Tolly was almost full size and tying a driftwood marker to the sack of beer that he had sunk in the sea.

The Big O had been dead a good while, and revived musically several times since. The great stuff just keeps coming back, Raf reckoned. David remembered those promotional photos of Orbison with his blank, pasty face, and dark glasses to hide his eyes. And the voice giving it all away. When their picnic was over, when they were back at the centre leaving only tyre tracks and orange peel in the rushes and gravel, then maybe the Big O would still be bouncing 'Pretty Woman' across the sound and up the slopes of the bushed hills that enclosed it.

A launch was going steadily up the sound towards Havelock and, because any boat at all was a rarity, it held their attention. It hit the chop with regular reverberation and a person in a blue anorak went and stood at the stern for a brief time and then disappeared. 'If I was in that,' shouted Jock, 'I bet I'd catch some bloody fish. This Pan Bay is hopeless: too shallow and with a mud bottom. Useless.'

'You've not got what it takes, that's all,' said Tolly.

A picnic is a dangerous, insubstantial thing once childhood is past, for it sets expectations that are never achieved, and an institutional picnic is the least favoured and most predictably disappointing of all. Like an artificial Christmas tree, or an orphanage reunion, it mocks the very feelings that it attempts to uphold. Abbey playing chess, Jock fishing, Gaynor stooping for a palely pink shell, Mrs McIlwraith exposing her demure ankles to the sun, Tolly wading back without the sack, were surely all wondering when the quiet, but fiercely spinning earth would throw them off, yet no one said a word of that, and they came and gathered at the vans for the apparently significant division of those packed lunches marked with green felt pen, and those untouched by mustard. The launch had become a water beetle far away, and Gaynor's upper arms, well muscled from years of weaving, were already pink in the sun. 'There are some small, dart-like shells,' she said, 'quite nondescript on the outside, but with exquisite colours on the inside lip.' She had two like flint arrowheads in her palm, but only Abbey took a quick look.

As well as sandwich packs to bicker over, there was the imperative of choosing a banana that wasn't too badly blackened on the skin. David and Abbey caught each other's eye, but nothing was said. What purpose is ever served by the mutual recognition of such ironies?

'The thing I'd like to do is come back here at night with torches and spears. I reckon that there'd be a whole bunch of flounder on the bottom of shallow water here at night. You can pick them out with the lights, you know, and spear them easily. Flounder like a soft bed without much current.' Jock was having no luck at all with the thread line, but the vision of darkness, quick with flashing lights and spears, countered his failure. The slick mud was drying to grey on his legs, and his hair was spiked up like a boy's when he took off his yellow, floppy hat. How he would enjoy a night with Post Office Bev's floundering friend from Havelock, David thought. Maybe it was something he could organise.

On the hard, uneven shore, with just tartan rugs beneath them, many of the group slept in the afternoon while change was imperceptible: just the sea slinking back from the mudflats and the sharp shadows from the vans to tell the time. Those who were still awake were no longer urgent in action or conversation, and the murmur of their voices, the easy silences, the low laughter, were stitched to the noise of the breeze, a few piping birds drawn to the feeding opportunities of the receding tide, and the subdued snores of Tolly and Gaynor Runcinski. Although David faced Montgomery, who told of his plans to visit India once he was well, although he smiled and nodded even, he was by preference with Lucy, imagining her session with Schweitzer. Her unpainted nails had a trick of catching the light, and there were tendrils of dark hair at the nape of her neck which escaped the casual band she wore. Montgomery went off a few paces to find a more animated conversationalist, and woke Raf, whose face continued for a while to have the relaxed blandness of sleep. 'Sometimes the more I sleep, the more I want to,' he said. 'Maybe I'll die of it. Maybe it's a sign I should take notice of the life I lead.'

'Better than striking Alice Bee on a bad day,' David said.

'It's odd you mention her. Roimata Wallace told me yesterday that Alice spent her time at the end balancing on her hands with her feet in the air no trouble at all.'

Poor old Alice. She once told David, during a programme session in her block, that the very first thing she could remember was a golden Labrador standing in her kindergarten sandpit. The inside of its lips glistened, she said, and it had a feathered front foot in a red plastic bucket. What final recollection did she have when connected with the national grid through the dayroom plug?

Montgomery's talk of India was soon overridden by interest in the work of memory. Raf told them that neurological research increasingly suggested that all experience is completely recorded, and that it's only the access which is limited. He knew of a woman who suffered brain damage in an accident and who for several days had the exact sights, scents, touch, conversations word perfect, from happenings thirty years before, which had never until then been available to her conscious memory.

Raf's own earliest recollection was of being smacked for sneezing mucus into his sister's face without malice, or intention. He could still see the hokey-pokey ice-cream in her mouth as she opened it to yell, the concentric blue bands on the milk jug in front of him, feel the sudden pang of fear and anger that his mother should smack him hard and console his sister. 'What can you remember, Abbey?' Raf asked her. 'What's the very first thing?'

And Abbey told them, with the candour that illness can bring; Gaynor and Wilfe drew closer to her side of the van to hear it. The first image of her life was not of any familiar face, or place of childhood, but a basement she never entered in a house visited only once. Some acquaintance when they were travelling, and she stood barefoot, unsteady, on dry scratchy grass outside a basement door. A heavy man with evident nasal hair came through the door, struck his head, reeled back, came on again and struck again with an impact of great solidity. His smile was tugged away and replaced by such pain and fury, such full-throated obscenity, that Abbey panicked and ran. Beyond the brown lawn which curved endlessly away as she ran, was an equally boundless sea, she said, with a blue, eternal glitter.

'How could you remember it so exactly?' said Dilys derisively. 'It's a nonsense.' Abbey had no more to say, but David waited until he could catch her eye again, and then smiled. The world was full of Dilys people, and had so few Abbeys. What was his own first tableau of the world? Riding Billy Bunter, the pet lamb that had become gargantuan. The crimped wool on Billy's skin, the feel of muscles and sinews beneath, Billy's powerful stench of life, the comfort of his father's steadying hand. There had been a strong, low sun, hadn't there, which spread great shadows right across the world.

Raf decided on a walk for everybody before putting his mind to a barbecue tea. 'Come on, you loafers,' he called. 'Let's pull finger and get this show on the road.' Like a school field trip party they began a walk along the water's edge of Pan Bay, and only Jock and Montgomery remained behind: Jock to maintain the vision of himself as a confirmed fisherman, Montgomery because he'd had bad news from home and wanted to smoke the shit David had given him to assuage that news. But being left together brought them no closer. Jock waded into the sea once more with his thread line; Montgomery stood with studied indifference by the vans and gazed inland.

'Where are we going?' asked Tolly Mathews.

'Round to the point of the bay and back,' David said. 'Work up an appetite for all the sausages we've got.'

'It's just so hot,' said Mary Cross. She seemed to be swelling in her top, so that neck and upper arms bulged from the fabric.

'You North Islanders are learning a thing or two down here at last. We're between Nelson and Blenheim, and one or other of those has the sunshine record every year.'

'You can get too hot, you know,' said Eddie Simm, who was from Wanganui, but he was laughed down by mainlanders, and his fellow North Islanders in the group gave only half-hearted support, for, as well as being out of their territory, they were sick somehow, weren't they, and so old loyalties were weakened.

It wasn't a simple, firm shoreline to walk. The rushes and sea grasses hid slight undulations where the mud lay deeply, and every now and then miniature inlets pushed back towards the road. Some of the group picked their way fastidiously from vantage to vantage, others went as the crow flies, but plopping and stumping through whatever happened to be underfoot. Dermot Sweeney found the body of a large cod: much of its tail and fins had either been eaten or rotted away, but its eyes were quaking and reproachful. There were also several loops of nylon string, faded to a coral blue. Tolly and Wilfe strung some together, tied it to driftwood sticks and went whipping as if they were ten years old again.

'You flick me with that, and I'll thump you,' said Raf.

'Just a little tune-up to get you trotting,' said Tolly.

'Get out of it, you dozy prick.'

'Mush, mush,' said Wilfe, and he cast the nylon so that it lightly rapped Mrs McIlwraith's prim back.

'I shall give you just this one warning,' she said.

'Why is it,' said Raf, 'that any change of routine sets off some people to play silly buggers?'

At the point it was stony and without mud. Wilfe, Gaynor and Dilys, who arrived first, stood gazing across the sound as if the few hundred metres they had covered opened up quite a new vista of the bushed hills on the other side, or a sky of different colour above them. The others came up and added to the scrutiny for a while, and only when all the twelve had made the full trek was it considered fitting that they turn round and walk back the same nondescript way to the vans. Wilfe was mastering the use of his nylon and driftwood whip and he darted the cord out at almost everything he passed. Tolly had lost interest in his, and let it fall among the rocks of the point.

When they were back at Pan Bay no one bothered to say how much fun it had been. Montgomery had begun building up a rock surround for the barbecue fire, and put aside all evidence of cannabis except increased good humour and the smell on his breath. 'He's caught bloody zilch, of course,' he said mildly of Jock McPhie. Jock had his back to them and, out of earshot, fished on.

'Now for the barbecue,' said Raf. The Takahes gathered to him reluctantly, as there was no other messiah at Pan Bay that quiet, hot day. 'A barbecue's delightfully appropriate for us, because, like Harlequin, it's total atavism, you see.' Raf said that quietly, and glanced about to check that those close to him wouldn't be offended by what he intended.

'Through civilisation we pushed on until we had jugs which filled themselves and never boiled dry, fan ovens and microwaves, blenders and beaters, and now we ignore it and go out and stand up-wind to char meat and wrap it in bread to eat.'

Abbey and Tolly saw the darkly funny side of it with Raf; appreciated the parallel of eating habits with primal brain regression. What a sign of trust and tacit friendship their reaction was, though, accepting he should joke about a fatal illness and be free of it himself. Tolly continued to laugh and smile as he laid the sausages and chops on the heavy, black tray that he and David had set up over the fire.

'Who knows,' he said, 'maybe it's a therapy worth trying, to fight fire with fire. Come and dance around the barbecue, Abbey, and we'll make the vans like bongo drums and beat on them with sticks.'

'You just want to see my legs.'

'A glimpse of heaven,' said Tolly, gallantry put ahead of truth.

The sun was still bright, but heat shimmered away from the fire between them in strange, colourless whorls. Tolly and Gaynor across from David were distorted so that their outlines broke and shook, their faces convulsed in a fleeting mirage of expressions completely alien to them. Even as they mocked Harlequin, maybe he was moving almost invisibly among them.

'Jock, Jock,' Tolly called, 'we're keeping a place on the barbecue for the fish. Where is it?' But there was no real malice: they all admitted, to themselves at least, that they had no more success with their various salvations than Jock with his fish. Jock dismembered and put away his rod, and came and joined the others by the barbecue. He was one of the most prickly of Takahe's inmates, a successor to Howard Peat in his wounded pride, which kept him a bit apart. 'What chance of catching fish with the noise you ones are making?' he said with his fierce smile.

The novelty of the day, and the exercise, gave them more than usual appetite. The pallid sausages, the candy red and white chops, heaped in the chilly bin, were soon burnt and eaten. Tolly brought in the sack of Speights cans to a great reception. Even Mrs McIlwraith took one gingerly, though she was accustomed to chardonnay, and put can to mouth only when she realised no cup at all was available.

Raf had borrowed a half-size piano accordion for Abbey to play, and he brought the custom-made black and yellow carry bag from his van. Abbey cleaned her hands carefully of sauce and fat before beginning to perform. It wasn't Ahab and Pod, or any of the latest stuff, it wasn't even the Big O's 'Pretty Woman', or U2 still not having found what they were looking for, but they could have *Phantom of the Opera*; they could have Celtic ballads, couldn't they. Old familiar faces.

There was hardly any traffic on the road behind them. No one stopped, though Bryce gave a toot and a wave. Maybe it would have been more appropriate at dusk around the campfire. As it was, the sun still had a good deal of heat at seven in the evening, and they were clustered there singing to Abbey's accompaniment. In the end there was an audience of sorts: three children hanging on the pipe and netting gate across the road where the trailer sign advertised mushrooms and walnuts. Two prepubescent spindly girls and a younger boy, with legs twining like creeper around the pipes. They were too far away to be spoken to, but their body language was of embarrassment, whether for themselves, or the Mahakipawa guests, who knew.

Once they'd done the singing, most felt the picnic must be almost over. The tide was coming in again, but the channels were still obvious — mud free and the best places for a swim. Montgomery, Tolly, Gaynor and several others wanted a last quick dip, and David went out with them. By keeping to the nearest channel, only ankle deep at first, they were able to move quickly through the mudflats and wade well out into the sound. There was a noticeable breeze out from the shore and it paid to swim with it at your back so that the chop wasn't blown into your face. Montgomery, normally no model of preparedness, had swimming goggles which made him look like a First World War participant — a dispatch rider perhaps, or the pilot of a Sopwith Camel?

Only after admiring Montgomery's purposeful, awkward overarm for some time, did David realise that he had no intention of husbanding any strength to return. Had Montgomery been a better swimmer, he might have achieved release on his own terms, but Gaynor was a strong swimmer, and Tolly and David rather better than Montgomery. Gaynor overhauled him, kept him partly restrained, partly supported. When David caught up he endeavoured to change Montgomery's priorities by grabbing his hair. It wasn't a time for subtlety, even when dealing with a man whose wife had left him the week before. Montgomery's eyes couldn't be read behind the flat, misted glass of his blue goggles. They all swam back together and, when the bottom was underfoot again, David told his charge that those on the shore need never know, but both were aware that the pantomime had been clear even at that distance. Nothing was said of it, though, as they dried and changed. Although they were in the real and mundane world of Pan Bay, they were also in the world of Harlequin, which has allowances, deceits and conventions all its own, where suicide is no more disparaged than any other touted cure.

'Now, Monty,' Tolly whispered to him as they pulled on their underpants, 'how could we let you go? There'd have been only thirteen green bottles left and that's very unlucky.'

'I was in the frame of mind for it, that's all,' said Montgomery. 'Nothing personal at all. No reproach upon the company, or the day.' The weed, the circumstances, his wounded pride, necessitated some formality.

In other circumstances David might have been willing for him to have his wish: to decide on the direction of his own life, but at the Pan Bay picnic the responsibility of supervision was too direct. A loss of a patient would almost certainly have meant no more outings, and the assumption of dereliction of duty. His generous but illegal provision of the shit might have come out. 'No bloody gratitude at all,' said Raf.

Still under mute scrutiny from the children at the fence, they prepared to abandon Pan Bay. The special genesis of the group made it partly dysfunctional, as the professionals say, but it had some dynamics nevertheless. Who travelled in which van, for instance. Who preferred Raf and who preferred David. Who wanted a front seat, and who wanted to be first away. Who wanted to travel with a friend, and who wanted to avoid Jock's disdain. Who wanted to sing, and who wanted to be quiet all the way home. Who didn't really give a damn, but made a vehement statement anyway, just to assert a presence.

Montgomery was compelled to return from the picnic he had hoped would be his last. As David drove back up the slope to the centre, he felt an ache that came from the intractable isolation of existence. There was a glimpse of Montgomery's sad and distant face. There was a limit to what anyone could do for him. That was the truth of it. Maybe David should have been less selfish: let the goggle man go for it across the sound.

After sentencing, David was allowed some time for family and friends. A fair bit of time, in fact: maybe the police had other customers they had to wait for in the courts, but their goodwill could as easily have been the reason. Jocelyn, the married woman who was his lover, and his mother, both came to see him, neither showing the slightest response to the other as they passed at the entrance to the holding cells. A mother may well be expected to stick by her son, however clear the disappointment in her eyes, but Jocelyn's presence was something else. For the first time David felt an admiration for her unconnected with physical response: the way her nipples fluted when she was aroused, or the flexing muscles of her back. You dirty bastard, she would say, in a voice so low, indulgent, so utterly familiar in tone that it put inches on him just to hear. A pact of passion in mutual and open convenience was what they had. No strings whatsoever. No future plans. No interest in the circle of each other's lives, except for that one place where circumferences met and fused as their bodies fused in strenuous relaxation. There was still no future sought or required, but how much had she placed at risk by coming to open court, by asking to see him? Just to say goodbye. What strength and directness a woman can have. All to say goodbye.

'It was a blast while it lasted, wasn't it?' David asked.

'Oh, yes,' she said.

'Prison's not such a big deal, really,' he said.

'I suppose not, but don't let it make you hate yourself. Start off your life again just the same. You're no worse than anybody else.'

You're no worse than anybody else? Surely at that time in his life it had been true.

They knew they wouldn't see each other again, unless it was by accident. In one sense it was a convenient closure, instead of Jocelyn ditching him, or her husband finding out. What David remembered best that last time they met, was the first time they met — on the observation terrace of the restaurant reached by gondola. She was relaxed against the railing as her companion talked, and her long, bare arms were crossed far down at the wrist, and she knew that he was watching her, but showed neither unease, nor coquetry. She was tall, with a figure better than her face, and when she raised a hand to push her hair from her forehead, the evident muscles moved beneath the smooth skin of her long forearm.

'I want to thank you for coming,' he told her in the holding cell, aware of how little the banality of his expression *could bear the freight of his feeling. 'Jesus, you're the last person with any obligation towards me.'*

'Fuck a life which is all obligation,' she said. He thought then, briefly, that she was a woman he might have loved in other circumstances.

When David later saw the prisons of television drama, he had very little sense of affinity, or recognition. Those places were given fierce, dramatic undercurrents; aspects of terrible focus which drove lives along. Maybe Paparua lacked sufficient incorrigible, dynamic personalities, for poverty was his main impression: you have a poor life, and the life of the poor, in prison. Food, clothing and shelter sure enough, but they're all poorly presented, and your options are restricted. The environment is poor, the outlook is poor, the opinion others have of you and that you have of yourself impoverished. The staff are a reluctant part of the diminished life and seek to escape it. Everything is worn and communal, down at heel, and kept going at a minimum level.

There were few grand desperadoes in Paparua, no intricate baronial hierarchy that David was aware of: just a ghetto of opportunities neglected, mediocrity, failure and self-deceit. The shame of failure was stronger than any remorse. In prison what you despise in your fellows hasn't anything to do with criminality: it's their failure that catches in your nostrils.

Prison wasn't particularly dangerous, or violent — not for someone in for the run-of-the-mill crime of drugs — and David wasn't baby-faced enough to be bothered by more than the routine approaches for sex. Things did happen, of course, like the Auckland guy in the east wing convicted for snuff movies who was found with a broken neck. Yet oddly, it was like hearing of murder in a different part of the city. The thing was to keep your head down. The thing was to look out for number one, and not draw vindictiveness upon yourself.

In some ways prison was like a single men's hostel for

unskilled workers, or a drop-in centre for those misfits spun out of the competitive centre of society. David became a regular watcher of a great many ongoing television programmes, and the many hours at table tennis put him in the prison team which played and beat Christchurch club sides. A sense of futility, a scathing awareness of days wasted, was a common mood for him, but you didn't talk about anything like that.

And, having been incarcerated for dealing, he was surprised to find shit quite readily available within the prison, but you didn't talk about that to anyone on the outside either.

David had no pet cockroach, or window bar that worked as a sundial. He began a correspondence course of business and financial skills. After years of the humanities he'd ended in prison, so he settled for practical subjects, but didn't stick to them, despite coming across ideas that would have improved his success in the cannabis business. He became more interested in programmes run inside, which meant, in effect, by Mike Wiremu, a recreational officer and counsellor.

'We haven't got many graduates here,' Wiremu told him. 'Most of the guys were dick happy, or into booze and shit during their formative years, you might say.' Wiremu's square bulk filled one end of the small office; opposite was the door and a chair on which David sat. One longer wall had a particle-board desk with file boxes and above it a large year planner. The other had a slightly recessed window with a view of the boiler house obscured by slashes of birdshit and the hachuring of a security grille. Four colours had been initially used on the planner but, as the year had progressed, so the writing dwindled and the colour fell away. 'I could use you if you like,' said Wiremu. He had no file in front of him: he seemed uninterested in David's crime, or sentence. It was as if he were asking a fellow bridge player to serve on the grading committee, or a working bee to enlarge the bar. One of the cardboard file boxes was labelled in felt pen as — 'Fitness and Hygiene Yak Sheets'. 'There's

no money in it, of course, but it passes the time, gives you some minor privileges and looks good on the old parole report, eh.' Wiremu, like many of his race, was egalitarian by disposition. Superintendent Somerville, Pye the wife beater, the pigman who came on Tuesdays and Fridays, all received the same soft-voiced, slightly self-deprecating attention. *'As a matter of fact, I never finished a degree myself, but then I married early.'* His face was large and flat, with a mouth that went right across it and out of sight around the corners.

The boiler-house wall was used by kitchen staff for improvised fives. David could see two of them playing with a yellow tennis ball in their break. They were free men, but their slouching, leaping uncouthness was exactly that of the prisoners they served. Maybe they'd been on the chow line too long, and something had snaked back to them. Maybe it was the place itself that determined attitudes, rather than being criminals, or free men, within it.

'You could work out some personal programmes for younger guys,' suggested Wiremu. *'That way we could match them up with volunteers that come willing to help. Okay, most of them will tell you to get knotted, but that's the normal odds here. You know that pale guy without teeth who's come into your wing? He can't even spell his name.'*

'What is his name?'

'Poniatowski,' said Wiremu, the expanse of his brown face just the same. That's when David began to like him. That's when he decided to develop programmes with him.

Paparua Prison was progressive enough to have general counselling sessions. For some inmates it was a directed part of their sentence, and a few others came out of boredom, the hope of disclosure, or to score parole points. Wiremu did the organising, and a psychologist called Garvan ran the sessions. He was known inside as Mad Max, because of a professional calm that had become almost total unresponsiveness.

'My old man came home for Christmases and christenings,' Houghton said, 'and one led to the other. All of us kids were born in August or September.' It was one of Mad Max's sessions — on fathers. David wouldn't have come had he known the topic beforehand. He didn't want to talk about his family in front of any of those people; didn't want even Wiremu to know anything about his father. 'He was a top mechanic on one of the Formula One teams,' went on Houghton, who was in for burning down a cough syrup factory after he was sacked. 'No, not McLaren, but he sent back birthday stuff from all over the world. The right number of presents for the number of September kids, but he never tried to sort them out by age, or enclosed any cards. I can't remember ever having a talk with him alone, he was so much on the go. Once I got a flat ceramic house from Holland to hang on the wall — one time a green and red felt bird from Mexico with a button for an arse. I was fifteen at the time.'

Mad Max nodded consolingly and asked Houghton if any resentment remained.

'Resentment?' Houghton said, quite surprised. 'I just wish I'd done half as well. There's a photo of him in a book and he's standing behind Niki Lauda and Jody Scheckter at Brands Hatch.' Houghton relaxed after having his say, by giving a long, quiet fart like a cat's purr.

Bagger was next; in for a long career of stealing meat from works' coolstores and flogging it to city butchers. 'Was my Dad a bloody tartar,' he said with rueful admiration. 'Was he ever. A skinful every Friday and Saturday night and then he'd go looking for an argument in the pubs and take-aways. The Liverpool kiss was his favourite. He had so many teeth marks on his forehead you'd think he had a frontal lobotomy, but he never hit a sheila, not even mum. I seen him once handbagged in the face by Nancy Kingham, because he decked her hubby at the Celtic Rugby Club. The catch on the bag drew blood, but Dad just walked away, eh.' Bagger shook his head and cracked his knuckles in *wonderment at the mythology he'd created. 'Every bloody thrashing I got I had coming, and he never hit a woman. Kept fighting even in the home he ended up in. Cleaned up one of the male aides who was thirty years younger and kept changing channels when Dad was watching footy.' Bagger obviously hoped for such belligerent resilience in his own old age. 'He died only last year in Taihape, and I got special leave to go up to the funeral. He'd no hair at all on him in the coffin, but most of the scars on his forehead had faded. I had this beaut pork meal in a diner out from Wellington on the way back. The screw Forbes took me in and he told this waitress that I was the underworld King of Paparua. She kept looking at me over the coffee machine.'*

'Do you dream about your dad?' asked Mad Max.

David knew that there was nothing he wanted to say about his own father — not to Houghton, Bagger and the others, not to Mad Max — but, even had he wanted to speak, his love and sadness would have choked him. 'All that crackling,' Bagger concluded, 'and the pork fucking tender so that it just falls apart. Bloody beauty. And this waitress slut scared shitless.'

The fact that David's father had done a thesis on Lucius Cornelius Sulla was no hindrance whatsoever to his skills as a farmer. He could have killed Bagger's pigs better than the next man and dressed the carcases almost as neatly as a works' butcher.

He had a favourite knife, slimmed in the middle from sharpening, and so keen at the blade that flesh seemed to flee before it. 'Always cut away from yourself,' his father told him. 'Then if the knife slips you don't slice yourself. And never try to work quickly with a knife when you're tired.' He could peel the pelt from a dog tucker ewe, or table hogget, like a banana skin. The inside of the pelt had a pearly sheen, and in winter steam would drift from it, and from the carcase swaying slowly beneath the tree, suspended by the metal hook beneath the tendons of the back legs.

'Best to kill an animal when it's relaxed,' his father said. 'A frightened animal spasms and the meat's never as good.' He hated cruelty and suffering. Death was another matter entirely; just like the sun and rain which made the farmer's world.

A mother's love is demanded and a father's love sought, Mad Max told them. One of the circle said his father never said anything at all within the house, but that he would sing and talk to himself behind the locked door of the garage. The shed is a male domain, Mad Max told them, and preferred for suicide.

Drought was the punishment for an east coast farm. David's father had paid no attention to the showers that only laid the dust, but a sweet, persistent rain brought him out to watch his land's release, even if it came at night. He would wake to the sound of it, lie listening and, if it set in, then he'd get up from his single bed and go quietly out, taking a parka from the hook at the back door. David had sometimes heard the click of the gates as his father went down to the yards, and from the window he could see him under the overhang of the tractor shed, or the pines, listening to the rain, taking a quiet pleasure in his land drinking after drought.

There was nothing that David wanted to say about his father at Mad Max's session: nothing that he would willingly share. Not that he thought himself better than Houghton, Bagger, or Paewai, in for assault, who had a tooth turning black as coal in his upper jaw, but that his father was too good for them and him, and by a mile.

'Why is that, do you think?' Mad Max had asked equably after Richards said that his father never allowed his mother to sit in the front seat of the car.

The Romans were a very violent people, David's father told him, but, unlike some other violent peoples, they were creative: and valued dignity of mind.

TWENTY-ONE

Schweitzer's secretary buzzed through to Takahe just a day or two after Easter. Was David able to come over? Some time between eleven thirty and noon if possible. The greater the gap in status, the less it needs to be emphasised. David thought Schweitzer was beginning to take something of an interest in him. He'd used his name at a staff meeting, which was something in an organisation so large; he'd sent a memo specifically asking him for a report on Dilys Williams's condition after the business of heckling phone calls to the mayor of Picton.

Once, when out jogging, Schweitzer had come over to where David and Abbey sat on the verandah. He did his warming-down exercises, and talked in his quiet, fluent way: his language never self-important, but supple, original, responsive to his listeners. He hadn't become overwhelmed by his own achievements. Abbey was so blessed by his attention that she breathed through her mouth to be noiseless, and her eyes widened in the regard of him. Schweitzer had a smooth scar on his left knee: a burn probably. Sweat darkened his hair, and his throat was noticeably pale, because he habitually wore a tie.

He said that he sometimes saw David rowing out in the dinghy to go fishing. 'I can see the sound from the office and I look up from my desk and there you are, enjoying the distraction I often wish for myself. Perhaps it's another keen fisherman, of course. It's too far to tell, but I know you're often there.' Abbey said meekly that sometimes she went out in the boat too, and so reminded David to introduce her.

That day, however, soon after chocolate eggs and an increase in visitors, when David was shown into Schweitzer's office after waiting less than fifteen minutes, he could see the reduced pink float marking the favoured fishing spot, and there was no one there at all. The director's office was unlike that of any of the other administrators, and not just in favoured size and location. Some modern philosophy of management determined that the evidence of a chief executive's day-to-day responsibility be hidden. No stacks of files, no in tray and no out, no bagged sandwiches, no heavily scored wall diary, no obsolete monitor relegated to a corner. No adhesive smudges, darkened sellotape tracks, or pin holes on the sheened walls. No white, warped plastic hanger behind the door. Not even framed qualifications with the rich, wax seals of approval.

Just the quiet heart of efficiency and decision. The arrangement of fennel and chrysanthemums on the expanse of the desk, a Grahame Sydney print of tussock land behind it, a buttoned, dark blue leather sofa and three matching chairs, so that Schweitzer could choose to abrogate his status behind the burnish of his desk and come to sit with his visitors. He didn't go quite that far for David.

No pretension, however, no arrogance. Schweitzer's talents required no such protection. It was the programme of challenge therapy that interested him, he said, and David was happy to talk about it, though Schweitzer could have picked a better day. David had a cold so severe that his sinuses were stuffed with mucus thick as rope and throbbed with the heart's pulse. Schweitzer wore a wine-coloured suede waistcoat with his grey suit trousers; the coat hung in the closet by the drinks cabinet. 'I have to fly up to Wellington after lunch,' he said. 'There's a big push on for more funding. Money coming in makes the politicians' mouths water, but going out makes their eyes water.'

'And is throwing money at Harlequin the way?' asked David.

Schweitzer didn't answer that at once. 'No matter what your profession, growth of responsibility means in the end your main task is ensuring resources — making money. And you're in competition not only with others like yourself, but with those whose speciality was money in the first place.'

'But what else has the shock value of Harlequin?'

'Shock value?'

'Doesn't fear loosen the purse strings?' said David. His voice sounded strange to himself because of his trivial illness. Schweitzer nodded gently and sucked air through his teeth. His eyes rested for a while on the bushed hills across the sound, before coming back to David, candidly. 'But how much do we want to scare them?' he said. 'That's the question making me sweat at nights. Scared people are dangerous.'

Perhaps if David had got married, he might have worn a waistcoat on his wedding day, but no other situation had prompted that small, sartorial experience missed. The wine suede was trim, elegant almost, with a close line of silver buttons. And the shirt was the pale pink of the bleached craypot float at the fishing spot. And Schweitzer's burn scar was hidden by the quality fabric of his trousers, while David had a shirt with a worn collar and breathed through his mouth. All over the world was a juxtaposition of setting and circumstance which would never quite exist again, despite the apparent repetitions of everyday life. Things were for an instant, then toppled into the abyss.

'I wish I knew the best way to tackle Harlequin Rex. Jesus, yes,' said Schweitzer.

'I've never heard the Rex added.'

'Nothing. Just a foible usage of mine,' said Schweitzer. 'But anyway, you learn that any approach takes money.' He was looking at David appraisingly, as if he'd been told things about him and wanted to see if they fitted. David had reasons for not wanting too much enquiry, despite his respect for the director. 'Tony Sheridan tells me that you and Raf Hewson are accomplishing a good deal in Takahe with people who could turn out to be among our successes. There's resilience and intelligence there.'

'And despair.'

'All of us dealing with Harlequin have that acquaintance, don't you think?' said Schweitzer. That was true enough, but had David known him better, or been less junior in his organisation, he would have questioned the lumping together of those who treated the symptoms of Harlequin with others who were afflicted with it. Almost every night, just before David slept, his true, unguarded self rejoiced in being free of the disease: an emotion stronger than any commiseration with those who suffered. He knew he couldn't bear to change places with any of them; no, not even Lucy.

'Anyway,' said Schweitzer, 'what I wanted to ask you was whether you'd be prepared to co-ordinate an extension of your programme throughout the centre? Perhaps initially develop a presentation for supervisory staff. Dr Mousier, or myself, would help kick it off, and Tony Sheridan's willing to set up an ongoing medical appraisal as to its benefit. There's some initial research evidence from France that Harlequin may be ameliorated by emotional distraction: a sort of psychological displacement therapy which inhibits attacks.'

'Or maybe it's just patients clutching at anything to take their minds off this appalling illness.'

'Quite, and maybe even that's a justification for your programme.' Schweitzer never pretended that he had a handle on Harlequin; that there was no crisis, that a cure was at hand. That lack of pretence was one of the likeable things about him. Another was his ability to put aside most of his specialised jargon for a time and still assume intelligence, as he did in his continued conversation with David about the programme. The desk buzzer sounded several times, but the director took no notice of it. He had the mild mannerisms of swaying forward to smile, and smoothing his eyebrows in reflection. 'And where do these ideas come from?' he asked. 'They're new to me, but I gather that you've been overseas a good deal.'

'They come from prison and military rehabilitation courses,' said David.

'Ah, then no wonder they fit snugly round here,' and Schweitzer gave a laugh of genuine delight, but didn't press any more about origins. Another thing that David appreciated.

When Schweitzer had to leave, he took his suit coat from the closet, running his fingers under the side pockets to make sure the flaps weren't tucked in. He had yet to drive over the Rai and Whangamoa to Nelson Airport. 'My door's always open. Well, figuratively,' he said, smiling as he closed it behind them. His secretary had selected two letters of particular note from the latest heap, and she held them up like an auctioneer's chit, and the director took them with the use of the same smile.

Schweitzer and David went down together towards the main entrance, and David saw an opportunity for a question. 'Where do you think it comes from?'

'I know where it comes from. It comes from the same place as Lassa fever and Ebola — it comes from Africa. Man came out of Africa, and now perhaps his nemesis is taking the same path.' Schweitzer raised a hand to Louise at the reception desk, and went and put his head around Mousier's door. 'I'm off,' he said. When Schweitzer talked of Harlequin he might have been talking about David's head cold, or the fishing that he was wistful about, but never had time to do.

You can become accustomed to talking about something even as hideous as Harlequin. Familiarity, evasion, optimism, impotence, all play a part. As the Jews debated orthodoxy while waiting for the gas chamber.

'And how did it get here of all places?' asked David.

'Better questions, and I've no answers,' said Schweitzer. They had come out of the main door and to the parting of the ways, but the director paused briefly, just his words speeding up because he was short of time. 'You know the real thing is to find how to stop the bastard in his tracks: bring him down.' He rarely swore, certainly not in the staff meetings. The vehemence was heartening somehow. 'We're not anywhere close to cracking it at present. That's the truth,' said Schweitzer. He shrugged and raised his palms in apparent apology, for his inability to give better news perhaps, or the need to leave at once. David watched him walk up the slope towards his house: the posture impressive, the stride benefiting from the regime of jogging. His black shoes, highly polished, shone in the sun; his jaw, closely shaven, was gun metal blue.

Another busload arrived that day; newly arisen Harlequins after Easter.

TOLLY'S VIEW

Is becoming Harlequin's view, for he is at the arched entrance to an episode. Maybe soon he will blow, or be driven to a fit of compulsive gymnastics on the cool, perky grass of the night. The world is as each individual sees it, and Harlequin sees it with ancient, such ancient, eyes. A dangerous and exhilarating release spreads through Tolly's system as the checks and balances of thousands of years fall away, and jaunty, with simian insouciance, old brain steps out again to claim his subject — Harlequin Rex, demon hunter, primal lord.

The face is a familiar map for the neurologist. The lion

visagè of Alzheimer's, the tic grimace of Tourette's, the averted eyes of autism. Schweitzer has dubbed Harlequin's expression 'the scenting face'.

Tolly has it now: restless, inattentive to any verbal language, his head tilted up and mouth half open. He stands in the night by his telescope on the Takahe verandah. The receding voices of rationality and temperance give way to sharp awareness of possibilities around and within. The distant majesty of stars, which have no fragrance whatsoever, is not enough. Oh, the scents of the night, and the tastes borne on the air to the acute tongue in his open mouth. His head lifts in the luxury of it, and lips draw back. Bathroom fittings and investments are nothing to him now: he cares bugger all for the responsibilities of family or friends. No pallid restraint of dignity, or convention. Fierce appetite and dread, curiosity and stimulation — self, *self*, above all.

Tolly starts to hum: basic, stripped down forms of the more sophisticated music he loves. Music is a link between old Tolly and new Tolly. In terms of Harlequin, of course, the old Tolly is the new Tolly and the new Tolly the old.

He knows that Transylvanian garlic has been crushed in the kitchens, and that kumara is being scrubbed up. The meat tomorrow will be pork. He knows that in his own block both Abbey and Gaynor are menstruating, that Dilys Williams has apples hidden in her room, that David has a fresh stash of prime West Coast shit, that the caretaker's Samoyed is running free on the gorse slope. He knows that Evan Beal sprayed Roundup hours before, because the poison is sharp in his nose. He hears rats in the ceiling by the water cylinder, a hedgehog in the gardens, and the rustle of thin, upright branches of broom on the hillside. His vision sharpens too: there are distinct vehicles in the car park, and swimming togs draped on the edge of the verandah. He sees the lights from the windows of other blocks blaze like campfires. Woodsie from Hoiho is far down the covered walkway going home. Tolly cannot recognise a face at that distance, but the posture, the mode of locomotion, are simple for Harlequin to identify.

He feels a flare of animosity for that shallow, pompous bastard, Woodsie. Maybe he should go to Woodsie's block through the night, and give him a good thud or two. Yes! Woodsie's well-merited pain and confusion; the impact of Tolly's boot on his tender balls. The establishment of primacy by force. Maybe he should visit Amelia Struthers of Weka to put his mouth to the large tits he saw by telescope the night before. He imagines all the natural and roguish smells of her, the pleasing roughness of her nipples to his tongue, his grip on the heavy flesh of her shoulder. Harlequin in this simulation has no way, or wish, to give him the artificial fragrances of soap or perfume.

Maybe he can evade the curfew check by Raf, or David, and walk down to his dinghy, launch it into the sound. He imagines trailing his hands in the cold water, cupping one so that he can sip from it and taste not just the variety of salts, but an array of other flavours as subtle yet distinct as a fine bordeaux.

Tolly's humming grows louder. He starts to jig a little, and steps into the grounds. What is going on within his territory here at Mahakipawa? What is here for interference, gratification and pain? What are the imperatives rising from deepest parts of his brain to take the helm again? Tolly takes off his shoes and his jersey, which have become too much insulation for him. He needs to feel with his hands and feet. His shirt goes then, although he wasn't hot before. He needs to have skin open to the world. What? What? What is there for him amid all the jostling possibilities of which his senses are aware? He feels the air moving through the hair of his chest and back, smells his own sweat as he keys up for fight or flight. Fear and threat and pain are strong in Harlequin's world, but so are vengeance and victory, precedence and power. The millionaire of bathroom fittings begins to jog away into the night. The astronomical commentator baboons to the moon, and does a cartwheel on the scented earth, crushes late flowers to his face. Tolly is well away, following his nose in search of mischief and excitement.

No harm will come of it — tonight.

TWENTY-TWO

In the constant passage of nights and days, no two were quite the same. The world might hinge a little at dawn and dusk, showing something of what was coming and something of what had gone before.

Privacy is a rare and special blessing within institutions. At the centre there were off-duty times when David would go up the hill behind the grounds and buildings. At gloaming often, when there was a hiatus between sea breeze and shore breeze, and the soft valleys of the hills across the sound were the colour of a bruise as night came on, when the lights of the block windows began to draw the eye, and cattle on the road flat bugled to those on the hill, with the smell of prime, crab-bearing mud, and the spent greens and browns of broom and gorse fading with the light. David felt at those turning points of twilight experience ineffable, something significantly beyond and greater than himself. A message was given then, wasn't it? But always just out of earshot, or beyond his comprehension.

Then came the night itself — Harlequin, perhaps, in his original guise. All those who have unleashed heady self-indulgence, breathe more easily in the darkness — murderers, hunters, lovers. Night isn't the same stage devoid of light, but a whole new play, with those that remain from the cast of day having entirely different roles. Some flowers open only to the moon and consummate with fumbling moths. New paths are used and old ones taken over by fresh populations. The stoat and weasel are about their work; eels flourish on the land amid the dew, mutton-birds fly in from the ocean, wherein creatures of ominous bulk drift towards a darkened surface; the mudbanks wink and glimmer as the crabs use pincers to signal to Tolly's stars. The land breeze replaces its cousin from the sea. Big eyes are king. The silken possum eats out the heart of the native trees, and the morepork glides and glares above it all.

A quiet joint beneath an overhang of scrub, quite out of sight of everyone, yet where he's able to enjoy a far, soft view. It reminded David of times and places at Collegiate and at Paparua, which had privacy as their instigation as well. David's was a tripartite experience of institutional life: boarding school, prison, and then the Slaven Centre. In some ways antithetical, they were in others disturbingly alike, for there are features of close community which exist in all examples of the form.

The character of an organisation is like that of an individual, in that each presents an image to the world, gives lip service to some beliefs, professes principles, while the life within is far more complex and volatile: urgencies and priorities never proclaimed are nevertheless served in full, and occupations of little formal title wield subtle power. The Honours Boards record the scholarships and Heads of House: the names of the bullies who ruled the grounds and dorms are cut into the hearts of Old Boys scattered through the adult world.

At school and Paparua however, David was part of the clientèle. Life was altered at the centre because he was staff. Not an executive like Alst Mousier, not a professionally qualified member of the medical team as was Tony Sheridan, not even the possessor of additional de facto influence like shapely Polly Merhtens who had captivated Dr Hassim. Yet he was staff, and on the other side of the divide from those who bore the stigma of being guests. Guests knew that they were there to get the treatment, as were boys at Collegiate, or the inmates of Paparua.

There was an irony, wasn't there, that after that Kaikoura business he was at risk in society at large, and safest in the centre. Who would think of looking for him in the skirts of Harlequin? And maybe he had saved the justice system the cost and effort of putting him out of circulation again, by doing it myself. Incarceration may be a state of mind.

There is power and satisfaction in seeing without being seen; in watching people when they imagine themselves alone. When no reaction is required of you, the focus of concentration is especially sharp. Just occasionally, when David was sitting on the hillside in old man gorse or broom, smoking some prime West Coast shit, there were pantomimes played out for him in the grounds of the centre.

There was that fight between two guys behind Weka block, which had a good deal of formality in its shaping up, but just a couple of punches in execution, which left one man sitting and coughing on the evening lawn, while the victor walked back inside. The sitting man stopped coughing after a while, but didn't get up. In time David went quietly back to his room, taking the long way through the car park, so that he wouldn't be heard, and leaving the guy sitting in a posture of abnegation as the dusk gathered. Maybe he was coming to terms with his defeat; maybe he had moved on to matters entirely distinct.

In an evening with more light he watched Melanie Harcourt dancing to her Walkman on the concrete slab in front of Beal's tractor shed. Melanie was from Titi and recognisable at a distance because she was rather large, yet usually wore the multicoloured tights of Columbine, Harlequin's mistress. Could she be unaware of the irony in that? Melanie was a surprisingly good back-of-the-court volleyball player. She hadn't gone to the shed to hide, just happened to be passing when the right tune came on, so she took advantage of the smooth surface. She had the Walkman at her already considerable hip, and the lead to the earphones swung out as she danced. She held up her arms, her head swayed side to side with them: the colours spun on her legs. David couldn't hear the song, but the rhythm she had going seemed to be the real thing. He found myself smiling, and swaying slightly to synchronise. Go for it, Melanie, wherever you are.

David knew where Jigger Fraser was — buried in the small headland cemetery at Havelock because the body wasn't claimed, yet on the low tablet headstone it said he was the much loved father of Jeremy, Blythe and Chelsea. He'd told Lucy that he'd not wanted to have a daughter called Chelsea, that sooner or later there'd be the joke about her having a bun in the oven. Jigger had long hair and a full beard. His hair was ginger blond at the crown and deepened down the length of his head until it had the colour of deep, damp rust. A broad face like that of a lion in a ginger and rock desert.

Anyway, Jigger had climbed through the fence and well up the hill to find a place among the grass and gorse not far from David's own, and sat there talking and praying alone. His sandy mane gave him good camouflage. 'Lord Jesus, take this cup from me,' Jigger said from some scant, ecclesiastic memory, 'but nevertheless, not my will, but thine be done.' Below them a group of people were laughing, and walking from the main block towards Hoiho. There is a jackass quality to laughter in which you have no part. 'I don't want to go out like this,' Jigger told Jesus more colloquially. 'Not in the grip of this thing. If it please you, Jesus, Chelsea's only three, and Brenda doesn't make that much of a mother, because she's into some jag about setting up a herb and dried flower shop.' Jigger held up his clasped hands in entreaty; the posture from soft-cover Sunday school booklets. 'Just let me be okay again and I'll be a true believer. I swear it.'

David never paid his dues as far as religion went, and so he couldn't in conscience make any prayer to Jesus, but as he listened to Jigger, as the laughter died away among the buildings below them, he felt a fierce joy to be alive, unsentenced, crouched in the gorse and brittle grass.

'I'll give anything, anything, for the chance,' said Jigger. He began on a clumsy and inaccurate version of the Lord's Prayer, growling away like the ginger lion he was. Jigger's abasement wasn't meant to be heard by his peers. David would have gone away if that was possible without revealing himself, but he had to wait until Jigger left instead.

David knew that Jigger was a fitness freak, and the next morning he went to the gym, where Jigger spent an hour on those days he was well enough. After hearing him pray, David felt that he should make some gesture of comfort, or support, without giving the game away. Jigger was working out on the wall bars. Sweat darkened his green singlet: the ginger hair of his armpits gleamed like chutney. His lion's face hung on the rack above the shifting tendons and long bones of his body. Rather than bestowing grace, physical stress had hobbled him, and he jerked on the rack with grimaces of determination. David invited him to the poker school at Takahe that night, but Jigger's vehement refusal shook sweat onto David and the smooth wooden floor of the gym. 'You're wasting your time,' Jigger said. 'I'm not interested in buying any of your shit, see. You'll have to make your profit elsewhere.' David hadn't realised that Jigger disliked him, that he knew of the dope brought in for friends. It happens like that sometimes. You reach out to someone, and you find all along they've disliked you, and you've given them the opportunity to display their enmity.

'Suit yourself,' David said. He found it difficult to match up the Jigger who was exercising, with the man praying aloud on the hillside just the night before. Neither prayer, nor physical jerks, did Jigger much good as it turned out. He may well have been happier with some of the hooch he thought David was pushing that day, for surely in just a few months he'd be forgotten at Mahakipawa as he'd been forgotten by his wife and children, and no one would recall his ginger-blond crown, his russet beard, his home-made prayers, his fears of Chelsea's bun.

TWENTY-THREE

Despite all his experience to the contrary, David still sometimes assumed that his decisions had some effect on the world. He had come to start a new life at Mahakipawa, and hoped fortune would respect that. It didn't, of course, yet he was still surprised when Simon Cryer came to the centre, almost as if Cryer had broken a promise. Cryer had worked in the freight section of Christchurch Airport and had got a lot of stuff up to Hamilton and Auckland, but always at top kickback.

In the dining hall the staff ate in a section by the windows, reserved more by custom than decree. Lunchtime, and David had finished his meal and was pressing his little finger on the table to see how much inflammation remained from an infection around the nail. He glanced up to see Cryer watching from deeper in the room, eyebrows raised for attention. Cryer was one of those guys of shallow, conventional handsomeness, whose personality soon makes you regard them as plain to ugly. He must have remembered all about the court case and the prison term. What else did he know?

David waited for the dining hall to clear a bit before

going over to Cryer and shaking his hand. 'Long time no see,' said Cryer eagerly. 'God, it's a small world.'

'Isn't it.' Too small, when Cryer could claim a walk-on part without invitation.

'How long's it been then?' Cryer's hair was combed back from his face, and he smoothed it with the palms of both hands as he talked. He smiled, too, and nodded in agreement with himself as he spoke. He told David that he was on sick leave from the airline; that his doctor had insisted he come into the centre for while, when there wasn't much wrong with him. 'Phoney bastard doesn't know shit from clay,' he said, the tendons showing in his thin wrists as he stroked his hair back. 'So, Jesus me. Fancy you being on the staff here.' He smiled at David, wondering what the angle was. 'You pushing stuff in here, or what?' he said quietly as they went out.

'No,' said David. 'I've given all that away. I get a bit in for myself and a few friends, nothing else.'

'Good one. Good one.' Cryer had no doubt that he was among those friends. 'I'm in some bloody unit with a Maori bird name,' he said.

'They're all bird names. Who are your live-in staff?'

'One's called Moffat.'

'You're in Weka then,' said David. 'Probably the worst volleyball team in the place.'

David stopped walking by the covered way to Takahe, to show that he wasn't going to invite Cryer back to his room. The Cryers of the world reminded David too much of what he feared in himself. A life restricted to physicality. Some animals see only in black and white, while others are allowed a rainbow world. There was a compassion and sanguinity in such as Schweitzer, Abbey, Raf and Lucy, Post Office Bev even, which was quite missing in Cryer.

'You'll get me some decent West Coast head?' asked the very plain man.

'Yes, okay.'

'Good one. For old times' sake, you reckon.'

'Yes,' said David.

'I guess people here don't know the things that went wrong for you?'

'I keep it all pretty quiet. It's over now, and I have to earn a straight living here.' What else did Cryer know, apart from the dope and prison? Did he know anything about Kaikoura — a small room, a large bed, a lost Gran? 'A good lurk gone wrong, eh,' said Cryer, nodding in self-affirmation.

Tolly came past from the dining hall and stopped, met Cryer and wanted to know how long he'd been at the centre. Cryer began asking questions about Harlequin, but offhandedly, as if he wasn't worried. He told them about the fits starting, and laughing jags at work, and then beating up television sets in the Riccarton Mall. Some games show was on and a contestant irritated him and he punched out several 26-inch Black Diamond screens before anyone could stop him. 'Weirdest thing,' he said. 'Gave me a buzz at the time.'

'You've come to the right place, definitely,' said Tolly.

'What is it we've all got?' asked Cryer, starting on his hair again. 'I mean, Jesus, I'm right as rain, and then I hear the frogs fucking talking to me out of the ditches, I can smell a dozen different shampoos on the office girls in the bus, at four in the morning I have to get up and go running like a fucking boy Scout, and my wife says I get over horny. Mind you, with her, a little always went a long way.'

'You've come to the right place,' said Tolly. 'Not that you'll get cured, mind you, but you'll fit right in with the rest of us.'

'I reckon it's just overwork,' said Cryer.

David left them talking about symptoms. No doubt Cryer would tell Tolly and others about knowing him before. Newcomers like to make such reassuring links. David was well down the path when Simon Cryer called out, and David looked back down the walkway with its shade cutting across the lawn. 'You won't forget the — you know — stuff, will you?' shouted Cryer casually.

David gave a half-weary, half-easy wave before going on, but he wished him elsewhere. Cryer was an unwelcome overlap from his life before the centre. The guy belonged to the freight depot and storerooms of the airport. David could see him clearly, taking the pylon insulators, stock drench, whatever they'd decided to send the stuff up with, and saying, 'You leave it to me, chief. Just leave it to me.' He had some purpose there, and was kept in his place by functional responsibility and greed. David wanted him still there among the freight, confident despite his plain face and thin, smoothing hands, but no, Harlequin had coughed him up at the Slaven Centre: some part of David's living past to die in his present, or future, and endanger him maybe before doing it.

TOBY'S VIEW

Detective Senior Sergeant Toby Cook looks out over the police car park at the Nelson headquarters. It's his day-to-day view from his office on the second floor. Most of the cars are Commodores, or Diamantes, although the newest ones are smaller Nissans, part of a fleet purchase for the South Island. Cook is a bit of a car nut. He drives an Audi: an indulgence that he can afford because of his seniority, and because he isn't married. Every time Cook sees a car, he makes an involuntary comparison between it and his own, and almost always he's reassured by the superiority of the silver Audi, which has air-conditioning, air-bags, beacon location/navigation and leather upholstery — not a turbo, though, for Sergeant Cook considers turbos are for boy racers, and hard on maintenance as well.

But Cook isn't thinking of cars this morning, even though he holds the car park in sight automatically. He's thinking about the Slaven Centre at Mahakipawa, and the conversation he had with the superintendent before the latter went over to Blenheim to a meeting on the major fire at the Woodbourne Air Force base. The super had returned from a Wellington conference on Harlequin only days before.

'There's apprehension about it long term, Toby. No doubt about that,' the super had said. 'So of course they're looking to spill as much responsibility as possible our way. Nothing new in that, of course.'

'No,' said Cook with the expected smile.

'Just the politicos as usual.'

'Yes.'

'How many deaths at that place in the last year?' asked the super. At his elbow he had Cook's file, which had gone with him to Wellington.

'Over two hundred and eighty.'

'And some very odd ones among those, for Christ's sake, weren't there? How many more people admitted in the last two months or so?'

'Nearly two hundred.' The detective senior sergeant knew his own report well enough to have given the exact figure, but he didn't want to appear a smart arse. Smart arses didn't go down well with the superintendent, who went on to tell Cook more about the high-level Wellington apprehension concerning Harlequin: the effects if no reassuring advance was made in its treatment; the establishment of two more centres in the North Island. The superintendent had been told to draw up contingency plans without the Slaven Centre medical people being made aware of all the objectives. Toby Cook was delegated the task of gaining the information needed, under the guise of setting up a more effective police response to the centre's needs when Harlequin patients stretched the hospital's resources, or broke out into the surrounding communities during episodes.

'I've talked to the director,' said the superintendent, 'and he's to arrange that you have the co-operation of the 2IC there, Dr Mousier. You've dealt with him?'

'Yeah, a no nonsense guy.' Cook realised that the job was a delicate one; that if it was botched it would mean the careers of them both. The super was reposing trust in him, not because of the detective's MA in business management from Massey, but because he thought Cook had judgement. It was a significant opportunity, and carried that element of risk that such opportunities have.

'Easy does it on this, Toby,' said the superintendent.

'Right.'

'You understand the sensitivities?'

'Right.'

After all, the superintendent has done quite well. Cook can admit that, even if his boss has only a regulation big Ford. There have been the expenses of the private schools for his son and daughter after all, and the retirement home on the hill above Ruby Bay. The super has a deep voice, suited to command, but physically he's unimpressive: slight for a policeman and with glasses on his desk. He seems to be drying up gradually from the outside, so that his pale skin is flaky. His hair, once dark and springy, has faded to grey and sticks up sparsely from his scalp like drought grass. Only a stubble remains of his eyebrows. When he opens his mouth though, his palate and tongue are moist and red, the teeth brightly, whitely capped, and his voice rich from the resources husbanded within. 'It's a delicate job, Toby,' he had said, 'and one that I want you to do, working directly with me.'

Cook had agreed, of course, but he'd also told the super that while preparing the Slaven Centre file it had occurred to him that maybe they should look at the place for other reasons as well. It was conveniently cut off in many ways, wasn't it, a world apart. Perhaps the answers to some backlog cases could be found there; maybe whatever the Harlequin disease was, its first inclinations may have been criminal. 'I'd like to have a close look at patient personal records,' he said, 'without making my reasons obvious at all.'

'And the staff, Toby. Don't forget them. All sorts are employed out there, and as you say, it could be a neat little bolt-hole. Yes, that's good thinking. Two birds with one stone, and neither of them the ostensible reason for you needing to work with Mousier. Easy does it, though — you know how prickly the medicos get about patient confidentiality.'

The superintendent is right, and so Cook in his second-floor office overlooking the car park is using his computer to compile a list of people whose whereabouts he would very much like to know. People concerned with cases so serious that a good cop never completely gave up on them. And Toby Cook is a good cop. He hopes on his visits to the centre to make an acquaintance or two who can, without quite realising their usefulness, be his ears and eyes there.

Cook finds his part in policing the Nelson district interesting and challenging. His previous posting was in Auckland's North Shore, but he doesn't disparage the provincial criminal. Nelson lacks the persistent city crime, the subtleties of high-level white collar corruption, but it's full of intense individualism and intransigence — alternative beliefs, craft obsessions, powerful historical convictions, are all jealously maintained. On Toby Cook's bad days the whole area appears overrun with glassblowers, potters, silversmiths, black sheep or kunekune pig breeders, screen printers, aromatherapists, naturopaths, Christadelphians, Montessorians, lesbian drop-in centre sponsors, flat fish dragnetters, idealistic Dutch migrants, cannabis growers and the proprietors of struggling boutique wineries. All of them doubtful of the need for a conventional society, and suspicious of a police force which claims to regulate it. Cook has come to the opinion that an individualistic community is just as resistant to good policing as one which maintains the united front of institutional crime.

On his visits to Mahakipawa, Toby Cook has an impression that there, too, people pretty much go their own way, that medical aims are put before any civic obligations, and that the authority which he upholds is poorly represented. Such a place would benefit from professional scrutiny from time to time, the senior sergeant thinks, and he will provide it. After all, if illness is permitted special dispensation, then half the buggers everywhere would get away with murder.

In the eighteen months that he served of his sentence, David was visited three times. Once by Chris after his own release from the new prison at Warkworth after a shorter term than David's, because he hadn't been the owner of Beth Car. Chris said that he was going to move to Wellington and get back into the business, but in a more subdued way. The police were increasingly losing interest in cannabis, he said, and political will was fading. They'd just been unlucky, he reckoned: perhaps got into it in too big a way.

Neither of them said much about prison at all, even when their conversation took place within one. They spoke of school, sport, Sharkey and Sneaky Pete: they spoke of overseas, women and whether Wellington would be a good place to live. They said nothing directly of friendship, or obligation, nothing of fear, remorse or apprehension. The bounds of their friendship had been prescribed a long time ago, and they never thought to alter them. Chris's hair was still short from his time inside, and his neck had the beginning of habitual creases. He talked with very little movement of his lips. For the first time David realised that he and Chris weren't young any more — not old, not even close to middle age, but not young any more, and the thought was a sour one. He wasn't where he wanted to be by that time in his life.

'You keep your pecker up,' said Chris. 'You haven't got that long here now yourself.'

'I'll be okay.'

'We're not finished yet, don't you worry. A year or so to set up, and I intend to be away laughing,' Chris said. What had happened to his art skills, his love of Modigliani, whom he used to call the brightest alcoholic of them all? What had

happened to his pinch of Asia looks, and his strut before the world?

The other visits were from his mother, who came all the way from Auckland. She told him again that she wanted that clean break with the south. 'I wanted a complete change, otherwise I'd make no effort to start again,' she said. His father had made a clean break too, hadn't he, without ever leaving Beth Car.

Against logic, his mother was growing taller and thinner with age. You can't fatten a thoroughbred, was his father's saying. Her shins were all soup bone, her neck soaring, her hands and wrists such obvious articulation, even her teeth seemingly enlarged and packing out her mouth. It meant she was able to wear clothes with style, despite her age. On her second visit, in the July cold, she wore a black suit and a cherry red cape.

'Let's not talk of your father,' she said when pressed. 'He's gone. A good father and provider, but he's gone, David. Don't sadden yourself with comparisons between then and now.'

She showed no embarrassment to be in the prison; no doubt she would have come more often if she'd lived closer. There was no thought to deny him. She had come to terms with her disappointment in a practical way. David's criminality was like polio, or retardation: it had to be acquiesced in. She must accept also that because of it he'd never have the same opportunities and attainments as other people. Love and allegiance were still there, but also disappointment that he was weak, lacking in judgement and responsibility. 'Can I help in any plans you have for your release?' she said.

No interest in his life in the place itself: how the long nights might be passed, whether he gagged on the fatty chops. No interest in his fears and apprehensions, which motherhood might encompass even if male friendship did not, because after all he'd chosen his own way. No interest in his work with Wiremu among the younger prisoners. No interest, above all, in the guilt he bore drawn tight like catgut around his heart, the origin of all the things he was. Guilt that lay further back than anything which he'd done wrong; the powerful, grieving guilt that comes from divided love.

Guilt's consequence is the failure to any more see yourself as deserving.

'I'll just keep my head down for a while when I come out,' he said. 'Get some simple nine to fiver for a living.'

'Come and live with me if you wish.' What more pelican flesh did she have to give from that spare frame? 'I mean it. Come if it's any help to you. There's a spare bedroom and a view across the sea.' Love is never quite burnt out, no matter what is lost to age, to sickness, to disappointment, to years apart. And when he asked about her own life she said, 'Things must be let go, or they tear out by the roots. All my good friends are dead.' He was sure she intended the second sentence to defuse the first. Her cheeks were concave, as if the pressure within what little cavity her body held, was less than on the outside. Her black and red were in defiance of the visiting room's regulation furniture, and the display of convict art at $250 a pop. The pictures were painted by Turtle Watts who jerked off into the mixed colours of his palette because the woman instructor told him to put more of himself into his work. As a result of a petition from the local arts society, Turtle was allowed to paint in his cell. He tore out magazine landscape photographs and set them up by his easel to copy.

What was permitted in the visiting room was defined by exclusion — no smoking, no liquor, no cellphones, no groups larger than three, no eating, no exchange of clothing, no carrybags beyond the door. But presumably you could be operated on for piles, or form barber-shop quartets. 'Are you happy at Herne Bay, Mum?' he'd asked. The thick hem of her cherry coat trembled as she sat in the tubular chair, and her hands shook slightly although her voice was strong. 'I'm on the committee of seven organisations,' she said.

Three weeks after that second visit, Wiremu came and told him that she'd died. His hair had been cut just an hour before and, as Wiremu told him about his mother's death, David ran his hand up the back of his neck and there seemed to be bristles right to the top of his head. 'I asked the cause of death for you,' said Wiremu, 'and evidently she had Parkinson's disease, but it was a fast blood cancer that killed her. Nothing to be done even if they'd found it earlier, they said.' Wiremu sat on the stool and David on the bed. Maybe it should have been dusk for such news, or a rainy day. Instead it was a bright, cold morning with a knife edge between the frost and the green grass further from the wall, and with a fine-cut mix of his own hair drifting before his eyes. 'All her stuff is going to her sister's in Devonport for the time being,' said Wiremu, 'but I've spoken with the office and you'll be eligible to go up for the funeral.' Eligible maybe, but not inclined to be the organ grinder's monkey for the gathered relatives.

At the time of his mother's burial — what thin bones they'd be — David was filling out a video order form for Wiremu, and he slowly and deliberately wrote down the titles of the idiot films approved. What composed greeting would his mother and father have when they met again? He remembered her sudden laugh as she prepared to leave the visiting room. 'What appalling art,' she said of Turtle Watts' seminal works. 'The man has no eye for country at all. No sense of structure beneath the surface. Limestone country, for instance, has a completely different look to the clays.' The coat hem and the skirt quivered; her back was straight. Had he kissed her? Surely yes, he always did on parting. The barrenness of the room, the guilt, the gaze of others, the chokingly inarticulate history of his love — none of those things would have prevented him. That's all right then. Body Count, Amazons in Space, Challenge the Reich, Alien

Holocaust — *all of those would give the sort of active unreality that was popular to distract inmates from their failure.*

Surely the most savage and unforgiving grief is that felt for those you have both loved and betrayed.

There's an inescapable nakedness to life in prison. You can no more hide the death of a parent than you can the nature of your crime, whether you're prepared to take it up the arse, or if you believe in Baby Jesus. Grocott was an emotional dwarf from the next cell and felt a need to commiserate at lock-up time. He came close to his grille to talk, although there was no way he could see David. 'Mother died, eh?' said Grocott, who particularly enjoyed a time of sorrow, or weakness, in anyone else's life. 'The old mumsie six feet under, eh, and not going down too bloody happy about it either. And you buried her, Stallman, you bet you did, you useless bugger. You buried your own mother because you fucking amounted to bloody nothing. All she did for you was thrown right back in her face, and it killed her right enough. Too right. You buried her by growing all that shit and selling it. You buried her by being a useless cocksucker even though you went to some useless wankers' school and then farted around at university.' *He was standing right up beneath the grille and his voice was muffled a bit by that and his sniggering.* 'So how does it feel now, Stallman?' said Grocott.

'Oh, shut your trap, Grocott,' shouted Lund from across the corridor.

'You think you're as smart as a shit-house rat, Stallman,' said Grocott, 'and you're no better than anyone else. Worse, because you didn't even go to see your mother turfed over, although you buried her all fucking right, no doubt about that.'

That's how it was when David's mother was buried — a day that finished with a homily from Grocott the dwarf, and what was the use in making any reply, because an expression of grief and pain was what Grocott wanted above all, perhaps because he wasn't able to generate any emotion of his own.

TWENTY-FOUR

Raf had drunk a good deal of Speights, and moved on to his cheap flagon port again. He was in one of his lost opportunity moods, so David said just enough to keep him jogging along, and gave most of his attention to his own thoughts.

'Maybe this is where the world begins to end for all of us,' said Raf. 'Not in a war zone, not in a city riot, but here at Mahakipawa with Harlequin let loose.'

'Humans have proved bloody persistent.'

'Sure,' said Raf, 'but you never know. The thing that gets us all might have started as simply and oddly as what we're dealing with here.' He had his new shoes off, and the colour from them had stained his light socks in contusions of blue and brown. The light smell rolled about the room on the convections from the two-bar heater.

It was possible that Harlequin would finish them all, but present tribulations always seem greater than those of the past. People thought that the Black Death was the big one, but it passed. 'Someone will make a reputation by coming up with a cure,' said David. 'Most likely our own hero, Schweitzer, and he'll get a knighthood and his own stamp.

You and I will establish careers on the strength of being on his staff.'

'It's the counter-attack of the old brain,' said Raf. 'That's what I reckon. We've got to the stage in evolution at which we're effete, and Harlequin lets loose that underlying, cunning old brain again. Maybe there isn't even a virus, but just some weakness in development.'

'Maybe.'

'The dinosaurs went because they were too stupid: maybe we're going because we're too sensitive. Crocodiles have the idea. A crocodile doesn't go in much for self-analysis.'

'The boffins will come up with something,' said David.

'No bugger has a clue about it, and I reckon if the numbers climb much higher there'll be panic action.'

'Shoot on sight,' said David gravely, but Raf, even with plenty in, knew that he was being had on. He grinned and had another slice of the corned beef he'd got from Pauline in the kitchen. It had a coarse grain like quickly grown, cheap timber.

'We'll see in a few months,' he said. His underclothes and dirty shirts were in a plastic bag by the door to go down to laundry. A paua shell wedged in a margarine pottle was his ashtray, and as an ornament on his desk was a piece of greenstone, polished on one side and with a whitened, oxidised rind. There was comfort in the ordinariness of such things. 'Maybe Harlequin's the one we don't crack, and man goes down like the dinosaur,' said Raf.

Tony Sheridan had told David earlier of an article in a psychiatric journal, which suggested that the worldwide and extreme celebrations of the new millennium had brought on Harlequin.

'You must be kidding me?' said Raf.

'No, evidently it's all there in very staid language.'

'Jesus.'

'Some argument about fundamental effects of mass hysteria.'

'Jesus,' said Raf wearily.

Darkness was on the way. The wind gusts were hunting over the ridges and gullies above the centre, and the waves broke with muffled intensity below. Those were the sounds of the place long before Harlequin, and they would be there long afterwards. Not everything has to do with people: not all is subject to the dominion to which they answer.

'Anyway,' said David, 'you're too thick to get Harlequin. It hits the most talented and sensitive.'

'Like Simon Cryer and Woodsie, I suppose.'

'Exceptions, and anyway they never had anything but a primal brain from the start. In their case, the whole world's coming back to meet them.'

Raf was pouring more port when a tap came on his door. Without any loss of concentration on his task, he asked who was there. 'Dermot,' said Dermot Sweeney, and when the door was opened for him, he stood there in his worn towelling dressing-gown with the sash of a different garment altogether. 'I'm on the way up,' he said, his tone both apologetic and fearful.

'How bad do you reckon?' said David.

'I can smell the wet bracken on the hill and Tolly's breath from two doors down. I can see moreporks on the wing, hear a stoat behind the car park and the sound of blood pumping behind my knees.'

'When was your last episode?' asked David. It was his duty night.

'Shit,' said Dermot, 'corned beef. I knew there was something else and I couldn't place it.' He took up the knife and cut himself a wedge. 'Silverside. Don't you love the strands when it's cold, and the bits of white fat in the body of the meat? This is what we had hot yesterday, isn't it?'

'I should be doing a round anyway. What's the time? Did you see anyone else about?' David got no answer, Dermot had assumed a protective half-crouch to eat his corned beef, as if the others might snatch it from him.

'You have a wander then,' said Raf. 'Dermot's in the aura. I'll go with him down to the main block.' He took up the clipboard with the duty sheet on it, and wrote in Dermot's report. 'What else tells you Harlequin's on the way?' he said casually, and then, 'No, no port,' as he caught Dermot's glance.

'Well, I'm hyped as hell, of course,' said Dermot.

'You always are, old son.'

'True, true.' Dermot was delighted with the compliment. 'But not with the sense of striking power you get from this, eh.'

'Colours?' asked Raf, hand and biro poised.

'I've been on the verandah, and the building lights where they fade in the night are the palest blue that you see in very old skim milk, and there are clouds as clammy as puff balls. But it's the sounds this time. That's the thing. You realise that the wind's no more one sound than a bloody orchestra is. The whine from a corner guttering is quite different from the wind noise through the gorse, flat across the grass, or barrelling across the water.'

'Maybe you can hear the steers farting in their sleep,' said Raf.

Dermot laughed more than the other two, his shoulders shaking furtively.

'Yeah, but some day you guys may have to go through it. And what a frigging business. I tell you this, though, there's something dead on Hitchen's property. I can smell the guts of it coming over the hill. That's probably your steer.'

'Or tomorrow's lunch,' said Raf. 'You want to go over now?'

'I think I'd better,' said Dermot. 'I could blow pretty soon.'

'Okay then.' Raf put on his shoes, and navy blue jersey. He flipped his pony-tail free from it at the back.

At the main door of Takahe David watched the other two go on down towards Treatment. He listened to the wind, trying to identify all the elements Dermot was aware of, but it was just the same indiscriminate swirl, and when he sniffed he could smell nothing from Hitchen's farm that wasn't from every other direction. The sea, the mudflats, were what the wind bore for him. He didn't know whether to be relieved or not, and went back through the corridor to do his first night check. Chime time and all's well. Outside the rooms at least: who wanted to pry further?

It reminded him of Paparua, when the screws Petrie, or McMurdoe with the limp, would be doing the rounds, and David was one of those to be accounted for. McMurdoe had a son who went to the Olympics as a wrestler. He didn't win a medal, but his father's pride was a compensation for the job he did, lessened his limp, reduced his whining complaints about the prisoners' recalcitrance and ingratitude.

David would have spent twice as long in Paparua to avoid being a patient at the Slaven Centre. As a prisoner you could always kid yourself that you were falsely accused, or unfairly punished, but there was no logic, no deceit, and little future when Harlequin pinned you. Only luck saved you, or perhaps prayers superior to those of Jigger Fraser. David stood at the smaller, far door to hear the wind buffeting the sides of the building and bounding over the grounds. All manner of threats might be out there, but how much worse was treachery from within for Dermot and the others: with Harlequin able to turn intelligence, emotion, even, perhaps, the soul.

ABBEY'S VIEW

Is from the blanket storeroom on the third floor of the main block. On impulse she took the key from the lock two months ago and, after a cautious delay, has made the place a refuge. It isn't that she feels persecuted, or even particularly unhappy most of the time, although she knows she may be dying. What the storeroom gives her is privacy: it allows her the heady feeling of being unlocated within the consciousness of the institution. Not Abbey is in her unlocked room, or Abbey is playing the piano in the Takahe lounge, or Abbey is swimming with a supervised group, or talking to Roimata Wallace, or halfway through the Thursday Neapolitan lasagne, or seeing a vision of the last supper of the great composers. Abbey is where no one knows, even if no one really cares, and she hugs that sense of secret location to herself.

There are two varieties of issue blanket: a straight wool in yellow-cream with machined edges, and a slightly more therapeutic sky blue wool-acrylic mix, edged with blanket stitch in a darker blue. Abbey needs some of each to perch high enough to see from the single window. Her vantage point gives an unusual view of the long-run roofing iron used for the walkway covers, the sloping grounds with garden plots, the ridge running down to the sound. What Abbey does among the blankets and pillowcases, the table covers and throws, is to let her socialised face go — all the reassuring play of responses which make her so approachable, civilised, comforting even. Her face instead becomes utterly introspective, both older, in the unhindered sag of flesh, and younger, in an expression of quest, innocence and vulnerability.

Abbey has loosened the dark blue edge stitching of the blanket she sits on, so that she can put fingers beneath it absently as she considers things. When she puts tension on the strand she sees her fingertips whiten, as the blood is forced from them. She doesn't imagine that there is any personal malice in her affliction with Harlequin: nor anything of punishment. Though she hasn't told the others lest it seem to be dealing in despondency, she thinks that Harlequin could well be the nemesis for them all, the catastrophe.

And, if so, wouldn't it be just the further descent from the paradise of childhood? Abbey's father had been a reader in chemistry, and her mother a professor in the same discipline. Their marriage was a close and happy one, both of them preternaturally sensitive to passing good fortune. 'Look at the full moon, Abbey,' her mother would say, with her husky voice, to her only child. 'How it glows for us, don't you think?'

Her father would press his lips close to Abbey's hair as the three of them hung blissfully in a Queenstown gondola, or walked with her pony through the silver birches of the property at Pigeon Bay, or sat on their tiled patio in bleeding sunset. 'Never forget this moment,' he'd whisper. 'Look at the kingfisher, Abbey,' he'd say. 'Look at the lights in your mother's hair.' 'Listen to the sound of the ocean in the distance.' 'See how high the thistledown is carried, like pale flecks in the sky.' 'Can you smell the fleeces on the sheep, Abbey. Can you?' For he was a man highly educated, and vulnerable to transience.

Look, listen, smell, feel, taste — and oh, never forget, never forget, and there would be in their eyes tears for the unbearable happiness that was passing. And the thing was that she never did forget, so that nothing afterwards had quite the bloom, or ecstasy. Not even the post-childhood gift of sex was sufficient compensation. Hers was a largely self-conscious performance, a localised and brief carnal pleasure. Her lovers tended to end up as friends, then seek new lovers elsewhere.

There was nothing, not even Mahler and Grieg, that could stay the descent from childhood: the dimming of the colours. Listen, Abbey, to the sound of Canada geese across the lake. Look, how the puddle ice is fractured in a glittering web. The adult world is more compromised and compromising, and that temperate cynicism which is called maturity holds sway. And Harlequin? Maybe she had unwittingly summoned him, and he had come with his second childhood of terrible dimension.

But Abbey isn't thinking of this at present in the storeroom, as she looks out across the grounds. She's thinking of her mother, retired in Tauranga with an honour for services to science and education, and the despair her mother feels because of Abbey's illness. Her father has been saved that agony by a cardiac arrest which killed him while he picked lemons. Remember this, my darling. Always remember this — and his whisper at her ear, his arms lifting her up so that she would have a better vantage point from which to view the world. Look, oh, look at the kingfisher, Abbey; see the blue sheen of it, and the dark, strong beak. So she's thinking also of her father, and she's enjoying her bird's-eye view over the grounds of the centre and the slope to the sea. The rushes there are like the morning bristles of a landscape face, and the road loops over the ridge by the one farmhouse, Picton one way, Havelock the other. The sound lies like that kingfisher's wing, outstretched between the hills.

Abbey sees David helping one of the laundry staff manoeuvre a trolley through the door of Takahe, and then stand, half turned to talk to someone out of sight, while the trolley is taken noiselessly down the ramp and towards the main block, just as the larger trolley carrying Jane Milton must have travelled. Abbey likes to talk to David, particularly after a serious episode, for she feels as if he suffers from Harlequin himself without the symptoms. He has empathy with her anguished powerlessness: transfixed like a butterfly, but still with an ache to take wing.

He isn't soft at all physically. His well-muscled neck is the feature of which she's most conscious: the sinews, the shoulder muscles sloped away, the blue arteries on each side of his windpipe which swell and pulsate beneath the skin when he plays volleyball. What she doesn't like is the loose, dark hair that too often needs a wash, his passive cynicism, the drug habit that he makes no effort to break, and even provides for in others — Tolly, Raf, Montgomery, Lucy Mortimer, who's his lover, they say. How could you do that to someone you loved?

She hopes David won't be around if she blows, and is surprised by the thought. Maybe when you die a stranger to yourself — and isn't that Harlequin's way? — it's better to go in the company of strangers.

Who can know the truth before it happens? More and more her mind lurches and breaks free, akin to the sudden racing of the heart. Hasn't she begun the withdrawal from other people which is necessary before you die? No more curiosity, or envy, in hearing of other pianists, no more casting into the future. Does she want her mother's hand over hers? Let's not forget this day together, Abbey. Look how the sky tucks down behind the hills.

Don't come. Of all the visitors warded off, her mother most of all. Abbey fears she will arrive to sit with her in her bedroom, or ringed by her fellows in the lounge. What would her mother choose of Harlequin's world to seal away in recollection?

In her special place among the blankets and linen, Abbey is already beyond official ken. She can float her consciousness away towards the shore with mud and rushes, the crabs flexing on the shining curvature of mud, or up to the ridge line with its rough pasture amid gorse and broom. If she focuses, if she holds herself very still, she becomes a held note of the clarinet, part almost of the music of the spheres. Never forget, no, never forget. Surely there is nothing now of her to be seen at all: nothing even for Harlequin to set his sights on.

And in her case the doctors are so optimistic, aren't they?

'No shit?' said Lund.

'So the man said. All of us gets to eat this slap-up feed for free, because the woman's son died in here last year, on the same fucking day that we get to eat the feed, and he only had a few weeks to go they say.'

'No shit. What name?' said Lund.

'The name,' said Bowden sharply. 'What fucking name's that then?'

They were sitting along the sides of the rec hall on metal chairs screwed to wooden slides, three at a time. For videos and addresses the slides could be pushed out into the body of the hall. Tick, tack, tick, tack, went the light, hard table-tennis balls. David sat with Lund and Bowden, and sometimes he watched the table-tennis players who weren't that good, and he half listened to Bowden on about the memorial meal.

'The name of the guy who died in here,' said Lund.

'How would I know? Who gives a fucking toss. We're not talking about any fucking names here, we're talking about a free feed on Thursday. We're talking about the menu, man, not the whys and wherefores of some old woman wanting to do it. And I hear it's turkey, no fucking question: absolute primo Tom fucking Turkey.'

'No shit.'

'You heard anything about Tom Turkey, Stallman?' asked Bowden.

'No,' said David. 'I just heard that the guy's family had been given permission to have a memorial dinner if they paid for it.'

Tick, tack, tick, tack.

Bowden had a large quince face, sallow and with full cheeks at the jawline, but he wasn't a soft man at all. He had a considerable stretch ahead of him for embezzlement from his union and an assault from which the woman nearly died. 'And a choice of puddings and bubbly with it all, I heard,' he said. 'Fucking oath. Now isn't that the sort of mum you'd like to see every prisoner fucking have, eh?'

Tick, tack, tick, tack.

This was the consequence of cannabis first tried in the old band room at Collegiate, and later cultivated as something of a rural industry at Beth Car. Had David realised what diminished opportunity, what boredom, his punishment carried, just maybe he'd have thought twice. But then it too passed.

'I seen the menu in the mess office,' said Bowden. 'All

set down by the guy's mother, and for the whole fucking wing, eh. And the dinner's to be fifteen minutes earlier than regulation time, out of respect and to mark it special. And anyone who's been playing up misses out. Let's remember that one.' Bowden played with the dense hair at the top of his chest as he talked, making curls of it around his strong, blunt fingers.

'But you don't know the name,' said Lund.

'I tell you the name won't make no fucking difference to that Tom Turkey, nor lemon meringue pie. It'll go down real easy without any fucking name.'

'You're right.'

'Of course I'm fucking right. Aren't I, Stallman?'

'You're right all right,' said David.

Tick, tack, tick, tack.

'Anyway, the guy went out because of some very dodgy fucking poppy, but they never told the family that, of course. That's what I heard,' said Bowden. He blew his cheeks right out and stretched his arms casually towards the roof.

'No shit,' said Lund. Would the man's sense of wonderment never leave him.

Tick, tack, tick, tack.

David didn't care about the menu for the free memorial dinner. No way was he going to think about the elderly mother spending her money on a dinner for guys in the wing where her son died. He wasn't going to consider that her motive might be that other prisoners would remember her son, and value that remembrance. He wasn't going to consider the pathos and the history and the agony which might lie behind the old mother's fucking Tom Turkey. He waited for an opportunity to replace one of the table tennis players. The movement and the competition helped him to forget his circumstances. But always, in the fortress of his heart, he continued to exalt honour, friendship, loyalty and love — the very attributes he found most difficult in life.

Bowden stretched again and worked his shoulders.

'Christ, my fucking guts are bound up these days,' he complained.

'No shit,' said Lund. *'Maybe that dead guy's Tom Turkey will do the trick. You know the name doesn't mean a thing to me — just can't place him.'*

Bowden caught David's eye, and blew out his big cheeks in exasperation.

TWENTY-FIVE

They couldn't meet in their rooms as often as they wished, in case what was readily accepted by their friends became known to other people at the centre who would move against them. Often at night they talked on the phone: the extended, trivial, and discontinuous conversations a poor representation of the intimacy they shared as lovers.

Lucy's illness, too, came between them, and days went by during which they had no contact at all. David was angry and perplexed that circumstances prevented them from being together more often. It was likely that they had little time allowed them, and they were wasting it by keeping to petty decorum and self-consciousness.

Lucy's birthday was celebrated at Kotuku: a cake from the main kitchens, a present from fellow inmates, some carbonated bubbly, a few messages of uncertain tone — congratulations, best wishes, many more happy returns? — the hollowness of being surrounded by well-wishers chosen for her by Harlequin. How quickly things change. Only a year before she'd been with family and friends, with more than three hundred faxes and emails from her viewers. David was at the most recent birthday in a conventional role, singing the song, keeping a smile, ensuring that nothing in his glance towards her disclosed for others his love, or, more importantly, revealed to Lucy herself the pity he felt for her and the sense of his own powerlessness.

Surely he could at least do better for Lucy by way of celebration: some special time away from the institutional cake and fellow Harlequins of the Slaven Centre, the communal ablutions facilities and the video operating instructions in blue felt pen on a card. He asked Roimata Wallace for help, and she suggested she take Lucy with her on a visit to Roimata's family at Blenheim, where David could appear unofficially and put on a special night as a surprise. Not ethical, of course — again — for either the doctor or himself, but David didn't give a damn about that, and Roimata thought the deceit worthwhile if Lucy gained by it.

'You be sure she has a good time, and just be careful,' she told David as they made plans. 'I won't have her upset.' Roimata was one of those thin, beaky Maori women who break the physical stereotype of her race, and are sufficiently numerous to suggest some genetic alternatives far back in Polynesian history. Her smile was like a slash in her dark face, and she took no nonsense from anyone. 'Don't make me sorry that I'm doing this,' she said to David. He got the message that the motivation for her kindness was the benefit of the sisterhood, and not his interests.

Yet it was kindness, and she put herself at professional risk. On the Saturday of the weekend stay in Blenheim, Roimata took Lucy to some of the wineries. 'Even my family has planted some grapes,' she said, 'and now we sell our crop of chardonnay to Hunter's. When medicine gets too much for me, I'm thinking of retiring to the property and becoming a winemaker. I'm already doing a course from Massey.'

'Let me come with you as publicist for the family business,' Lucy said. Maybe Harlequin would let her leave the Slaven Centre if she had someone to vouch for her. She could get pissed among the vines and few people, perhaps, would know. She could become famous as a wine 'nose' — a back-handed gift from Harlequin.

In the afternoon Lucy and Roimata drove up the Wairau Plain to the old Cresswell settlement and the new vineyards there, with a rose bush end to each carefully staked row. They took a cheeseboard and a bottle of sauvignon blanc to the wooden seats on the sloping lawn: the one green patch, by courtesy of sprinkler, in the dun, surrounding grasses. And Roimata made some excuse to leave Lucy sitting there; went back to the car park where David waited. He was surprised how awkward he found it to thank the doctor, and how awkward she was in accepting his thanks, as if both of them had a sense that their acquaintance was too slight to bear the burden should anything go wrong. 'Anyway,' she said, 'I've got to start back for Mahakipawa early tomorrow afternoon, so you'll need to drop her off at home by lunchtime.'

'I'll have her there by twelve. Jesus, just to have some time together out of that place. You know? Everyone does a good job, but you can't forget what you're there for, what's happening around you.'

'You help Lucy forget for a while then, David. You give her a good time until tomorrow afternoon, but remember how things are. You wouldn't do anything silly like going off, eh?'

'No,' said David. How often he'd thought of that, and always reluctantly admitted to himself that Lucy wasn't up to it, even if she'd wanted to make the break.

'Anyway, Lucy'll be wondering what's going on. Go on out to the lawn and let's hope she's pleased to see you.' Roimata Wallace drove away with just a flash of that smile from a face so sharp it always seemed to be one profile or the other, and David locked Raf's car, yet another favour, surely, of which he was scarcely deserving, and hurried past the tasting room to be with Lucy.

found it an effort, though, being always alert to subtle signals, affirmations that contained denials, apparent disinclinations that were coded for rapprochement. David watched Lucy closely, sat close on the wooden bench seat, squeezed her hand in his. He promised himself — he promised her without declaration of it — that he'd make their time together the very best within his power. Pledges and resolutions are easy enough, aren't they, but so often circumstances change, and it seems that a compromise is in order.

There were other people at tables on the slope of the vineyard, with their own intentions and histories, their own illnesses and causes for celebration, but David didn't give a thought for them. He was concerned only with Lucy, and his own life. In any case, his background made him resistant to any glamorisation of rural land use.

The vineyards attracted the townies. The staked rows above the dry soil so familiar from the holiday programmes on television, the tasting shops and tarted up storage areas for the oak barrels, the artfully created pond with a few clipped geese, the gravelled car park big enough for tour buses, the restaurants offering a ploughman's lunch, or chicken kebabs in pockets of pita bread, the large, colourful signs at the frontages shimmering in the heat, the careful rusticity of vineyard and label titles.

David was more drawn to the diminishing number of conventional farms: the closely cropped dry pasture with sheep dung in scatters, the tracks meandering to the concrete water troughs, the lopsided tractor sheds, the implements among the nodding brown-top by the fence. No tour buses there, just the memories of a different Marlborough and a different life. Up the drive, however, might come that northern yuppie money, and another family farm reward its founder's descendants in a manner that even the most perspicacious had not envisaged.

'Why aren't there more people?' asked Lucy. An observation rather than a criticism.

'It's late autumn,' he said. 'Some wineries will have closed for the year already.'

'Around Auckland these places are busy all the time, just about.'

They were, and David disliked it: a gaggling, superficial engagement with the countryside as entertainment. How could he explain to Lucy that the fewer people he had around him, the more clearly he heard the voice of the land. How could he express the satisfaction it gave him to be quite solitary among hills. And part of the difficulty was that he suspected such feelings originated in arrogance and selfishness. 'Isn't it better here, without so many others about?' he said mildly.

'Yes, maybe it is,' she said. What did they care for other people anyway: each of them had reason to be blocking out much of life.

'Sit closer to me,' she said. 'It makes me feel good that you went to so much trouble to be here with me — you asked Roimata for help, you arranged things.'

'I wanted you to have something for your birthday that was absolutely apart from the Slaven Centre — except me, of course.'

'It's great to pretend we're normal, isn't it?' Lucy said. 'Sit here as if it's an afternoon break in a conventional life. You could be a vet — you've got that half inside, half outside look about you, and I could be a teacher.'

'Your tits are too good,' said David. 'Women teachers never have a decent pair. It must be something that's determined in the selection process.'

'Even my tits are getting bigger. It's all that institutional food.'

'A joke. I'm kidding, right?'

'I know,' she said.

He did sit close to her. He cut gruyère and blue vein, he toyed with dark olives, which the folded card stated were grown near at hand. They talked in that oblique, relaxed way used by people who have let down some of their defences. They spoke when they felt like it, and not because of any need to prevent silences, for the spaces when they weren't speaking filled up with concern and affection and the pleasure of being together. They stayed there until all other visitors had left, until both the autumn sun and autumn temperatures dropped, then they drove a few kilometres back down the Wairau Plain to a farm that had converted its married couple's quarters to guest rooms. Lavender plots and rose bushes had replaced a vegetable garden, but there was still, by the steps, the large horseshoe used years before by workers to get their boots off.

They sat on the small verandah in old cane chairs painted yellow. The chair backs were shredded by cats sharpening their claws, and a tabby watched them from beneath the lavender, gradually indistinct as night came on. David had brought some shit, and they smoked it there away from the sea, away from the institution, away from people they knew, away, for the moment, from Harlequin itself.

'Jesus,' said Lucy, 'now this is prime stuff.'

'Isn't it, though.'

'You're the candy man all right.'

'Happy birthday,' he said. The lavender had lost its bees and colour; just a tail from the shadow remained of the tabby. The hills across the Wairau had become a sharp, flat backdrop.

'Let's not get heavy,' Lucy said. 'Any crap about what might happen to us. Not tonight, eh?'

'Okay. Anything you like.'

'I'm going to drink and drag and you can keep me amused.'

'Okay, sure,' he said.

That was the way to live in difficult times perhaps: concentrate on separate moments that held their own satisfaction, and not allow all of experience to be linked with some ultimate despair. David took a long, slow pull of his best West Coast shit, and watched Lucy do the same. She was relaxed in the cane chair, her legs extended and crossed at the ankles. Her head was back, and her broad face quietly content. He was giving her a good time, wasn't he? She was happy?

Yet happiness accentuates the rest of life, as a candle in the still night draws attention to the darkness all around.

TWENTY-SIX

David knew from experience that if you treated the police as fools, then eventually you suffered for it. Although for a time you could look good because you chose alternatives for which they had no planned response, persistence by you, and them, almost always had the one result. That one mad gunman shoots the president, guarded by the whole FBI, isn't evidence they're all numbskulls, just the difference between the ease of selective initiative and the impossibility of covering every contingency. David didn't much want to play silly buggers any more, but in agreeing to take Tolly Mathews to the national symphony orchestra in Picton he knew there was risk. At first he'd resisted the idea, but after a few joints his fondness for Tolly won out. Abbey had been taken in the small, official group to the Nelson performance, and been impressed. Tolly didn't harp on to David, which only made his wish to go more importunate.

'You're going to get me into trouble. You know that?' David told him.

'Bullshit,' said Tolly. 'Picton's nothing these days. There's no trouble to get into since it lost the ferry. It's all computer buffs, tourist chalets, goat cheese and yachts now, and women making natural dyed skirts so thick you can't get your hand under them.'

Yet in winter's dusk it looked so much larger than it was: the lights a trembling margin of reflection at the port before the dark sea, and higher skeins of street lights, and the clustered yellow glow of the houses. All mundane and explicable enough, but David felt again that quick frisson of wonder at the diamond scatter of the lights on the plush of the night.

How Tolly looked forward to their breakout: a chance to hear Bartok and Schoenberg, to slip for one night free from the host of Harlequin perhaps, and be one of a normal, enviable assembly. Odd in a way, for Tolly's economics degree, his catch as catch can business pragmatism, his wealth, his physicality, his love of fishing at the float, all entrenched him against any refined art. But music was something entirely different, and more in keeping with the hours he spent with his telescope and the sky. 'No, fair go,' he said, 'only Abbey and I in that place have any clear love of music. It's the one pure language, isn't it?' He even took a tolerant interest in Raf's jazz, as a parent might encourage a kid with comics, so as to draw him on to books.

With no attention to the lights of Picton, Tolly was tapping the dash top of Raf's Mazda, and humming extravagantly. 'A quiet night, Tolly. That's what we agreed. No nonsense, remember. We're bunking and can't afford to be noticed.'

'Just some good music. Nothing else. I'm a pussy cat,' said Tolly. 'Nothing coming up from the depths at all.'

'Otherwise we could both cop it.'

'Yeah, I know you're putting out for me, but no sweat, really.'

Tolly was wearing a dark suit and a tie with diagonal stripes of red and blue. A quality suit and quality tie, which he wore easily. David had never before seen him so close to his pre-Harlequin self of successful manufacturer, and it made him aware of his own off-the-rack slacks and casual jacket with a stamped metal button missing. Some sort of role reversal in terms of responsibility could so easily occur.

There was a park behind the pie factory and from there they walked to the hall, which had a facelift entrance of glass and tiles, but a gaunt, wooden interior. Tolly had paid for two of the best seats, but could find little advantage in them. 'At least we're not behind a bloody pillar,' he said loudly.

The concert was such a splendid novelty for Picton that there were speeches beforehand from the mayor and the chairwoman of some regional arts organisation. Each commended the other's part in achieving the event, and both were given applause only mildly derisive. Bartok began the programme.

David enjoyed it all, but largely as spectacle, because he had little musical understanding; no standards of skill for attainment, or comparison. What he saw was as memorable and as absorbing as what he heard: the variety of appearance and response in the audience and the orchestra. Those who were musical showed their affinity for the performance in their posture, their faces, with stirrings and whispers at the mention of their special gods. In front of David was a thin woman with grey hair piled up rather elegantly, and her neck became pink during a second movement. The oboe soloist had the forearms and fingers of a pit-sawyer, dark hair mole sleek on the backs of his hands, yet when he rose and played, the great plate of his face was full of tender pride because of the sounds he could create. One of the lead violinists had a necklace which she moved adroitly on her smooth neck each time she was to begin, and as she played her body swayed in its slim dress as a cypress does.

In times of exhilaration during the programme, Tolly quite ignored David, as if his musical incomprehension made him invisible, and communicated with complete strangers around him in a temporary bonding of musical appreciation.

The catching of another's eyes, nods, eyebrow flashes, small sounds of accord with the performance which were half grunt, half sigh. David noticed that Tolly became increasingly restless; not at all from boredom, but rather that he wanted to express his involvement and pleasure in ways more immediate than clapping. His face became almost comically animated, and his hands were an avian flutter as the tremors through his body ended there. David had seen it many times before — the first puckish breath of Harlequin through the system, which might be all that was manifest, or the sign of tempests to come.

After the concert, Tolly imagined that the orchestra would be delighted to see him, that he had a summons which would give him entry, but David talked him out of the main doors and into the Picton streets. 'Take it easy,' he said. 'You could be heading for an episode if you don't steady up.'

'Oh, knock it off. Just because you've no feeling for music, you think I'm sickening for something.' Yet he had a very high walk, poised on the balls of his feet; his spread fingers combed the night; his eyes were expansive, and glittered with each street light as David looked across at him.

'What am I doing at that bloody place of yours?' Tolly said. 'Eh? A family, a business, enough money to burn, and I'm tucked away at your bloody Scout camp at Mahakipawa. Where's the sense to that?'

'Pass,' said David. He wondered how those refinements of musical appreciation and astronomy had come to be among all those pragmatic aspects of Tolly's nature.

Around them moved many others of the audience on the way to the car parks. The majority were women, and Tolly Mathews suddenly slipped off among them, flicking up dresses and skirts with almost balletic dexterity, his soft hands half glancing from, half impacting on, thighs and buttocks. It was done so quickly as he eased past, that the reaction of most was a startled laugh, or a bewildered clutch at their own clothing. Tolly passed beyond threat so smoothly, was so well dressed, that most of the women didn't realise what had caused their skirts to lift, and looked at companions, at the surroundings for snags, at the ground for some air vent and grille.

David made no attempt to follow. He didn't want any association with what was going on, and besides, he knew that even a whiff of Harlequin could provide enough juice to keep Tolly well in front. Just let it not be the start of an episode, that's all he asked. He walked to the car but, after a few minutes during which Tolly didn't come, he went back into the shopping area, walking down towards the lawns at the edge of the sea and the jetties. Tolly was sitting on the wall, looking out over the sound: quiet, so well dressed, almost as if he were the one being kept waiting and too tolerant to mention it. 'I could do with a cigar,' he said.

'Haven't a thing,' said David. 'Jesus, it's cold here.'

Yet he sat down beside him, conscious that the wall and the lawns were a transition between the lights and movement of the town, and the darkness of the sea and the hills beyond. Not a flat, backdrop darkness, but one that had gradations of depth and colour, and winds that carried scents and sounds from a long way off in the capacious night.

'Not even any shit?' asked Tolly.

'I never carry it in a vehicle.'

'I'm dying for one.'

'It's all that playing silly buggers: putting your hand up skirts. You'll have the cops on us.'

'They loved it,' said Tolly.

'That's your story.' What was that fragrance on the dark air? 'You feeling okay?' asked David.

'Ah-h, stop worrying. I'm just glad to be out of the bin for a night. You know what pisses me off?' The concert audience had disappeared. There were just a few less purposeful folk on the street: some young people laughing, and ambling towards the fast food outlets, a few men changing pubs, a skinhead giving his Dobermann some air.

'What pisses me off,' said Tolly, 'is that five years ago nobody had heard of Harlequin, and now I'm likely dying of it. When they can't get you with any of the regular things, then they come up with something new. Christ.'

Somewhere macrocarpa was burning: far back, perhaps in time rather than space. David had the unmistakable smell of the resinous smoke, and it hit him so hard for a moment with the farm and his father, that he turned away from Tolly Mathews so that the street lights wouldn't show his face.

'Ah, Jesus, the old macrocarpa, eh,' said Tolly quietly, as if he knew all that was David's legacy of it, and had his own as well. They were quiet for a time, and when Tolly spoke again he'd moved on to other topics. 'Gaynor Runcinski did have someone run over by a bus, you know,' he said. 'It's the fatalistic hazard, the cliché, isn't it, but Gaynor's aunt, or whatever, really was run over by a bus when she was coming back from a holiday in Fiji.' Tolly couldn't stop himself laughing, though he didn't mean to be unfeeling.

David's father had sold one of the oldest windbreaks for firewood, and when the contractors had finished they bulldozed all the rubbish around the stumps, and the next summer David and his father lit the piles, which smouldered on and on to become the scent of that year's drought. And it was back again, oddly out of season, just suggestions of it on the wind across the sound and across the years. Great stumps smouldering in the ground.

'You never bloody know, do you,' said Tolly. He gave a shiver; a brief animation which went from top to toe, as a cat's-paw of wind travels a paddock's long grass. He stood up and wiped the seat of his good suit trousers. 'On our way. On our way. There's no more music tonight,' he said.

'Do you want a beer before we go?'

'I'd rather have a joint in the bin.'

'You'll be moaning in the car that you want a drink,' said David, but Tolly was already walking back into the streets.

Maybe he was in search of more women to goose — would he walk over parked cars and trash them? Did the placid window of the naturopathy shop seem an opportunity for mayhem? David put on a spurt to catch up but, as he did, Tolly sensed his apprehension, slowed to say, 'It's okay. Nothing's going to happen. Harlequin's not coming out tonight after all. The music's just unsettled me, and now I feel grotty.'

'We'll go straight back.'

'As if I've been sleeping on a hot afternoon, and wake feeling absolutely crappy, you know?'

On their way to the car, they heard a man shouting in the distance — an urgent, ugly sound — and then the siren of a police car. They stopped to listen, but soon the town was quiet again. 'It's not my night,' said Tolly, perking up a bit.

'It's a wonder after you and those women. You could've got thumped, or picked up by the police.'

'Some very nice skin,' said Tolly as he waited for David to unlock the car. 'Very nice skin, and one of them had a lacy petticoat. Now that was a touching surprise.'

He was quiet while David drove out of town, gaining height on the hill above the old ferry terminal, and with the lights spread in the night again. Those lights had dropped away over the hill, before Tolly asked for a joint again, and got the same answer. David's caution was justified when, on the first flat stretch, there was a police car and two cops with beckoning torches beside it. No worries about a stash in the car, but for David there were dangers greater than that.

One of the cops came over and asked politely if they would step out of the car. Some spot of trouble in Picton, he said. His mate stayed back, by the police vehicle, towards which the others came. Tolly stumbled, and David explained that he was a bit under the weather. 'Some sort of a do, was it?' said the back-up cop, as Tolly's immaculate suit became evident in the car light. An older cop, with heavy, regular breathing even when standing still.

'The New Zealand Symphony,' said David, and he got the programme from his friend's pocket. Tolly stumbled again on the loose shingle at the road edge, and began conducting the dark foliage of the bank. His eyes were lit for a moment in the younger cop's torchlight.

'Oh yeah, the concert,' said the back-up, and he glanced at the programme.

The younger cop established that David was driving, even though he knew it. 'Yes,' said David. 'I'm the non-drinker for the night.' He said it with a laugh, hoping that way it wouldn't sound wowserish, but just the shrewd, masculine compliance of someone who'd have his share another time.

'Can't smell anything on either of you,' said the younger man pleasantly.

Any moment Tolly might start saying things that would suggest Harlequin. The police wanted their names, and David's licence; just routine, of course. That was the thing which worried David. He had a trick licence, the photo fitted, but he didn't want any enquiries made. 'So what was the trouble back at Picton?' he asked. Wasn't that the expected thing to do?

'A fight and one guy got knifed,' said the younger cop with the easy manner.

Another car came from the dark hill that cut them off from Picton, and the older cop stepped out into the greater arc of approaching light. His big face, with salt and pepper moustache and neck bulge at the collar, leant towards the driver's window as the Honda Civic halted. It was natural, just for a moment, that they all looked in with him, and glimpsed a woman's face, mouth half open, beaver teeth exposed. Then the other cop brought attention back to the smaller focus. 'And your licence?' he asked David, having taken down his name, and Tolly's, who stood unobtrusively supported by David's hand.

'We're only a few k's down the road, you might say,' said David. 'At the Slaven Centre.'

'You're doctors there?' Tolly's suit was surely a professional statement in itself.

'Block supervisors. Live-in supervisory staff,' said David.

'You think that the bright boys there have a handle on this regressive brain thing?' the cop said. The car lights prevented David from getting his night vision, and he felt crowded into the space that was lit. The fine dust of the Beaver's car was in his lungs and the air. Her voice and the other officer's were still going.

But Tolly had scent of things further off. 'The mudflats are in the air,' he said. 'Storm kelp is in decay, and there's a faint drift of eucalyptus smoke that must be from the last Australian bush fires. The koalas must have fried with them.' David tightened his grip on the good cloth of Tolly's coat.

'A hard case when he's had a few,' David said. The cop checked the number plate again, and told David to have his licence sighted at the Picton police station within a few days.

'Strap your friend well in,' he said, 'and I hope we haven't held you up.'

He would check with the centre, wouldn't he. Probably not that night, but the next day. David would have to cover it, and also take in his licence. The moonlit sound lay like a sword blade between the hills as they drove back to Mahakipawa.

'The string section was the only weakness, I reckon,' said Tolly gently. 'Especially the violas.' What further anxieties could a man have who knew Harlequin.

They had a joint together in Tolly's room before turning in. They sat in a companionable silence and focused on the strands of smoke spiralling up to the ceiling. 'I had a great bloody night, David. Thank you,' Tolly said finally.

'It's okay.'

'No. Let me thank you. You took me because you knew how much I'd love the music.' Tolly moved the joint before his face, playing with the smoke. 'Music and the stars,' he said even more gently, 'are the ways I hold out against Harlequin.'

David went to see Tony Sheridan early in the morning. At the price of a homily on following procedure, he agreed to confirm that two supervisors had been at the concert. His conscience stretched that far. And a day later David took his licence into Picton. Neither of the two cops who had stopped him were there, and the desk guy was only interested enough to find David's name on a clipboard sheet, see that his face matched the photo, and sign to prove the document had been sighted. David was relieved to see that he didn't record any information, because that meant that almost certainly no checks would be run.

'And I hope that you pick up whoever did the stabbing,' David said as he went out. 'No call for that at all, right?'

'Not from where I'm sitting,' said the desk man, barely looking up. He had ears that seemed made from bacon rind, and a face weary of crime.

TWENTY-SEVEN

With Schweitzer's blessing, David offered a relaxed discussion programme on Thursdays: an hour and a half in the Takahe lounge. The block guests had agreed to the venue by consensus, though some still grizzled at the usurpation of their common space.

Thursday afternoons were also visiting time for Weka and from the lounge windows, the verandah if the sun drew them out, the discussion group would see and comment on the relatives and friends moving from the car park to Weka. A small parade of passing interest when the group's own topics flagged. David encouraged such apparent distraction, for often it led on to more unguarded and significant expressions of opinion than those which began from their own loose agenda.

Like Mrs McIlwraith waving to Dawn Loomis's sister, whom she had met socially. 'An original Wanganui family,' said Mrs McIlwraith. 'Such a lovely voice, and she's lost weight as well. Dawn was the deep one of the family, but it hasn't saved her from this affliction.'

'I knew a Loomis once,' said Montgomery.

Mrs McIlwraith continued, in disregard of his

information, although her hearing aid was well attuned. 'When I last talked with Dawn a few days ago, she used the words salutary and innate very naturally and precisely. I always feel, myself, that some command of language is so very important.'

'The favourite word of the Loomis I knew was fuck,' said Montgomery cheerfully.

'No possible connection then,' said Mrs McIlwraith. She was partly affronted, partly angry. Her face lengthened, the lips turned out in disdain.

'No, fair go. She used it for people's names she couldn't remember. You could hear her halfway down the street. "Fuck's here," she'd shout to her husband in the shed behind the garage, or, "Fuck's going," when some visitor left.'

Mrs McIlwraith excused herself. She recalled correspondence to attend to in her room, she said, but the new, unconnected Loomis seemed to interest the rest of the group.

'Was she typical of the neighbourhood, then, Monty?' asked Tolly.

'Her husband made garden gnomes in his shed, and fired them in his own kiln. All undeclared income of course. When he got caught up with a Pentecostal church against her wishes, she fired some dogshit in his kiln, ground it and filled the pepper pot. The poor bastard used it for ages without knowing. She'd push it over to his plate with a wifely smile.'

'You must be kidding,' said Wilfe.

'God won't be mocked though, you'll see,' said Dilys.

'She was a piece of work, I tell you, was Noreen Loomis,' said Montgomery in a tone of grudging respect.

The Loomis of original Wanganui family and her companions got into a Range Rover and drove away. She had no idea that she had sparked a conversation at Takahe, or that she had so rapidly been passed over in favour of a namesake. The discussion group were happily away on their recitation of outlandish personal foible. Gaynor told of a guy whose gastric noises were so loud and ongoing that he was formally banned from the bridge club, but won a court case on the basis of discrimination, and had to be readmitted, and seated by the open door.

Mr Sarasvati, in his serene voice and impressive English, told of a colleague in his insurance office named Boylan, who sold pardons in the name of the Medici hedonist Pope Leo X, yet was perfectly normal in all other ways. Boylan wrote the pardons on pages from a Warrior school exercise book, and his sincerity was so patent that people rarely ridiculed him. Many even paid the money so that they could be absolved of venery and idolatry, and have something to dine out on as well. Boylan put the money in a green velvet Edwardian hat-box, and when he died there was over $17,000 there, which his widow took and invested in a successful small business making Anzac poppies.

'Not paper poppies?' said Wilfe.

'No,' said Mr Sarasvati evenly, 'Oh no. The fabric ones with separate petals.'

'Can't stand the paper ones — disrespectful in some way,' said Wilfe.

'The poppies grow in Flanders and in Gallipoli,' said Gaynor. 'Isn't that a wonderful thing? I've seen them there, and on the day we spent at Gallipoli it rained for the first time in ages, the taxi driver said.'

It was warm in the lounge, and the triviality of their conversation, their knowledge of each other, encouraged them to relax. Two small children bobbed past outside with their parents. Children were a novelty at the centre, and made Abbey and Gaynor smile.

Nothing had been said of Harlequin for half an hour.

Abbey once had a successful accountant as a neighbour whose house was quite unremarkable on the outside, but within was given over almost entirely to an aviary for budgies. Whole rooms, she said, aflutter with pastel blue and green, tiny scallop feathers and seed husks drifting in the air, and just narrow netted corridors, a kitchen and a bedroom for the unmarried accountant. She asked him once if he wanted the birds to talk, and he said that they had a language already.

'Was he bloody foreign?' asked Paul Coussins, who was comparatively new to the block and keen to fit in.

Abbey said she didn't think so.

'I reckon most of the weirdos are foreign. They shouldn't be allowed,' said Paul. 'They come here and start bloody telling us what to do, going on about how things are done some place else. Pigs can't fly, nor sheep neither, but your foreign buggers don't know we've got mutton-birds down here, do they. Isn't that so, Peter?' Peter's iwi possessed the right to all the mutton-birds, but he just smiled at the small joke.

'Are you thinking that I am a bloody foreigner?' asked Mr Sarasvati, his face suddenly creased with agitation.

'No, not you of course,' said Coussins cheerfully. 'You know the sort of ones I mean.'

'People can't be sent home now,' said Mr Sarasvati. 'No use bolting the stable door when the horse has closed. Not at all.'

'And we wouldn't want to be cut off from the rest of the world,' said Gaynor. 'Openness in a community is a virtue surely.'

'You can't mix oil and water,' said Paul with finality. 'That's a fact, isn't it, say what you like.' That was the truth he had gained from his life; his heartfelt philosophy; his hobnailed Leviathan.

But, with Mrs McIlwraith gone, the discussion group was in a mood to find humour in prejudice, though Dilys made a mental note of any personal revelation for future accountability. Harlequin gathered there, in the warm institutional lounge, people who would otherwise never be sharing their lives. A bathroom millionaire and a fish filleter, a builder's stopper and a textile artist of renown, young Peter

Just for a moment, as he approached across the lawn, before Lucy's attention, her recognition, caused any response in her, David perceived her as objectively as he found possible. She had put on some weight since coming to the centre, as she frequently complained, but she could carry it in her tall, loose-limbed way. A certain assurance and confidence had been beaten out of her by Harlequin. She wore little make-up, or jewellery; her clothes were comfortable rather than smart. She no longer felt it important to make a statement to others by appearance. Her attractiveness remained, but her focus had moved elsewhere, and her expression was one of closed vulnerability.

But when she saw him there was such quick pleasure that David felt the afternoon grow brighter, illuminated even, though there was nothing he could promise against her illness. He experienced a pang that was compounded of both joy and despair.

'You bugger,' she said, 'you planned this all along, didn't you.' Her even, capped teeth showed in a wide smile, and she reached for his hand when he sat down.

'Roimata made it happen really. I don't think she's all that taken with me, but she'd do anything to please you. Just remember to give me a good report tomorrow, or she'll be on my case.'

'She does all she can for me — she's a friend as well as being staff. I wish she hadn't gone so that I could thank her right now. You didn't make her go?'

'Nobody makes Roimata do anything, you know that,' he said. 'She wanted us to be alone when we met, I guess. It's a woman's sensitivity, isn't it? Even when you're as tough and realistic as the good doctor.'

Maybe that was how men should learn to be more responsive: observing the tender perceptions that women show in their dealings, the small vibrations through a web of emotion more delicate than the gossamer of spiders. He

Taiaroa and old Mr Sarasvati, who both had noble lineages and courtesy, but little else, in common. A woman who had given overseas concerts in the course of a career, and a man whose zenith had come in the seventh form at Te Kuiti when he was captain of the first fifteen. And David himself in refuge — possessed of health and education, but bereft of Beth Car, family, and on the run. Yet he'd found for the first time someone outside family to love. He'd found Lucy Mortimer, and that maybe was worth all the rest.

'Who else has a story to tell?' he asked, sitting in the circle of matching chairs, while the sun gleamed on the chrome knobs of the Zip above the bench, and the Weka visitors ambled back and forth along the path outside, glancing sometimes with self-conscious curiosity into the lounge.

David knew that almost all in his group were dying. They must have been far more keenly aware of that than he was, yet they talked and laughed there in Takahe. They coped as best they were able; they persisted, for that was their nature. They tried to live out the fullness of their lives no matter what the circumstances.

'Who else has a story?' he said, and they were willing to speak and to listen: to hold on to character and narrative which linked them to the world.

SCHWEITZER'S VIEW

Culhane has the letter from Alessandro Bellini in his hand as he turns the swivel chair at his desk, so that he can look directly over the slope and across the sound to Tolly Mathews's dinghy at the fishing spot. Who is the solitary person in it? He's not close enough to tell. Probably David Stallman, or wealthy Tolly himself. Schweitzer readily substitutes himself for the distant figure so that he's able to feel the broad, free moving and heavily scented breeze over the sea, hear the slap of the small waves on the clinker-built hull, see the hand line refracted and shimmering down into the depths.

But it isn't that taut line that his fingers hold; it's Bellini's letter, which leads in a quite different direction. The letter is deliberately circumspect and understated, using a casual medical and personal shorthand which the research colleagues and old friends fall into, but to Schweitzer the significance is quite clear: he and Bellini have been carriers of Harlequin from the Congo to their homelands. The incidence found by Bellini in his own part of the world has a correlation convincingly similar to Schweitzer's findings in New Zealand. They are leading experts in the aetiology and treatment of Harlequin, and they now find they are also propagators of it. It isn't a confirmation that Schweitzer welcomes, and not one that he would publicise, but neither is he distraught, or self-accusatory. Other lines of introduction are discernible, even though the carriers aren't identifiable; Harlequin was bound to come out of Africa, just as the old brain it released had moved out millions of years before in an earlier colonisation. Schweitzer and Bellini possessed no inkling of Harlequin's transmission during their time in Central Africa; and isn't it likely anyway that it can occur spontaneously as a result of environmental factors, or the culmination of some genetic evolution? It's not the exposure to Harlequin that's the real issue, but the identification of susceptibility — why do some minds succumb and others apparently have immunity? Why is childhood a protection?

Schweitzer is aware of irony rather than guilt. All his skill and energy devoted to the cause, yet almost certainly he's a seedhead himself. Maybe the consolation is that he seems safe himself from Harlequin, at least for the time, and so can work even harder, make greater sacrifice to help those in his care. He has passed on nothing that he hasn't exposed himself to in the course of duty. It's too late for any form of quarantine anywhere in the world, the specific means of communication is still unknown, and to pass on what he and Bellini suspect would cause alarm and create no benefit. Schweitzer is optimistic — not for himself, or Lucy, not for the present population at Mahakipawa, but for his species, which has survived a whole series of brutal challenges before now.

Schweitzer is buzzed by his secretary who reminds him that Dr Sheppard is coming for his professional development interview at two. Schweitzer can hear half-muffled laughter between Sandra and Elaine, who has come in with letters from the main office. He has worked in institutions all his professional life, yet he's still struck by the ease with which staff detach themselves from the plight of the patients. There are hundreds of Harlequin guests at the Slaven Centre. Most will never recover, several of them are dying as the director thinks of the probability, yet Sandra and Elaine laugh, and Dr Sheppard takes the opportunity to discuss the possibility of advancement. David Stallman, or maybe Tolly Mathews, fishes quite out of reach of any cries, and Schweitzer himself can sit with Bellini's letter and ponder the degree of responsibility he bears for Harlequin's spread. People are hardened by the suffering of others as well as their own: war, prisons, bad families, hospitals — Schweitzer recalls Orwell's dispassionate accounts of his hospital ward in the 15th arrondissement of Paris. The pitcher goes too often to the well: sympathy isn't inexhaustible. The capacity for such selfishness is part of the psychological strength of the species. In the same day Schweitzer must die with one patient, and be reborn in another. There's a natural tendency for each generation to expect the end of the world to coincide with its own demise, but Schweitzer believes that in ten years Harlequin will be subdued, and later a harmless Slaven Centre will be pointed out on the hillside to passers-by, just as former tuberculosis sanatoria were two generations ago. And Schweitzer's name might play some anecdotal role in the stories of Harlequin.

Nothing is real once it has happened, and complex truth is corrupted by summary. Without memory there's no civilised life, yet any documentation of the past bears a similar relation to it as the wedding photo does to the nuptials. The mother's smiles belie the anguish she expressed at breakfast; the best man's central place in the grouping conveys nothing of his utter uselessness on the day. Each of us has only a facet of happenstance, but takes it for the whole.

Chance may flick out into the everyday and create small, random immortalities, perfect in their way. The Australian au pair girl turning up on a winter's morning to hammer in vain on the door of Sylvia Plath's suicide. Polenka, the coachman's bruised daughter, passing Vladimir Nabokov on the little station of Siverski, Christmas 1916. 'Look, the young master does not know me,' she said. Neil Armstrong as a boy crouching beneath the bedroom window when Mrs Gorsky told her husband he could have oral sex when the kid next door flew to the moon. The Nelson magistrate, Thompson, who gave the order to fix bayonets at Tuamarina, and was later found with his hands full of hair torn from his head in the agony of death.

Schweitzer's six-year-old daughter drowned in their home pool. There are still times, both waking and dreaming, when he feels his daughter's small, strong hand resting on his palm; when he smells the chlorine on her cheek, watches her run to meet him. All his brains and all his professional success haven't freed him from being a hostage to fortune as is everybody else. Only occasionally, when fully concentrating on some subtlety of his profession, or even more fiercely focused as he fucks Lucy Mortimer, do the shackles fall briefly away. Yet he knows that sex is an appetite, not an achievement: a recurring hunger, and not the enduring possession that is parenthood.

'Come in,' he says, and stands from his desk to welcome Ormond Sheppard, comes from behind it, and sits with him looking out towards the sound and dinghy. If Harlequin is the herald for the end of the world, what does Ormond's status in the centre matter, or his remuneration and, if there is a longer term, don't those things remain profoundly insignificant within the process? People are dying in the treatment rooms as they speak, are in a flux of mental dissolution, the ferocity of which is appalling even to clinicians, but Schweitzer gives Dr Sheppard his attention. It's possible that Ormond Sheppard might be the one who makes the breakthrough in the puzzle of Harlequin, whose name goes down in history, while Schweitzer is forgotten with all the others. All sorts of ironies are possible, and Schweitzer fully expects them to be played out against himself. He has brought Harlequin home with him, hasn't he? He built a pool for his family's pleasure, didn't he?

When his colleague has gone, bolstered by support for his advancement, Schweitzer allows himself a few more minutes with Bellini's letter, before the meeting with combined ancillary staff which Mousier is to chair, and on which he has promised to sit in.

Schweitzer worked for two and half years with Bellini at the Rushmilt Institute in Kinshasa, Zaire, and in the Democratic Republic of the Congo, attempting to determine if there was a history of Ebola in certain indigenous groups. They even went to the Kitum Cave on Mount Elgon together to take samples, protected almost like astronauts. Bellini's long, seigneurial nose had its end pressed against the glass of his visor.

The last time they met was eleven months ago, at Ventimiglia close to the French border, and they drove up to Tende in the Vallée de la Roya for a couple of nights, before Bellini went on to Genoa, and Schweitzer in the other direction to Paris. The mother of Bellini's ex-mistress had a small hotel in Tende, and although the ex-mistress vowed to knife him, she was never much at home, and Bellini and her mother got on well. It was autumn, with few tourists, but a chill quite different from the coast. The old village was squeezed between the mountains. 'It's French now,' said Bellini, 'but its people and its history are more Italian,' and he showed Schweitzer all the Italian names in the high cemetery.

Schweitzer took a small gift from Ventimiglia for the mother of the ex-mistress: a basket of clementines with the fruit still attached to twigs of greenery as was the local custom. In the small hotel there was always the sound of French or Italian coming from one direction or another. He found that foreign languages, indistinctly heard, tended to be reformed by his ear into echoes of English, or perhaps the universal rhythms of conversation. Almost intelligible phrases would make him turn with a smile of recognition, only to find as people neared him that both they and their language were strange to him.

He and Bellini sat in a sunny nook away from breeze, and drank espresso as dark as used car oil. The conversation of old friends recognises no distinction between what is personal and what is professional, so the talk of Harlequin and performance contracts was mixed with talk of food and women, mutual acquaintances and common enemies, trivial and august recollections of Africa. Before leaving they walked in the steep hills above the village, where old terraces, the labour of centuries, were almost all abandoned to a beautiful encroachment of wild plants. The late autumn colours were far more varied than any part of home that Schweitzer knew. There were firs and chestnuts on lower slopes, but blues, yellows and greens of low-growing plants mottled the heights, with the smoke bush standing out a sharp red against the others and the pale alpine rock.

Bellini's face was lined, there was a tinge like grey slate beneath his eyes, but his hair was still dark and thick, left long so that it fell almost in tresses. He told a typical Italian joke, which was both political and sexual, and laughed at it so spontaneously that it was almost as if Schweitzer had told it, and he himself caught unawares.

'You can't see any way forward?' asked Schweitzer. 'Nothing new?'

'Only in palliative treatment. Oh, and of course we're making great strides in the description and prediction of symptoms, but little in the way of causes, or cure. The worst thing here in Europe is that because legitimate science is failing, then the quacks, the con men, the modern necromancers are moving in. The colour therapists, monkey gland and herbal people, cliques with doctrinal remedies, hypnotists. There's even a muscular Albanian who claims that he can fuck it out of people. A twenty-first-century Rasputin, I suppose.'

'Someone will crack it though,' said Schweitzer as they walked single file through lavender. And he remembers how Bellini turned back to face him, shook his long hair and said, 'The thing is, I've found that I've got it myself.' The steep fall of the mountain slope was colourful with hebes, smoke bush and lavender. *'Che minchia* – what a bastard,' he said.

It's time for Schweitzer to go to the meeting. He puts Bellini's letter away. The tide is going out in the sound, and the dinghy is pulling for the shore, but still too far away for him to see who is rowing. A soft belly of mud is growing beyond the rushes. It is all a long way from the Vallée de la Roya and the ex-mistress's mother in Tende. Bellini said he may retreat there and set up a hospice in the time left, and when they parted he quoted Pliny the Elder: *ex Africa semper aliquid novi* — There is always something new out of Africa.

Almost always, those of our friends with the true sense of humour are the sad people too.

Schweitzer will ring his wife in Wellington after the meeting, and much later Lucy will come through the darkness and use her own key to the side door of the director's house. She will cook him pasta and they will talk of staff and patients at Mahakipawa; they will extend to each other the comforts that friends and lovers have to offer and there will be no talk of his daughter, or of Lucy's future.

Schweitzer will ask her if she knows the origin of the corrupted name Mahakipawa, and go on to tell her how the people of the place set fire to their pa and fled when they knew Te Rauparaha and Ngati Toa were coming. Te Rauparaha exclaimed that he saw smoke rising — and that was the origin of the name. 'So maybe there's a curse on the place,' Lucy will say, but believe no such thing. Harlequin has brought all the powers he needs to this place of fire and smoke.

Wake-up time. And the light from the high cell window was the colour of the bath water for the last brother in a large and poor family. Maybe David had been dreaming of Jocelyn Parks; maybe of separating out the head from some prime cannabis grown behind wind sacking in the shelter belt; maybe of happy companionship at Llama Heaven; maybe of Beth Car and the separate but undeniable love his mother and father gave him there. Maybe he wandered the steep, cobbled streets of Gattinara: visited the squat, old church that was scarred with bullet holes yet still protected its nondescript, saintly relics. Whatever. At wake-up in Paparua such personal treasures must be packed and stored in a fortified place.

The grey light would manage a glimmer on the stainless steel rim of his lavatory, and show the tourist mountains of his calendar in a dim parody of sunrise. How well he knew the routine of the day — quite stuffed with lack of opportunity. The cell check and ablutions block, the breakfast amid the clatter of both cutlery and the broken language of his peers, the mail call that brought nothing personal — ever. The proximity of Grocott, and the almost companionship of Lund and Bowden. The table tennis, which was a dreary exercise, but helped to pass the time. The television programmes, which were so antithetical to his frame of mind that there seemed no distinction between fact and fiction — the Lotto celebrity and the talkshow celebrity no more real than the languid stars of soap opera. Maybe in his day there'd be the comparative peak of a reading recovery session that went well, or a chat with Mike Wiremu. Maybe a hail storm, and the novelty of the ice blocking the gutterings would pass an hour or two of his sentence.

In prison two of the most melancholy and sapping convictions were able to flourish side by side. One was that precious, irreplaceable time was being wasted: the other that it couldn't be wasted fast enough, such were the boredom and reduced possibilities of life there.

Books should have allowed him a form of escape. Wasn't that the advantage his education provided? And through Wiremu's kindness he had access to books quite out of the ordinary. They didn't do it for him, though: he seemed always aware of the base level noise of prison life around him, a vibration of disquiet and resentment and disappointment which never ceased; which was present day and night, as if Paparua were some blunt cargo ship pushing on to God knows where.

Mike Wiremu had a rare judgement which allowed him to be at times completely open about feelings and opinions, without the intrusion that might cause awkwardness when the two of them met again. Apart from the programme they did together, the things they talked about were quite distinct from crime and punishment and rehabilitation. Wiremu was a country boy as well, from the Hokianga, and they yarned together about landscapes, family ties, seasons, stock and the habitual political neglect of heartlands. Wiremu talked also of his time as an army officer: the range of character and incident he'd run across, the stints overseas as a United Nations observer.

How very few were the positive things David experienced during his time in prison. There was the passing but accepting friendship of Mike Wiremu. There were those sustaining images of better times which came to succour him during the night, and which he packed away at each grim wake up.

TWENTY-EIGHT

Tolly Mathews and Montgomery were planning to get their own back on Hoiho's Woodsie because he was a whining bore who had complained directly to Mousier about the drug-taking at the centre — the non-prescribed variety. Rife was the word Woodsie used continually, liking its pejorative flavour. Others in his block said he had journalistic affiliations and was planning to do an exposé on Mahakipawa for one of his home city magazines. Auckland was the city. For Tolly and Montgomery 'Auckland' was far more pejorative than 'rife'.

Tolly called Woodsie Form Monitor, and sometimes, by extension, Lizard. Woodsie's Harlequin episodes had the unusual symptom of being prefigured by his awareness of feral animal noises, and Montgomery had taped some from a television programme on the Serengeti. It was vindictive and inexcusable, of course, but then they all existed in a bat-wing door saloon life: care and comfort becoming at a stroke the free fall of terror. 'It's combat conditions here, isn't it?' said Tolly. 'Even our bloody recreations have to be heightened to compete with Harlequin.'

'It might flip him,' said Raf. He was reluctant to put a

damper on the fun, but his position demanded at least the protestations of fair play and caution.

'So?' said Tolly.

Woodsie liked espresso coffee: it provided an opportunity for him to talk about his experiences in France. A week in Paris had made him an oracle on the culture. Montgomery and Tolly got hold of some coffee and thimble cups. They set up at the car park end of the Takahe verandah, and hid the cassette player in the facing azalea garden. Montgomery had the remote. The nights were becoming warmer: the buildings seemed to expand in it, and the lawns drifted into the shadows.

Such was the complacency of Woodsie's self-esteem that he accepted it all at face value — the invitation, the authentic coffee, the Dutch cigar that Tolly amiably extended, the presence of Montgomery, Raf and David. 'Don't mind if I do,' he said. His eyebrows were dark, theatrical tufts, and he tilted his head to the left whenever he was about to speak.

'Coffee, Woodsie?'

'Don't mind if I do. Jeez, the stuff here! Don't you find?' Woodsie pouted his lips to moisten the end of his cigar, and fetched up a tidy burp. 'In Europe, though, now that's coffee. This smells good.'

He wore pale, linen slacks, and pale, summer shoes that could have been woven in rattan. Without eye contact, David and Raf sensed each other's aversion. Yet the Monitor stretched out his legs in the warm dusk of the verandah, displaying his drongo shoes, quite undismayed, made the small noises, himp, himp, himp, as he drew in strongly to begin his cigar. David had the quick thought that perhaps Tolly's vindictive humour had extended to lacing Woodsie's cigar with cannabis resin.

'So Woodsie, how's it hanging?' said Montgomery, but Woodsie didn't pick the false idiom, or the genuine contempt, and began without any attempt at paraphrase on the story of his battle as Hoiho block representative against a few intransigents there.

Tolly grunted occasionally as a social lubricant, Montgomery fingered his concealed remote, Raf and David smoked and, although maintaining the physical presence, seemed to project themselves out somewhere above the garden plots, drifting in the warm and expanded night.

'But how are you in yourself?' said Tolly finally, the in-joke since the visit by the parliamentarians, and he stopped balancing the ash of his cigar and let it drop like a small dog's turd to the boards. 'Eh? In yourself.'

Woodsie didn't catch the ironic repetition, and he wasn't offended by the interruption because it didn't take the initiative from him, just gave an invitation to continue with a different aspect of his life. 'A good patch, actually, I'd have to say. Nothing threatening for a couple of weeks. Roimata Wallace says I'm fortunate—'

There came clearly from the azaleas the sound of spotted hyenas all stirred up about something. Woodsie's face puckered, and he looked behind him to the Takahe lounge, although he knew the sounds weren't from there.

'So Roimata Wallace seems quite happy with you?' said Tolly, his voice not raised at all despite the hyenas.

'What's that bloody racket?' Woodsie had forgotten his cigar, and his shoulders were hunched a little in defence.

'Racket?' said David. He leant forward as if to listen more keenly. 'What sort of racket?' The laughing of the hyenas stopped, and just the echoes scattered for a moment through the darkened grounds.

'Sometimes you can hear the laundry machines at night,' said Montgomery helpfully.

'More like bloody animals shrieking,' muttered Woodsie. 'You hear anything?' He turned to Raf, who shook his head.

'Anyway,' continued Tolly, 'you reckon you're having a good trot — maybe even a pink form release coming up.'

Woodsie tried to relax in his cane chair, and he took an

interest in his cigar again. 'Well, it's early days of course, but with my motivation and professional backgr—' There were lions coughing menace from the flower bed, and the challenge of a baboon troop. Woodsie stood slowly, with immense self-restraint, and went to the edge of the verandah. He leant forward from a post into the night. 'You heard *that*.'

'What?' said Tolly.
'Not a thing,' said Raf.
'Describe it,' said Montgomery.
'What are you on about?' said David.

'Jesus. Lions and stuff, that's what,' said Woodsie. 'No bugger hears it?' His voice was harsh with fear. The others didn't reply; just continued with cigars and coffee. For several more seconds the lions and baboons were joined at Mahakipawa by wild dogs and zebra. 'Then it's bloody Harlequin's menagerie,' said Woodsie in the silence that followed. With a formal and unexpected dignity, he thanked Tolly for the coffee and cigar. His textured shoes were plaited across the instep. 'I'm going down to the treatment block in case something's coming on,' he said. His left cheek twitched despite his tight control.

'Do you want me to come?' asked David, but the Monitor went off down the walkway, first one then another of his multiple shadows gaining dominance as he moved from the province of one light to the next.

Woodsie's punishment had gone according to plan, but there was less satisfaction in it than expected. Tolly knew that David and Raf felt a measure of professional guilt. 'Don't be sorry for him,' he said. 'He had coffee and a cigar, didn't he, and think of the trouble he's stirred up by whining to Mousier. The guy's a prize prick.' Woodsie's opposition to drugs, apart from alcohol, nicotine and caffeine, reminded Tolly of his stash, and he brought out his tin of joints.

'I suppose I expected farce,' said Raf, 'but seeing Woodsie trying to cope with the noises wasn't all that funny.' David felt the same, and rather regretted going along with it.

'Come on,' said Montgomery. 'Just because some of us are on the way out, doesn't mean we have to tolerate Woodsie. A pain in the arse is what he is, sick or not. You guys will be wanting us all to join hands and sing, next. Maybe it'll come to that, but not yet, eh Tolly, not yet. If the jungle comes for Woodsie, then that's his lookout.' Montgomery stood up and went off the verandah to the far limit of the light which spilled from it. He looked into the night, as if he thought that Woodsie might have circled around and be out there somewhere, then he went further into the dark to the azalea plot and retrieved the cassette player. His disembodied voice preceded his return. 'Those hyenas, eh, and those lions. How about that, then?'

'Spot on,' said Tolly and he lit up, drew in with prolonged satisfaction.

Woodsie stayed only one night in Treatment for observation and there wasn't any episode, but ten days later he heard elephants while in the main foyer, and then the big cats started again while he was in a therapy session painting a still life of quinces, oranges and mangoes. David was told that it was all over in a few days: one of the quicker meltdowns the centre had had. Woodsie had a hooting contest with a baboon troop and then a full-scale battle. No relative came to claim the body, despite Woodsie's wide professional acquaintance, just the punctilious, bald-headed Picton undertaker and his offsider who whistled Beethoven with some skill on each visit.

TWENTY-NINE

There were mornings of such natural serenity at Mahakipawa that even the dying couldn't be downcast, and for those not under immediate sentence, their lives stretched so far ahead that the end was diminished beyond threat. The sky was intensely blue in its centre and paled on all sides without losing lustre. The sun laid a blaze of silver on the water which fragmented in a dancing shimmer on the blue of the sound further out. On the far side, the dark, forested hills held the blues of ocean and sky apart and trembled with the strain of it. Bird and stock calls, and the laughter from the laundry, carried as sharply as percussion caps.

It was the world's display of eternal permanence, harmony and indifferent beauty. The trance might hold for an hour or more, then people fell back on the familiar focus of themselves — bellies and bowels, bank balances and basket weaving, bickering and bleating. Was there a letter from the outside? How dare Mr Paycock use their floral cushion on the verandah. And the chance that day of being called to dance with Harlequin.

That morning the dance master would call for Takahe newcomer Rachel Ellison, but David and Raf didn't know it as they checked the rooms, and reminded people it was laundry day. 'There's a Maori man with a bowler hat on the foreshore,' complained Mrs Tunney as she put out her own washing despite injunctions which forbade it: no nightdress, but pyjamas with faded sprigs and flowers like an old wallpaper.

'Tolly Mathews is telling dirty stories again,' said Dilys, 'and, what's worse, the women laugh. But God won't be mocked, you know.' She wanted to be clearly heard, yet at the same time keep the door sufficiently closed to hide the box of Roses chocolates on her dresser, in case she was expected to share.

Peter Taiaroa had already been for a run, and was warming down on the verandah. David found it hard to accept that someone so young and solid and strong should need to be with them at all. 'All the way to the point again?' he asked.

'And a plunge at the end of it,' said Peter, continuing his exercises as he spoke. A sea plunge after a sweat-up didn't sound ideal, but what could it matter.

Mr Sarasvati was fully dressed, but sitting neatly on his bed like a day one boarder. It was his wife's birthday but, as he was coming down from an episode, he couldn't be with her. He was waiting until it was the right time to ring her. It was a good day, wasn't it?

Mrs McIlwraith was outside, putting bread and butter on an ice-cream lid she had wedged into the fork of a crab apple tree for the birds. 'A great morning,' she said vehemently. David nodded. 'What we used to call a real gas of a day,' she said recklessly. Her face, still without makeup, had a peeled look that reminded him that once she must have been young. She stopped fiddling with the food when she remembered something she was meant to pass on. 'That tall, staring man from Kotuku came over earlier. He said to tell you that Lucy Mortimer has had a bad turn and is in Treatment. Not such a gas that, I suppose.'

The tall, staring man was Tilling, the noted soil scientist who had a room next to Lucy. He occupied his time by doing his own research on Harlequin, with Schweitzer's blessing. Why shouldn't his hypothesis of soil toxins be as good as any other? And it offset to some extent his sense of helplessness. Tilling must have known that David and Lucy were lovers, yet not once had he departed from his good manners to mention it. He had added to that courtesy by coming over and leaving his kindly message undemandingly second-hand.

The blue, the gold, the silver and the far, deep green still cradled Mahakipawa as David walked down to the treatment block. He imagined Lucy lost to self-possession and ease, lost even, perhaps, to awareness of who she was. She was nominally one of Tony Sheridan's patients, and David went to his office, gave his name to the secretary, sat on a padded bench in the outer office which served as a waiting room. Sheridan's door had a glass panel, and David could see part of a Gary Larson poster on the doctor's wall. A stag, standing on its hind feet, with arms akimbo and an expression of American candour. The murmur of Sheridan's professional voice was even and reassuring. After a very long time of about five minutes, Sheridan accompanied his patient to the door, opened it to farewell her, rather than giving dismissal from his desk.

David didn't know the woman; didn't give a damn about her except that she was preventing him from finding out about Lucy. A bony woman with a face so worn by humdrum domestic repetition that it was as plain and true as a breadboard. He stood up as a sign that he regarded her pause in the doorway as a trespass.

'Thank you for your time, doctor,' she said. Sheridan had already crooked a finger and turned back to his desk; David stepped past her to follow. By the time he had closed the door, Sheridan was already on the phone to Treatment to get an update on Lucy. David sat: the stag still stood with persistent candour.

'I meant to tell you,' said Sheridan when he'd spoken with the nurse, and crossed his heavy legs with an effort. 'She came in at three this morning, but I've been absolutely flat out since breakfast.'

'How is she?'

'Bad is how she is, David. A pronounced degree of hyperactivity during the early morning, and by the time we got her down here, she was really stirred up and had a massive seizure in Treatment.'

'Jesus.'

'All of us are going to have to be more careful, but before she's always had an aura warning of an episode. Not this time. She's done no great damage to herself, but we've had to give her a fair cocktail to counteract the extreme vivacity of the attack.'

Even with some understanding of professionalism, David wondered how Sheridan could talk about Lucy in a way that made her one among others, rather than the unique focus she was. 'Can I go up?' he asked.

'Would she want you to?' said Sheridan awkwardly, but it was a fair challenge. David was thinking of his own need, his own fear and love, rather than Lucy's needs. They so rarely talked about the illness, preferring when together to create an exclusion, proof against even Harlequin itself for much of the time. Lucy had told him to keep away when she was sick. Would she want to be seen in the aftermath of an episode?

'I would've expected the two of you to have come to some agreement on that,' said Sheridan. 'Sooner or later it was going to happen, wasn't it?'

'Can I just go up and see her?'

'Okay, but not by yourself, you know that.'

Sheridan took a few minutes from his appointments to go up with David, who was too selfishly involved to appreciate it. The doctor talked of the number of treatment admissions there'd been that morning; more and more there seemed to be some cyclic predisposition, he said. Off duty, Tony Sheridan could seem ineffectual, slightly bewildered even, like a bear who has lost his growl, but on the job his sincerity, judgement and concern were reassuring.

'If you were anyone else,' he said, 'I'd tell you how young and strong Lucy is, how important those things are in any prognosis, but you know that, with this illness, physical condition doesn't really come into it. The brain is the battleground with Harlequin, and if too many lights get scrambled there it doesn't matter a toss how strong you are. You know that. On the other hand, think how few episodes like this Lucy's had, and Culhane's supervising her treatment personally.'

Sheridan and David went past the nursing station, and into a small room where Lucy sat listlessly by the one window. There was a high view over the centre's grounds and down to the sea. The perfection of the morning was all still there, undimmed, but Lucy seemed to be watching the glass pane itself. She looked up at David and Tony Sheridan when they came and stood beside her. Her expression was ambiguous, as if one film negative was laid over another of similar definition yet different significance.

'Ah, shit,' she said quietly, 'my inseminators are here. Schweitzer before breakfast and now Davy boy.' She turned her face away when David stooped to kiss her.

'How are you?' he said weakly. Schweitzer had been before him in ways he had to face up to, but not now, not now.

'As you see.' She was picking at her lips as if quite alone in the room. Her posture, the ugly splaying of her knees, the loss of self-consciousness concerning appearance, weren't part of any Lucy he acknowledged.

David put his hand where her neck met shoulder, but she gave no response. 'I came as soon as I knew,' he said. 'You've had a real rough one. I can sit with you for a while.'

'Not while I'm in this shithouse,' she said. 'Fuck off. I've nothing for you, David, and you've nothing that's any use to me.'

Sheridan had moved back towards the door to give them space, and he motioned to David to follow him, shook his head to discourage him from prolonging a conversation. 'Is there anything you want?' asked David and then saw in her face the recognition of the complete fatuity of the remark. There was so much she wanted, and so little he could give her.

Even the medication hadn't completely blocked out what had happened. How easily and utterly Harlequin could strike. As David was urged from the room by Sheridan, Lucy gave him a farewell without turning.

'It's not funny when it's you,' she said. 'There's no good way to deal with this shit when it hits. You could do to remember that.' She kept looking at the window and her shoulders were hunched in a way that reminded him of a sick bird. 'Don't come here looking for me,' she said. She wasn't the Lucy he loved: she wasn't even the startling jack-in-the-box Lucy that Harlequin released. She was a limbo Lucy harnessed and sickened by drugs.

Sheridan told him in the corridor, and again in the lift, that he should remember that Lucy wasn't herself, not responsible for the things she said because of the treatment and the severity of her episode. 'Why am I telling you this, when you work here every day,' said Sheridan with a short laugh when they reached his office again. He screwed his face up in unprofessional chagrin at not being able to offer something more personal and insightful, and said that, although he had a patient due, he could meet David later, perhaps have lunch in the grounds. 'Damn,' was the last thing David heard him say, self-referentially, at a distance, closing his door behind him.

What David felt was not so much pain, or even sympathy, but grief, which swelled his chest so that when he'd tried to say a few words to Sheridan, those words had trembled before utterance, threatened to topple into shuddering incoherence, and he'd closed his mouth without allowing their weakness to escape. He walked from the main door into the sudden sunlight and left the path quickly in case he met someone, pressing on into the institutional neatness and display of the gardens.

Must so many be struck down at random, with no regard to culpability? Lucy was a goner if she kept getting major episodes like that. Was she on the way out, and nothing that he could do in redress? David's fingers cramped and his chest constricted so that he had difficulty in drawing breath. The things around him were distanced and diminished. The buildings hugged the ground, even the voices from the volley-ball courts seemed to be coming through glass. The sun still burned gold in the unquenchable blue, the silver blaze still lay across the sound, but everything — the lights and colours, the voices and shapes, the buckled hills, the smell of laundry, the barking of the Samoyed — had about it a dying fall.

When he first came out of Paparua he moved around a good deal, the freedom to do so giving the pleasure of novelty for a while, but then he got a job with Samuels Bros. Transport and drove sheeptrucks, and loads of hay, cereal crops and super throughout North Canterbury. The towns and districts became familiar through the distortion of the summer heatwaves, and then the frosted clarity of winter: Cheviot, Culverden, Parnassus, Waipara, Hundalee, Hawarden, Waiau, Hurunui. Drugs and prison may have hardened his attitudes, but his hands had grown soft again, and he had townie blisters for a time, which shamed him, but in a few weeks his fitness came back to him; he could feel the even and economical pull of muscle and sinews as he worked with bags, bales, cartons and pallets, on and off the deck. His senses sharpened so that he was conscious again of the slight soapiness of draught beer in the mouth, of the birds in a sky far too bright to scrutinise, of the aroma of sheep shit and oily fleeces, the easy song of the big diesel when its revs suited both load and road, the uneasy squeak of corrugated iron on the sheds in the feared nor'-wester. Only occasionally, on flat Sunday afternoons when regrets crowded in, did he lie in the Samuels' bach at Gore Bay and smoke shit, until the water stains on the makeshift ceiling became most elegant decoration, and his decline from private school, university and ownership of part of the country itself, seemed the most natural and blameless of careers.

After all, what would be left of the sense of achievement if everyone went up in the world?

And twice a week he had a run to Kaikoura where he took general freight for the stock firms. There he noticed Rebecca, who was a hairdresser in the small salon across from the hotel: next to a second-hand caryard ringed with netting and aflutter with red and green bunting, where the salesman played his fingers into the tread of tyres with the fervency of Thomas exploring the wounds of Christ.

As he ate his quiche and fries, drank Old Dark, David could see Rebecca talking to the middle-aged women as she washed their hair, cut it, sat them under the driers — or, rather, responding to their talk with a smile and few words of her own. She had a round, nondescript face, but over two or three lunchtimes David noticed that she was tall and solid, well able to bear the weight of a man, and the signs were that she had good hips and tits beneath her rather loose-fitting smock. Sometimes at a slack time she would stand looking out into the street, and catch his eye across the thoroughfare. Her bland, doughy face never altered its expression, but neither were her eyes quick to disengage. Long hours in the cab, the reviving fitness and loneliness, made David keen to get to know her.

On a still day, when the heat had drawn a sea mist into the town, he crossed the road after his lunch and stopped in the doorway of the hair salon. 'Any chance of a quick cut?' he said. 'It's not only women, is it?' He spoke to Rebecca, but she transferred the question with a glance to Jeanne, who owned the salon. 'No problem,' said Jeanne. 'Rebecca can take you in fifteen minutes or so.'

David knew he could return the favour in a good deal less time, but he just smiled and thanked them, and went down to the foreshore shingle, which was immediately behind the shops. He'd never found playing the smart arse to be a very productive line. He enjoyed the surge of the sea air and watched the whale spotting boats at a distance. He thought of Jocelyn Parks whom he'd first met on the observation platform of the gondola restaurant, and united with so often after: the strength of her long, pale arms on his buttocks as she urged him into her; the regretful gasp she gave when he drew out of her for a time to forestall climax; the low laugh when he went in again. The greatest aphrodisiac is a partner's pleasure. In Jocelyn's spare bedroom had been a quality print of Raeburn's 'Mrs Scott Moncrieff', and so often was it in his line of sight while locked in extremis, that the painting became utterly suffused with an almost unbearable eroticism.

How many loving and generous women could he expect? Let there be prayers of gratitude for Mrs Parks, but he didn't dare hope that Rebecca would be any, or sufficient, consolation. He knew that he was coming down in the world.

'You want much off?' said Rebecca later. She was washing his hair, and the shaped lip of the basin tipped his head well back. The swell of her breasts under blouse and smock bumped his cheek in a practical way as she massaged shampoo in.

'Just a good trim,' David said. There were all the warm, blatant scents of the salon, but, when she was closest, a slight whiff of meat pie and instant coffee. She and Jeanne talked together as if, being prone, David was invisible, and only when he'd been placed upright in front of a mirror did he have any opportunity to start up a conversation. Rebecca obviously found his tale of twice-weekly visits to the town

less interesting than Jeanne's account of the Lucas wedding reception at which the cake stand had collapsed upon the bridesmaids.

'Oh, yeah?' Rebecca said when David told her how he'd seen her from the hotel. 'Is that right?' she said, after he offered the obvious flattery in his opinion that she was good at her job. When there wasn't much hair left to be cut, he asked her if she had a coffee break and if she'd like to share it. 'I'm married,' she said matter-of-factly, and she held up the hand with the ring, as if it would make some difference to his intention.

'Just a coffee,' David said. 'Someone to talk to before I start back again.'

'No thanks,' she said.

'Maybe next time I'm up?' but Rebecca began to talk to Jeanne about the Lucas wedding again. Mr Lucas paid for a helicopter to take the couple to Hanmer for the first night of their honeymoon, and the bride threw her bouquet out. It burst in the rotor swirl of air and the flowers fell over the guests, Jeanne said, so that a score of women were able to claim they'd be next.

David was close enough to Rebecca to confirm that she had a plain, heavy face, but also that her legs and arms were shapely in a large-scale way, that her powerful neck rising from the pale blouse and worn, blue smock, was smoothly white, had a slightly waxy sheen, like the core of a fresh leek. He imagined his mouth there, the pulse quickening, a slow flush rising.

Over several visits he continued to call into the salon, at first just putting his head around the chipped, blue doorway for a few words with both of them before going over to the hotel, but then Rebecca began going for a coffee with him on her break.

'Just as long as you realise you'll get nothing out of me, you know. I'm married.' And she held up a large hand with its very modest band. 'All clear on that?'

'Sure,' said David. 'It's just nice to have someone to talk to on the days I come through.'

So it was, but David imagined that Rebecca must often have been bored with hairdos, in a town of a few thousand people whose claim to fame was the sperm whales passing offshore. He told her stories of Australia and Europe, some of them his own, some borrowed to impress. He knew he was making progress when she asked him not to come to the salon any more; that she'd meet him at the beach frontage, or the corner past the hotel. It showed that she'd become aware that it could seem they were meeting for sex, and, because she persisted despite that, the possibility of it being so was tacitly admitted. 'I don't mind meeting to talk,' she said, 'just as long as you know you won't get anything out of me.' Again he avoided the cheap and obvious rejoinder.

In a prosaic sort of way she was quite interested in his life: where he lived, how efficient a housekeeper he was for himself, why he had given up farming, the expense of travelling overseas. Her own talk was of the salon, and gradually, increasingly, her home circumstances. There wasn't anything else. Jeanne was okay to work for, but there weren't any opportunities, Rebecca said, no future in it, not at all. Her husband was a crayfisherman, but didn't have a boat, or quota, of his own. Fishing was getting tougher. 'It's all a percentage catch sort of thing,' she said.

Sometimes they sat on the marram grass and shingle bank by the sea; sometimes they would sit in the truck cab at the lookout, or by the seal colony. The more it was obvious they had little in common, the more he relaxed, and the more she appealed to him. He wanted only one sort of contact with her; nothing else to give purchase on either side for sensitivity, or obligation, or pain.

Rebecca's Nan was in her eighties, almost completely cut off from life by Alzheimer's disease. We begin by being enshrined in our bodies, and end by being imprisoned there. She had a small unit by the overhead bridge, and David and

Rebecca first met there on a day the southerly made it too cold for the foreshore, or even the cab of the truck. 'I have to do her hair later, you see,' said Rebecca as additional justification.

'Is it a stew today?' asked the old woman as David entered the living room. 'I hate any meat disguised with a gravy. You never know what's gone into it, do you.' She wasn't sick, but her voice had the terminal hoarseness of old age, and her stockinged feet were uneven and discoloured, like a bag of marbles.

'She thinks you're Meals on Wheels,' Rebecca explained.

'No, no, meat should be cooked alone and plainly visible,' said Nan firmly, as though Rebecca had been sticking up for stew.

'Nice to meet you,' said David.

'I'll just make your bed, Nan, then we'll have a cuppa together.'

There was just the toilet-cum-bathroom, a sitting room with its annex kitchenette, and the one single bedroom into which the old woman's country marriage bed was shoehorned so that there was barely space to walk around the walls. Rebecca's Nan talked of the eleven pieces of junk mail she'd received that very morning, while David followed her granddaughter into the bedroom.

'Stop it,' said Rebecca when he came close behind her and gripped her hips, but all that was gathered in the room of hopelessness, loss and decay became the powerful incitement to defiance. 'She's just out there, and I have to be back to help Jeanne by two,' but she was easily toppled from the alley alongside the bed on to the handmade quilt of her Nan's life, which smelled of Deep Heat, unwashed wool and exhalations of bewilderment. 'What on earth would I want with power tools, even at half price,' said Rebecca's Nan. Rebecca tried to close the door completely with a kick, but David was already sitting on her to undo her salon smock, her blouse, her skirt. She knew it was no

use showing him her wedding ring again.

'Easy on now,' she said. 'Easy on. Nan's just out there.' *She had a wide, white belly with the umbilical twist like a small delicacy on an uncooked pastry top, and a pink welt beneath her breasts from the edge of the bra.*

'They clog up the box for the good mail,' said the old woman. 'I don't want any hot-air balloon rides. I don't want country and western music, exercise bars, or trolleys to wind up garden hoses.'

Rebecca made little noise during it. Her head went progressively back with an open-mouthed smile. The old woman's walking stick tapped with unaccustomed and poltergeistal energy on the bed end where it hung, and Rebecca brought her heavy arms and legs around David's back to restrain his efforts to get maximum height for each plunge.

The pleasure was greater than he'd anticipated: but then it always was. Such joy exits only in the moment of attainment.

'Did I see the man bringing me a dinner?'

'I'll get you something in a minute, Nan, when I'm finished here.'

Had a Basque with a bomb, a serial garrotter, a charismatic evangelist, the ghost of Christmas past, come in to do the three of them mortal harm, they could not have broken from their preoccupations — David and Rebecca striking the sparks of life itself, and Nan sifting the embers.

'Alan never writes to me at all,' said the old woman firmly.

'He does, Nan. You know he does.' *Rebecca's breasts were impressive, covering all of her chest, even when she was underneath. David tried to wrestle her on top so that gravity would show them to best advantage.*

'Junk mail's all I get. Nothing personal at all. Stuff you're supposed to spend money on. Nothing from people you really know.'

The walking stick smartly struck the moments and

movements of the struggle, many more than a grandfather's twelve, until they were locked together, quite still, in that instant which the French call the little death, and the only sound was Rebecca's sigh and his deep breathing.

They dressed with difficulty in the ditch between bed and wall, and then went back into the living room, waking Nan so that she started in the chair. 'My goodness, where did you come from, Rebecca? How long have you been in there?'

'I was making your bed, Nan. You know.' Rebecca went to the kitchenette and began to make a cup of tea for all three.

Nan put her hand on David's with surprising speed. 'Not out on the boat today?' she said. 'That's nice. You should have more time with Rebecca.'

'I'm late for the salon as it is,' said Rebecca.

David just smiled. To find pleasure in life was quite enough without expecting logic with it. When reason can't be found, rhyme is some satisfaction.

'What was it I was saying?' asked Nan.

'Don't think that you're going to get that out of me again,' said Rebecca, giving him his cup. 'I'm happily married.'

'Do you think the postman's been?' asked Nan.

He did, though. Not every time that he made the round trip, not as often as he wished, but on occasions enough to keep him hopeful, she agreed to his suggestion that they should visit her Nan in the lunch hour. Tidying the bedroom, Rebecca said, and through the partly open door she would maintain a sort of desultory parallel conversation with the old woman, both of them caring little for the words they used, and with their interest elsewhere. Each time there was the same ritual. He would snare her in the confined margins of the Deep Heat room: each time her small resistance to support the pretence that his intention was unexpected, each time the faded salon smock removed to show the large nipples, darkly compressed beneath the fabric of the cups. She grappled him in the same way each time, no interest in variety, until the expanse of her white belly had a thick sheen of sweat and their thighs smacked like paddles. No tender and mutual absorption, but instead straining face to face as if in dispute concerning his cock between them.

It was what he deserved, wasn't it? It was all that he was capable of offering. He had given up any idea of love in regard to a woman: that far place in poetry and homily, which continued to recede. Love wasn't for the likes of him, was it? And always close behind love was the pain of its betrayal. Family had taught David that.

They were at it when the crayfish husband came one sunny lunchtime, when the sea had let him down perhaps, and he heard the noises even before he began to talk to Nan, and walked straight on by before she could begin to wonder how he managed to arrive twice — right into the bedroom with so little space to stand that he climbed onto the bed with them in his amazement and anger. A fisherman knows how to use his hands and, even in the tumult of the struggle the three of them made, there on Nan's marriage bed, he wasted only a few blows on David before concentrating on his wife. David ran in shirt and boxer shorts past Nan, put on his trousers in the confined porch — where he could hear the noises from the bedroom — ran three blocks more to his truck. Tears of fear and remorse were driven back towards his ears. 'Turn the television down,' complained Nan in the empty sitting room. 'How can I hear myself think with such a racket.'

All the way back to Gore Bay, David disciplined himself to keep within the speed limit, and he spent just long enough at the bach to lift his cash and stash of shit, a few personal things that had survived prison, and leave a note for Samuels Bros. that he'd been called away by sudden family illness. He then began hitching back the way he'd come, hoping to confuse anyone interested in his movements. He passed through Kaikoura before dark with a refrigeration engineer and his family, already becoming accustomed to a new name, and oblivious to the children's game of guessing the colours of oncoming vehicles. The through road to Blenheim didn't pass the salon, where Jeanne still told of the helicopter wedding perhaps, or the unit by the overbridge where Nan's incapacity for short-term memory would surely save her from everything except the first shock.

What had happened there, dear God?

'Green, green. Yes.'

'It isn't. It's blue.'

'Green. Green.'

'Bloody cheat.'

'Just shut up.'

'Cheat.'

'I've won, and you can't take it.'

'Knock it off, you two. I won't tell you again.'

Some people seem to get away with expressing their weaknesses without much consequence; others have no luck. Or maybe it's that they don't learn their lessons fast enough. He'd done it this time, David knew. No more chances to put things behind him, to straighten himself out — all the platitudes to excuse a past. He'd gone too far to be able to return and make any more than a pretence to be like those people who could live frankly and with some self-esteem. Acid from his stomach rose to the back of his throat; his hands clenched as if he were in some free fall and knew, even as he counted, that there was no rip-cord. He felt his body throb with an agony which was part remorse, part horrified sympathy for Rebecca, but most essentially just pity for his own predicament.

'Do you do much fishing yourself?' *asked the refrigeration engineer as he drove along the rocky coast, past surfcasters and crayfish stalls. His wife was inspecting her nails, his boys were selecting jubes from the bag — again by colour.*

'Not a lot, no,' *said David.*

'Heading any further north than Blenheim?'

'No, no plans for that,' said David, but he had: he wanted to reach Wellington where Chris lived, someone he could rely on for help.

THIRTY

From Tolly's dinghy at the pink float, well out in the sound, the buildings of the Slaven Centre were pleasantly distant, but the greater satisfaction was that no solid ground linked them. Between the two in the boat and anything that happened at Mahakipawa, was a disconnecting fluidity. Other times, other selves, as well as other places, could be kept at some remove by the green and sinuous ocean arm of the sound. The weak chop apologetic on the dinghy, which sidled on its anchor rope in response. The bright sun sharply metallic in faceted reflection from the water: both David and Lucy wore dark sunglasses and relaxed against the bleached canvas cushions. Were they hidden there perhaps? Were they out of sight and out of mind for the world, for Harlequin, for any past and any future?

Lucy had caught one large, blue cod, which had come up dark and spiralling from the depths, and it lay on the slatted bottom of the boat, its passionate colours drying and beginning to fade.

David stroked Lucy's warm forearm and said he felt like making love. She reminded him of Tolly's telescope: quite possibly half of Takahe were clustered round it, and they'd be visible from other vantages in the centre too. When he asked where those others might be, Lucy just smiled and her eyebrows lifted at the rims of her dark glasses. Did she want to talk about Schweitzer? David had just themselves on his mind.

David recognised that, for the first time in his life, he was in love. What else could he call it? Not anything as crass as simple happiness, but an aching focus on another person, and on the unbearable awareness of the simultaneous power and transience of *now*. Love is that singular form of suffering which moves concern from yourself to another, so that you are freed a while from stultifying selfishness. More than anything else, he wished he could do something to protect Lucy from Harlequin, but there was also his desire to move to her there in the dinghy, fiercely bringing them together as one. And simultaneously there was a need to lie absolutely still and talk to her in a trusting way that was quite apart from sex. Isn't all that part of love's jumble, so that poise, caution and common sense are upset? He could smell the sunblock on her skin, see the winking, silver studs in her ears. There was that pale scimitar of a scar on the underside of her left arm.

'Schweitzer suggested that each week I make an hour-long video of things going on around the place, and copies be sent to all the blocks,' she said. 'I thought that it could sort of tie in with your own group programmes — something we could work on together. Now that the numbers are increasing so much he thinks there's a danger the sense of community could be lost.'

'What would we call it, Harlequin's Parade? Thalamus Review?'

'More Mahakipawa Mahappy Days,' said Lucy.

'Think of the feature sections we could have: Episode of the Week, Most Prolix Personal Abuse, Volleyball Highlights, Victimisation Prize, Trite Condolence Award.'

'It's bloody marvellous out here,' Lucy said.

'It is, isn't it.'

'So warm, but that dry heat of the South Island rather than the muggy stuff.'

'We'll come out again some time,' he promised.

They would begin the regular video reports together, they would have more weeks together as friends and lovers, they would be concerned for each other, attentive by turns and then pissed off for reasons which were at times quite beyond the control of either of them, and which at other times arose from those weaknesses and fallibilities that are retained even by those in love.

But they would never be there together again at the blush pink fishing marker, so happy in the bright sun with their dark glasses on, and Tolly's dinghy nudging and shifting on its deep tether. Talking there, laughing there, with no solid connection at all with the rest of the world. David told Lucy about the island of Burano in the lagoon of Venice, an upstairs room so low he couldn't stand upright, and the small birds flocking in over the flat water to roost in the one big tree in his view, swooping and wheeling in the twilight, and the shrill babble of their congregation, which seemed to have some Latin pitch of excitement and provocation greater than the birds of Beth Car's pines. Until at last the darkness subdued them and, looking out at the tree against the pale sky, he saw the still birds outlined there like a thousand small cones on the branches, and farther in the perspective of the night the leaning spire of the island church.

Lucy told David about going to Kuala Lumpur several years before as part of the TV coverage of the Commonwealth Games. They stayed in an old-fashioned but rather grand hotel with heavy, brass-handled wooden furniture in every room. All night, with little change of tempo, the traffic hustled on Jalan Kuching across the Gombak River. She wondered what was so different in the sound, and then realised that it was the waspish domination of mopeds and small motorbikes. One day in heat that was almost liquid, they were taken to the butterfly gardens and saw them as big as birds on the hibiscus flowers. Gaudy blues and greens in the shimmering wings, and bodies banded red and black like plaited pipe cleaners. And when Lucy peered through the lush leaves she saw that some of the huge butterflies had died, and lay spread on the earth like stained glass ornaments.

That is how life goes, things held in unique juxtaposition for a moment in time and space — Burano and Kuala Lumpur, small birds in the night and great butterflies in the light, the dinghy on the sound and the buildings on the slope, David and Lucy talking, generous intentions and slender gains — then all whirls on again for a different throw.

THIRTY-ONE

Abbey and David wandered towards the latest accommodation block being built in the sloping pasture behind the car park. The expansion of the centre was forcing gorse and cattle steadily higher. The activity on the building site drew Abbey: a natural curiosity about the workers as much as structures, for there was a novelty in seeing non-Harlequin people getting on with their lives. The new block was to be larger than any of the earlier ones, and was growing in a series of great, empty, load-bearing oblongs, so that even at the beginning of its life it had the appearance of a ruin, with fissures and broken seams, with raw concrete, and protruding ringed reinforcement rods already rusting. Unlike the earlier residential blocks, it reared up several storeys and the ground floor was still as barren and derelict as the third, on which the men were working. Harlequin had become a growth industry: disease was providing job opportunity. The workers had dark singlets and yellow helmets and shouted and gestured to each other like Italian brothers. Somewhere within the great concrete slabs, the scaffolding, the wooden boxing like patches, drills or grinders were working, and their wailing was like some harsh, territorial cry which drove the farm stock still further back.

Abbey and David continued to talk of Alst Mousier's proposal for a concert, but both knew they were thinking the same thing — that Harlequin was set to make some sort of breakout in the general population, and that the level of care provided by the Slaven Centre and those at Omapere, Whatatutu, Mayfield, would have to be discarded as a luxury. Already there were plans for old army camps and long disused sanatoria to be prepared for emergency use. 'Nothing's doing any good, is it?' said Abbey, coming to the point at last, and the drills wailed from the monolith. 'It'll become one of those great epidemics beyond control, and no one knows what to do.' The workmen shouted and laughed, unperturbed by the reason for their employment, or the likelihood that they'd inhabit the rooms there soon enough.

'Schweitzer still thinks there's some genetic inhibitor for most people, and no children under twelve get it at all, so there must be reasons.'

'But nobody knows,' said Abbey.

Nobody did know, and understanding would probably follow the event, so that years afterwards, when it was too late for the sufferers, Harlequin would be in the history books and medical texts, and readers would be mildly surprised that it killed so many people before a cause and cure were found. How could you expect those living it, though, to be objective? It was like enjoining a Flanders infantryman to consider that he was taking part in the last great example of static trench warfare.

And if Harlequin was *it*, the conclusion of that short evolutionary experiment which was *Homo sapiens*, only those at the very end would know.

David's own grasp of the generalities kept slipping, yet he wasn't a Harlequin. He could respond only to the particular, the personal, one thing at a time. Lucy, who was the one really precious thing he had found; his other friends at the centre, such as Abbey beside him. What else could matter? His role as an aide was, after all, little more than a convenient camouflage of his past.

He and Abbey moved back from the building site, with its ashen concrete and red plastic tape perimeter, its yellow hard hats, shouts and wails. They went together across the car park, the seal broken in places by the recent passage of heavy machinery, the surface scattered with cakes of pale clay from the caterpillar treads. On the lawn, and paralleling the entrance road, was a line of quick-growing birches, with tissue bark curling from the slender trunks like cigarette paper and vibrating in the breeze.

'I reckon you're going to be all right, Abbey,' David said.

How much quieter it was there. He had been talking to Tony Sheridan about Abbey's good spin, the probability of her release, but he hadn't realised how strong was his conviction of her remission until he voiced it. He felt an assurance that was so much more than the doctor's opinion, yet not dependent on wishful thinking at all. 'I know you're going to be all right,' he said again firmly.

'Oddly enough, so do I,' said Abbey, and she put her small hand on his arm. It was the first time she had touched him in such a deliberate way. 'The last episodes have been different: even though I can't stop them coming, I don't get pushed out completely any more. I have some influence left, even if it's only that of a bareback rider.

'You'll be able to go home soon, and all this will lose its grip.'

'It doesn't pay to look Harlequin in the eye,' said Abbey. 'Just some good months, some remission, would be enough.'

Apart from Lucy, who better than dear Abbey to beat the odds, and walk out of the shadow to carry on her self-contained life in her own quiet, stubborn way: playing music for herself and anyone else who would shut up long enough to listen. The joy of being reunited with her mother to share all the memories of family yet again: Look, Abbey, the snow is falling on the sea, remember, remember this.

And Abbey did go home three weeks later, on a fine Sunday morning when the construction site was silenced, and called for by her aunt who wore a similar cardigan, and an expression of complacent superiority because she had a husband with her. No one stood on ceremony: to do so would only heighten the awareness of her fellow patients that they must remain. Besides, Abbey had been too much the intellectual and too little the gossip, to be widely popular, though her fellows at Takahe had given her a small presentation the night before. A biography of Franz Schubert with his boyish face on the cover.

Sheridan, Raf and David represented the staff, and Tolly Mathews and Gaynor Runcinski came along as friends, as Abbey left Mahakipawa. Dilys Williams did go as far as the lounge window by the Zip, and stuck her head out to shout, 'And God won't be mocked, you know. Give him thanks, Abbey, for deliverance. Oh, give him thanks, or he'll smite you with the jawbone of an arse.' Abbey's aunt and her husband were startled; the aunt overlapped her cardigan across her bosom for protection, the husband gripped the suitcases more securely, but no one else was at all disconcerted, and Abbey called goodbye to Dilys, as though the jawbone of an arse was an everyday farewell.

A parting rarely expresses the truth of feeling we wish for it. What should be said is lost amid petty practicalities and our fear of the vulnerability that honesty inflicts. The aunt and her husband fluffed about the car with the cases, Jock, walking back from the shore, felt obliged to join in the farewell, Tolly told anecdotes to save himself from awkwardness. Abbey became more and more subdued.

David kissed her cheek. It was soft and downy, and he could smell no make-up or perfume, just the quality soap she used on her skin and the dry, grassy smell of her hair. She looked away to lessen the intimacy, and conceal her need of it. She got into the back seat and gave a soft laugh that had nothing to do with humour.

'Thank you all for your help,' said the uncle, and almost ran over Tony Sheridan in backing out, despite the doctor's clear bulk.

'Nice to meet you all,' said the fatuous aunt.

So at the end David and the others found that their last words were being taken by complete strangers, when they cared only for Abbey. David put both hands and both thumbs up and he called out loudly as the car went, 'Good luck, Abbey.' She looked back and he saw for the last time her plain, decent face, which disguised sharp intuition and talent insufficiently acclaimed. Abbey had a curious half-smile, like that of a child who sees, from a train, circus clowns and animals practising in a field still untrampled.

Chris was living in a wooden villa in Hataitai, the house on a steep slope above Evans Bay, which allowed the wind full access to buffet it until the place boomed like a drum. He never asked David why he wanted to keep his head down for a bit, and was happy enough to see him. Chris was still distributing shit and found Wellington the natural place to operate from — a bottleneck if it wasn't handled right, he told David, but a money tree if it was. After what had happened with Beth Car, he was keeping it very much low key, he said.

But Chris was living with an older, divorced woman who worked in one of the city's rehabilitation units, and she made it plain that she expected David's visit to be very temporary. She disliked drugs because of what she saw of the effects at her work. She thought Chris was an occasional user only, and that his job was something to do with cargo transfers and Trade Aid imports. She had one of those half ugly-half beautiful southern European faces — all rearing nose, cheekbones, and lipstick — and the green veins were like intricate road maps on the underside of her pale arms and wrists.

'We need the time together to build up our partnership,' she told David, as if she and Chris were in business together.

'And then there's the renovations. Working through each room. We're stripping back to the wood. I wouldn't be surprised if the doors are solid kauri. My boss said that some of the villas of the twenties and thirties used a lot of kauri, because it was freed up when metal-hulled boats became the thing and so demand fell off.'

'Quite a job ahead,' said David. Such conversations reduced him to a helpless despair. He tried to keep the existing place in focus — the Hataitai villa leaning towards the sea, Chris and Antonia definite in their own life, but insubstantial in his, for they gave way so easily to Rebecca on her Nan's marriage bed, to the crayfisherman as crucifix in the doorway, to the blows upon his wife's body, to Nan's bewildered face as David ran through the sitting room, her lips lifting oddly away from her teeth. In the paper it said that the woman died from internal injuries, that the police confirmed their enquiries suggested it was a crime of passion, with alleged perpetrators still at large. It was happening again: the complex experience of his life being reduced to a public cliché which permitted no mitigation.

'It's not that you're not welcome for a few days, like. No, old friends are nice,' said Antonia. 'It's just that we have to prioritise at this stage of our lives.' And unemployed old friends with vague pasts, and even more vague prospects, who turned up on the doorstep were low priority in anyone's book. David could understand that, would feel the same way if the situation was reversed.

Yet it was Antonia who unwittingly provided the means for him to move on. The three of them were having Caesar salad for tea, in an evening which cast the hill shadows across the bay. She said that the rehab had been sent a circular for staff about vacancies at the Slaven Centre at Mahakipawa in the Sounds. Residential positions both medical and ancillary, and well paid too, but of course it was the place that took people with the new disease — that regressive behaviour thing which was popularly called Harlequin's *disease, because it got at the brain with such bizarre, ill-sorted effects.*

'Mad cow stuff, isn't it?' said Chris.

'You mean Creutzfeldt-Jakob Disease,' she said. 'No. Bill Stenness says it's a regressive brain disorder: atavistic, involuntary behaviours.'

'Jesus — atavistic? What's that when it's at home?' said Chris.

'The oldest parts of the brain take over again, I think.'

'So, mad caveman disease.' Chris became increasingly cheerful. All those people gathered up by Harlequin, while he was nicely set up in Hataitai with a villa, a low-key distribution business, and a divorced woman adequately keen on bed sports.

'What's so bad about it?' asked David.

'No one's sorted out how you get it, have they,' said Antonia. 'It could be contagious, and the whole place is that isolated, stuck away up the Sounds somewhere. No wonder they struggle for staff. The rehab's no picnic, but I wouldn't have a job in a Harlequin place for any salary you could name.'

'Out of sight, out of mind,' said Chris happily. 'Who wants people like that living next to them. A sort of Halloween for real, eh. I bet the authorities wish they hadn't closed down all those loony bins now.'

David had a letter from Mike Wiremu, commending his assistance in Paparua, without explicitly saying that David had been himself an inmate. And Antonia left the headed notepaper of her rehab unit on the sunroom table, allowing David to create more support for his quasi-counselling skills by forgery above the name of Dr William W. Stenness, Director.

Such modest credentials were sufficient to bring an invitation for David to go to the Slaven Centre at Mahakipawa for an interview which should confirm a residential aide position. The letter came from a Dr Alst

Mousier and was direct and candid. 'Working with our patients requires resilience of body and spirit,' he wrote. 'This is no place for the faint-hearted.'

Although Antonia had unwittingly provided for David's chance to go to ground, he told her nothing, and when he said he was leaving Wellington, her relief expressed itself in an affectionate attention which increased as his departure grew closer. 'Old friends are nice,' she said, flaring the nostrils of her Castilian nose as if to keep from being overcome at the thought of parting. 'I said to Chris that no one could say you've been any bother.' No more need she attempt to smother the involuntary cries from their bedroom. Be loud, be loud, you gorgeous bitch, Chris would say. No more would David distract her from determining if all her villa doors were solid kauri. No more would she hide her pay packet under the tissue box in the top drawer. No more would his long friendship with Chris be any possible threat. Nor did he give any destination when he parted with Chris, and he wasn't pressed. That was the sort of life they had — and understood. Didn't everyone when moving on have reasons why it was better not to leave a forwarding address?

David did ask for Chris's Picton contact, so that he would know how to get hold of the prime West Coast shit that he liked best. 'It seems to be giving you a real edge,' he told Chris, as they walked up the hill from the pub for the last time.

'I've got to keep it out of Toni's sight,' said Chris. 'Anyway, I've got together a few bucks for you, and some tinnies. You need anything, you know where I am.'

'I'll get back to you in time.'

'We had a good set-up, didn't we?'

'Yes,' said David.

'I reckon it was just bad luck. And maybe we got into it in too big a way. The real bugger was that you lost your farm because of it.' David had nothing to say to that, and the two of them walked on up the slope. 'That's probably *the only thing that I feel bad about,' said Chris. 'You know?'*

'There was always that risk,' said David. 'I don't think about it much now.' What else could they say? The significance of it made them uneasy and, after one keen meeting of glances between them, they let it drop. They had been friends for a long time, and the claims they made on each other no longer needed the advocacy of explanation. Beth Car, the place of his family, was gone. His mother and father were gone. The early, easy expectations he had assumed as of right, were gone too.

David took a flight to Christchurch, so that, if it should ever become known, there'd be little indication that he was heading for Mahakipawa. That's how he came to be on a bus from Blenheim which came over a small rise, fringed with red hot poker plants, and there was Havelock, the dipping main street little changed at first glance from the place he had visited as a boy. That one short stretch of clumsy, honest buildings, the steep hill behind them, the glistening mudflats at the head of Mahau Sound, the inevitable association with a grandfather who had never lived there.

THIRTY-TWO

Some people want more than anything else to be listened to. David remembered his mother telling him that some time after she'd retired to Herne Bay. She delivered Meals on Wheels, and said that a piece of mutton in cooling gravy was okay for old people if their teeth were up to it, but more important was the contact she briefly gave, when they had no company apart from their own voice and those of television. How they wanted to talk, she said, how they longed for the indulgence of a listener. Yes, just like Rebecca's Nan.

Sickness could take some people that way, too, as well as causing others to withdraw from the world. Dilys Williams was one of those determined to be heard. She saw the entire hierarchy of staff, from Schweitzer to pot scrubber, as being in her employ, and at her disposal. Her regular sessions with medical staff were not sufficient, and she waylaid Raf and David as her particular Takahe functionaries, and jawed at them endlessly. Her fellow guests could use their equality of affliction as an excuse, and walk away, or tell her to shut up, but David had to take a certain amount.

'It's the turning away from religion that's done it. God

won't be mocked, you know: not outright and not all the time, He won't. When I was young the church meant something, and the vicar was a person of influence in the community. All that's gone. The church's got no clout any more — no status. For myself I'd say only the Catholics get to the top of the heap, because no one asks about people's religion any more. As long as you love the Maoris, and people in same-sex marriages, you're away laughing. But God won't be mocked is what I say, and it's true without a shadow of a doubt. Think of all those plagues in the Bible and how they punished people.' David asked her as inoffensively as he could why she had Harlequin, if it was a penalty for unbelief. 'Tainted by my husband,' Dilys said, 'who was a sinner day and night. There's no distinctions made in the bonds of marriage.'

Dilys was petite, attractive enough in old age, with her unblemished skin and nimble way of using her arms and legs — walking, sitting, folding, crossing, gesticulating. In time, though, her voice drove out any other awareness of her presence, as disembodied as the whine of a mosquito in a cheap Barcelona bedroom. 'I went to hear Billy Graham when I was a young thing,' she said. 'Thousands and thousands, like a rugby game, and streams going up to pledge themselves. Not that he was C of E, but Protestant, of course. Ask young people today about Billy Graham and they're as blank as a lodge wall, aren't they, but God won't be mocked is what I say. This Harlequin's the result. No doubt, absolutely none. No doctors can find any physical reasons at all, can they.'

David and Raf were having a Sunday joint — very traditional, Raf said — but Dilys had rapped on David's door until he opened it just enough to allow her monologue in, and the fragrance of hooch out. The two aides wanted to drift a little, talk a little, keep Harlequin beyond their door.

'What's that smell?' said Dilys.

'Raf's got his sneakers off again,' said David.

Dilys wanted to stay and tell them more of the decline of religious observances, but the Reverend Weymouth, the Anglican minister from Blenheim, was taking a service in the conference room of the main block. He was popular because of the jokes he used, and once a month was about right for ecclesiastic humour. Dilys was a stalwart of the services he held at the centre.

'Guess that service must be due to start right about now, Dilys,' Raf said.

'Staff should be setting an example,' said Dilys, 'and what's that smell in there?'

David shrugged and smiled. He held the door so that her narrow strip of vision grew no larger, and she went off, grumbling, to be a Christian.

Later Montgomery tapped on David's door, then opened it and put his meaty head into the room. He silently enjoyed the aroma for a while, then told David that there was a call for him. David went to the corridor phone, and found that it was Schweitzer. As he heard the voice he visualised the director in his high office, the smooth desk of executive responsibility, and the view which suggested escape from it over the broad sound to the pink fishing buoy and beyond.

'Everything all right?' asked Schweitzer. Do you love her? David wished he could ask, but the line was quiet between them, though the Reverend Weymouth and Dilys must have been about their Father's business not far from the director. 'I've had a call from the Nelson police,' said Schweitzer in a voice quite devoid of dramatic inflection. David took a step or two as release of anxiety, which stretched the close spiral of the telephone lead, then moved back into the alcove.

'Yes,' he said. Jason Brown had left his name in green biro on the wall, and in his mind's eye David saw the Harlequin fires of the night on the hill.

'Someone here has told them about you, and they're coming up late in the afternoon. The superintendent contacted me as a courtesy.'

'Do you know what time?' He had no need, or inclination, to ask what Schweitzer had been told.

'He just said late afternoon, but he did ask the dining room times.'

'Right.' Nothing was audible of Weymouth's far Sunday service, but David could hear Wilfe's laugh from the lounge. In that strange, tangential way the mind works, the idea came to David that Abbey should be playing at the service. He missed Abbey and, with a turn of his heart, he knew that soon he'd be missing Lucy, whose loss meant so much more. 'I appreciate you letting me know,' he said.

'I haven't told anyone else at all. I'm the only one officially who's to know. You understand?'

'Yes, thanks.'

'In some ways, David, I wish they were coming for me. Anyway, good luck,' and he hung up before David had a chance to reply. Schweitzer's use of his Christian name had a kind of intimacy in it, but the greater sense was that of finality. And why would Schweitzer half wish the police were coming for a different catch? But there wasn't time for speculation.

David didn't want to involve any of his centre friends and acquaintances, not only for their sake, but because of the pain of farewells. Who in the whole outside world knew of him, cared enough to act quickly, could be trusted? Post Office Bev, he decided with a sudden confidence, and he rang her straight away.

Raf wandered off without question when David went back to the room and said he needed to go down and see Tony Sheridan. It was mid-afternoon: already the police would be on the road from Nelson. Even with his fear of being caught, and the agony of leaving Lucy, David was aware of the weary dullness that is the breath of a Sunday afternoon. Wilfe and Jock in the lounge laughed on at the television; Mrs McIlwraith's patrician voice from the verandah gave instruction in the pruning of roses she was no longer able to oversee. The scent of banality hung in the air, as did the smell of the sluice room.

David put on his best shirt and jersey, and his jacket over that; his new jeans and the hand-made Last Footwear Company boots from affluent times. He carried all his money and all his stash in his pockets, and nothing besides. Raf's room was open and empty when he passed it, and he took down the calendar there and wrote on the back — 'Take anything in my room you want, cheers' — and left it lying on the bed.

He went out of Takahe, set against attempting to say anything to Tolly, Gaynor, Montgomery, Tony Sheridan, or Raf, who was another of the friends whom he'd made and lost through the years. Life was like a war, wasn't it, and the longer you served, the less inclined you became to draw close to your fellows. He just had to slip away from the place to save himself, leaving the dance of Harlequin to go on without him. He'd just be the latest in a long line of departures one way or another.

The wind surprised him with its gusty force across the grounds as he walked over to Kotuku. Simon Cryer was idling about the door of Weka as he went past, confirmation in David's mind as to who had given the police the nod. 'Hey, chief,' said Cryer, 'haven't seen you for a while.' He made as if to come over.

David kept walking. 'I'm on a promise,' he said. 'Can't stop.'

'Way to go. Yeah.' Cryer held a thumb up, made a tongue clicking noise, man to man.

Lucy wasn't in her room: he could see that while walking the garden side of Kotuku and looking through her window. Propped against her light blue pillow was the smiling rag doll she'd been given when she left television. David went in because he wanted to be close to her place, her things, one last time. But he made no attempt to leave a message. A phone call would be the best thing, when he was well away, and any Mahakipawa interrogations over.

The indentation from Lucy's body was clear on the duvet; on the floor beside the head of the bed, the biography of a ballet dancer made a small chapel, spine up. Lucy was unlikely to be seeking strength from the Reverend Weymouth. More likely she was with Schweitzer, although that had never been acknowledged. Perhaps she had been standing there with him when the warning call was made to Takahe just minutes before. And if that was so, why should he feel anything but thankfulness that his desertion, his freedom from Harlequin, his inability to be of help, might be the less painful for her. No adult can fully bear up the life of another.

On Lucy's cupboard was a photo of her mum and dad with her in the studio — what ordinary people they seemed, to be the parents of such a woman — and her clothes for the laundry were in a soft, draw-top bag by the door. Just for a moment he put the fabric bag to his face so that he could have her smell. He took the stash from his jacket pocket and slipped it half under dolly, half under the pillow. He allowed himself one aching moment of love and gratitude and grief before he left, whirled away again by life which was, perhaps, just Harlequin writ large after all. 'Ah, shit,' he said softly to himself as he went back into the wind again.

Old Sidey, ranting to himself, was coming up the path in his electric chair, which was so silent in the wind. He reduced speed with a twitch of his abbreviated arm, not so that he could be heard, or hear, but that he might catch David's eye for a moment with a keen sardonicism, then, still talking for himself, he was past.

David walked up behind the caretaker's cottage and climbed over the four-strand fence and into the poor grass and rubbish of the hill. The broom tossed in the wind and, as the cloud lowered, some gusts were damp and cool on his face, precursors to a sweeping drizzle. He carried on uphill for a while but, when hidden from the centre, he veered off, dropped over the ridge line and down towards the sea and the road. Where the stock tracks came together in breaks through the scrub, the ground was bare and deeply pock-marked by the passage of cattle. He crouched in the pigfern on the bank above the road. He was hidden from the centre, but able to see the swimming place where he and Raf had gone often. The full, buffeted tide covered the mudflats, and the bright rushes vibrated on the shoreline like a thousand batons. Tolly's dinghy lay on its side there, with the anchor rope leading up to slightly higher ground.

David tried not to think about much as he waited. He began to close down. It was something he'd resorted to during his prison time, and after Kaikoura, and when he realised what was in store for Lucy. He could still see how things were, often with greater clarity than he wished, but he allowed them no easy purchase on his feelings.

LUCY'S VIEW

Is the study in Schweitzer's house, not his office in the admin block, and because his wife and family live in Wellington, that flight away, the only womanly touches are those Lucy brings to it herself — the dark roses in the pale vase, her fingers across the shaving path of his jaw, which feels as if there is sand on the surface of his skin. 'In some ways, David, I wish they were coming for me,' he says before putting down the telephone.

Lucy understands why that is said. She knows all about Bellini and Kinshasa. Isn't that her own wish — that someone was coming to take her away from Mahakipawa, even though she loves two men there?

One is David. She's not at all surprised to find that the police are coming to call on him. She knows there are things David can't share, tight coils of some experience which trap part of him inside himself. Something ails him and he can't talk about it to her. Deep down and a long way back something has gone wrong. He can't allow himself to be fully known, as a man with a withered arm manoeuvres always to present his good side.

And Lucy also loves Schweitzer, who manages to relieve his guilt, who gives more than he receives. Neither love is any less for not being exclusive. Only moralistic convention denies that it's possible to love more than one person at a time, and convention is nothing to Lucy now that Harlequin has her life — now that all is day to day, and episode to episode.

She and Schweitzer understand that the warning they give to David is a farewell too, but that's not the reason he rang. He's done it for Lucy, of course, but also for David. Her grief in that is tempered by relief, for any later form of parting must be worse. Lucy knows from the progress of the disease that she won't follow Abbey back to a life outside.

'Do you want to go down and see him?' asks Schweitzer. He takes no pleasure whatever in finding that the police are after David: no satisfaction in knowing that he will slip furtively away. Schweitzer is so devoted to his work that it's only there he has time for relationships. Each woman has had his friendship and his passion at the periphery of his true dedication. How clinically that was established at any outset. What right has he now to see any other man as rival.

Lucy doubts if David has as civilised a tolerance, and has never put it to the test. She feels no guilt in that. She must give and take all that she can now as Harlequin comes closer. To David she gives more; because his need is greater, from Schweitzer she takes more, because he has strength and confidence — and resignation. 'I may do something silly if I go down,' she says. Her hand traces Schweitzer's on the fabric of the chair. 'Like going off with him,' she says. 'I'm sure that would have happy outcomes.'

Schweitzer smiles and puts his free hand over hers, so that there is a pancake of three. 'I suppose it's the cannabis they're after him for, though it seems a big deal for that.'

'Maybe. It's difficult to tell with David. Something's gnawing away there.'

'Where will you get your stuff if he goes?'
'You?'
'If we started on the run of drugs I've access to, Lucy, you really would ride the roller-coaster. Good try, but no luck.'
'So what then?'
'Alessandro Bellini told me that there's an Albanian doctor with a clinic in Paris who claims to cure everything with sex.'
'Theoretical, or applied?' says Lucy.
'Maybe there's a New Zealand franchise available.'

They can talk on like this for quite a while, but what is really happening is the light pressure of their hands, a warmth of contact nothing to do with sex, and their eyes meeting in recognition of those things impossible to discuss, incapable of solution.

A little later, while Schweitzer prepares to visit his office although it's Sunday, Lucy sees David leaving Takahe. He wears his best boots, which she has always thought too yellow by half, and leans slightly into the strong wind. He walks in the direction of Kotuku, which is out of sight, and yes, she does want to be there.

'He's going, I think,' she calls. A voice louder than necessary to reach Schweitzer in another room, almost as if the cry is for David.

'Are you sure that you don't want to go down?' says Schweitzer, quickly back to be with her. 'Quarter of an hour won't be any danger I wouldn't think. It's going to take the police a while.'

She watches David, his longish hair blown up in the wind, his boots resplendent, until he's out of sight behind Weka. He's going to her room and will find it empty. If she'd been well, she could be there and they could hit the road together, like the conclusion of a bitter-sweet romance, but she's sick isn't she, Harlequin's bride, and if she wasn't then she wouldn't have met David, or Schweitzer, anyhow, so a script didn't work either way. And if she can't go with him, then she doesn't want to say goodbye. She thinks of the last really good time they were together, and it wasn't to make love, but fishing in Tolly Mathews' dinghy. Only a light breeze then, but salt in the sea air, the boat rocking, the large blue cod on the slats mouthing for water and finding air which provided nothing. They had told stories against themselves, and exchanged memories, laughing so much together that they almost forgot their fears, just as some mornings she woke happy and complete, had a moment of her former life, before it was overwhelmed by the realisation of where and what she was.

David had seemed relaxed there, as if most securely insulated from the reach of what troubled him in the world: together in the boat, the sea around them, the third embracing protection of the quiet hills of Mahakipawa. He had even talked of visiting Havelock as a boy to stay with family friends, of shimmering summer afternoons spent hunting the crabs and butterfish, nights on an open porch with moreporks sounding the chiming hours, waking to the touch of a breeze moving up Mahau Sound. In all the time they spent together he rarely talked of the past.

'What do you think he'll do?' asks Schweitzer. He has four more minutes he can spend with Lucy, before he must go to his office to talk with Alst Mousier and the contractor about the official opening of the amenities extension. Maybe he'll be interrupted there by news of the police raid which he's had to keep quiet about.

'Go back to Christchurch, I suppose,' says Lucy, 'or overseas again. He gets by okay wherever he finds himself. I don't think that his expectations are that high.'

'Then he was damn lucky here to find you, Lucy.'

'Did the police really say nothing about what he's done?'

'No,' says Schweitzer. He smiles and waits for her next question.

'Did you ask them?'

'No,' he says. Both of them still look out of the window,

although David had long vanished behind Weka, and is unlikely to come back that way. Schweitzer moves behind Lucy and holds her loosely, rests his chin on her shoulder, looks out at the grounds. 'Stay here as long as you like,' he says. 'Make yourself something to eat. What is it down there on Sunday nights anyway?'

'Salads and cold meat,' says Lucy, but she's wondering if David has left any note in her room, how he's getting away from Mahakipawa, if this is how it ends: watching a lover being driven out, knowing it's for the best and hurting like hell. She goes with Schweitzer to the door. They don't kiss there, but he squeezes her hand in his, before leaving for the main block. 'Don't worry too much,' he says. 'What else could we do for him at such short notice?'

And what else, what more, could she have done for him when notice wasn't so short? It's what happens to couples, families, communities when they're harried too much by life — they split up and make a run for it as individuals, partly to survive, but more importantly because they can't bear to be a witness, or have a witness, to the way things will end. There have been those close, heightened times, though, haven't there? Moments when some real contact was made between them, and not all, or even mainly, physical. Nothing could take those away. Lucy imagines David slipping away from the Slaven Centre: his closed, quiet face as he becomes solitary again, the wary resilience in his regard of the world. He has his dis-ease too, as she has Harlequin.

Lucy will stay in Schweitzer's house a while, which is her entitlement. She will cry and swear, she will smoke shit and think of David and Schweitzer. She will try to remember the way her life was before she got sick. She will twist on the hook, but nothing will change how things are for her. She will wait till Schweitzer returns, and take and give what comfort is left. But after David, after Schweitzer even, Harlequin Rex will be her final suitor.

That great pied piper of malady.

THIRTY-THREE

He was there, still and quiet, watching the empty sea, when Bev came and parked on the seaward road edge, which was extended somewhat where a culvert ran underneath. David recognised her at once, but he waited to make sure there wasn't a car close behind, then scrambled down the bank and went over. She wore her old-fashioned wasp stripe trackpants, and a New Zealand Post top. 'You okay?' she said.

'I'm on the run. Just like in the movies. The police are coming over from Nelson.'

'Lie down in the back then, and we'll go straight back.'

'You're sure?' said David.

'Put that tartan rug on top. You can convince me of your innocence later.' Bev looked into his face keenly. 'I hope,' she said after the pause. The bright scar by her eye didn't crease when she smiled. They turned around and headed for Havelock. What a brief acquaintanceship they had, and yet his trust was quite complete. She had a down-to-earth sympathy which instinctively responded to individual need rather than civic generalities.

The space between back and front seats was hardly big

enough for David to lie down but, with the rug over him, a quick glance from a car going the other way could well miss him. He could see a muslin rag under Bev's seat, and a red, boiled sweet with a fuzz of carpet strands, and a small, black plastic shank that he recognised as the clicker from a cheap biro. That was his view as he passed the centre where the Reverend Weymouth was finishing his service with a mildly feminist joke; that was his view as they passed two police cars on the Mahakipawa Hill. Senior Sergeant Toby Cook, travelling in the rear seat of the first car, gave Bev just a glance — the ageing Ford without a passenger barely merited that.

'Two cars and a fair bunch of gendarmes,' said Bev. 'You must be popular.'

'All from a long time ago.'

'That's peachy then. I guess you're all reformed now.'

'Absolutely,' said David. His voice came muffled from beneath Bev as she drove, and the oddity of it caused her to laugh.

That is what he had to do, wasn't it? Not allow himself to stay physically or emotionally with Lucy, pretend no concern with either past or future, and just concentrate on himself in the present, move by instinct as a survivor should. He thought that was the quarry Harlequin would admire. Maybe all of it was just a fox hunt, and making a good run was all the satisfaction you could expect.

All of life is the play of sparks between the poles: night and day, men and women, life and death, ignorance and recognition, community of spirit and essential isolation, sadness and joy. How urgent are the sparks between them — flash, flash — electric colours that singe the air and leave the charged ions drifting there. Flash, flash they go.

As he lay ingloriously on the floor of Bev's car, borne away from Mahakipawa, it came to David, with strong conviction and without premeditation, that he would get out of his own country and never come back. If he left the old places behind, maybe he could leave the worst of the past there, and the best, which could never be recaptured. If he came to foreign places determined to stay, maybe he could find a new language of experience.

It seemed fair to him that, having no control over the beginning of his life, he should attempt mastery of its end.